D0909215

DOUBLE DEAL

Also by Michael McClister

Victim's Choice

DOUBLE DEAL

Michael McClister

Thomas Dunne Books / St. Martin's Minotaur ⋈ New York

THOMAS DUNNE BOOKS.
An imprint of St. Martin's Press.

www.minotaurbooks.com

Design by Heidi R. J. Eriksen

Library of Congress Cataloging-in-Publication Data
McClister, Michael.
    Double deal / Michael McClister.—1st ed.
      p. cm.
    "Thomas Dunne Books."
    ISBN 0-312-26562-X
    1. Attempted assassination—Fiction. 2. Governors' spouses—Fiction.
  3. Kidnapping—Fiction. 4. Governors—Fiction. 5. Tennessee—Fiction.
  6. Cults—Fiction. I. Title.

PS3563.C34157 D68 2000
813'.54—dc21   00-031767

First Edition: October 2000
  10 9 8 7 6 5 4 3 2 1

Ingram
10/00

Acknowledgments

The author wishes to acknowledge two nonfiction sources that were helpful in the writing of this book: *The Silent Brotherhood,* by Kevin Flynn and Gary Gerhardt (The Free Press, 1989), and *Gathering Storm,* by Morris Dees with James Corcoran (HarperCollins, 1996).

The
Days
Before

The first question was, would Elmo Finn agree to assassinate the governor? Though he had never accepted such an assignment, Finn immediately said yes.

Which led to question two: Could he actually pull it off? On this point, opinions were furiously mixed.

Yes, if . . .

No, unless . . .

Maybe—it depends.

Seizing on the turmoil, Finn's pal Graves set up a calcutta and the wagers poured in—Finn wouldn't get on the grounds, he wouldn't get past the metal detector or the troopers, he wouldn't make it upstairs, he'd never even lay eyes on the governor.

Or he would.

And side bets. Finn would face a drawn gun, feel the cold

pinch of handcuffs, blacken his hands on a fingerprint pad, suffer the trashing of his glossy reputation on the talk shows.

Or not.

Everyone haggled over odds and terms, especially the spy crowd, who knew Elmo Finn from Vietnam. They'd seen him do some things. The various cops and ops weren't as picky. They'd seen Elmo Finn do some things, too, but different things. George Graves merrily played each clique off against the other, egging everyone on to sweeten the pot, and soon was e-mailing weekly "Snuff the Guv" updates to all the far-flung gamblers. Although George was operating his casino right under Elmo's nose, from the guest room of Finn's sand-colored villa on Longboat Key, he decided it was safer to keep Elmo himself in the dark. Couldn't predict his reaction—Elmo Finn the purist who might stand on some principle no one else could even divine; Elmo Finn the perfectionist who had once refused a six-figure reward for capturing a serial killer (he insisted he should have caught him sooner); Elmo Finn the . . . everybody had a story.

The gamblers cyberdickered over every conceivable detail except how the wagers would finally be decided: by Finn's own account of what went down. Elmo Finn would tell the truth—no one questioned that. George Graves covered everything that anybody wanted to lay off, then shut his gaming window at thirty-six thousand dollars and bought a ninety-day CD.

Elmo went into his cocoon to plan the job. He cut back the golf schedule to eighteen holes a day—a three-hour forced march at sunrise when the course was empty. "Redneck golf," George sniffed, emitting great groaning yawns and pointedly refusing to share the coffee in his silver thermos. After golf, Elmo labored alone in the high-ceilinged office with the lazy overhead fans, ignoring the postcard view of the Gulf, ignoring George, ignoring Sandra, ignoring the menagerie, ignoring everything . . . whisking through cyberspace on his souped-up modem, e-mailing god-knew-whom, downloading God-knew-what . . . and transacting long, late-night phone calls with the louvered doors closed and the Miles Davis up. George and Sandra stubbornly refused to ask how it was going. Elmo Finn's two closest friends were sorely miffed—Sandra because her sabbatical from the Broadway dance studio was running out, and her idiosyncratic lover had selfishly cocooned himself; and George because he wasn't in on it, whatever it was.

Elmo appeared for most of the meals and never missed cocktail hour, but for weeks no one had even proposed a fuck-dinner toast, much less insisted on a vote. Life at Finn's had become "just too goddamned British," George groused: drinks at five-thirty, dinner at seven, back to the war room, tut-tut.

Sandra and George lazed through the torrid afternoons under a ring of umbrellas on the narrow Longboat beach. Watching the pelicans soar and dive and swallow. Knocking back icy straight Absolut from George's silver thermos. Wading out far enough into the bathwater Gulf to find the cooler currents. And calling Elmo Finn vile names. They had a storehouse of vile names, and agreed that for someone who believed God created day and night largely to accommodate golf and sex, Elmo Finn was sacrificing both ends of the hourglass. They discovered he had even spent an afternoon prowling the Palm Avenue galleries, and two full days in the Selby Library among the drudges.

"At least you get to sleep with him," George muttered to Sandra one afternoon. "Doesn't he say anything?"

"About what, George?"

"About anything. Whatever. Who cares? Go do a flip or something."

Sandra stretched her dancer's legs and assumed a pose of indifference. But couldn't hold it. "George, seriously, could he get shot or something . . . some state trooper hiding in the shrubbery? How dangerous is this?"

"How would I know? Seriously?"

"Did all those guys bet on it?"

"Those sonsabitches'd bet on anything."

Even Elmo Finn's menagerie was out of sorts. Dr. Watson, the lopsided English bulldog who according to George "looked like Churchill and acted like Stalin," spent most of the day lying flat on the cool tiles in the foyer, his jowls spread forlornly around his face like a bib, his bloodshot eyes despairing. This was Dr. Watson's normal state of misery when Master Elmo was on the road, and apparently it applied to cocooning as well.

Falstaff, the red-and-green "imperial cockamamie" who could croak out several Shakespearean classics—including "Out damn spot" and "Kiss me Kate"—was definitely backsliding. Without his daily tutoring from Elmo, he had fallen back on an old standby—mimicking the cat. His perfect meows always fooled Macduff, the cross-eyed orange tabby, who would saunter into the den, spring to the back of the sofa and then to the top of the birdcage, and perch there for hours as if he had conquered something, while Falstaff fluttered and orated on his trapeze.

"Serve him right if they all just dropped dead," George groused to Sandra after Elmo had vanished following another desultory cocktail hour and dinner. "He's paying no more attention to them than he is to us. The goddamn dog is severely depressed, needs constant meds for his gas, the goddamn bird is severely confused from all that Shakespeare, and the goddamn cat is just severely stupid. And the great goddamn Elmo Finn is severely . . . ungrateful."

"Ungrateful for what, George?" Sandra asked, giggling.

"Go do a flip."

Then one innocent morning after the sunrise eighteen, Elmo drove the golf cart back to the first tee, where the starter waved him on. "Thirty-six, anyone?" he asked cheerily. "Finally," George said with a tiny twitch-smile, "finally a full round of golf." Inspired, George finished birdie-par-birdie and won eighty dollars. Then they revived another custom that had lately surrendered to the cocoon and went to the Colony for a late lunch. The customary flirty hostess. The customary table looking out on the skinny beach and the skinny pier and the great blue Gulf, flat and still as a lake. The customary lunch—Amstel Light, conch chowder, shrimp salad. The customary talk—embroidering the good shots, rationalizing the misses, musing whether the latest fad, stroking short putts with one's eyes closed, was Zen-inspired or true madness. George thought it had possibilities.

The two men looked like brothers. Mid-forties, give or take. Elmo Finn was about six-one, trim, at one-eighty just ten pounds above his Vietnam weight, with an angular face and gray eyes softened by warm gold flecks, and a cleft in his chin like a bullet hole. George Graves was as tall as Finn, a little stockier, with musician's hair and a thin mouth that could twitch a range of smiles but which always settled into a turned-down expression of doubt or irritation or worse. Depending on the lookee.

Elmo put away his leather notebook after recording his calories and fat percentages, which he could estimate with annoying precision. Without looking up: "George, can you go tomorrow?"

George drained the second Amstel to cover his shiver. "So it's on."

Elmo nodded pleasantly. " 'The game is afoot.' "

George glared for a moment. "That's not the Shakester—that's Conan Doyle."

Finn shook his head. "King Harry said it first. 'Once more unto the breach' and so forth. I think. I'm pretty sure."

"Don't cudgel your brains about it. Pack big, pack small?"

"Small will do."

"I'm already packed."

"I assumed so. 'The readiness is all.' "

"Hamlet."

Elmo inclined his head a few inches.

"Act Five."

A few more inches.

"Hamlet telling Horatio, I'm ready for Laertes. Bring that dipstick on."

Elmo's eyebrows shot up and he made a full-fledged bow. George took another sip from the empty glass. His mouth turned down to the maximum.

"Sandra will certainly be pleased," George said.

"She settled for Bermuda. Said it was the perfect hideout for assassins. If you and Angie don't come, we'll have you kidnapped and brought. That'll be a snap after snuffing a guv-nah."

George flashed an indulgent smile, followed by another dry sip, followed by another plunge of the mouth.

"If it's not too much bother, Colonel Finn, perhaps you might give me some tiny little hint of what is expected of me. Since I am not in the goddamn loop. Since I ain't snuffed all that many guv-nahs lately. Since the readiness is all, don't you know. Forsooth."

Elmo was chuckling and smiling broadly. "Combat rules, George. Need to know. Thought you'd want it that way, all those bets you've been covering."

Nashville, the capital city of Tennessee. A metropolis of a half-million people, home to empires in medicine and publishing and insurance and education, yet whose image remains country music, whose image to many, according to the mayor, remains *Hee Haw.*

A West Nashville neighborhood of boxlike old houses groaning under ancient oaks and elms, houses once deemed mansions, where the upper crust had lived, where the Sunday afternoon streets had been cruised by legions of the envious in newly-washed cars. A mixed neighborhood today—half the mansions sliced into apartments, half the residents retired, the Sunday streets yawningly empty after church.

Two men and a woman sit inside a cream-colored van with opaque windows parked diagonally across the street from one of the old three-story gray-shingled mansions. Unlike its dark and shuttered neighbors, the house is brightly lighted inside and out. A broad porch extends along the front and down one side.

"Lit up like fuckin' Disneyland," the woman code-named Red says from the backseat. "I don't know, Blue. Where can you hide on that porch?"

"You can see *everything* from right here," the driver, White, says, glancing back at the woman called Red. "Everything—the front hall, the whole porch—"

"Looks like a fuckin' movie set," Red says.

"It does! It sure to hell does! Take some cojones try to hide on that porch," White, the driver, says. "Even you, Miz Red, with your very righteous pair."

Red ignores the driver and scrunches forward into the space between the high-backed seats, her eyes cocked toward the other man, the silent man. "It *is* pretty well lit up, Blue, that's a fact."

Blue still says nothing, forcing silence from the others. Then he sighs heavily to convey his mounting exasperation. When he finally speaks, his voice is softer than theirs, barely modulated and thus more sinister, and he does not look at them but continues to gaze at the bright house across the street.

"On the side porch, past that planter thing. Down low. Nobody can see you there even with the porch lights on, and the porch lights will be out. *The porch lights will be out.*"

After a moment Red asks, "Which room did he hang himself in?" She shivers a little.

"Top floor. Center."

"Jesus."

Another long silence. Then she says, "Is the first commercial in the eleven o'clock news always at the same time?"

"Close enough," Blue says.

"What's the cat's name? I never can remember that name."

"Baskerville. Baskerville. But the cat's name don't matter. The cat matters." Blue checks his watch, luminous in the dark. "Speaking of which."

"Is it time?"

Within seconds the door to the bright old house opens a few inches, then closes.

"See him?"

"Hell no!" White says.

Red says, "I saw a blur. I think." She scoots over to the window.

"You just saw Baskerville."

"Son of a seacook, that ain't much time!" White grips the steering wheel with both hands.

"It's enough," Blue says in a biting whisper, still staring at the house. He realizes he should have expected their jitters. "Be quick but don't hurry. You get it? Be quick but don't hurry. Take a deep breath and push right in. I know for a fact it's enough time. Look—look—that's her. Right there on the porch. Sometimes she comes out for the air."

A small woman bundled in a long robe walks to the edge of the porch and looks downward. She is mouthing something, apparently talking to the cat.

"And she's always alone?"

"Always," Blue says. "Always. I 'spect she'll need more than air, you two get done."

They laugh, as he intended. Better. Jitters are normal. Should have expected it. He can talk them through it.

"They can hear out there, you know. There's no privacy like in the Mansion . . ." Nikki Gannon, the First Lady of Tennessee, lay sprawled on her back on pale yellow sheets in the California king, her arms flung wide. She stared at the high ceiling.

"They're down at the other end of the hall, Nikki, they can't hear. And I really don't think the Tennessee State Police are trying to eavesdrop on our bedroom. Just bear with it—we'll be back in the Mansion before long. Behind all those nice tight soundproof doors." Governor Lucas Gannon was stretched out on a flowered chaise in a corner of the spacious room, a stack of documents on his lap, a four-line telephone on the antique table at his elbow.

Nikki folded her arms tightly across her chest and let out a long low sound. She shuddered and curled under the goose-down comforter.

Luke Gannon said, "What's to hear, anyway? It's not like there's been any action in this room lately."

"I know, I know, that's what I mean! They listen out there and they don't hear anything and spread it around that the governor and his wife . . . I can tell from their faces."

"Oh, now I get it—you *want* them to hear something? Okay, Nikki, fine, let's give 'em something to hear, let's give 'em somethin' to talk about, the First Couple actually coupling! We can wail and moan and—"

"Why are all these extra troopers around all the time, Lucas? I'm not blind, you know, I see them, all the extra body men. Have there been more threats? Tell me!"

"No, Nikki. No more than usual, every governor gets threats. Mostly crackpots, you know that."

"Mostly crackpots. Mostly! Oh that's comforting, Lucas. I feel *so* much better now. No more than usual! *Mostly* crackpots."

He closed his eyes and stretched for a long moment. His voice softened. "We're in a rut, Nikki, a bad rut. No quality time. My schedule's murder, your schedule's murder, the goddamn legislature . . ." He laughed sourly. "The polls say we're *very* popular."

Governor Lucas Gannon got to his feet, allowing the documents of state to slide to the floor. He squared his shoulders beneath the silk robe, which seemed to fit tighter. He drew in

9

his stomach. Then he threw off the robe and got into bed beside her.

"You and me against the world, babe," he whispered. This was their pledge, their compact, their mantra since a certain European history class at Vanderbilt twenty-five years before. "Can't let the bastards get us down."

"When it's us against the world, Your Highness, bet on the world."

He nudged her. "I didn't hear that."

"I didn't mean that." She nudged back with her hips.

"Am I getting fat, Nikki?"

"No. I don't care, I just miss you."

Nuzzling her soft chestnut hair, stroking her thigh. "I miss you too."

"Put on a CD."

"I thought you wanted them to hear."

"They'll hear enough—*Lucas!* Music first, soothe this savage beast. Then you can do that again. You better do that again."

He rolled to the bedside table, selected a compact disc, and inserted it in the player. The music surged from the twin speakers.

"Oh how fitting. How perfect. *The King and I.* You fucking governors."

"Isn't that what you wanted—a fucking governor?"

Closing her eyes, turning to him, pressing hard. "So who is she, Your Highness?"

Kissing her eyes, a wet kiss. "Just another nymph, darling. They flock to power. Nothing to worry about, it's only raw sex. Now, Your Wenchness, may I ask, who is *he?*"

"Oh, nothing to worry about, darling, just another Adonis. A *real* body man, young, hung, and stupid, just the way I like—"

They fell to each other hungrily.

The First Day

On the takeoff from Sarasota-Bradenton, Elmo Finn and George Graves sat side by side in the first-class cabin of the Delta MD-88, observing their comfortable superstitions. George as always in the window seat, peering down to count swimming pools and sand traps; trying to break the record, which he could never remember. Elmo as always in the aisle seat working the *New York Times* crossword in red ink, his fire-flecked gray eyes never glancing up unless a flight attendant was passing. Two veteran air travelers, apparently, slouching their six-one frames into attitudes of unconcern in the roomy seats, mixing doubles with the miniatures of vodka and whispers of tonic from a shared can. Perhaps two businessmen in sweaters and jeans who had no appointments upon arrival. Two freshly tanned golfers returning from a Gulf Coast junket. Two political consultants who had just reinvented another candidate. Certainly not assassins. Neither Elmo nor George would kick off his shoes until the plane reached cruising altitude, a ritual with a practical basis—can't crash out an exit window or walk a burning wing in your socks. When the shoes did come off, they would complete the takeoff ceremony by assuring each other they had absolutely no fear of flying.

George went through each of the steps, which were second nature, but he was still stewing. Silently he rehearsed how he would needle Elmo. Didn't we serve together in Vietnam—two tours—including twenty months in the controversial Phoenix Program? Didn't the Director of Central Intelligence personally award each of us the Company's highest medal in a secret ceremony? Haven't I trudged along beside you for twenty years as your faithful Boswell, shooting a thousand rolls of videotape to catalogue your grand adventures as a consulting detective, and in the process been shot at three times and hit once? So don't you think, Colonel Finn, don't you think that maybe, just fucking maybe, good old loyal George can be trusted with the operations plan? But George bottled his irritations inside and said nothing. Down deep he knew Elmo Finn was right, goddamnit. Combat rules. Need to know.

They had a stopover in Atlanta, where Elmo cheerfully reeled off the next verse of their obligatory litany. "Die and go to hell, you'll change planes in Atlanta." Then they high-fived like ballplayers, to the amusement of the people-watchers along the vast Hartsfield concourse. Two washed-up jocks with nothing left but the strut.

One hundred minutes later, carrying two bags each, they stepped through the electric doors of Nashville International Airport onto the broad walkway outside. It was bright but cool for September, fall in the air, people hurrying in and out. An ancient black-and-white Checker cab began rolling toward them across the Arrival lanes and squeezed in at the curb. The driver jumped out and opened the trunk. His nondescript baggy clothes didn't fully conceal the coiled muscles beneath. With a start, George realized it was Roy. Elmo was really serious.

"Contingencies?" Elmo asked as Roy maneuvered the Checker back into traffic and headed for I-40 West.

"No, sir. Everything's just as you figured. Hi, George."

"Roy."

"All right, gentlemen," Elmo Finn said briskly, "here it is. They're renovating the Executive Residence—the Mansion—so the governor and the First Lady are living temporarily in their old house, their private residence in Belle Meade. Security's not as tight. Tomorrow is Tuesday, and the governor will start his morning workout at eight-thirty in his home gym. Second floor, far end of the hall, off the master bedroom. Nikki won't be there—she visits her mother on Tuesdays, leaves at eight-thirty sharp. At eight-fifty, Roy will drive us to the front door in this fine old Checker cab. Well done, Roy, this is the perfect vehicle. The housekeeper or a state trooper will greet us. We'll have a gift for Governor Gannon, who we will insist is expecting us. We will insist. Several possibilities at this point, George, we'll review them tonight. You're my personal assistant and, by the way, we're homosexual. Practice your mincing."

"*By the way,* I didn't bring the proper ensemble to play gay. You could have warned me."

"Clothes don't make the dandy." He rolled down the window and inhaled. "Hope it's like this tomorrow. Good assassination weather."

"Speaking of tomorrow," Roy said, turning to grin at his passengers in the backseat, "the weapon is state of the art. These new alloys—I don't think even the hand-held detector will pick it up. And it breaks down perfectly inside the frame of the painting, which won't fit through the X-ray machine."

"So," George sneered, "we're borrowing trinkets from Langley again."

"Good, Roy," Elmo said, beaming. " 'How oft the sight of means to do ill deeds makes ill deeds done!' "

"Forsooth," George muttered, his mouth turning down despite their laughter. He was still furious that Roy had apparently been operational the whole time while his own role was merely to play the sissy assistant. He almost wished he'd laid off his two large *against* Elmo Finn's assassination plan, whatever the hell it was.

Someone a hundred fifty miles east of Nashville, in a remote hollow that snaked between wooded hills and crags, a tall, thin, unshaven man dressed all in black sauntered down a gravel-and-dirt lane. His arms swung oddly, stiffly, as if the elbows were locked. Despite the late-summer chill, he wore only a black T-shirt covering his torso. His arms were sprinkled with tattoos of spiderwebs in all sizes. His head was shaved bald. Riding low on his right hip was a Glock nine-millimeter semiautomatic with a seventeen-round magazine.

Fifty yards up the gentle grade behind him, cut into a stand of Scotch pine and hickory, stood a ramshackle compound. A dozen mobile homes, all single-wides. A dozen cars and a few pickup trucks, some of them up on blocks, and several vans. Two clotheslines strung between thin trees, dark-colored clothing hanging limp. A gray polyurethane hut surrounded by stacks of firewood and mounds of sandbags. Another hut, this one constructed only of stacked bales of hay, with tin sheets for a roof. A cookout area with picnic tables and a rusting children's swing set. A few dogs sleeping in patches of sun.

The only imposing structure was a large, remodeled barn, fully enclosed on both ends with new planking and painted a resplendent red. Windows of ersatz stained glass had been installed, tinselly red and green and gold, and the huge loft windows, once open to nature, had been fitted with heavy glass panes and curtains. It was called the Ark. A flagstone walkway lined all four sides, and from the angle of the roof where a weathercock once stood, a blood-red cross of steel stretched crassly to the sky.

An observer high in the surrounding hills with strong binoculars—and there had been many—would have seen that instead of Tennessee license plates all the vehicles bore hand-lettered pasteboard plates reading *God's Country*—and in smaller letters beneath, *The Promise Land.*

The man in black continued down the gravel-and-dirt lane, avoiding the high weeds sprouting between the vehicle tracks. The lane served as a hundred-yard driveway connecting the compound to a narrow blacktopped county road with no center line. At the end of the lane stood a weathered chimney-shaped guardhouse, like an elongated phone booth. When the man in black got close enough, he stooped to pick up a handful of stones and with clumsy, unathletic push-tosses rained them one by one against the sides and roof of the guardhouse. The dogs ignored the dull plinks that penetrated the stillness of the hollow and the hum of a distant generator. One of the stones clunked against a plywood sign that was propped against the front of the guardhouse, toppling it forward into the dust.

As the man in black bent for more stones, the guardhouse door flew open and a squat, square man in camouflage fatigues, his head also shaved, charged out. He scanned the blacktopped road, his head snapping left and right, then spun into a crouch and with a two-handed grip swung his Luger up to point directly at the tattooed man in black.

"That's it, Hi!" the man in black yelled. "That's it! Son of a bitch, you come out of there fast! Drew down, too!"

The squat man came forward with a tentative swagger, fitting the Luger into the holster on his belt. "Drew down, dint I, Spiderman? Come out of there fast!"

"Damn fast, damn fast, Hi. Best yet."

Grinning a snaggletoothed smile, Hi hitched up his camouflage fatigues and took a wide-legged gunfighter's stance, his hand poised above the holster.

"Better get the sign back up, Hi. Joshua's overdue, he'll be back any minute."

"Whoa!" Hi scurried to reposition the three-foot-square plywood sign against the front edge of the guardhouse. In hand-painted block letters, white on black, the sign read:

GODS COUNTRY
the Promise Land
ARYAN'S ONLY

The two men stood beside the guardhouse, peering regularly down the blacktopped county road.

"He was visitin' with Linda," Spiderman said. "Probably why he's runnin' late."

"Lin-da the law-yer, Lin-da the law-yer," Hi sang in a child's falsetto. "I don't see why he has to visit with no lawyer if we ain't livin' under no law."

"We use the law, Hi, *their* law, when it's to our advantage. Linda's all right, she's one of us, not one of them. She's like our spy."

"I hope Joshua remembered 'bout my name change."

"He will if there's time, Hi. He's got a lot on his mind right now." Spiderman picked up another rock and push-tossed it at a dog which had meandered down to the road. "Did you understand exactly what Linda said . . . about your name?"

"Sure I did. Sure I did. But it still sounds like '*Hi* Hitler' to me, I've played the videos over and over and over, she said it was really '*Heil* Hitler' but I said it sounds like *Hi* to an American. Hi Hitler. When'd you stop wearin' white laces, Spider, you a nigger-lover now?" Hi manufactured a giggle.

"They're dryin', back there on the line, fresh and pearly white. We were only *born* American, Hi. We live in God's Country now."

They heard the car before they saw it. The gray hatchback sped into the driveway kicking gravel and dust, past Hi's stiff-arm Nazi salute, and shot up the gentle grade to the Ark. Spiderman and Hi trundled along behind.

"Why does Mother drive right by us like we're not even there?" Hi said, huffing for breath.

"Hah! She's mad at *him,* not *us.* That's why she goes along to Linda's every time, draggin' that dirty little baby with her. She's afraid Linda and Joshua got a little more goin' than a lawyer-client relationship."

Hi sputtered an uncertain laugh. When they reached the gray hatchback with the homemade God's Country plates, the driver, a slender woman wearing black jeans and a cowboy hat and carrying an infant wrapped in a blanket, was already striding toward a silver trailer set back in the trees. Waiting for Hi and Spiderman was a tall, well-built man of sixty with chalk-white hair and radiant, ice-blue eyes that made him look years younger. The blue eyes were impossible to stare down. Everyone always looked away. Everyone always remembered the cold blue eyes.

"Boys," Joshua said, exchanging stiff-arm salutes with the two men, "Linda's come up with a beauty. A beauty. So simple, like all beautiful things. Like an AK-47."

The men waited a little breathlessly, nervous as usual in the presence of their leader. Like Spiderman, Joshua wore all black—black suit, black shirt, even a black tie, starkly setting off his white hair and eyebrows. On his right hand was an onyx ring that gleamed from regular buffing. Now his luminous pale-blue eyes widened and brightened and took them in.

"You know those Adopt A Highway signs along the roads—where people do their civic duty and pick up trash once a month? Well guess what? God's Country is going to adopt one mile of highway—one mile of highway *officially"*—his voice deepening conspiratorially—"and as many as we want *unoffi-*

cially. You get it? It's Linda's idea. And while we're all dressed up in our little Adopt A Highway ball caps and T-shirts, pickin' up a little trash here and there, we'll be checkin' out the codes on the backs of all the road signs, and changin' 'em, or paintin' over 'em—"

"And throw a monkey wrench in the New World Order!" Spiderman, grinning broadly, pounded his hand with a fist.

"One king-size God's Country monkey wrench, comin' up!" Joshua beamed. "And when The Day comes—*when The Day comes*—the blue helmets will get totally lost! And confused! And scared as hell! But we won't be lost, will we, Spiderman?"

"No, sir, Joshua! No, sir!"

"We won't be confused, will we, Hi?"

"No, sir! No, sir!" He snapped each arm up and down in alternating Nazi salutes.

"We won't be scared of the Crips and the Bloods and the mud people and the Jewnited Nations in the blue helmets, will we?"

"No, sir, Joshua, never!" Spinning in a circle, mouthing sound effects, Spiderman finger-fired at imaginary targets.

A dozen women and children had emerged from the trailers and huts and were drifting toward the three men, but only a boy of nine or ten came close enough to be noticed. He was spindly and moved jerkily, and wore hand-me-down clothes many sizes too large.

"Eighty-eight!" the boy shouted in a high-pitched twang. His arm flew out and up, his hand hidden by the overlong sleeve. Hi clicked his heels and returned the salute. "Eighty-eight, Jeremiah, eighty-eight!"

Smiling, Joshua turned to Jeremiah and waved him back. The boy danced sideways, then scampered away. Joshua watched him for a moment, then turned back to the two men, his pale-blue eyes settling warmly on the squat figure in camouflage fatigues. "I am glad to tell you, Soldier Hi Hitler, that Linda will be bringing out the papers for you to sign—to make it official."

Hi Hitler snapped another salute. "Which name do I sign, sir, Glenn Forbush or Hi Hitler?"

"She'll know just how to do it, Hi. There's an illegal fee that the state charges, of course, but I've already paid it for you, even though it's against our policy to pay any tax or tribute to the occupying government. But I am making an exception in your case so you can have your chosen name." He put his hand on the militiaman's shoulder. "Soldier Hi Hitler."

Hi Hitler's stiff-arm flew up yet again. His square face was bright and moist. Spiderman clapped him on the back as Joshua smiled broadly and smiled also with the relentless blue eyes that enveloped the two men like an embrace.

"Now I must go to Mother. You know how she gets around Linda. As you were, men. Eighty-eight!"

"Eighty-eight!" Hi Hitler and Spiderman boomed in unison.

On his way to the silver trailer, Joshua paused to greet the small knot of women. The young boy Jeremiah ran in among them, then raced away toward the hut made of stacked bales of hay. Joshua drew each woman to him and kissed her full on the lips.

The cream-colored van follows a serpentine course, turning left, right, left, backtracking, before it finally closes to the target and cruises past the three-story gray-shingled house with the wrap-around porch.

"The porch lights are off," the woman code-named Red says. "Just like Blue promised. How'd he do that? All right, no problem now." She shivers and squeezes her arms across her chest.

The driver shakes his head rapidly. "No problem, no problem." He checks the mirrors. "Did you see that man back there?"

"That was three blocks back, doll. I mean, White. He's already home by now, inside one of these dark old houses. Having his graham crackers and milk. Don't go too fast."

"I meant he's the only person we've seen on the street."

"These people go to bed early. They're old, like Louise. I guess we'll have to help Louise get to bed, won't we, Mr. White?"

He manages a high-pitched laugh. "Early to bed, Lady Red. And ever so late to rise." They giggle anxiously.

White parks the van on a side street only two blocks from the target house. They walk side by side along the cracked sidewalk, keeping to the shadows as much as possible. He carries a fully packed Kroger's grocery bag with stalks of celery peeking from the top. Their black running shoes make no sound. They scurry under a fading streetlamp which casts a cloudy half-light.

A noise in the trees makes them pause.

White peers into the blackness. "What was that?" he whispers. "Was that a door?"

"No. Could be anything. It's nothing. Just keep walking. No problem."

Suddenly a dog barks nearby—a staccato woof-woof-woof-woof. Both of them flinch. He repositions the grocery bag.

"It's okay," she whispers. "That's Henderson's dog. He can't even hear it."

"If we see anyone, we abort—that's the plan."

"I know!" She exhales sharply. "We've rehearsed it, White. Now let's just do it."

When they reach the target, they turn smoothly into the walkway and mount the steps quietly, angling into the shadows of the side porch. Their breathing is rushed and heavy and it takes several minutes to compose themselves. Then, on her hands and knees, Red moves forward until she can scan the neighboring houses. No inside lights; only a few outside lights shining bleakly here and there in the trees, and none nearby; no one on the sidewalk; no cars on the street. At 10:50 P.M. the neighborhood is as placid and drowsy as Blue had insisted it would be. From the Kroger's bag, Red and White carefully extract a roll of duct tape, a lump of cotton wadding, an unlabeled medicine bottle, and a syringe, and prepare for the first commercial in the eleven o'clock news.

"How about this one?" Roy said, looping a flowered lavender necktie around the collar of an even brighter lavender shirt. "Says sissy. Says out of the closet. Says gay pride. Says—"

"I'll take your word for it, Roy." George Graves, his mouth turned down to the maximum, fluttered his eyelids.

Roy cackled and drew some stares from the other customers in the twenty-four-hour Wal-Mart just off Charlotte Avenue in West Nashville. The store seemed busy for one o'clock in the morning. A uniformed policeman with a nine-millimeter on his belt was stationed at the front, just inside the electric doors.

George picked up the lavender shirt and tie and studied them again. "This'll do, won't it?"

"George, you'll be a credit to your race and the entire fairy community."

"Wear it with my navy jacket . . ."

"What race is it, George, exactly, you belong to?"

". . . faded jeans. The Music City look."

"Let's get some rhinestones—go full-bore Porter Wagoner."

They headed to the front of the store. On a clearance table near the checkout lanes was a jumbled pile of children's raincoats, clear plastic with huge red polkadots. George scooped one up as he passed.

Out of the side of his mouth, he said, "Elmo should have told me more. I've been completely out of it."

"I didn't know much either, George, just my little end."

"Completely out of it. I thought you were in the Caribbean somewhere. Diving for doubloons."

"Chief of security, thank you, for a salvage ship. We were looking for sunken treasure."

"They fire you?"

"I fired them."

George chuckled. "Well, you've been more involved than me. I've just been lyin' on the beach waitin' for Hamlet to make up his mind."

"Well, he sure made it up."

"Yes he did. He did that. I have to admit it's pretty good."

Only one cash register was open. A few customers were ahead of them. The policeman eyed them mechanically.

George paid cash for the shirt and tie and plastic polkadot raincoat, and they left the store. In the Checker cab, Roy said, "The only thing, George, that nags at me, a lot can go wrong. Mo usually has more rehearsals. Every detail."

"You're tellin' me. But he wants us fresh, not stale. You got a problem with somethin', Roy? There's time to change—"

"I got no problem, George. How could I have a problem— I'm just the hackie. You gay blades got all the grindin'."

The Second Day

As much as she relished her "free spirit" image in the media, Nikki Gannon, the First Lady of Tennessee, in reality was a creature of habit. Disciplined. Organized. Predictable.

Every Tuesday morning, unless she was traveling with the governor or making an official appearance as First Lady, she visited her mother Louise, who lived alone in the old gray-shingle family house with its three stories and fourteen rooms. Hazelnut coffee, home-baked croissants, political gossip—and sometimes personal talk. The Garden Club, they called these mother-daughter, staying-in-touch sessions, though there was no longer a garden out back. Just an overgrown arbor behind the big drafty house where Nikki had lived from birth until Vanderbilt and which still attracted Sunday drivers who stabbed fingers at the third-floor room where Nikki's father, the judge, had looped a rope over a beam and hanged himself.

The unmarked black sedan rolled up to Louise Gannon's house at eight-forty-eight, right on schedule. It was an accustomed sight in the neighborhood, the state police car with its line of aerials sprouting from the trunk, rear window, and roof, and only the diehard political junkies bothered anymore to carp about taxpayers' dollars wasted on chauffeuring the governor's wife. As she always did, Nikki insisted that the trooper spend the ninety minutes at a nearby coffee shop, where he loved to comb the sports section over biscuits and cream gravy. As he always did, the trooper offered a perfunctory protest, then declared how much he appreciated it, how thoughtful she was, how he'd return at ten-thirty sharp, how she could ring him earlier on the cell phone if necessary. Yes yes, she said, go go, you guys work long enough hours, no sense sitting out here all morning and giving the neighbors more to bitch about. As the police sedan pulled away, the tall and spirited First Lady of Tennessee, whom her mother still called her "horsey girl," loped up the familiar walk and took the stone steps in two strides, ignoring the gentle rain that was spotting her dark green exercise suit.

"Baskerville, you still out, you been spoonin' the night away, you old tomcat you? Come on in, it's rainin', Gran'mere Louise should have your breakfast ready." Nikki laughed. Her mother often cooked breakfast for Baskerville—eggs scrambled with milk and bacon, a few buttered pinches of a croissant. The sleek gray tabby brushed past Nikki's leg and disappeared around the corner of the porch.

"So you're stayin' out a little longer! You naughty little—I guess both of us got lucky last night." Giggling, Nikki wiped her feet on the woven mat and pushed open the heavy front door, which was always unlocked for her arrival. As she stepped jauntily inside, something seemed—

White slammed her hard from the left, clamping her nose and mouth with the chloroform-soaked cotton, his powerful hands encased in surgical gloves. They fell violently against a narrow table, smashing an antique lamp and scattering bric-a-brac across the floor. Terrified, Nikki fought instinctively against losing consciousness, struggling to pry the iron grip from her face and lashing out wildly with her strong legs. Catching someone in the thigh, someone else in the midsection. Faintly hearing a muttered curse as White lost his grip on the cotton wadding, feeling something sting her forearm, hot, searing, then the rough smothering of her nose and mouth again, falling now, fading now, still another sting higher on the arm, duller now, still another. Tumbling into deep faraway blackness as Red plunged the hypodermic into the pectoral muscle, yanked it back, and stabbed wildly again and again.

"Stop! Stop!" White whispered hoarsely, releasing Nikki from his headlock. She slumped heavily onto the faded Persian rug, motionless, silent. Exhausted, Red and White fell onto their backs gulping air.

Twenty minutes later, White drove the cream-colored van to the front of the house, and he and Red hoisted the rolled Persian rug onto their shoulders and headed down the walkway. The rain had stopped.

A tall, pear-shaped man with a British military mustache was standing on the sidewalk next to the van. He held a leash attached to a sturdy brown springer spaniel.

"Another cleaning? Already? Louise just sent that rug out a fortnight ago. Can't imagine—"

"The cat had an accident," Red mumbled, avoiding eye contact with the man and hunching inside the collar of her coat. They loaded the rug through the rear doors of the van, handling it carefully to protect the tight roll, angling it from corner to corner to make it fit.

"Baskerville had an accident! Well, answered prayers, answered prayers—transacting his business on the towelhead carpet instead of my lawn. You hear that, Chesterton! Answered prayers. I think I'll give Louise just the tiniest goose about this. What's in the bag—pilfering groceries, are we?"

"She's sick. Mrs. Perry is sick. She went back to bed." Red hurried back to the house and locked the front door. Keeping her head down, she trotted back to the van and got in.

"Louise Perry is sick? Another damn miracle." He moved closer to the van. "You people always wear gloves just to pick up a bloody A-rab rug?"

The van roared away from the curb. The pear-shaped man thought of noting the license number, but at that moment the springer spaniel pulled hard on the leash as Baskerville the cat appeared on the porch, then shot away.

It was drizzling when Roy chauffeured Elmo Finn and George Graves into the driveway of the Gannons' private residence. Past the guard's kiosk, which they knew would be empty. Past the closed garage with the Mercedes roadster, which neither the governor nor Nikki dared be seen in, lest the political wrath of the United Automobile Workers descend. Past the tiled pool covered by a bright blue tarpaulin. Past the bent-grass putting green that the governor's enemies loved to ridicule.

Roy stopped the Checker cab directly in front of the big white two-story house. A black sedan with two whiplash aerials was parked in the turn facing out.

"Still raining, perfect," Elmo Finn chuckled. "All right, gentlemen. 'Be bloody, bold and resolute.' "

"Don't cudgel your brains about it," George muttered.

The huge painting in the ornate frame had been wedged diagonally into the spacious rear seat of the Checker. George's video camera, covered by the child's red polkadot plastic raincoat, was in the trunk. Elmo and George got the painting out and shuffled with it through the soft rain to the stoop, which was poorly protected by a tiny overhang. George went back for the camera while Roy stayed in the cab with the back door open, a point they had debated only a few hours earlier.

Elmo Finn, his fire-flecked gray eyes masked by shiny black contact lenses, wore a navy blazer, oxford-gray trousers, striped pink-and-white shirt, and no tie. He gave the brass doorknocker four loud whacks. George, standing to the right and behind Elmo, balancing the polkadotted video camera on his shoulder, was buoyant in navy blazer and lavender shirt with a half-tied flowered lavender tie, only the wide end of the tie visible, flowing down from the neck, no knot. Roy had called it the mod West Village pansy-deco look. Red-white-and-blue Gannon for Governor buttons shone in their lapels.

The door opened and a brawny, sandy-haired figure in gray glen plaid stared down at the two six-footers.

"Top o' the morning!" Elmo boomed in a sham accent, which George had pronounced "exquisitely hairdresser" during rehearsals. "The painting is *finally* here! Lucas told us—I mean the *governor* told us—to deliver this *today*—you must be Clay, are you Clay, Sergeant Clay Jennings, he said you'd probably be on the door, you're one of the body men, isn't that the term?"— giggling and winking at the trooper—"it's the painting of Lucas testifying before Congress, that *wretched* committee, I'm sorry it's taken so godforsaken long, so much longer than anyone could have imagined, if you only knew, Clay . . ."

As he babbled and bobbed and weaved, Elmo gradually turned the painting so the strapping state trooper could see it. It had been produced from a black-and-white photograph by a Sarasota artist and framed by a certain craftsman, and was truly horrid. But, as Roy said, truly huge.

"Clay, Sergeant, may we get this in out of the rain—Lucas said he would be doing his exercises—the *governor*, the *governor*—we've known each other since college—Clay, I'm so nervous that he won't like it—I forgot to introduce myself, forgive me, Clay, I am Dr. Constantine Lemay—surely the governor has mentioned—this is my dear friend and associate, Dante, who will not reveal his last name and I suspect may not even have one, Clay"—Elmo giggling again, George smiling and bowing mincingly from the waist—"who wants to take a picture of the painting, some film, actually, *tape,* video*tape* to be precise, of the painting with the governor and the First Lady, speaking of whom . . . perhaps Nikki could look at it first, her eye is so good, if we've made the most awful mistake we will just simply vanish into the fog before the Honorable James Lucas Gannon finishes his morning nip-ups . . ."

Suddenly looking stricken, Elmo ran down like a wind-up toy. He swallowed air and shot desperate looks at Sgt. Clay Jennings and George, then fondled the painting like a pleading lover. "Do *you* like it, Clay? *Do* you? I've been so frantic—James Gannon—he was James in college, not till all this *politics* came along did *Lucas* appear on the scene—cool hand Lucas, for the love of the Almighty—but I knew him as James, James always said I had more talent in my little—I'm so nervous, Clay, I didn't even have the cab driver close the door, so we could escape if—Clay, does this have to fit through that odious contraption, oh *sweet* suffering Jesus of Nazareth! I mean cheese and crackers!" Elmo performed a little jig of panic.

The sergeant's hard eyes had lost some of their wariness and his rigid shoulders had relaxed. Two uniformed troopers were standing in the hallway behind him, looking on with cold cops' eyes. He waved them away. He looked at the ancient Checker cab, its rear door open in the gentle rain. He looked at Dante's untied lavender tie and the video camera in the ludicrous red polkadots. He looked at the massive painting. He looked at Constantine's moist, agonized face.

He motioned them to bring the painting around, not through, the metal detector. This was the part Elmo and George had rehearsed until three-thirty.

From the trooper's viewpoint, the next two minutes must have looked like this: Constantine and Dante lugging the painting from the rain-speckled stoop into the foyer and to the left of the metal detector, Dante whisking the video camera in by the same route as if it were obvious that no camera should be x-rayed, Constantine and Dante backtracking on tiptoe so they could glide through the detector themselves, still on tiptoe, then an ever-more-frazzled Constantine gripping the painting with one hand and tilting it forward for the swipes of the sergeant's hand-held metal detector, a process interrupted by Dante, who swooped up the video camera and began shooting footage, Constantine suddenly imploring the trooper to intercom the First Lady before alerting the governor, no, that was too divinely insipid, just get it over with and call the governor as *soon* as possible, then suddenly requiring and charging into the foyer bathroom (which had been outlined in red on Roy's hand-drawn chart) just as George shifted the painting a few crucial inches, balanced the camera on his other shoulder and launched his own plaintive whine about Dr. Constantine's beastly mental strain, the ordeal of art, the agony of rejection, the unwholesome effect on one's bowels, finally urging the trooper not to call *anybody* until Dr. Constantine could refresh and compose himself. "A splash of water, you'll see a wondrous change."

What Sergeant Jennings didn't see, when he turned to answer the phone on the narrow desk (as Roy's cellular call rang through right on time), was Elmo Finn in stocking feet shoot silently up the stairway, hidden during the crucial seconds by the great garish painting. He made no noise, but George's histrionics would have drowned it out anyway.

With Elmo safely away, George leaned the painting against the banister, deposited the video camera on the floor beside it and sat down to occupy Sergeant Jennings. Grinning inanely, his hands fluttering through a wide orbit, he nattered on about Dr. Constantine's breakdowns and his personal conviction that

God's true message to the modern world was one six-letter word: Prozac. Finally, Sergeant Jennings, who had grown edgier and edgier as the minutes passed, got up and went to the door of the bathroom. The sound of running water was audible. He tapped on the door twice, then three times. The phone rang again and Jennings hurried back.

"Front," he said crisply, his anxious eyes fixed on the bathroom door. His shoulders became rigid again as he listened.

"What? What? Are you—" Now the eyes were furious slits aimed at the mincing Dante. "Yes, sir! Yes, sir! Yes, sir! Goddamnit to hell!"

Jennings dashed to the bathroom, opened the door, and turned off the water. Returning, he allowed the glen plaid jacket to fall open. The butt of the big nine protruded from the shoulder holster. Clay Jennings was left-handed, as Roy had reported.

"You assholes."

George Graves shrugged. The mincing look was gone.

The trooper's face was blotched red, the big vein in his temple pulsating visibly. With a violent motion, he pointed toward the stairs. George began climbing, half expecting a blow from behind. At the top, they went down a wide hallway, past alcoves and closed doors, finally stopping at the last door on the right. Jennings tapped twice, then opened it.

Elmo Finn and Gov. Luke Gannon were relaxing on exercise benches, drinking mineral water from plastic bottles.

The governor, in gray shorts with a white towel around his neck, no shirt, looked the way George remembered. Perhaps a little less hair and a little more gray, perhaps a few more pounds. Winking at George, he bounded forward and put his arm around Sgt. Clay Jennings's shoulder.

"We've been had, podna, *had*," he said with a lilt. "Not just you, Sarge. The both of us."

"Governor, if—"

"Sergeant, I asked for this. I didn't tell you. I didn't tell anybody. When those first threats came in, I called Elmo Finn and asked him if he would analyze my security operation, see if we had any weaknesses, make recommendations. This is how he does things like that. Clay, meet Elmo Finn and his faithful pansy companion George Graves. They just snookered us. And please don't let anyone shoot at that crazy cabdriver. He might shoot back." Turning to George, he threw a mock punch before pumping his hand warmly. "Nice work, George. You son of a bitch."

The florid Clay Jennings was unmollified. He began arguing that such a "charade" couldn't have occurred in "real life," and the governor cut him off.

"Clay, pal, this *is* real life. I was lying on this bench doing flies, and suddenly Elmo Finn just opened the door and said, 'Houston, we have a problem.' Then he pulled out a gun to prove it."

Suddenly Roy appeared in the doorway, grinning sourly, his favorite lockpicking tool dangling from his fingers.

"Second wave," he said. "Good morning, Sergeant Jennings." From behind his back he produced a grim-looking black automatic with a monstrous suppressor.

"Jesus Christ, this ain't no fuckin' game!"

The big state trooper lunged at Roy, dropping his right shoulder and coming in hard behind it. Roy spun like a matador and slammed the automatic into the back of Jennings's head, then kneed him hard in the face. The trooper went down with a sharp cry, but scrabbled to the side and started back up. Roy glided around him, eyes bright and predatory, flicking a jab that largely missed and a followup that largely didn't, then dived for the floor and exploded upward in one motion, levering Sergeant Jennings up and over and down. The big trooper was soft beneath all the swarthiness, and his remaining wind whooshed away. He fell back, gasping for air, as Roy glided away and dropped to one knee, still holding the black automatic like a club.

"Break it up, goddamnit! Roy!" the governor yelled. "Roy! This is crazy! What the everloving fuck are we doing!"

Roy rose liquidly from the floor without using his arms. He picked up a towel and wiped the blood off the automatic. "All due respect, Your Excellency, fuck you. I work for Elmo Finn."

Luke Gannon glowered for a furious instant, then let out a whoop. "Okay, Roy, okay, please don't ever change, Roy, for Christ's sake please don't ever change!"

The governor picked up a gold-and-black Vanderbilt Commodores T-shirt and slipped it on. Sgt. Clay Jennings, who had made it to his feet but was still holding the wall, lowered his right shoulder as if he might charge Roy again. But he was merely checking for range of movement.

"My fault, sir," Jennings said, looking at no one.

"Sergeant . . . thank God this time it was a game. And we lost. It's *my* fault. But these guys are friends, we were in country together. They'll help us get it right."

Jennings pushed off the wall and left the room without closing the door. The others listened as his footsteps died out.

"Okay, okay," Luke said, clapping his hands twice. "This little unfortunate scene is over. Let's clear the tension away—just exhale it." He closed his eyes and took some patterned breaths. The other three men shared a quick glance. This was a side of Luke Gannon they had never seen.

Over coffee and bagels in the bright kitchen, Elmo told the governor how they had assassinated him.

"Almost everything we needed to know was in the papers. And the papers are online."

"Wait, I want Nikki to hear this."

"She's at her mother's, Luke. Garden Club."

Luke glanced at his watch. "Of course, Tuesday morning—was that in the paper too?"

"Several times. Those 'Day in the Life' stories. And a feature on your security detail, complete with pictures. We knew all the body men by sight. It took three phone calls to get the private number at the front desk downstairs. It was just too easy, Your Exaltedness."

Luke Gannon's mouth was fixed in a grim line, his teeth clenching over and over.

Elmo said, "George, how much did you lay off?"

"Thirty-six large."

"Goddamn!" Luke said. "Anybody bet on me?"

"Sure. Some of the Phoenix people thought that if any governor would be well protected, it'd be you."

"I want to hear everything, every hideous detail. And Nikki too—she's really been upset about all these threats. I want her to know that we've got some holes in our security but we're going to fix them. How about dinner tonight? My treat. All you can drink."

"Sure, Guv. We'll try to reassure Nikki."

"Just tell me one thing—what was the hardest part?"

"Getting the gun in."

"How'd you do it?"

"In the frame of the painting. In three pieces."

"Jesus. Where'd you assemble it?"

"In the loo."

"Jesus." Luke Gannon looked off somewhere, then jumped up, clapping his hands again. "We'll fix it. We'll fix it. You don't have that Sandra with you by any chance? Nikki really likes her. You still have that nasty parrot that quotes Shakespeare?"

George made an ostentatious gesture of checking his watch. "Yes, Governor, I'm afraid he does. The accident hasn't occurred yet."

Luke and Roy let out horse laughs and Elmo grinned broadly. "George," Luke said, "you haven't changed a particle. None of you guys. Damn, we got plenty to talk about tonight. Till the dawn kills the moon—or the brandy runs out. And the brandy doesn't run out when you're governor."

At ten-forty the trooper got out of the black sedan parked at the curb. He looked at the gray-shingled house with the big front-and-side porch. There was no movement anywhere except the gray tabby slinking near the door. This was odd. Nikki Gannon was dependable, predictable, not like her husband. She was always in the designated place at the designated time. The cat darted away when the policeman's boots thudded on the steps.

He rang the bell, then knocked sharply on the door. No answer. Peered inside. Walked around the house; the overgrown backyard was empty. Knocked on the back door; nothing. Anxious now, he hurried back to use the radio in his car.

"Oh, there you are." Louise Perry, Nikki's mother, was standing on the front porch holding the gray tabby and stroking his fur in rapid jerks. "She's already gone, Officer. Such a nice morning, she went ahead and walked to the capitol."

"Walked? All the way to the capitol? By herself?"

"Sure. She's a good walker. I gave her a little piece of gossip and I think she wanted the governor to hear it right away."

"She's walking by herself to the capitol? Across the bridge? The Church Street bridge?"

"About a certain senator." Louise winked twice, then again. "She'll be fine, Officer, she didn't want to disturb your breakfast. But I'd love to hitch a ride to the capitol, if you're going." Abruptly she dropped the cat and hurried to the black sedan.

———

The three teenagers wore black shirts and jeans with silver chains and buckles, and leather bandoliers across their chests. Their heads were shaved, and two of the three had tattooed arms. One was balancing a huge boombox on his knees that was blaring heavy metal.

"You know who sat right here?" Spiderman grinned, scanning the boys' attentive faces. "Turn that down some. Turn it off. Can't understand the words anyway."

The skinhead turned off the boombox. "That's 'Third Reich' by RAHOWA. Racial Holy War. Can't hear 'em on the radio. They're totally fly."

"Right where we're sittin' now, lookin' out over Lake Joshua. Right here at this very table."

"Who?"

"Don't know, do you?" Hi Hitler said.

One of the boys seemed embarrassed, as if he ought to know the answer. "Randy Weaver!"

The others laughed until Spiderman's scowl quieted them. "I'll tell you but it's top secret. Top secret. Don't be jokin' 'bout Randy Weaver—Joshua'll skin you."

"Skin the skinheads!" Hi Hitler boomed. His voice carried across the flat blue lake that had once been a rock quarry and reverberated faintly off the limestone walls.

The teenagers leaned forward with eager faces. Spiderman looked behind him, then all around, then once more over his shoulder. He turned back to the skinheads.

"McVeigh."

The boys gasped as one. Grinning, Spiderman bent down to pick up a stone and push-tossed it toward the lake. It fell short.

"What was Timothy McVeigh doin' here?"

Spiderman nodded importantly and selected another stone. "Just visitin'. Just passin' through. He knew all about God's Country."

The three skinheads were sitting on one side of a wooden picnic table, facing the two militiamen on the other bench. A few red and brown leaves, early perishers, lay around their feet, stirred occasionally by the breeze.

"Lots of people come to God's Country," Spiderman said, crossing his tattooed arms.

"Bank robbers come here for Professor Spiderman's bank-robbin' school," Hi Hitler cackled.

"You robbed a bank?"

Spiderman reached for another stone. He winked at Hi Hitler, who let out a high-pitched giggle.

"How long was McVeigh here?"

"That's classified. That's above your pay grade, soldier. Never know where ZOG is. None of you wouldn't be no ZOG agent, would you now?"

The teens laughed nervously. "Who is ZOG again?" one said.

"Zionist Occupation Government. FBI, BATF. Federal Reserve. Jews! Know your enemy, soldier."

"Is it true the governor was FBI? I heard that. What's the pigfucker's name?"

"You heard correct," Spiderman said. "Gannon. James Lucas Gannon. He was FBI *and* CIA. Once an FBI, always an FBI. Once a CIA, always a CIA. Once a ZOG, always a ZOG. But Governor FBI CIA ZOG fuckin' Gannon better watch out! He better watch out real good."

Hi Hitler smirked, then giggled as Spiderman elbowed him playfully.

"ZOG, ZOG, ZOG," Hi Hitler drawled in a guttural baritone, leering wickedly at the teenagers, then finger-shooting them one by one. "ZOG, ZOG, ZOG."

"Did McVeigh do the bomb?"

"ZOG did the bomb! ZOG did the bomb! And pinned it on McVeigh! To throw suspicion on militias and true patriots and places like God's Country. So they could u-zurp more of our rights."

Urged on by Hi Hitler, Spiderman drew himself up and went into the spiel he had learned from his white-haired, blue-eyed prophet, Joshua. The secret Jewish gang that controlled the American economy. The New World Order's secret plan to conquer America with foreign troops and urban gangs who were already conducting maneuvers in black helicopters. The coded deployment orders on the back of the highway signs. Spiderman droned on until the young boy named Jeremiah came running along the path to the compound. He stopped short when he saw the group, a tiny shapeless figure inside the vast baggy clothing.

"Eighty-eight!" he yelled, snapping a stiff-arm salute, his hand and arm swallowed by the comically long sleeve.

"Eighty-eight!" Hi Hitler shouted back.

"Eighty-eight!" said the others.

The boy ran on. His overlong jeans caught under his heel and he fell. Everyone laughed. The boy jumped up, looked back at them, then ran on, faster.

"Ain't that the kid lives in that straw house?"

"Like the three little pigs."

The skinheads laughed louder. Then the boy with no visible tattoos said, "Show us some of the guns, Spiderman. Let us shoot one. You promised last time."

"You wanna fire a weapon, do you? I'll let you fire an AK-47 if you can tell me what AK-47 stands for."

The teens looked at each other. One said, "We don't know. Let us shoot it anyway. We know it's Russian."

Pedantically, Spiderman intoned, "*A* is for assault rifle, *K* is for Kalyshnikov, who invented it, he was a tank mechanic, forty-seven is for 1947, when they first made it. Got to know your history, soldiers."

"My granddad was born in 1947," a skinhead muttered. "That's an old gun."

"Still the best," Spiderman said. "The Armalite don't compare."

"Let us shoot some."

"We're startin' a gun class, you come back then, you'll get to fire 'em all. We're gonna have targets shaped like mud people and Jews and UN troops with blue helmets. We just ordered a thousand Official Runnin' Nigger Targets."

The teenagers whooped and shouldered imaginary rifles, burping sound effects as they fired at imaginary prey.

Frowning, Spiderman motioned them to be quiet. "I'm gonna teach SPIKE classes too, like they do out west. Specially Prepared Individuals for Key Events. SPIKE—you get it?"

"What's a key event? Like an assassination or something?"

"Like an assassination or somethin'. A kidnapping or somethin'. You all know what ricin is? Know your weapons, soldier. One speck of ricin on the tip of an umbrella—that's how the KGB did it! You ever seen a rattlesnake? Ricin is twelve thousand times more poisonous than a rattlesnake. One speck on the tip of an umbrella—jab jab—bye bye."

"God! Where do you get it?"

"I know how to make it," Spiderman said archly.

"Jab jab," Hi Hitler giggled.

"How'd you earn your spiderweb tattoo?" a skinhead asked.

"Classified," Spiderman said. "Top secret. Above your pay grade, soldier."

"Nigger was chasin' him," Hi Hitler said.

"So what happened?"

"He caught me," Spiderman said. Hi Hitler's wild laugh echoed off the rock face above Lake Joshua.

———

Elmo Finn and George Graves were seated in a booth in the coffee shop of the Crowne Plaza, discussing ways to spend an afternoon in Nashville, when Roy came rushing in, elbowing his way through a group of senior citizens dressed in identical cowboy attire who were filing into nearby booths. Roy's eyes were wide and shooting lasers. Elmo Finn knew something was very wrong.

Roy's breathy whisper came in spurts. "Colonel, Luke just called"—grabbing air, looking intently from Elmo to George and back—"this is what he said—exact words. 'Phoenix dying but rising from the ashes.' "

An icy shiver ran through Elmo Finn. He glanced at George, who was dumbstruck.

Elmo dropped his head and looked at the floor. "Roy. You're sure of those words, those exact words . . ."

The waitress appeared, a coffeepot in each hand. "Who was decaf? I can't remember my name today."

"He said those exact words. Then he hung up."

"Let's go to my room." Elmo handed the waitress a twenty, her lips forming a question but the men brushing past her, sweeping to the elevator, crowding inside, scarcely able to abide the tortuously slow ascent, the intermediate stops on the lower floors. Scarcely able to stifle their roiling emotions in the presence of strangers. Grimly reaching deep within. Questioning. Feeling. Remembering . . .

An impossibly green jungle turned to fire and gore. A Phoenix operation betrayed. Seven Americans escaping in a chopper, all of them bleeding, one of them dying, shooting their way up and out, screaming over the rotors and the crackle of the guns. Mason falling dead over the M-60, his trigger finger locked in place. Roy prying him off, seizing the gun as George Graves fed in a fresh belt. Henry Wood wrestling the controls, fighting heavy torque, yelling 'Wipe the blood from my eyes!' Cecil Beech hurling grenades. Elmo Finn and Luke Gannon working the machine gun in the

opposite door. Lifetimes thundering in their heads. Then the star-
tling miraculous whoosh of cold air and impossible silence and
safety, and the fingers pressing Mason's carotid artery, and the
spoken and unspoken prayers, and finally the solemn bitter pledges
in tears and blood. Pledges for life, for all of their lives. Six men.
The code came naturally. Dying, then rising. Like a phoenix.

Not once in all the years since had the code been invoked.

In the corridor Elmo Finn said, "What in hell could have happened in forty-five minutes?"

Roy shook his head.

George was hoarse. "It has to be real bad, the worst thing since the valley. Since Mason died."

Elmo Finn said, "This is the first time we've ever heard the code. And four of us are already here. What the hell does that mean?"

"It means we're still lucky," George Graves said. "I hope."

The Sikorsky was idling noisily on the bright yellow helipad with the corner-to-corner black X, thirty yards from the executive parking lot. Jogging to the helicopter was the drilling company's chief executive officer wearing a roughneck's canvas shirt and jeans instead of pinstriped boardroom attire. As the pilot ran down his checklist a second time, the CEO climbed aboard and worked his way forward to the co-pilot's chair.

"Wild blue yonder, Henry, my man," he said, and began strapping in. The pilot smiled and spoke into the headset.

"Ready for takeoff, Babs baby."

The CEO slapped the pilot's knee and grinned. This was the best part of his job, choppering out to the field, climbing the rigs, wasn't no goddamn oil to be struck under his goddamn desk. And riding second seat alongside the heavy-lipped pilot with the smooth African skin, with the dark suspicious eyes, with the sloped shoulders and barrel torso beneath the khaki bush jacket. Henry Wood might have been a mercenary in any war in the world. He was the most competent man the CEO had ever known.

Babs was saying something. The pilot's hand froze on the stick.

"Say again, Babs."

"Somebody named Roy called. He was very rude, actually, I sure hope he's no friend of yours, Henry. *Very* rude. Demanded to talk with you personally, *demanded,* but I said absolutely not so he made me promise to tell you that the governor of Tennessee had died, *died,* but was rising from the ashes like Phoenix. Made me promise to say it exactly like that. The *governor of Tennessee!* Phoenix isn't in Tennessee. He was really quite rude, and I'm a Texan."

The chopper's big rotors slowed as the engine whined down.

"Henry, what's up? What the hell's happening? Roy the fuck who?"

The black pilot had already twisted off his helmet and was halfway out of his seat.

"I've got to go, Mr. Kelleher." His dark eyes shone.

"Got to go? Henry—the fuck you've got to go! I'm the one who's got to go!"

Climbing into the back, wrenching the handle violently, Henry Wood shoved open the narrow door.

"I'm sorry, Mr. Kelleher."

"Henry, can't this wait? Goddamnit, this is bidness!"

"This is personal, sir."

"Personal, goddamnit, Henry, how'm I gonna get to Galveston?"

But Henry Wood was gone.

The small, wiry man with the Pancho Villa mustache crossed his legs and lit a nonfiltered cigarette. He was sitting with another man at a corner table in a hotel bar on the west side of Manhattan.

"Hope you don't mind." Cecil Beech pulled the ashtray a few inches closer and held the cigarette between his thumb and middle finger, palm up.

"No, no, it's fine. Used to smoke myself. Mr. Beech, if we could just review, since there's to be no written contract . . ."

Cecil Beech made a small wave with his cigarette hand, still palm up. "Mr. Shapiro, I will summarize once more. You fear that your company's computer can be penetrated by your competitors, perhaps *has* been penetrated, despite the assurances from your encryption people. My team of paid professional paranoids will test your security by trying to hack into your system. On the extreme q.t. Our fee is fifteen thousand dollars in cash—half down, half upon conclusion, whether we make it in or not."

Cecil Beech took a palm-up drag, an affectation he had picked up from a Noel Coward movie.

The other man leaned forward a little, tracing a circle on the table with his cocktail glass. He spoke hesitantly.

"Mr. Beech, I have confidence in you, personally, the job you did for . . . our mutual friend . . . he was most pleased, most pleased, but just who exactly *is* your team, though, is the . . . what I'm getting at."

"Mr. Shapiro, my team is two Japs. Tojo and Sushi. They are the best hackers in the world who are not currently in custody. You must realize, Mr. Shapiro, that the top résumés in my line of work often include a category called *time served*. To catch a thief, you understand—"

A woman came up to their table, startling Mr. Shapiro. She handed Cecil Beech a folded note and left.

Cecil leaned back, his expression alert above the drooping mustache. He read the note.

Nashville. Phoenix dying but rising from the ashes. Roy.

He thrust the note into a pocket, stubbed out the cigarette, and got up.

"An emergency, Mr. Shapiro. I must go."

"Who was that woman? How did she—"

"An associate. I'll call you later, when I can."

"But when—"

Cecil Beech had disappeared.

"What do their husbands do, Harlan? *What do their husbands do?* Just walk out, just say "Oh excuse me"—or do they like to watch, Harlan, do they kneel down over in the corner and watch while the great mighty Joshua takes care of their wives? Slam bam oh thank you Joshua God bless you Joshua! Oh—"

Noreen McConathy, her anguished face streaked with tears, flung the plastic container of margarine against the stove and bolted from the tiny kitchen. Joshua reached out and caught her arm, twisting and wrenching so powerfully that she came off her feet and fell heavily on her back on the stained linoleum floor.

"Oh! Oh! Oh!" Noreen screamed, a fresh flow of tears erupting. "Oh, that hurts—that hurts—let go of me! Let go of me, Harlan!"

The white-haired Joshua, his pale blue eyes glinting angrily, did not move from his chair at the rickety dinette table. He tightened his grip on Noreen's arm and pulled her up.

"Ohhhhh . . ."

"You mustn't call me Harlan, Noreen. Ever again. Ever again. My name is Joshua. I've told you."

"Let go . . . please let go . . ."

"What is my name, Noreen?"

"Oh oh . . . Joshua! Joshua! Your name is Joshua!"

He twisted her arm and slung it like a rope. Her agonized scream exploded in the narrow trailer. She screamed again, then folded the arm softly into her body, like a bird's broken wing. She slumped to the linoleum floor and fell against the counter, probing her arm, weeping silently.

"Noreen, your suspicions are . . . unfounded. As the high priest of God's Country, I must minister to members of the flock from time to time, there is nothing wrong with that, there is no impurity in that. You must control your imagination. I remember your daddy always said your—"

"My daddy! Don't you mention my daddy! I wish he'd never given you all this land!"

Joshua slowly laced his fingers together and rested his hands on the spindly table. He had been gazing steadily at her streaked face, but not once had she looked up to meet his relentless ice-blue eyes.

"Your daddy, Noreen, could see what was happening, your daddy was not blind. The Jews. The mud people. Waco and Ruby Ridge, Noreen, the New World Order! ZOG! ZOG! He could see, Noreen, he could see the sheeple being led around by the shepherds of Satan—"

"No! No! That's not what he could see. What he could see was a thousand acres to be used for the glory of God, for building a Christian community, nice homes, and a Christian school, and the woods and the lake and the mountains and the woods, good Christian people living here, peaceful, good neighbors, raising their children, not these head-shaved tattooed . . . *misfits!* How many homes have you built, *Joshua,* not one, *not one,* just these filthy old trailers and that awful hut made out of bales of hay, *hay,* people living in a straw house like the three little pigs, and all your guns and bombs! No, no, my daddy thought this was going to be God's Country, not Harlan's Country! *Harlan!*"

Banging her head backward again and again against the cabinet, harder and harder, wailing now, her face wracked in torment.

Then for the first time looking directly into her husband's cold eyes.

"I saw you kissing them, Harlan! Right out in the open, one after another, those were real kisses! I saw you! *Ministering to the flock!*"

His lip curled but she was looking down again.

"And that Linda!" she whispered brutally. "I know all about you and Lin-da the law-yer, Lin-da the law-yer. The way you look at her . . ."

He laughed sourly and extended his arms beatifically.

"Come, Mother."

She looked dazedly at the stained linoleum floor. She reached out and rubbed a dark speck near her feet.

She said, "Why do you need to *adopt* a highway, just go paint over the signs or the codes or whatever it is. Linda dreams up this stupid stuff."

"Come, Mother."

"They make fun of me, they call me Mother—and you don't make them stop, you do it too."

"Come."

"God *could* be a woman, or part woman, or both man and woman, it's *possible,* Joshua, Daddy said it was. That's why they call me Mother of God, just to make fun of me, and they're just common trash . . ."

"Come."

She slumped forward on all fours, then jerked back her wounded arm. Using her good arm, she bumped across the narrow space and fell onto his lap, whimpering mournfully.

He stroked her hair.

"Oh Joshua."

His hands found her face and rubbed gently at the tear streaks.

"Noreen, the real kisses are for you. You know that. Not for

Linda, not for anyone else. You know that. And calling you Mother of God is a measure of respect—for you, for me, for baby Esther. You know that in your heart. Your daddy would have been very proud. Now I'm going to tell you something I've been saving as a surprise. We're going to start building those homes for God's Country, soon, very soon, there's just one more job to do first. One more job—and I want you to drive."

She raised up abruptly and stared at him.

"You said no more. You said no more. You said no more." Her voice was a wail.

"It's not a bank, Noreen. I said no more banks. This is something much better, much easier. You're our best driver, Noreen. I can't spare one of the soldiers to drive. After this job, this one last job, the homes will start going up. Homes for God's people in God's Country, I want that more than anything. Just like you. Just like your daddy."

A baby was crying in the rear of the trailer. Noreen struggled to her feet.

"You said no more, Joshua. Not after Esther came."

"Just one more, Mother. It's *for* baby Esther."

"We meet again." Sgt. Clay Jennings of the Tennessee State Police uncoiled his six-four frame from the ornate chair in the private corridor next to the governor's private door. His face showed the effects of the tussle with Roy.

Elmo Finn's gray eyes flashed. "The governor wants to see us, Sergeant. Right now."

"I know." He stuck out his hand. "You guys were pretty slick this morning. Taught us a lesson. Guess I got carried away."

"We all do, Sergeant. Forget it." Elmo and George shook hands quickly with the big state trooper.

Elmo said, "We do need to see him, Sergeant. Right now."

"Sure." He flopped his large hand on the polished doorknob, then turned back. "Mrs. Gannon isn't with you?"

"No."

"You haven't seen her, by any chance?"

"No."

Jennings took a deep breath, his hand still on the doorknob, his big shoulders rising and falling. "This ain't our day. First you guys manage to get next to *him*, then we lose *her*. And they call us the body men."

"We really do need—"

Jennings turned the knob, pushed open the door, and ushered them into a small anteroom. He went across to another door and knocked twice. Gov. Lucas Gannon opened the door at once.

"Mo, thank God."

Elmo and George hurried into the office.

"Governor," Sergeant Jennings said, catching the closing door with his hand, "I've just eaten some more crow about this morning, I wanted—"

"Clay, we're running late here—"

The big state trooper edged forward into the doorway. His face was flushed. "Governor, we haven't located Mrs. Gannon. Her mother said she was walking over here—"

Lucas Gannon shrugged and made a vague gesture. "Nothing to worry about, Clay."

"Governor, if you want me to resign, just say so."

"Hell no!" Luke made a sharp dismissive gesture. The trooper nodded and backed away, allowing the heavy door to close.

Elmo and George had never seen the governor's spacious office, thirty by thirty, with its antique desk, marble fireplace, and twin chocolate leather sofas. Perched on one of the sofas was Louise Perry, small and gray and pale, wearing a navy pants suit. She was massaging lotion into her wrist.

The governor moved briskly to the fireplace.

"Okay, boys, here it is. *Nikki's been kidnapped. Kidnapped.* You remember Louise, Nikki's mother, she'll give you the details of what we know as of now. There's been no demand, no contact yet from the kidnappers—"

Another door, behind and to the right of the big desk, opened abruptly and a slender young man in a pinstriped suit popped in with a stack of folders. He stopped short when he saw Luke Gannon shaking his head emphatically. "Nothing now, Eli. Nothing! Seal me off." With a wide-eyed nod, Eli Korn took everyone in, then backed through the open door and pulled it closed.

"It was diabolically simple," Louise began hurriedly. "Last night at a few minutes past eleven, the late news had just started, when the first commercial came on, I opened the front door to let Baskerville out. The cat. That's how we do it every night, he was already waiting at the door, he knows when it's time. As soon as the door opened, they barged in, I don't know how many of them, it was over in just a few seconds. They grabbed me and put their hands over my mouth and I just went out. They were obviously waiting on the porch and they obviously knew what to wait for." She began applying lotion to her other wrist. Both had deep red marks.

"That's all I remember. They knocked me out pretty fast, I showed Lucas the needle marks. Almost twelve hours. They knew Nikki would come this morning, they had to know. When I woke up, I was upstairs in my bed, four-poster bed, trussed up like a prisoner with duct tape. It took me a long time to get loose. That's when I found the note. It was pinned to my robe."

Luke turned to the mantel and drew a half sheet of paper from behind a vase. He read it aloud, a flutter in his voice.

" 'We have Nickie. She is in danger. Tell no one except the Governor. NO ONE.' "

Elmo went over for a closer look. "Lined paper, handprinted. Obviously, a second message will come. They misspelled *Nikki*."

"Lucas!" Louise stood up, her hands fluttering. "You told Eli to seal you off. He takes that very seriously—nothing can get in here now."

Luke picked up a phone and punched two numbers. "Eli, be on the lookout for a letter or a delivery of some . . . bring it in! Now!"

Hurrying to the staff door, Luke said, "City Delivery just brought something."

The door opened and Eli Korn rushed in almost charging into the governor. He handed over a large orange-and-blue envelope, his intelligent eyes scanning the room.

"Eli, zip us back up. Total blackout. I'll explain."

"Yes, sir." Eli spun and disappeared.

The governor ripped at the narrow tab.

"Careful, Luke," Elmo said.

Luke fished out a smaller envelope, opened it, and extracted another handprinted half sheet. He propped it on the mantel and read it aloud as the others gathered around.

Governor Gannon,

We have Nickie. She is safe and will be returned safe if you meet our demand. A political prisoner named Randall Tice must be released from Brushy Mountain. Work it out however you want—but work it out fast. You should not want publicity in this matter and neither do we. If there is publicity or if you call out your jackboots, you will never see her alive again. Get busy, Governor, we will be in touch. Nickie is safe for now.

There was no signature.

Luke was pale. "Oh Jesus, this is a nutcase. A nutcase! Who the hell is Randall Tice! *Political* prisoner? What does that mean, political prisoner? How can I release a convict—the governor has no power—"

"Lucas!" Louise's hand fluttered to the governor's arm. "Lucas, I know who Randall Tice is."

"Who? Who?"

"Surely you remember Randall Tice."

"No! Who is he?"

She stared up at her son-in-law. "You've just forgotten the name, son. About three years ago, or four, a state trooper was killed. The police were sure this Randall Tice did it, they arrested him for murder—"

Now Luke was nodding his head. "And the judge threw out the case. He got off."

"Yes," Louise said softly. Her face turned scarlet, as if she had confessed to a crime.

"I don't understand," Elmo Finn said.

Luke put his arm around his mother-in-law. "The judge who threw out the case was Nicholas Perry. Louise's husband. Nikki's father."

Louise's clasped hands were working furiously. "We got such awful mail. We even had to change our phone number."

Luke said, "The police found the gun—the murder weapon—in Tice's trailer. But Judge Perry ruled that the search was unconstitutional, Fourth Amendment, and the D.A. was so furious he nol-prossed it. Had a press conference and said Judge Perry should be impeached."

"There was so much impeachment talk," Louise said. "The papers were full of it."

"I still don't understand," Elmo said. "Randall Tice shoots a state trooper, he isn't prosecuted because Judge Perry makes a ruling—but Tice ends up in prison anyway."

"He wasn't prosecuted for *murder*." Louise began pacing in a small orbit, her hands shaking at her sides as if palsied. "But about a year later, Tice was arrested again, this time for bank robbery. He was one of those fanatics, what do they call . . . God's Country! God's Country, it's some kind of cult. They were robbing banks to pay for their . . . whatever, and this Randall Tice got caught." She grabbed the governor's arm. "Lucas! Those fanatics have got Nikki—and they want to swap her for Randall Tice!"

She was bouncing on her toes, a vigorous presence at five-foot-two. "You *can* pardon him, Lucas, you're the governor! We've got to save Nikki—this is no time for politics!"

"Politics? Screw politics! Screw the governorship! But it's not that easy to just pardon somebody. You can't just open the doors of a maximum-security penitentiary and close your eyes while a felon strolls away."

"You do want to save her?" Louise stood rigidly in a pose, her hands still working at her sides. "You do want to save her?"

Luke's glare was venomous. His voice became low and bitter. "Louise. What are you saying, Louise? Nikki and I may have had . . . I'm not going to answer that question. Sit down and shut up."

"Oh I'm sorry, I'm sorry, Lucas. I'm just—"

"Sit down and shut up."

Elmo Finn went to the sideboard, poured a glass of water from the crystal pitcher, and drank down half of it. "All right, all right, we seem to have a terrorist kidnapping. The ransom isn't money, it's releasing a convict named Randall Tice who's a member of some kind of cult. Luke, can you get the complete file on this Randall Tice—without asking anyone?"

Luke thought for a moment. "No."

"Without asking anyone?" Louise put in. "Of course he'll have to *ask* someone."

"Hold on, Mom."

"Is the prison system computerized?" Elmo asked.

"Yes. Department of Corrections—it's a model program. Other states copy it."

"George, get Roy."

George went out through the anteroom. As the heavy door

opened and closed, Elmo saw Eli Korn huddled intently with Sgt. Clay Jennings, who eyed Finn with the expressionless look of policemen everywhere.

Elmo Finn said, "Louise, we ought to find out what sedative they used on you. How can we get you tested without raising anyone's suspicions?"

Louise and Luke began discussing ways to do this. After a while the door opened and George and Roy came in. This time only Eli Korn could be seen in the background, stock-still, his rolled-up white shirtsleeves exposing matchstick arms, a scowl on his face.

"Roy," Elmo said, "this is Louise Perry, Nikki's mother."

Roy nodded perfunctorily and took up a sleepy-eyed, slope-shouldered stance near the door, his hands loosely behind him. To most observers, he would have appeared innocent, even deferential. Not to those who knew him.

"Enemy contact, Roy." Elmo's voice was flat and unemotional but there was a light in his fire-flecked gray eyes. "We need to hack into the state prison system's computer, read a file, maybe alter it. Where's Cecil?"

"On his way, sir. Henry too."

Luke said absently, "I haven't seen Cecil Beech since we were in country. He couldn't make the wedding."

Louise Perry went shakily to the corner sideboard and opened a cabinet. She took out a bottle of gin and filled an old-fashioned glass to the brim. Tremulously, she said, "Lucas, I want you to call the police—this is my daughter here, and your *wife,* not some game you play with your old commandos. Who lost a war."

"Mom, shut up. That's the game you're going to play right now. Just shut up."

She froze halfway between the bar and the sofa, then tossed off a big slug of gin and stared at her son-in-law. Her hands began to drift again, and gin sloshed out of the glass.

"Louise," Elmo Finn warbled in a pacifying tone, "let me try to reassure you. We know this isn't a game. We aren't old. We didn't lose a war. The commando part's right."

"So do something!" The glass shook in her hand.

"We *are* doing something. We're considering breaking into the Department of Corrections computer to find out about Randall Tice, and we're going to find out about these God's Country people, and, if they have Nikki, we're going to devise a plan to make them release her—"

"*Make* them! Make them *how?*"

"I see three ways. Undoubtedly others will present themselves."

"Three ways! I'd like to hear just one!"

"All right. We get Tice released and then kidnap him ourselves, and work out an exchange for Nikki."

Louise's face softened a little. "Fight kidnapping with kidnapping. Break the law ourselves."

" 'Our strong arms be our conscience, swords our law.' " Elmo looked at the governor. "That's just one scenario, Luke. You'll call the shots, obviously."

" 'Swords our law'? I like that," Louise said.

"The well-known vigilante, Shakespeare," Luke muttered.

Louise put down her glass, crossed the room and embraced her son-in-law, who was a full head taller.

"I'm sorry, son, I didn't . . . oh Lucas, last night I went up to the judge's room. The first time in months, and now this happens. Why did I go up there?"

"Mom, Mom," he whispered, "we'll get her back. I promise you, we'll get her back safe and sound."

"Oh Lucas, let's fight kidnapping with kidnapping! *Swords our law!* Oh, Lucas, please don't bring the police in, whatever oath you took! Use Elmo Finn—use the commandos! *Swords our law!*"

"Nikki comes first, Mom. That's my oath."

As Louise turned away and went into the governor's private

bathroom, Lucas put his hands to his neck like a noose. Elmo, George, and Roy nodded as one. They remembered the tragedy of Judge Nicholas Perry, after whom his daughter Nikki was named, a liberal jurist who had abhorred capital punishment and refused to impose it, but who, with a perfectly tied hangman's knot at the end of a length of rope, had made an exception for himself.

From the capitol complex on the high bluff above Broadway and the Cumberland River, the red Toyota pickup dropped down to Interstate 40, headed east for a few miles, then swung south on I-24. Traffic as usual was heavy.

"How far is it?" Louise Perry asked, her heart throbbing so loudly she was sure it could be heard.

"Not that far," Sgt. Clay Jennings answered. "It's a little out of the way, but no one will get wind of anything, especially those damn reporters, pardon my French. That's what the governor wanted, why I'm usin' my private vehicle. How long you been feelin' poorly, Miz Perry?"

"Oh, it's . . . off and on. I don't think anything's too terribly . . . but you know Lucas." She folded her hands together to hide the trembling.

"Yes, ma'am, the governor sure wouldn't want you to get sick on us. You do look a little peaked, but it's comin' up fall. Change of season, affects everybody. I get the worst hay fever."

Louise nodded several times. "It's just some allergy, probably, but you know Lucas. Traffic'll move better after Harding Place. I hope."

They crept along in the rush-hour crawl. The late-afternoon sun streamed through the right-side windows. Louise had not pulled down her visor.

"Your daughter sure gave us a scare today, Miz Perry, walkin' all the way to the capitol, crossin' the Church Street bridge. I *guess* that's what she did, nobody's actually *seen* her that I know of—"

"Oh I saw her, Sergeant, I saw her, she was in and out, had a million things on her mind. Sometimes with all the security and everything, you know, all you body men around all the time, she just has to . . . assert herself. She was always independent." Louise ran the last few words together, coughing loudly to cover the break in her voice.

"I never noticed her bein' too independent, she's always co-operated with us. But we're just doin' our job, Miz Perry, there's some crazy, crazy folks out there. You know about the threats been comin' in. This mornin' at the residence . . . you hear about that? This has been a day. These cowboys showed up out of nowhere, old buddies of the governor, Vietnam, pretendin' to be a pair a cupcakes, and they sure put one over on us. Testin' our perimeter. Almost got my nose broke before it was over—they're damn lucky we didn't shoot 'em."

He glanced quickly at Louise, who was staring straight ahead.

"So I guess we're a little on edge today."

Glancing over again.

"So you did see her? At the capitol?"

"Oh yes, she breezed right in . . . what do y'all call her, her code name? Horsey?"

"Yes, ma'am."

"That's from me. I always called her my horsey girl because she was a little . . . homely, I suppose, when she was young, a little ungainly, people called her things like 'horsey,' the boys all ignored her—" Coughing again. "Then one summer Nikki just blossomed, just *bloomed,* you should have seen the boys then, Sergeant! All tongue-tied and stammering around! And now my horsey girl is the governor's . . . wife . . ." She turned to the window.

"What time did she breeze in, Miz Perry? More or less?"

Louise coughed and rubbed her eyes. "Oh, late morning, I'm not exactly sure—must have been eleven or so."

"Eleven or so."

They drove in silence for several minutes. Then Louise said, "Sometimes she comes in through the body man's station, sometimes through Eli's office, sometimes through reception . . . see, the traffic's better now, I knew it would be."

After a while the Toyota left the interstate and wound through a maze of suburban streets. The sun was lower in the sky and cast a warm, golden light.

"Is this Murfreesboro?" Louise asked.

"Not quite."

They left suburbia and took a smooth but curving country road. Before long they came to a long white rectangular building with stunted columns in front, two smaller buildings behind, and wide parking lots stretching along both sides. The complex was bordered on three sides by fenced, rolling pastures with high-roofed barns and gleaming silos. Sergeant Jennings pulled in and proceeded to the rear.

"A funeral home? In the middle of nowhere. Good Lord, Sergeant . . ."

Clay Jennings laughed. "The perfect cover, Miz Perry. My sister works here part-time. She's a nurse."

"Good Lord, what's that?"

"That's the crematorium. They've got pretty much a full-service operation here. They'll put you in a box in the ground or up on the mantelpiece in a jar."

"Good Lord. A crematorium in the boondocks. Why does a funeral home need a nurse?"

Another chuckle. "She's just the organist. But they have a room where . . . I guess you could say it's well equipped. And Joyce will have her bag."

"I won't have to see any dead bodies, will I?"

"No ma'am, no ma'am, absolutely not. I made sure."

"I didn't know nurses had a bag."

They went in through a rear door and were met by a woman in her thirties with a two-inch streak of gray through her hair, as if she had suffered a deep trauma that singed her head. She was wearing a nurse's uniform and a plastic name tag: Joyce R. Jennings, R.N. They were in a quiet, dimly lighted corridor with closed doors along both sides.

"Mrs. Perry, I'm Clay's sister, Joyce. If you will just take this and go right in there, we need a urine specimen first. Then I'll draw some blood and that's it."

Louise took the paper cup in both hands and looked around suspiciously. "All right," she said meekly, and went into the bathroom marked Employees. She closed the door and slumped against the wall. She went to the sink and turned on the faucet, then tiptoed back to the door and pressed her ear against it, straining to hear the conversation in the corridor.

Joyce Jennings was saying, "I couldn't believe it when you called. How'd this happen?"

"Governor said she's takin' too many downers, he wants a chemical analysis without her knowing it. Said she's been feelin' bad anyway, so he talked her into doin' it this way because her regular doctor's out of town, have to keep the press in the dark, blah blah blah . . . so I volunteered you."

Joyce Jennings laughed. "So this is a drug test."

"That's the plan."

She laughed again. "Always glad to help state government." And laughed again.

In the bathroom, Louise smiled a tight smile. She had pulled it off. For the first time since waking up a century ago this morning, bound to her bed, terrified, certain she had expired and passed on to infernal regions, Louise felt a tiny but insistent bloom of hope. They would get her back. A vision of her horsey girl flashed into her mind's eye—Nikki at her first school dance, a head taller than all the boys, waiting in vain along the wall to be asked onto the floor; and Louise, one of the chaperones, recruiting the neighbor's boy with a secret bribe. And how Nikki had beamed and pranced. And now the governor's wife, the First Lady of Tennessee. Tears flooded her eyes, but she suppressed them, her clenched teeth making a grinding noise. Hold on. Hold on for Nikki. God's Country wouldn't be crazy enough to harm a governor's wife. But they were surely crazy, how crazy is enough . . . stop!

She used the paper cup and prepared herself to go out and meet the nurse and the body man.

Elmo Finn said, "It's your call, Luke. Bring in the state cops and the FBI and go by the book—or go it alone. It's a tough one. And every second counts."

Luke got up from his high-backed chair and came out from behind the antique desk. He went to the corner cabinet and fixed his second weak Scotch and water. Elmo Finn and George Graves sat on opposite sofas, sipping bottled water. Roy leaned against the wall near the trooper's door, nursing a bottle of beer.

"You had to make the same choice, Mo. How long ago was it?"

"Eight years."

Luke Gannon was one of a dozen people who knew the full story. Elmo Finn's fiancée, the only woman he had ever been sure about, the only woman he had ever wanted to marry, carjacked . . . raped . . . murdered. By a brutal sadist entitled to carry a detective's shield. Elmo and George tracking the killer down, pushing themselves day and night, their manhunt aided and abetted by anonymous tips from certain cops. Finally, near a remote mountain cabin close to the Canadian border, sighting him through powerful lenses. Felling trees to seal off avenues of escape. Closing in. Several police officers had been there at the end. No charges were filed.

"Mo, what's the best . . . way . . . to . . . rescue . . . Nikki? That's the only question. The only question. I could pick up that phone right now and have an army of detectives, techs, FBI agents—hell, I *was* an FBI agent—combing Mom's house, canvassing her neighbors, interviewing City Delivery, tracking down everybody who ever knew Randall Tice. And invading God's Country, which should have been done long ago."

He looked around challengingly. No one spoke.

"That's what I *should* do—to fulfill my oath of office. And the statistics show . . . I know what the statistics show. I was on two kidnapping cases with the Bureau, our line was it's always better to call the police, don't go it alone no matter what the threat is." He rubbed his eyes with his fingers, then with the heels of his palms. "The statistics show that a lot of kidnap victims don't make it. I know the statistics. But it's not the statistics, it's not my oath of office. The question is getting Nikki back. If the cops get involved, I'm afraid it will leak, accidentally, and those media bloodsuckers will never sit on this story, whether Nikki ends up dead or not!" He took in some air. "And those God's Country fanatics—I think they'd carry out their threat, I think they'd kill her if this leaked."

The phone rang and Lucas answered.

"Tell the senator . . . Eli, tell the goddamn senator I'm not . . . Eli! Goddamnit! Zip us up!" He slammed the phone down and exhaled heavily. "My oath!" he snarled. "I'll have to resign." He stared blankly at the limp flags of Tennessee and the United States in their heavy brass stands behind his desk.

"Maybe not, Luke," Elmo Finn said. "But probably."

"Screw the governorship! Screw the oath! This is it, Mo, the only question . . . can we lay on an operation without the police, without my staff, without the FBI—I can't believe I'm saying this—without the Department of Corrections, which runs the prisons, without the press, without the sympathetic outpouring of public opinion—what I'm asking, Mo, can we find Nikki and get her back ourselves?"

"I like the odds better."

"You don't think the cops will catch 'em?"

"Sure they will. Catching 'em is number one for the cops. For the Bureau. But they might not completely protect Nikki in the process. That's number one for us."

The room became so quiet that their breathing was audible. Luke said, "Everything's different when it's your own wife."

"If we do it ourselves, Luke, we'll take some chances the cops wouldn't take. Maybe bend the law a little. Maybe break it. But if the goal is to get Nikki back, *period,* I like doing it ourselves. Us against the world."

Something crossed Luke's face, like a shadow. "That was our motto. *Is* our motto. Since college. *Us against the world.* Last night Nikki said if it's us against the world, bet on the world." He sat up, rolled his chair forward. "The debit side, Mo—what's our biggest problem?"

"What you already said. They're fanatics. 'Political prisoner.' 'Jackboots.' They aren't asking for money—they have a cause, they're true believers. Can't predict 'em."

"Do you take the threat against Nikki seriously?" He grimaced. "Of course you do. We have to. I don't know what I'm saying." He came over and sat down next to Elmo and pressed his fingertips into his temples.

Elmo said quietly, "There's something else, Luke—if this leaks, we lose the option of releasing Randall Tice and snatching him ourselves, or planting a transmitter on him and following him. Or anything else. You can't possibly let Tice go if everybody's looking—even if we've got a play on."

"I know, I know. That's the best reason to do it ourselves."

"How about this, Luke? Keep everything zipped up until we

learn more about Randall Tice and more about God's Country. You can always go public after being private, but not vice versa."

Luke jumped up and went to the corner bar. He packed a highball glass with ice, then filled it halfway with Scotch.

"You want something, Mo?"

"I just want to get going. As soon as possible."

Luke Gannon guzzled half of the drink and set the glass on the sideboard. He wiped his mouth and picked up the glass and finished it. He rattled the ice cubes and set the glass down again and looked off somewhere.

"You think they'll hurt her, Mo?"

"We have to assume they won't, like you said. There's every reason to believe they'll keep this deal. If they get Tice back, which is what they say they want, why wouldn't they return Nikki and balance the books? They figure you'll have to keep it quiet to remain in office. But if they *don't* keep the deal, they know you and about a million cops will never rest."

"But they're fanatics."

"Yes, apparently, but the deal they've offered isn't fanatical. It's a straight swap. It makes sense."

Luke turned back to the bar, filled another glass with ice but added only water from the crystal pitcher. He gulped it down. "I took an oath, Mo. Hand on the Bible. Faithfully execute the laws."

"Luke, you took an oath to the state of Tennessee but you also took an oath to Nicole Perry Gannon. I was there for that one."

The governor of Tennessee crossed the office to the high windows and looked out. He was silent for a long time.

Finally he said, "I keep thinking how scared she must be. How alone. Helpless. She must be terrified, I just want to find her and hold her . . . my heart's pounding, Mo, it's like combat. Like that last helicopter ride."

Elmo Finn moved a few steps closer to his old friend and comrade in arms. "People adjust, Luke. Prisoners adjust, just like in war. And Nikki's strong, she's smart, she's resourceful. They've got one tough lady on their hands—they might want to send her back early."

Luke let out a grim chuckle and turned back from the window. "She is tough, I'll say that. We have to trust her to hang on. To stay tough."

" 'Could I come near your beauty with my nails, I'd set my ten commandments in your face.' "

"Oh she would. Yes." He looked at Elmo Finn. "Mo, you love a fight, you love the combat. The chase. The game. And I know you want to help, that's who you are. Could your judgment be . . . overzealous maybe?"

Elmo said, "I've already asked myself that question, Luke. I'm not objective on any of this, I can't be. So I may be wrong. That's why it's got to be your call."

They stared at each other across the plush carpet. Then Luke Gannon clapped his hands sharply several times.

"Swords our law, swords our law. Let's lay it on, Mo."

A modest office in a modest building on a side street in downtown Nashville. Dimly illuminated by overhead fluorescent bulbs, most of them faint or burned out. Faded beige and tan linoleum flooring in a diamondback pattern. Four framed photographs on one wall: Randy Weaver, the survivalist hero of Ruby Ridge in Montana; David Koresh, who died at Waco with eighty of his Branch Davidian followers; Pete Peters, the Christian Identity minister and apostle of white supremacy; and Adolf Hitler.

A wooden desk was angled across a corner of the room. Behind it, in an old-fashioned wooden swivel chair, sat a big woman, bulky but not fat, wearing olive drab fatigues, a military-style web belt, and a khaki shirt with epaulets. No makeup or jewelry. Camouflage boots.

"I have no sympathy for you, Mrs. Cherry," Linda Pearson, attorney at law, snapped. "None at all. None at all. And very little time."

Facing the desk in a metal folding chair was a round-faced woman wearing a shapeless dress, a white cardigan sweater balled up in her lap. Her face was flushed and damp.

"Mrs. Pearson—"

"Miss."

"*Miss* Pearson, you're a lawyer, an educated woman—do you think my Jeremiah should be living in a house—in a *hut*—made of bales of hay? A *straw hut*? Not going to school—"

Linda Pearson slammed her hand on the desk. "School is held every day in the Ark, Mrs. Cherry. Every day. The children are learning the four Rs—readin', 'ritin', 'rithmetic, and race! And race! Joshua himself teaches, I teach, Mother teaches, the Professor, Popeye, Spiderman, even Earl—"

"Earl!"

"Your husband, Mrs. Cherry, is a God-fearing white Christian patriot. Earl Cherry teaches from his own experience, from his own life, from his own vision—"

"Earl didn't even finish seventh grade, for God's sake! He can't teach—he can't even read Joshua's sermons, if you can call them sermons, all that poison—"

The hand crashed down again. "Infidels had better watch what they say in this office. About our beliefs. About Joshua's teachings. You breeze in here threatening your husband—my client—with a custody fight over little Jeremiah, who is doing so much better with Earl than he ever did with you, and calling names and trashing God's Country—do you even know what God's Country is?"

"I was there, Miss Pearson! I saw it! Oh I know what it is!"

"You were there for one week. Until Joshua banished you."

Helen Cherry half stood, her face twisted in rage. "*Banished* me—how about *raped* me! *Raped* me! He makes all the women . . . even you, Miss Pearson, they all talk about you, Linda the lawyer, and Joshua!" Her hands were tearing at the white sweater.

Smirking but red-faced, Linda Pearson leaned back and locked her fingers behind her head. "What a grotesque little sheeple you are, what a slanderer. You will never get custody of Jeremiah—"

"Have you seen his clothes! They're so big, they were Earl's clothes, he just falls out of them. I sent him—"

"You sent him unsuitable clothing and it was burned."

Slumping back onto the metal chair, Helen Cherry broke into sobs. Her hands pulled and twisted the sweater. She curled forward into a ball and wept silently. At length, she drew herself up and absently fixed the white sweater about her neck like a scarf. Forcing herself to look across the desk. Forcing her eyes to meet the smirk of Linda Pearson. Rising slowly to her feet.

"What does eighty-eight mean? Will you tell me that? Why do they make Jeremiah say—"

"No one *makes* him say anything—he *wants* to say it. It's an honor to say eighty-eight!"

"What does it mean? Please tell me what it means!"

"It's very simple, I'll tell you. I want you to know. What is the eighth letter of the alphabet, you sheeple? H. Eighty-eight is HH—*Heil Hitler! Heil Hitler!*"

Linda Pearson's brittle laugh echoed in the corridor as Helen Cherry ran sobbing from the room.

The young man with the rolled-up shirtsleeves and the thin arms stood before Luke Gannon's antique desk, shifting his weight from foot to foot. Shooting quick glances at the strangers in the room to whom he had just been introduced. Hearing but not comprehending what his boss was saying.

"Special project . . . vital project . . . totally confidential . . ."

A thousand thoughts and variations of thoughts and permutations of variations of thoughts whirled in Eli Korn's agile mind. One of his faults—one of his few faults as chief of staff to the governor of Tennessee—was a tendency to overexamine and overanalyze. "Eli, my man," the governor told him once, "sometimes I'm afraid you chew more than you bite off."

"Like Henry James," Eli Korn had answered, smiling, just to show he knew the quote.

"Eli! Listen, goddamnit!"

"Yes sir, sorry, this is just so unexpected, I'm just not sure—"

"Eli. When you and I started down this political road, you asked me to make one promise. Remember?"

"Yes sir."

"You wanted the right to challenge me. About anything. The right to say your piece. And I said yes—hell, I *wanted* you to challenge me—you're a better politician than I'll ever be. But now I have to break that promise, and I'm asking you to trust me until I can explain."

"Yes sir, yes sir. You got it. May I ask one question?"

"No."

"On another point."

Luke Gannon gestured impatiently.

"Governor, we've gotten several calls for Nikki, and we can't find her. Jill's a little upset."

"Tell Jill that Mrs. Gannon is out of town for a few days. On a private matter. Don't let the press find out. It's simply an unannounced trip—just take messages."

"Got it."

"Now, Eli, what kind of shape is the headquarters in?"

"The headquarters? Not too bad. Use some cleaning up—nobody's working there much."

"I want you to get the top floor ready for these men. They'll live there and work there. Whatever Elmo asks for. If it takes all night. The whole floor—no questions asked. Use my private Visa card for whatever you need. Then forget all about it and keep everyone away. Will you do that for me, Eli?"

Eli Korn squared his shoulders and met the keen eyes of the politician to whom he had pledged his fortunes. Until he himself ran for something. And until he ran for something, he would continue to serve loyally as Lucas Gannon's Yes Man. *Will you do that for me, Eli?* Eli Korn always said yes. Then found a way.

"Yes, sir." Rapping the antique desk for emphasis, spinning away, hurrying to Jill Dennison's office to brief in breathless whispers the governor's executive assistant, Eli's colleague and rival and now his ally in this strange new game with these strange new people; then a beeline to the permanent "Gannon for Governor" headquarters that occupied all four floors of a nondescript office building two miles from the capitol. His mind inventing, sifting, tabling explanations of the governor's curious conduct. He would analyze it and figure it out; he always had. In the meantime, the Yes Man would deliver; he always had.

"It was too dangerous. I told you. I was more nervous than at the house."

The woman code-named Red finishes her coffee and signals the waitress to bring a refill.

Blue drums his fingers on the tabletop, watching Red intently. Jitters before, jitters after. Everything going so well and still all this hand-holding.

He says, "Even if anyone remembers you, your disguise was perfect. And nobody at City Delivery will remember. Stop worrying so much."

"It was too dangerous. Stop being so defensive."

The waitress comes and pours fresh coffee. After she leaves, Blue says, "How's White holding up? Is he panicking too?"

She leans toward him, cocking her head and challenging him with a hard look.

"Nobody's panicking, damn you." Her harsh whisper is loud; she softens it. "You ever hear of constructive criticism? White and I are just fine, we rolled with all the punches, *we were quick but didn't hurry,* we got it done. You weren't there. We were there. And I got it done at City Delivery, but it was too dangerous. *Could* have been. We're taking enough risks, no point in unnecessary—"

He decides to lose the argument.

"Okay, I admit City Delivery was risky. You're right. That's why I used them first. Every delivery's going to be different. The others will be safer. Foolproof. I'll handle most of 'em."

She raises her cup halfway to her lips, then replaces it in the saucer without drinking. Her face is red. He looks out the window at the traffic.

He says, "Isn't Randall Tice worth it? Worth the risks?"

She waits for him to look at her but he continues to stare out the window.

She says, "I'm sorry. Let's stop fighting among ourselves."

He finally turns and reaches across the table and they shake hands awkwardly.

"I'll handle the next delivery. Is it in the trunk or on the seat?"

She snorts. "What do you think? The trunk."

He checks an impulse to flare back, then contents himself with a satisfied nod. And sticks out his tongue like a child.

Grinning, sticking out her tongue in return, she says, "Guess what. Her name's written on the inside. Victoria's Secret, 34C, Nikki Gannon. Her fucking name—like summer camp."

———

"Sandra, I want to learn the merengue. Do you know the merengue? Surely a professional dancer . . ." Elmo Finn's cheery voice suddenly ran down.

"Yeah, sure, I know the basic steps . . . is everything okay . . . sure. Okay."

They hung up. They had rehearsed this procedure several times but had never needed to employ it. Elmo waited ten minutes and dialed the number of a pay phone outside a Publix supermarket on Longboat Key. Sandra answered on the first ring.

"What is it, Mo? Are you okay? My heart's pounding."

"I'm okay. George is okay." Then he told her what had happened in Nashville.

"My God, poor Nikki. She must be insane, if she's still . . . do you think . . ."

"I think she's still alive. That assumes we're dealing with rational people, and perhaps we aren't. But I'm an optimist."

"Yes! We must be optimists. Give Luke my love. Do you need me, Elmo?"

"I may, Sandy. I may need you. This is . . . I don't know what this is."

"I'll be on the first plane."

"What about the studio? All your little Isadora Duncans?"

"It'll keep. They'll keep. You shouldn't even ask that, Mo. When I called you that time . . . I owe you one."

"No you don't. You don't owe me anything. But you're right—I shouldn't ask."

"I'll be the judge of my debts."

They continued to talk for several minutes. Elmo Finn was standing at a pay phone outside a Mapco convenience store on busy Hillsboro Street in West Nashville. A stream of customers, mostly Vanderbilt students, came and went.

Elmo Finn said, "Explain things to the menagerie, pal, if you

68

can. Maybe read Falstaff a little *Hamlet*. Or *Romeo*—he likes *Romeo*."

"Falstaff's doing fine, Mo, and Macduff too. But Dr. Watson—Dr. Watson is deeply disturbed. His jowls have just about melded into the tiles. He's the saddest dog when you're gone."

" 'Every dog will have his day.' "

"Were these creatures ever normal?"

"They seemed normal until George started the experiments."

Sandra cackled. "Oh, how can I laugh? I feel so terrible thinking about what Nikki's going through. Will you call me?"

He gave Sandra a list of items to be air-shipped to Tennessee.

"Now I'm really scared," she said.

"Just normal preparation. 'Discretion is the better part—' "

"Quote me no quotes, Colonel Shakespeare. Why do you need the vests?"

"We don't need the vests. We just want them handy."

"In case you need them. Goddamnit, Elmo."

"We'll be careful. I love you, pal."

"Promise me."

"I promise. Cudgel your brains no more."

"Promise you'll call me."

"I promise. And I promise we'll still go to Bermuda. Where I promise to smother thee with kisses."

"I want that one in writing."

"Can't you read my lips?"

The Yes Man delivered. Suppressing his doubts about the boss's unprecedented behavior, Eli Korn summoned six of his diehard campaign volunteers to the capitol, three "studs" and three "dolls," terms that offended the politically correct, which was why Eli used them. He had one of the body men usher them into the governor's conference room, where amid the trappings of high office Eli confided to them that certain "emergency strategy sessions" would be taking place at the old headquarters and the governor needed their help. Right now. Eli's sly half smile conveyed the perfect sense of intrigue, investing the janitorial assignment with the glow of insider status, and within hours his energetic little band had dusted, vacuumed, mopped, and rearranged most of the fourth floor of the idle "Gannon for Governor" headquarters. They paid special attention to the big corner office that had been Campaign Manager Eli Korn's command post in the last campaign. Using a piano dolly, they rolled out a half-dozen locked filing cabinets and jammed them into a storeroom. Yanked everything off the walls except a giant map of Tennessee showing the counties color-coded in red, white, or blue. Pulled down all the window shades, taped them fast to the sills, drew the curtains, stapled them tight to the frames. Cleaned out Eli's old L-shaped desk and set up worktables and folding chairs around the walls. In the farthest corner they positioned the computer, which they had first installed in a separate room, then relocated at the behest of the wiry man with the drooping mustache and the foppishly held cigarette. They managed to wedge it all in—computer and monitor and laser printer and fax and scanner and external backup—and neatly tied off the umbilical wires beneath the table with bungee cords.

The other rooms on the fourth floor became a dormitory with rollaways and rented linens, a makeshift kitchen, a darkroom (fashioned from a janitor's closet), and a supply room into which the bush-jacketed black man and the mysterious Roy dragged military-looking boxes and duffels, then drilled new clasp holes themselves and secured the door with heavy padlocks. Eli's volunteers hung vinyl curtains in the purple-and-green-tiled showers of the two executive bathrooms, stocked them with linens and soap. And the strangers moved in.

Elmo Finn checked his watch. "Nine hours. They've had her nine goddamn hours."

Turning to the man with the drooping mustache who was working at the computer, he said, "Cecil, you got everything you need?"

Cecil Beech nodded, reaching down and tapping the locked aluminum briefcase at his feet.

"Brought my own software, Colonel. Can't get this at CompUSA."

"Is it illegal?" Louise was peering over Cecil's shoulder at the screen.

"Some places it ain't."

"Some places it ain't," she chirped delightedly.

Elmo Finn said, "Cecil, you need a DSL line or a cable modem, or more juice, or more whatevers, just say so. We'll get it. Borrow it or buy it."

"Or steal it," Louise added brightly.

Cecil growled, "Talkin' don't bother me a bit, folks, 'less you're talkin' to me." His hands flew over the keyboard in a burst of clicks and clacks.

The black man hung up the phone, tore off a page of notes from a scratch pad, and stuffed it into a pocket of his bush jacket. "Pretty good options, Colonel, I'll have a Cessna tomorrow morning. Weather looks okay. Plus, they got some surplus choppers, military and industrial, including one beautiful olive drab Huey with the machine-gun mounts still in place."

"We just may need it, Henry." The two veterans of the CIA in Vietnam looked at each other. "The Bell UH-1 Iroquois. Talk about old times, Henry."

"Roger that, Colonel."

They heard footsteps taking the stairs two at a time. Luke Gannon burst in.

"Man!" He was breathing hard, looking from face to face. "Man. You guys."

He embraced big Henry Wood, then little Cecil Beech, and the three men shook hands and hugged more or less at the same time. Henry said something, and as Luke tried to answer the words caught in his throat. They all embraced again, silently, awkwardly. Louise turned away and wiped her eyes.

Elmo Finn said, "Luke, you bring the map?"

From his inside coat pocket the governor produced a bulky clump of paper. Henry took it and began unfolding it carefully. Louise got Scotch tape from the desk, tore off some strips, and they taped the big aerial map to the wall.

"Is that it?" Henry was pointing to a hand-drawn red circle.

"That's it," Luke said. "Jill Dennison had this in her files. My executive assistant. She's been monitoring God's Country for quite a while."

"She didn't ask why you wanted it?" Louise said.

"I told her the same thing I told Eli. Trust me."

"Can *you* trust *them?*"

"Eli and Jill? Mom, we've got to. Yes. I'd trust them with my life."

"It's Nikki's life we're trusting them with. Where's the body man?"

"Downstairs."

"Is it Jennings?"

Luke shook his head. "Moody."

"What does *he* think is happening?"

Luke shrugged. "Less explanation is better than more. I told all the body men that this was old home week for me and my Vietnam buddies. Eli's volunteers think I'm running for president and these guys are the vanguard."

Henry said, "I want to get another weather check." He gripped Luke's shoulder, then went back to the phone.

Luke said, "Food's coming. Eli called a caterer. And a refrigerator in about an hour. I haven't eaten anything since those bagels this morning, Mo."

"Let me be in charge of food, son," Louise said. "I need something to do."

"Sure. When will those tests be done?"

"I don't know. I thought it was better to play dumb. Sergeant Jennings thinks it was a secret drug test you ordered to see what horrible tranquilizers I'm taking on the sly."

"Good, that's what they were supposed to think. Why did Clay take you to a funeral home?"

"His sister works there, she's the organist but she's also a nurse. I saw the embalming room."

"Jesus, Mom. There weren't any . . ."

"No. I made sure first. It's a crematorium, too, way out in the boonies—they'll put you in a box in the ground or in a jar up on the mantel. Oh, I don't know why I said that."

With a little whoop that startled everyone, Cecil Beech pushed back from the computer table and lit an unfiltered cigarette. Holding it palm up, he took a deep drag, still peering constantly at the flickering screen.

"All right!" he said raspily, turning to the others who were waiting intently. A satisfied smile fought past the bushy mustache. "Pleased to announce that we are now through the firewall. We have *root privileges,* don't you know. I think I can toast this mother by dawn."

"Yes!" Luke began clapping his hands, chanting, "Ce-cil, Ce-cil." Louise ran over and gave Cecil a big kiss, momentarily discomposing him, but soon the cigarette was restored to its two-fingered, palm-up attitude.

"Cecil, you're the best." Elmo Finn bowed to him with both arms extended.

Cecil puffed on the cigarette and cocked his head. "All modesty aside, Colonel, this state government stuff ain't too pluperfect hard. Bureaucrats ain't got beaucoup imagination. But gettin' in is the easy part—it's hangin' around impersonatin' people that might get a shade touchy. May have to send for Tojo and Sushi yet. My super-Japs. Ain't nobody better who ain't behind bars." Another puff, blowing a ring of smoke toward the ceiling. "But I'm bettin' on dawn."

"Will Corrections be able to tell you've been in there," Elmo asked, "digging around about Randall Tice?"

Cecil wrinkled his nose. "Nah. We'll use a trapdoor, then we'll lay a little virus on 'em. Germ warfare. Destroy the evidence."

Footsteps sounded again on the stairs, someone jogging up. Luke yanked open the door just as George Graves arrived carrying a package wrapped in glistening red-and-gold paper.

"Eli gave me this," George said. "An anonymous call came in to the switchboard, Governor, saying that a special gift for you had been left under a certain bench in the capitol. Eli went and got it himself. Had it x-rayed. It's apparently harmless, but he's mighty curious."

Luke had already grabbed the package and was tearing into it.

"Easy, Luke," Elmo said.

"Let me do it, son," Louise said, and he handed it over. Her fingers suddenly lost their tremors and she quickly unwrapped the package. Inside was a shallow folding cardboard box of the kind used by department stores. Louise carefully removed the top.

"Oh my God. Oh my God." She looked fearfully at her son-in-law. "It's a brassiere, Lucas. It's hers. I know it's hers." She extracted the undergarment and fumbled for the label, on which her dependable, predictable daughter had printed her name in indelible ink, just as Louise had taught her in the horsey days. Nikki Gannon.

"Oh my God, Lucas, what are they doing to her?"

Enclosed with the brassiere was a half-page note handprinted on lined paper. Luke, his voice quavering only slightly, read it aloud.

To Gov. Gannon,

Communicate via classified ad in personals section of Tennessean. Use these codes—we are White Thunder. You are Blind Man. Nickie is Hot Stuff. Randall Tice is Ice. Hot Stuff is ok so far. Nice tits.

White Thunder

"Goddamn those scumbags," Luke whispered bitterly. "If they touch her. If they touch her. God, I want to kill 'em."

"We'll get 'em, Luke," Elmo said. "But let's get Nikki back first."

"Have they hurt her, Lucas?" Louise cried, clutching Luke's arm, then Elmo's. "Do you think they've hurt her? Oh God!"

Luke embraced his mother-in-law, the half-page note pinched in his fingertips. "Mom, we assume she's okay. We have to assume she's okay." He closed his eyes and his voice trailed off. "We have to assume that."

"Exactly," Elmo Finn said briskly. "Nikki's not only okay but she's working this very minute to remember everything—voices, sounds, smells, accents—everything. It's been almost ten hours—let's get back to it. And work as hard as she's working."

The door opened and Roy came in. No one had heard him on the stairs.

"You got something, Roy?" Elmo said.

Roy nodded. "The City Delivery clerk remembered the customer who dropped off the envelope. Woman, thirty-something, a little heavy, maybe wearing a wig, dark glasses. Had her hand in a bandage, so the clerk had to fill out the form. Avoiding prints, obviously. Paid cash."

"She's from that awful God's Country place, I know it!" Louise said. "Randall Tice's wife! Or girlfriend!"

"Could the clerk make an ID?" Elmo asked.

"She thought she could. My opinion, sixty-forty no."

Elmo Finn nodded and turned to George Graves, who was

leafing through a sheaf of photocopied pages. "George, give us a summary."

George propped his leg on a metal chair. "There's a good-size file on Randall David Tice in the *Tennessean* morgue. Here's the gist. Tice is thirty-four, a common redneck lowlife, white trash in the purest sense, high school dropout, even rejected by the U.S. Army when he tried to enlist. The U.S. Army doesn't reject all that many. Criminal record—a dozen arrests, mostly assault, two short jail terms. Then he fell in with God's Country and became a real felon. A gang of three or four hit a bank in Cookeville. They got away, but the cops somehow suspected Tice, tracked him down, and arrested him in a trailer at God's Country. He still had traces of dye on his hands from the exploding pack. But the money itself was never found, close to three hundred large. Cops searched every trailer at God's Country, every building, searched the property—as well as they *could* search a thousand acres. Tice refused to confess, even when they offered him a deal. So he's doin' eight to ten at Brushy Mountain. Served thirty-two months so far."

"Who was Tice's lawyer?" Luke asked.

"Woman named Linda Pearson, she represents God's Country and this cat Joshua, who's the head nutball. Listen to this"— Graves consulted his pages—"she asked Tice on the stand who could have framed him by putting the dye on his hands, and Tice said, quote, 'It was agents of the New World Order or the mud people.' Unquote. Jury started giggling, which made Linda Pearson ballistic, and she ranted and raved all this paranoid super-patriot crap until the judge had her removed from the courtroom. Prosecutor called her Loony Linda right to her face. She'd refuse to stand up when the judge came in, stuff like that. But to describe Randall Tice in a nutshell—take your basic illiterate redneck, mainline him full of William Pierce and Pete Peters and David Koresh and Randy Weaver, sprinkle in some *Mein Kampf*. Voilà—one dangerous dodo."

"This is the *political prisoner* they want back so bad?" asked Cecil, tugging at his mustache.

George shrugged. "Randall Tice is more than a bank robber—he's probably a murderer, too. Most of us know this story but it's worth repeating. About four years ago, before the bank job and not long after Tice first moved into God's Country, a state trooper named Travis Page was shot dead on Route 52, near Jamestown. Late at night. Cops are sure Tice did it—the theory is that this Page had pulled Tice over because his car had a homemade God's Country license plate—they refuse to register their vehicles because they claim they're a separate country. Travis Page didn't radio in a tag number, which fits the theory—there wasn't any tag number to radio in. Anyway, Tice shoots Page—seven times—and escapes to God's Country. When the cops get there, they storm into Tice's trailer and find him and the gun, a Glock nine, ballistics got a seventy percent match."

George took in some air and peeked at Louise Perry.

"Go ahead, George," Louise said. "It's okay."

"Judge Perry, Nikki's father, Louise's husband, ruled that the search of Tice's trailer was inadmissible, no probable cause, which ruled out the gun. Fruit of the poisoned tree. Then the prosecutor had a press conference and dramatically dropped the charges. Said Judge Perry's ruling made the case impossible to prosecute and the judge should be impeached. Some people say he didn't have a solid case anyway, with only a seventy percent ballistics match, and was looking for an out. But Judge Perry was roasted in the press, and there were demonstrations. Death threats, too." He looked at Louise Perry, who opened her mouth but nothing came out. Her hands were scrubbing nervously.

"Some state troopers were so pissed off they started laying for Tice in their off hours, like vigilantes. But then Tice got arrested for the bank robbery and ended up behind bars anyway."

Elmo Finn asked, "Any guess on why God's Country, or

somebody, wants him out of jail bad enough to kidnap the governor's wife?"

"One guess," George said. "The three hundred thousand from the robbery was never recovered. Maybe Tice stashed it somewhere and God's Country wants it back."

"Why'd they wait almost three years?" Elmo mused. "He's been in prison for thirty-two months."

George shook his head.

"Cecil," Elmo said, "can you hack into the Visitors Log at Brushy Mountain? Find out who's been to see Randall Tice over the last thirty-two months?"

Cecil exhaled a long puff of smoke and restored his cigarette to the Noel Coward position.

"One Visitors Log," he said, spinning back to the keyboard, "on toast. Comin' up."

"I love you, Cecil Beech," Louise blurted.

"Oh, he's nothing if not lovable," Elmo said, as Cecil struck a Valentino profile. "God's Country, George, you get anything on God's Country itself?"

George shuffled his pages. "If this place is God's Country, I don't want to see Satan's. It's a mishmash of the so-called Patriot Movement, which thinks the enemy is the U.S. government, the so-called Christian Identity Church, which thinks the enemy is blacks and Jews, and a touch of the other nutcase groups who think everybody's the enemy. It's a real screwball cocktail—of ignorance and hate and neo-Naziism and paranoia and assault rifles. Basically, God's Country attracts life's losers— uneducated, unemployed, unsophisticated, unhappy misfits who need to blame somebody else—some outside force—for all their problems. So they find a home in a superpatriotic hate group, which gives 'em beaucoup scapegoats for their miserable little lives—the Jews, the blacks, the Federal Reserve, the New World Order, whatever the hell that is, the Illuminati, the Council on Foreign Relations. And they get to join an army—at God's

Country they call it God's Swift Sword—where a loser in the real world can become a captain. But the leader isn't stupid at all, he's very shrewd and manipulative. Former door-to-door salesman named Harlan McConathy, calls himself Joshua. The Prophet. His father-in-law gave him—*gave* him—a thousand acres of pristine Boone County land to build a Christian enclave, modeled after that Almost Heaven place out west. His wife is an interesting study, too. Noreen McConathy. They call her Mother of God because she says God's a woman. And Joshua apparently is very charismatic, 'piercing blue eyes,' they say, and especially appealing to the ladies, who appeal to him as well. Like Koresh. Charles Manson."

The room was hushed and wary, everyone glancing at everyone else.

"You want more, Elmo?"

Elmo Finn nodded grimly.

George went to the side table and poured a cup of coffee, then came back to the center of the room, shuffled his pages again, and in a flat voice began reeling off more particulars about God's Country.

The tattooed ex-paratrooper called Spiderman, born Quincy Dean Klepper, who was kicked out of U.S. Army Special Forces with a general discharge, who wore white bootlaces to symbolize white supremacy.

The ex-delinquent and dropout named Glenn Forbush who insisted on being called Hi Hitler.

The straw hut made of bales of hay where Earl Cherry and his ten-year-old son Jeremiah lived, if you could call it living.

The cache of weapons confiscated during the manhunt for Trooper Travis Page's killer—AK-47 assault rifles, MAC-10 machine pistols, sawed-off Heckler and Koch semiautomatic carbines, Barnett Commando crossbows, throwing stars, blasting caps, one hundred sticks of Gelmax dynamite.

The four unsolved bank robberies that Randall Tice and

God's Country were still suspected of, although two witnesses had recanted their stories.

The converted barn called the Ark where Joshua conducted daily sunset services, which served by day as a schoolhouse and by night as a barracks for visitors—or, some said, a safe house for ultra-right-wing fugitives.

The thousand outlying acres, a craggy and forested Tennessee mountain wilderness with primitive cabins tucked here and there, a secluded valley shooting range, and crystal-blue Lake Joshua, formed by damming up a rock quarry. At several points along the irregularly fenced perimeter were hand-lettered wooden signs: God's Country. Trespasser's Will Be Shot.

"Why don't the cops just roust 'em?" Cecil demanded, rising from the computer desk and pulling at his bushy mustache. "The right to bear arms ain't the right to raise an army."

"Weaver fever, Cecil. Weaver fever. All the law-enforcement agencies are gun-shy after Ruby Ridge and Waco. When that FBI sharpshooter hit Randy Weaver's wife, who was holding her baby in her arms . . . caution infected the good guys. They're lookin' the other way on things like homemade license plates and unpaid property taxes. Weaver fever."

Again everyone was silent. George closed his folder and poured more coffee. Cecil returned to clacking at the computer keyboard. Luke gave Elmo Finn an eye signal, and the two went out into the hall. They walked to the end of the corridor.

Luke put his hand on Elmo's arm. "Mo, they took her clothes off. 'Hot stuff. Nice tits.' Goddamn it, if those bastards touch her . . ."

"This is the reaction they want, Luke. I don't understand it, why they want to infuriate you. It makes no sense. But we'll figure it out. 'Every why hath a wherefore.' "

"I know this is the reaction they want, my head understands all that, but in here . . . goddamnit, Mo, they're succeeding." He drove his fist into his palm. "Swords our law!"

They shook hands solemnly and went back inside the big corner office that was now the command center of an extralegal police operation being run personally by the governor of Tennessee.

Elmo Finn checked his watch. "Eleven hours, people," he called out. "Eleven hours since they took Nikki. Our working assumption is that God's Country has her, somewhere on those thousand acres. Let's go, let's go—I want to be on offense. By sunrise."

"I know y'all said 'hill country,' Joshua, but I'll tell you, these East Tennessee hills look a damn sight more like mountains, you ask me. A damn sight."

Joshua laughed and smoothed back his white hair with both hands. "Why we call it God's Country, Sarge. Go tell it on the mountain! Let's get you another cold beer, then we'll get down to business. Start makin' out a list."

The man called Sarge said, "I'll sure have another beer, Joshua, and I'm sure ready to do some business. But I sure ain't writin' nothin' down." He laughed stridently.

The bartender caught Joshua's gesture, set up a tray with three drafts in iced mugs and a stained carafe of hours-old coffee, and ambled over to the farthest booth in the backcountry roadhouse, where four men sat hunched over the table. He knew three of the four as residents of God's Country—the man in black with the spiderweb tattoos; the gaunt, tense, unsmiling man who seldom spoke; the engaging blue-eyed preacher who seldom stopped. When he first met Joshua, months earlier, the bartender had been attracted to his earnest, forceful, antigovernment harangues, and had once driven out to God's Country in his red pickup to attend a sunset service. But once had been enough. Conservatism was one thing—everybody was conservative in the mountains—but radicalism was something else, and to a country-cautious barkeep who'd served with the Ninth Infantry in Nam, God's Country was radical. Throw stones at the government, sure; big stones. But it was still the red, white, and blue. He'd seen too many pine boxes draped in the red, white, and blue. He'd take their business, though, even if the blue-eyed holy man sipped only coffee and his hard-eyed lieutenants nursed their beers like light-duty pussies.

He had never seen the fourth man in the booth. Heavyset, pig-eyed, balding. Forearms like a butcher or a blacksmith.

"You all want some music?" the bartender said. "Quiet as a tomb in here tonight, none of these big spenders gonna spring for no jukebox. I can't hear nothin' but you all a-whisperin'. Don't sound inter-estin' enough try to eavesdrop."

Joshua and Spiderman smiled. The heavyset stranger said, "Good idea, partner, give us some music. You got Merle Haggard, can't hear Merle on the radio anymore. Just that pop-country bubblegum shit."

"You can sure hear Merle Haggard on my jukebox."

"Now you talkin'."

Soon the shimmering twang of Merle Haggard and the Strangers filled the big barroom with a working man's lament.

Two men in coveralls with oval name tags sewn on the chest were playing pool in the back, singing along with Merle Haggard on the hookline. Fewer than half the stools at the long bar were occupied, most by solitary drinkers. There were no women in the bar.

In the corner booth the heavyset man leaned forward on his big forearms. "Y'all understand, Joshua, there ain't no credit in this business. Cash deal, I got to see cash money first." He smiled, showing a perfect row of teeth. "Even from a man of God. Even from a man of God's Country."

Joshua reached across and gripped the man's arm, the pale blue eyes homing in. "That is exactly how we do business, Sarge.

C.O.D. We have the money. The money's no problem. I just wanted to get our order in, make sure you can supply exactly what we need."

Merle Haggard reached the hookline again, the bass line descending in a syncopated push.

"Absolutely. Sure. I can sure supply it. If it's military ordnance, I can sure by God supply it."

"That's why we wanted to talk with you first, Sarge. There are others who claim—"

"I know, I know, you can hear any goddamn thing you want to hear. But I'm the only dealer called *Sarge*. You cain't be a master sergeant at Fort Bragg long as I was and not have some . . . special forces." He cackled harshly, his porcine eyes sweeping their faces, drawing tight smiles. "Special forces, you get it?"

"Spiderman is our minister of defense, Sarge. Earl Cherry here is deputy minister. They will present our requirements."

Spiderman unfolded a half sheet of paper he had been massaging in his hands. He looked around, then shielded the paper as he cleared his throat.

"One M-60 machine gun with ten thousand rounds. One rocket launcher with fifty rockets. Fifty pounds of C-4 explosive. One hundred Claymore antipersonnel mines. Two hundred antipersonnel grenades."

"Damn! Double damn! You all must be hittin' Fort Knox."

Joshua and Spiderman smiled.

"Can you hide all that stuff?"

"We got a thousand acres at God's Country alone, Sarge. And if that ain't enough, you ever hear of the Daniel Boone National Forest?"

"Goddamn. Don't you want no M-16s?"

"We prefer the AK-47. We've already acquired those."

"Goddamn." Sarge finished his beer. The Merle Haggard song was over and an edgy silence resettled on the barroom.

Sarge whispered, "Claymore mines? You gonna mine God's Country? With children runnin' around?"

"That's true." Earl Cherry spoke for the first time, his voice weak and reedy. He looked at Joshua imploringly, his narrow face pale and moist. "Jeremiah would step on one sure, I'd have to tie him up inside all day."

"Earl, you know I wouldn't place Jeremiah in harm's way, or any of our children."

"No sir, I know you wouldn't. No sir."

The jukebox started again and the four men, welcoming the noise, relaxed a little. Sarge grinned and rapped the table with a fat fist. "Boys, show you my good faith in this, I'm gonna give you a little present today, a token of appreciation. I got it right out there in my trunk. I wasn't sure how serious you boys were, but by God I am now, and I have no doubts that you'll come up with the money—"

"How much money we talkin', Sarge?" Spiderman said.

"I got to do some pricin' first, make some calls, but you'll sure get a discount, this much volume. I'll work out the best price possible. And this present I've got for you, I think you'll like it. I call it the Rat Trap." He sipped beer and beamed at them over the glass. "It's a radio frequency detector, you can strap it on you, wear it concealed. And it will detect a wire! It will detect a foreign transmitter. So if you got a traitor, God forbid, somebody wearin' a wire for law enforcement, some ZOG agent, this little beauty'll sure let you know. The Rat Trap, I named it myself. This ain't military issue. More like CIA."

The other three wore big smiles. Spiderman said, "We'll take that Rat Trap off your hands today, Sarge. And much obliged. I think we can do us some business."

"All right, all right. I knew we could, hell I feel exactly like you boys do, I saw a lot of what you would call treason, right there in Uncle Sam's army. Right there at Fort Bragg."

"When *The Day* comes," Joshua said, "we expect most of the American military to come over to us. Bring their weapons and fight with us."

"When the day comes," Sarge said uncertainly.

"It will come, Sergeant Maloney, have no doubt of that. It will come."

Joshua finished his coffee and fished a twenty-dollar bill from his pocket. He stretched it taut.

"See this?" He pointed to a tiny ridge, narrower than a matchstick, on the gray side of the twenty-dollar bill near the left edge, running vertically through the *U* in United States—the plastic security strip to prevent counterfeiting.

He began rolling and twisting the bill. "This is how ZOG works. This is how fiendish things have become in the Jewnited States. This little strip lets 'em count our money and track us by satellite."

He smiled knowingly as he worked the plastic strip loose and extracted it from the bill, holding it up like a prize.

"Goddamn," Sarge said. "I never knew that one."

"Fuckin' ZOG bastards," Spiderman said.

"*The Day* will come," Joshua said. "*The Day* will come."

They stood up and headed for the door. Joshua stopped at the long wooden bar.

"Harold, I've just kept the big eye in the sky off of you," he said loudly to the bartender, tossing the defaced twenty onto the bar. A few heads turned. "Now you do me a favor and come back to one of our sunset services. We had a real good one tonight."

"I'd like to, Joshua, that's a natural fact, I've been meanin' to get back out there. But that sunset service, I get most of my customers 'bout that time. We call our sunset service Happy Hour."

"Bring 'em all out. Do 'em good."

"Well, now there's an idea. Might have to bring a keg with us."

As Joshua and the other men left, the bartender glanced at the nearest customer and muttered, "Or two."

The customer, a wide-shouldered man in a plaid shirt who had sipped two draft beers over the last hour, said, "Mind if I look at that twenty, see what he did?"

The bartender slid it across the smooth surface of the bar. "He thinks it's coded with that little strip, so the gov'ment can count your money, or track you, or somethin'."

"What the hell for?"

"Oh, like the feller said, his toothpick don't quite make it through the weenie. You ought to hear him go on 'bout the highway signs, the stuff printed on the back to show when they need paintin' or replacin', whatever. Joshua thinks it's codes or signals or somethin' for the New World Order, so when they invade they'll know where to go. Their marchin' orders, for God's sake. I know a man used to work for Transportation, he said Joshua was one hunnerd and fifty percent full a shit. Said the Transportation Department don't even know theirselves what's on the back."

The wide-shouldered man laughed and asked for another beer. The bartender drew a full glass, drained off the head, and topped it off. He placed it in front of the customer, who offered his hand across the bar. They shook.

"I'm Gene Kessler."

"Just call me Harold, Gene."

"Good name for a bar. The Hog. You get a lot of bikers?"

"Used to. Friday nights that parkin' lot out there was wall-to-wall Harleys. They've mostly moved on. Sheriff took some interest."

Gene Kessler took a thoughtful sip of beer. "Harold, how many local people go along with this God's Country . . . way of thinkin'?"

The bartender stretched his arms behind him and looked curiously at the stranger.

"I wouldn't know. I wouldn't know, Gene. Wouldn't think too many folks goes along too much with 'em. I'll tell you what riles a lot of folks, they won't pay their vehicle registration and they put those cardboard tags on their cars like God's Country was a separate . . . whatever. Jurisdiction. Sheriff oughtta go after *them,* leave my customers alone."

"How often they come in, Harold? Joshua and Spiderman, especially?"

Harold froze for a moment. "You know 'em, do you?"

"Can you keep a secret, Harold?"

"I wouldn't be no bartender if I couldn't."

"You served with the Ninth Infantry. I was with the First Cav."

Harold cocked his head and stared at the stranger. "You were at Khe Sanh?"

"Longer'n I wanted to be," Gene Kessler said, taking a thin leather case from his pocket and handing it to Harold, who looked inside for a moment, then handed it back. They looked at each other.

"Guess Joshua'd call me a ZOG agent, Harold."

"Well, callin' you somethin' don't make you somethin,' Gene."

Harold went down the bar checking on each customer, refilling a few glasses. Then he came back and pulled over a high stool and conversed in low tones with Gene Kessler for a long time. At length, the wide-shouldered man stood up and reached for his wallet.

"On me, Gene," the bartender said.

"Wish you'd let me pay, Harold."

"Your money's no good here, Gene. You just do somethin' about those goddamn homemade car tags. People are gettin' highly indignant."

"I know you've heard the story," Louise Perry whispered to Elmo Finn, gripping his arm. "The so-called official story. But my Nicholas did not commit suicide—he did *not*. I will never believe it. *Never*."

She squeezed his arm tightly. They were sitting by themselves near the coffee machine in the fourth-floor command post. The only sounds came from Cecil Beech's computer in the corner.

"Nikki was named after Judge Perry, wasn't he?" Elmo asked softly.

"Yes," Louise said hoarsely, her hand darting to her throat. "Nicole. She came up with her own nickname—N-i-k-k-i—when she was seven years old." Louise gazed off for a moment. "Just last night, before those fiends burst in, I went up to the judge's study, I *never* go up there, but something made me go up there last night. I just looked around for a minute, I forced myself to look at the beam where the rope . . . I've been thinking maybe I could *feel* something . . . get some kind of . . . sensation. You must think I'm crazy."

"Not at all."

"Elmo. Elmo. He—did—not—commit—suicide. And he would never hang himself. *Never*. We were planning to take a cruise." She struggled with the tremors in her voice.

Elmo Finn said, "Do you sense some connection between what happened to your husband and what happened to Nikki?"

"*Yes! Yes!* I've been afraid to come right out and say it. But I know there's something, I can feel it but I don't know what it is."

"What does Nikki think about her father's death?"

"When Nicholas died, Nikki said she was almost relieved in a way. Because she couldn't disappoint him anymore. He wanted a son more than anything, Nicholas Perry the Second. Not Junior. The Second. But we had Nicole instead." Her eyes bored into Elmo Finn's. "Elmo, they started calling him the Hanging Judge—the prosecutor, the police, mocking him, mocking him after he was dead and gone which they wouldn't dare do when he was alive! Because he believed in individual rights, civil rights. Because he hated the death penalty. The Hanging Judge! But I know in my heart he did not hang himself. He did not."

Elmo Finn resettled himself in the metal chair and leaned toward Louise, who was perched on the edge of her chair like a child, her hands busily working.

"Louise, I've got an assignment for you. A very important assignment, and you're the only one who can do it without calling attention to it."

"Yes, Elmo, please, I want a job. I'm going crazy."

"Tomorrow morning, Henry and George are going to fly over this God's Country place in a spotter plane and take pictures. The first thing they'll do is radio back a description of every vehicle on that property. Not tag numbers—they don't have legal tags. But whoever kidnapped Nikki had to use a vehicle. I want you to take that list of vehicles and canvass your neighbors, one by one, very discreetly, very carefully, to find out if anyone saw a strange car or truck or van in the neighborhood that matches one on the list. Not just last night and this morning, but in recent weeks. The kidnappers have been there before—they had to recon the target. They had to get Nikki out of the house and into a vehicle in broad daylight. She's five-eight, one-thirty-five. Did they just *walk* her out? Did they use a wheelchair or a gurney? They had to get her out *unnoticed*. How? In a box? A trunk? Rolled up in a rug—"

"Oh! Yes! Elmo! That's it!" Everyone looked over. Louise jumped up, her hands intensifying their scrubbing motions. "That's what was wrong this morning! The *rug* was gone! The Persian rug! I was so disoriented I couldn't put my finger on it, but I knew something was different. Things were broken all over the floor. But that's it—the rug was gone!"

"Are you sure, Mom? We can go check." Luke Gannon was half standing behind the desk in the corner.

"Yes, I'm sure, absolutely, now I remember seeing the floor, all the broken figurines on the *floor,* not the rug . . . I was just so scared and confused . . ."

"Okay," Elmo Finn said loudly to the room, "assume that Nikki was sedated and carried away inside a rolled-up Persian rug. Louise will canvass her neighbors."

The room stirred, invigorated by the scrap of knowledge.

"Henry, when's sunrise?" Elmo asked.

"Six forty-four. That's also wheels-up. I've booked a Cessna 210, we leave for the airport at oh-five-hundred."

Luke came out from behind the desk, a yellow writing pad in his hand. "Okay, everybody, what do you think? *To White Thunder. Will swap Ice for Hot Stuff. Working out details. Please keep Hot Stuff safe. More information soon. Blind Man.*"

"I don't like 'please,' it's weak," George Graves said, reaching for a sandwich on the worktable laden with caterers' trays. Half the food had been devoured as soon as it arrived.

"George is right," Elmo Finn said.

"Okay, 'please' is out. What else should we say?" Lucas looked around at all the faces. "This tells them basically that we're playing ball. What else?"

"It's fine," Elmo Finn said. "Let's call it in."

Luke said, "We're too late for tomorrow's paper, goddamnit."

"Oh no," Louise said.

"It's okay," Elmo Finn said. "The next day is fine."

"I may have something." Cecil Beech swiveled in his chair and snapped a sheet of paper from the laser printer. "Just tapped into some departmental e-mail, Governor. Department of Corrections. Apparently, there's a mandatory release of prisoners in the works. Did you know about this?"

Luke nodded, his eyes brightening. "Sure, sure, of course. I should have remembered—this could be the answer!" He clapped his hands. "Of course! A few years ago, before I was elected governor, a federal court ordered Tennessee to reduce prison overcrowding by a specific number of prisoners. No matter what. No excuses. So the state had to cut deals to let a lot of felons out early—mostly nonviolent types, but not all. Even though we've built new prisons and have enough capacity, the original deadline is coming up. And all those early releases the state agreed to are coming due. The judge won't let us out of it—says a deal's a deal."

"So let's put Randall Tice on the list," Cecil said matter-of-factly. "Release him early."

"Can you do that?" Luke asked in astonishment.

"Indeed," Cecil said. "My working cybertheory is that I can do anything I can think of doing. All modesty aside. I've just been reading Tice's file at Brushy Mountain. He's been a model prisoner, reclassified from Maximum Custody to Minimum Restricted, even leading discussion groups in—guess what—patriotism, Christian Identity, and God's Country."

Everyone crowded around the compact, mustachioed hacker, offering congratulations and bowing. Cecil lit a cigarette and wielded it like a conductor's baton. Louise rushed over and kissed him on the cheek, her hands batting at the smoke.

When everyone calmed down, Elmo Finn said, "Let's think this through. What if some eagle-eyed prison official spots Tice's name and investigates? We need a contingency plan."

"There are no eagle-eyed prison officials," Luke said. "But I think I can handle it with the commissioner, if necessary. Tell him it's an FBI sting or something. He'd buy that—we're letting Tice out to lead us to bigger fish."

"Which of course is true," Elmo Finn said. "Luke, can you spring this big prisoner release at the last possible minute—so the Corrections Department will be less likely to notice the error? Maximize our chances?"

Luke pondered the question. "Yes. Hell yes. Gonna break the law, break the son of a bitch! Break the son of a bitch good! Swords our law! Nikki is the focus, nothing else."

The others nodded approvingly. Elmo Finn said, "Now, Sir Cecil Beech, Your Cyberness, let's figure out how to insert one of your thumbnail transmitters on Randall Tice's body or in his clothes. In case we decide to follow him—maybe all the way to Nikki."

"Yes! All the way to Nikki!" Louise said. "I'm fixing a drink."

"Me too," the governor said.

"Make it a round," Henry Wood said, and a fresh wave of exhilaration and energy washed over them. They fixed drinks and drank toasts to prison overcrowding and cybergod Cecil Beech.

"We're gonna get her back!" Luke said. "I can feel it in my bones, I can feel it."

"Oh, yes, son," Louise cried, squeezing his arm with both hands. "I can feel it too."

Squinting at his watch, Elmo Finn said, "I officially declare this operation on . . . the . . . offensive. Way to go, Sir Cecil—you beat sunrise by eight hours."

It was past midnight when three sharp knocks sounded on the command-post door.

"Oh!" Louise jumped up.

Luke opened the door and stepped aside to admit a beefy man of fifty wearing a shiny brown suit. He had brown hair going gray and a prizefighter's nose. He stepped into the room confidently, taking in everything.

Luke said, "Everybody, this is Colonel Floyd Hanner, commander of the Tennessee State Police." Luke's relaxed voice was at odds with the strain on his face. "We call him Bump."

Luke, raising his arm high and pointing to Cecil Beech at the computer in the far corner, called out Cecil's name like an announcer. Then he followed suit around the room with the others. Col. Bump Hanner, his jaw clenched, made brief eye contact with each person, nodding perfunctorily. When Luke got to Roy, Hanner half smiled. "Rambo," he said with a drawl. Roy's shoulders loosened a fraction. When Luke got to Elmo Finn, the last in line, Hanner said, "Colonel Finn. It is colonel, isn't it?" Elmo Finn smiled enigmatically. "Once upon a time," he said.

"Understand you folks met Sergeant Jennings this morning," Bump Hanner grunted, walking to the center of the room and lacing his hands across his front. As he moved, the flesh under his coat rolled and shifted, half solid, half soft. A tough cop going to seed behind a desk. "Made us look bad. Showed us up. Governor, I offer you my immediate resignation."

"Come on, Bump," Luke said wearily, looking to the ceiling for a moment. "Clay Jennings already offered me his resignation. You guys quit too easy." He dropped onto one of the metal chairs.

"All I needed to hear, Governor, all I wanted to hear. I can assure you I will fix what needs fixin'." Hanner's eyes flicked to Elmo Finn. "Colonel Finn, you and your boys showed us a weakness and we will fix it. Ain't nobody goin' to harm this governor or his wife on my watch. We are the body men and we take it seriously." With a contrived chuckle, he said, "Governor, I sure hope we can keep all this inside the tent. The media would . . . everybody'd look bad." He emphasized *everybody*.

"Case closed, Bump, forget it," Luke said. "Anybody who leaks anything will be fired. And Elmo Finn wasn't trying to embarrass you. Hell, I'm the one who's embarrassed."

"Well, for not tryin', Colonel Finn sure did a first-class job." He chuckled, with a hint of a snarl, and produced a small envelope from his pocket. "Sergeant Jennings sent this."

Luke took the envelope with a nod and stuffed it in his pocket.

Hanner said, "I think it's from his sister. Joyce. The nurse."

Luke nodded again, impatiently.

"Governor, this has been a day for us—a bad day—and I must admit something else. We do not have contact as of now with Horsey, with the First Lady. I was hopin' she was here with you. So my resignation is—"

"Bump, quit talkin' about resignin', goddamnit. I need you. Nikki's on a little trip. A private trip. Nothin' to worry about, you have my assurance. Even a governor and a First Lady have some right to privacy. We should have informed you, I admit that."

Bump Hanner looked around as if to make sure Nikki Gannon was not in the room. "Yes, sir, ah . . ."

"You just stand by, Bump, have everybody stand by, and when Nikki gets back we'll go on just as before."

"So she's out of town?"

"On a little trip."

"Well . . . that's not exactly the question, Governor."

"Well, Bump, that's the answer. That's exactly the goddamn answer."

"Yes, sir." His face coloring, Bump Hanner backed away a few steps. Abruptly, two sharp knocks on the door cracked like gunfire. Luke went to the door and opened it, and Eli Korn, a desperate look on his narrow face, flew in. He rushed past Col. Bump Hanner, who quietly slipped out and closed the door behind him.

"Governor," said the earnest chief of staff, his dark eyes shooting around the room, "we're getting beaucoup calls for the First Lady, we cancelled her schedule like you said but people are still calling, we say 'private trip' and everyone freaks, we can't find her mother, now I see she's over here with you, all these new people getting in the way of the state police, and strange packages are coming in the mail, turning up *under benches in the capitol,* anonymous phone calls, and you're holed up over here like there's some secret operation, and Jill's in the dark, and I'm in the dark, and the body men are in the dark, and the press is starting to sniff around—Governor, what in the everlovin' fudge is goin' on?"

The Third Day

Despite her sixty-seven years, Louise Perry took the three flights of steps two at a time, stopping only once. She rushed into the command post where Elmo Finn, Cecil Beech, and Henry Wood were bent over a worktable covered with photographs. It was ten minutes past noon.

"Elmo, Elmo, I found—" She hauled in air and half stumbled to the corner, where bottles of mineral water and soft drinks were packed in a round rubber trash can filled with ice. She twisted open a bottle of water and took a long pull, followed by a coughing spell. At length she composed herself.

"I found a witness, Elmo," she said, hurrying back to the worktable. "A witness who saw the kidnappers! *Saw* them! My neighbor, the viscount, Rupert Henderson, he's not really a viscount but we call him . . . he was walking his dog Chesterton and he saw them! Just like you figured, they were bringing the rug out from the foyer, rolled up on their shoulders, and put it in a van. Cream-colored."

Her eyes filled and she took more water. "That was Nikki, Elmo, that was Nikki inside . . . I almost broke down when he told me."

"How many of them?"

"A man and a woman. Two."

"Were you able to ask him what they looked like?"

"Oh yes, oh yes. But Rupert wasn't too sure what they looked like or how tall they were, said they were very dodgy, that was his word, 'dodgy,' he even thought about getting the license number but my cat Baskerville popped up and Chesterton got all excited . . . but they told him I was sick and then ran back to lock my door!"

"The van was cream-colored?"

"Yes! Cream-colored, off-white, beigy, nothing written on it. It had those dark windows you can't see through."

"Mo." Henry Wood's mahogany forefinger pointed like an African dagger at one of the aerial photographs of God's Country. "Might call it cream-colored."

"That's it! I know that's it!" Louise bent over to examine the photograph.

"Can't tell which vehicle goes with which trailer," Henry said.

"Is she in one of those trailers?" Louise whispered. "Do you think she is?"

Elmo Finn said, "It's possible, Louise. But it's a big place."

She let out a sniffle, then another, then brought her hands together in an animated scrubbing motion.

"Isn't there any way to—I don't know what! Did you learn any more about the chloroform and atropine?"

"Yes—you've got nothing to worry about. No side effects. Presumably they used the same stuff on Nikki. They wanted to knock you out, not hurt you."

"So that's a good sign."

"Yes. A very good sign."

"What's next, Elmo? Can I do something else? I need to do something else."

"Did you canvass everywhere?"

"No. After I talked with the viscount, I ran back here."

"Go back. Keep at it. Now you can be specific—a man, a woman, a cream-colored van. They stole your rug pretending to be cleaning-people. Maybe somebody noticed something odd, maybe somebody wrote down a tag number. Right now the van's more important than the people."

"I thought the God's Country vans didn't have license tags. Real ones."

"They must have a set of legal tags for jobs like this. Just ask around."

"Where's Lucas? Is he doing all right?"

"He's at the capitol, putting out all the little political fires, like nothing else is going on. He's amazing. George placed the classified ad, which will run tomorrow—then they'll know we're playing ball."

"Elmo, do you trust Eli and Jill?"

"Luke does."

"Luke trusts everybody." She was scrubbing vigorously. "Elmo, do you think Nikki's all right? I'm going crazy."

"No, you're not. You're going back to work. Yes, I think Nikki's all right because this is a political kidnapping. And we're going to find her, Louise, by working at it. Work works."

"Yes, sir! Colonel! Work at it! Swords our law!" She made an exaggerated trembling salute and rushed out.

The Commissioner of Corrections hurried into his office and buzzed for his administrative assistant. When no one appeared, he stabbed at the buzzer several times, then pressed it down and held it. Soon the private door crashed open and the aide appeared.

"Jesus, Clarence! What's up? Not another fuckin' riot?"

"Sit down, Lou. You got to hear this. And you can't say a word to anybody."

The administrative assistant warily took one of the chairs in front of the huge desk. He edged it a little to one side to create a clear line of sight past a desktop plant that had overgrown its vase.

The Commissioner of Corrections put his index fingers under his glasses and pulled the skin beneath his eyes outward. He blinked slowly, rubbed his eyes, pulled the skin once more.

He said, "Politicians are crazy, Lou."

"Crazier'n a jailhouse mouse. I've heard that already, Clarence, but I'll keep it under my hat."

The commissioner chuckled sourly. "I just came from the governor, Lou. He gave me an order—you won't believe this—to release all two hundred and twenty-six prisoners three days from today."

"Three days from today? The federal release? That's impossible, that's crazy, we can't—"

"With no advance notice to the public."

"What? How in the world can—"

"Listen, Lou. Listen. Then forget what I'm telling you. I looked him directly in the eye and I said, 'All due respect, Governor, I don't feel we would gain anything by just springing this prisoner release full-blown, without any warning, you might say, to the public. The federal courts are *making* us do this, we don't *want* to do it, we can put the blame on *them*, there's two hundred and twenty-six prisoners, including a few very serious felons, I must say, and I had planned to have a press conference and explain all this so you wouldn't get hit with the political fallout.' "

"Of course," Lou said. "He knows that. I've discussed it with Eli and Jill."

"I asked him if he wanted to bring in Eli and Jill and discuss it, and he said, 'Clarence, I do not want to bring in anyone. This is not a discussion. All due respect.' *All due respect*—that pissed me off. He said there would be no press conference until *after the fact*. The prisoners would be released three days from today, en masse, and if a word of this appeared in the press beforehand, he would fire me. The instructions to the wardens would go out only the day before. The day before! Top secret! He said to tell our people it's governor's orders—just release all two hundred and twenty-six felons and he would take the heat."

"He's crazy. He's fuckin' crazy."

"They're all fuckin' crazy. I thought maybe this one was different, but he turns out to be the fruitcake of all fruitcakes. Well, Lou, let me tell you, we're going to do exactly what he ordered. Exactly. And I am going to memorialize every word of this in a memorandum so our ass is covered when the legislature goes ballistic. And they absogoddamnlutely will."

"Ballistic? Senator Mullins will fly to Nashville on his own power. They'll impeach him! Of course, we could find a way to leak this strategically—"

"No leaks, Lou. I believe he would fire me. I *know* he would fire me. And I know he would fire you too. And I will kill you. Now, while I get all this on paper, you go figure out how—"

"Clarence, this is going to be one monster fucking Chinese fire drill—two hundred and twenty-six felons escaping all at once with no notice to the public, and we're the ones opening the cell door."

"No no, Lou. No no. Governor Lucas Gannon, former CIA agent, former FBI agent, supposedly tough on crime if you heard his campaign speeches, is the man unlocking the cell door. And if it becomes necessary, and I'll make sure it becomes necessary, the story will come out."

Blue has parked on the fringe of the spacious parking lot and is scanning the Nashville *Tennessean* classifieds when Red opens the door and gets in.

"It's not in there," she says, gently closing the door. "I read them three times."

"Where'd you park?"

She gestures behind her toward some trees.

"Legally?"

"No, Blue. Right in the middle of the road."

"He didn't have time to place the ad."

"Time! Governors don't need time, governors can get a classified ad into a newspaper. If they want to. Something's wrong."

"Nothing's wrong. Nothing's wrong unless you panic. Where's White?"

"Where do you think he is? Why do we have to always use these stupid code names? No one's here but us."

"Discipline. Is he panicking too?"

Red flexes her legs against the floorboard. She looks through the trees at the traffic streaming by on the four-lane boulevard. She looks back at Blue, her upper lip curled oddly.

"White doesn't like it and neither do I. We didn't have to do it, she wouldn't have caused any more trouble."

Blue's jaw clenches. He draws a deep breath and lets it out slowly. "You don't know what trouble she would have caused. She'd have gotten more dangerous every hour. What's done is done."

"Were you planning to do this all along? Were you lying to us?"

"No. It's just a change of plan warranted by circumstances."

"Change of plan. What if there's no ad tomorrow? Then what?"

"There will be."

"What if there's not? Another change of plan? What if every cop in the state is on this case right now, and they're keeping it quiet."

"They couldn't keep it quiet."

"You don't know what they could do."

"And you do?"

Red blushes. "No, of course I don't. All I know is there was no classified ad this morning, and a governor could get one in if he wanted to. Why use the newspaper anyway, why not call them from a pay phone?"

"Wait till tomorrow. Don't forget, they'll be getting another little delivery this morning."

"What time?"

"Before noon. Guaranteed."

"With no fingerprints on it."

"Sure, plenty of fingerprints. But not mine."

"Well I'll be goddamned."

Cecil Beech, the telephone clamped between his head and shoulder, shifted his unfiltered cigarette into an extreme palm-up, thumb-and-middle-finger position and pushed away from the keyboard. He leaned back as far as possible in his swivel chair, listening intently. The others were trying to eavesdrop.

"Well I'll be goddamned."

"What is it?" spouted Louise Perry, who had just returned from another canvass of her neighborhood. "Is it important— I've got to go knock on some more doors."

Elmo Finn motioned for her to go but she lingered, listening like the others to Cecil on the telephone. Everyone was frowning in concentration except George Graves, whose lips were forming a tentative grin.

Cecil said, "If we scan you the photographs—"

George Graves broke into a three-quarter-inch smile.

Cecil said, "Sushi, you are the supreme goddamnedest Jap in a world of goddamnedest Japs. God bless your devious little yellow heart. But I cannot believe, Sushi, that you are so petrified about one little airplane flight . . . Sushi, this is very suboptimal behavior . . . well goddamn it, send Tojo, he's a cosmopolitan Jap, he's actually been south of Jersey City—"

Cecil swung the mouthpiece above his head and whispered to Elmo Finn, "Sushi says he ain't ever been south of Macy's!"

George went into full one-inch beam.

"Sushi, listen to me. Tennessee is not the land of the Voodoo Rednecks, you little suboptimal hara-kiri devil, but just forget it—"

Cecil began tracing figure eights in the air with the Noel Coward cigarette, his upper body heaving in a sinister silent laugh. Finally he leaned forward and abruptly hung up the phone.

"Goddamnedest Jap."

"What is it?" Louise asked breathlessly.

"Sourest goddamn Jap ever was. He's come up with a thoroughly bogus plan, we'll have to see. Interestin'."

Everyone was silent for a moment.

"Is that all you can say?" Louise cried. *"Interestin'?"*

"It's—complicated, Miz Perry. Long shot. We'll know more tonight." Cecil swung around toward Elmo Finn. "Colonel, I happened upon something else pretty interestin' just before that sour Jap called. Never been south of Thirty-fourth Street, you believe that."

"I'm off to find another witness," Louise announced to the room at large. "Somebody must have seen that van."

"Good luck, Louise," Elmo said.

"Swords our law!" She breezed out.

Cecil lit a fresh cigarette off the butt of the old one and wedged it into the side of his mouth. His pianist's hands flew around the keyboard with a flurry of clacks until he brought up the page he wanted.

He announced, "Visitors Log at Brushy Mountain State Penitentiary. Randall Tice has had only eight different visitors during his thirty-two months as a guest of the state. And we know seven of 'em. Harlan McConathy, a.k.a. Joshua. Noreen McConathy, a.k.a. Mother of God. Quincy Dean Klepper, a.k.a. Spiderman. Glenn Forbush, a.k.a. Hi Hitler. Earl Cherry, no known alias except stupid. Linda Pearson, a.k.a. Linda Pearson, attorney at law."

"That's six," Elmo Finn said. "All from God's Country."

"Number seven is right interestin'. Sergeant Clay Jennings, governor's security detail, Tennessee State Police."

"Jesus, that dude gets around," George said as everyone exchanged shocked glances.

"Who's number eight?" Elmo said.

"The visitor who came the most, averaged about one visit per month. Gentleman by the name of Herman Page. Gave a phony address. Even brought Randall Tice a TV set for his cell."

"Who's Herman Page?" Roy said.

Elmo Finn leaned over for a closer look at the monitor. "What was the name of the state trooper that Tice supposedly shot along the highway?"

"Travis Page," George said.

"Herman Page, Travis Page," Elmo Finn said. "Might be coincidental."

"And might not be," George said.

"And might not be. Assume it isn't. Assume that Herman Page is related to Travis Page, the dead state trooper. Perhaps his brother. Why would he bring a television set to his brother's murderer in the state penitentiary?"

"If Tice *was* the murderer."

"He was," Luke Gannon said. "No question of that."

"And there's one more little item," Cecil said.

"Go."

"Just after the Branch Davidian tragedy at Waco, the fire and everything, there was a message to Janet Reno posted on the God's Country Web site. An open letter from Joshua." Cecil fished a page from the printer tray and read:

Dear Janet Reno: If you send your jackbooted, baby-burning bushwhackers to God's Country to confiscate my guns, pack them a lunch—it will be a damn long day. The Branch Davidians were amateurs. We're professionals.

"There's that word *jackboot* again—same as in the ransom note."

"Another little arrow pointing to God's Country," Elmo said.

"Goddamn them," Luke said bitterly.

Elmo said, "Cecil, keep surfing, see if you can find Herman Page. I want to identify the man who brought Randall Tice a TV set for his cell."

Cecil blew out a storm of smoke and struck his cigarette pose. "I'll bump that up to Sushi, he's got more firepower, sittin' up there north of Macy's. Sittin' on his Jap ass, won't go out the goddamn door."

Eli Korn slipped into Jill Dennison's office and closed the door. The two senior aides to Gov. Lucas Gannon looked at each other grimly.

"What the fuck's going on?" Jill barked before Eli could speak. She was described in the press as "tart-tongued," "blunt-speaking," "salty." And loved it.

Eli Korn slumped into one of the red leather armchairs across from Jill's desk, lacing his fingers behind his neck. Jill's pulse spurted. Eli never sat down in her office.

"Do you know what's happening in three days?" His voice was sharp, his demeanor challenging—the opposite persona from the governor's normally accommodating Yes Man.

"I don't know what's happening *today*," Jill shot back. "I don't know what happened *yesterday!*"

"We're releasing two hundred and twenty-six prisoners before their sentences are up. Including some hard cases."

"Who's releasing them?"

"The state of Tennessee. Governor Lucas Fucking Gannon. No press notice."

"The federal release? No press notice? What happened to the media blitz to inoculate public opinion—weren't we going to have a press conference and blame the pointy-headed federal judiciary—and stir up the pointy-headed rednecks?"

"Indeed, Miz Dennison. We had an excellent plan, which you yourself helped draw up, I believe."

Jill was on guard now. Eli never said *Miz Dennison* unless he wanted to be chummy, personal, serious. And she never said *Eli* except for the same reasons.

"Eli, what are you saying? We're just turning them loose? *In the dark of night?*"

"Clarence is having a press conference after the fact."

"They'll kill him. They'll kill us. They'll certainly kill His Majesty. What the fuck's going on?"

"I don't know! What are all these old war buddies doing on the fourth floor? Can't be politics—you and I would be in on that."

"You and I *should* be in on it, whatever it is. That one with the mustache is creepy."

"Sir Cecil, they call him, the chain-smoking computer geek. He *is* creepy—they're all creepy. Do you know about Elmo Finn? Luke told me some stuff one time—he's like a real James Bond or something. He's killed people—they've all killed people! They were in some Vietnam firefight and barely escaped in a helicopter. The black guy, Henry, was the pilot. And now they're all holed up over there on the fourth floor, and Lucas is right in the middle of it, whatever it is, and they're making the body man stay down on the first floor and what the hell is Louise doing, running in and out all the time?"

"I don't know, Eli. I don't know nothin'."

"Well, I have some ideas."

"What? Tell me."

"Okay, scenario number one, could it be Nikki? Say she's left him—wouldn't be the first time—say she just said 'Fuck you, Luke, and the white horse you got elected on' and just vanished, and the old Vietnam gang has ridden to the rescue, tryin' to find her and return her to the fold before there's political fall-out."

"But I thought they came in to test security. Because of all the threats. Talk to the body men, talk to Clay—"

"I have talked to Clay. I should say I've *listened* to Clay—he gets ballistic about it. Anyway, they *all* weren't here testing security. Some of 'em came later. And what are they doin' now?"

Jill produced a pack of cigarettes, shook one out, and lit it.

"Let me have one of those, Miz Dennison," Eli Korn said.

"You quit, Eli."

"I just unquit."

He got up to take the cigarette and leaned toward her for a light.

"Scenario number two," he said, exhaling smoke and coughing. "The old vets are really trying to release a certain prisoner or group of prisoners, because of some dark Vietnam secret or something, and Luke's speeding up the federal prisoner release to disguise it."

"Do you actually think Governor Law and Order could be talked into releasing two hundred felons—"

"He could be blackmailed into it. And they're *going* to be

released, no matter what. Federal court order. It's just a matter of how and when."

"Let's get the list from Clarence."

"Already sent for it. How much do you know about the Phoenix program? Big CIA covert operation in Vietnam, very controversial. All these creepy guys were part of Phoenix. Including our honorable governor."

"That was a long time ago."

Eli Korn spread his bony hands, palms up. "Got to be *some* explanation."

"Scenario number three," Jill said. "Maybe this is a CIA deal all the way. And Luke's going along because—"

"Because he's still a Company man."

"That makes sense, Eli. I forgot to tell you—Luke asked for the file on that God's Country cult—maps and everything. Maybe the CIA's got an operation—"

"Or the FBI! Luke has ties to both."

Jill lit another cigarette and tossed the pack to Eli. The phone buzzed. She answered and listened for a few seconds, then hung up.

"There's a Federal Express package for the boss. Marked Personal and Confidential. Should we?"

"No. I'd like to, though."

"He told me to trust him," she said.

"Same with me. *Trust him.*" Eli took some short, quick breaths. "First cigarette in a while, goes to your head."

"The press is going to go nuts over the prisoner release," she said. "They'll storm this place."

"The Judiciary Committee—can you picture Senator Mullins?"

Jill sneered. "Let's get drunk tonight, Mr. Eli Korn."

"Why wait, Miz Jill?"

Governor Luke Gannon, exhausted and jittery, his hands suffering tremors he could not control, impatiently endured the sluggish elevator ride to the fourth-floor command post. When the cab finally settled, he threw himself between the opening doors like a fullback and wedged his way out. He almost charged into Elmo Finn and the other ex-commandos, who were waiting to get on.

"Hey! Another message, Mo. Goddamn them." One of Eli Korn's volunteers was loitering in the corridor, smiling officiously, angling for a glimpse into the command post when the door was opened. Luke nodded and scowled simultaneously, and the volunteer scurried away. Luke showed Elmo the red-white-and-blue Federal Express envelope.

Elmo waved his troops into the elevator and went back into the command post with Luke. On the third try, Luke managed to extract a half sheet of paper from the inside envelope. He spread it on a table. The note read:

Blind Man,
> *A reminder to hurry! Hot Stuff is okay for now. Nice ass.*
>> *White Thunder*

"They sent her panties this time. Her name was on the label." Luke's voice was tremulous and tired.

Elmo said, "A Federal Express package arriving today had to be sent yesterday. They sent this at the very same time they were putting the other one with the bra under the bench in the capitol. I don't get it. Why all this calculated pressure—holding Nikki should be pressure enough."

"Goddamn them, Mo. If they molest her . . ."

"Luke, we're headed for the airport. Go back there and hit one of those cots. You can't think when you're tired."

"Eli and Jill are getting very suspicious, Mo, they think—"

"They're under control, Luke. They won't do anything. Get some rest. So you can help Nikki."

"Goddamn them, Mo."

"They're trying to break you, Luke, humiliate you. We can't stop their little games, pal, but we can stop their little games from stopping us. Thirty hours now. Let's stay focused, force the anger into a box and stick it in the corner."

"Exactly, Mo. Exactly." Luke Gannon's voice now vibrated coldly; his shoulders wriggled fitfully. "Stay focused, just like Nam. Just like combat. I'll stay focused on getting her back, Mo—nothing else. Thirty hours isn't that long. But in that little box over in the corner—when we do get her back, Mo, I sure want to open up that little box."

Sunset.

Sixty-five men, women, and children occupying wooden benches and folding chairs, slouching forward attentively. Wearing jeans and work clothes and modest dresses, their ages seven to seventy, their hands more hard than soft, their faces more lined than smooth. The children uncommonly still. Three black-clad teenagers with shaved heads straddling a bench near the front, their silver chains and buckles chiming as they shift and pose.

A smooth-faced, white-haired, pale-blue-eyed figure in black bending toward the pliant faces from a raised platform, his muscular shoulders square, his hands braced on a massive rough-hewn altar. On the wall behind him, flanking the altar, two icons illuminated by overhead spotlights: a silver cross and a red-white-and-black Nazi flag. Four men standing at parade rest at the four corners of the platform, dressed identically in brown shirts with shoulder patches and collar insignia, black neckties, bloused black trousers, boots, and Sam Browne belts. Wall-mounted spotlights throwing hard gleams around the vast Ark that had once been a barn.

"Tonight I'm going to talk about sex!" Joshua thundered, a ripple prickling through the crowd. "We have some visitors with us tonight, hearin' the message of God's Country for the first time, so to make 'em feel welcome I'm just goin' to go back and start at the beginning, and the beginning by God is sex!"

Another ripple, tight smiles, heads turning, huddled whispers. A small boy in an absurdly large shirt bouncing and fidgeting in the front row, his drooping sleeve riding up for a moment revealing silver handcuffs shackling him to the slender man on his right. Next to him, a woman holding an infant wrapped in a towel, her eyes cast down. At the end of the row, erect and florid, a big woman wearing camouflage fatigues and military boots.

"Now, Eve had sex with Satan! Satan! The serpent in the garden! And a son was born, and that son was Cain! And the descendants of Cain, my brothers and sisters, are the Jews, the Jews, the seed of Satan!"

His voice, strong and well modulated, echoed richly in the spacious Ark. The congregation was a hypnotized still life.

"And then Eve had sex with Adam, her husband, and Seth was born, Seth, the father of the white race. And you and I are the children of Seth, and the children of Seth are the true lost tribes of Israel. No, the ten lost tribes of Israel are not the Jews, not the Jews, the ten lost tribes are the descendants of Seth— the Anglo-Saxon race—our forefathers—who settled in Scandinavia and western Europe and came to America on the *Mayflower* and were inspired by God Almighty to write the Declaration of Independence and the Constitution. And had *sex*—and had *sex*—down through the years until you and I were created. We—we—are God's chosen people! That's how God's Country came to be, brothers and sisters! Sex! And only the chosen people, only the children of Seth can live in God's Country. The children of Satan can live in the rest of the Jewnited States! And die there too!"

A thunderclap of applause, surging, the pale-blue-eyed pitchman wiping his brow with a black handkerchief and leaning forward again, allowing the smile to dissolve into a stony gaze.

"Purity! Sex means purity! Do you know that we spend more money to make sure horses are pure than to make sure people are pure? Well, not at God's Country! Not at God's Country! No Californicators allowed!"

George Graves whispered to Elmo Finn, "That's his wife, front row, with the baby." Elmo and George were sitting by themselves on a bench in the rear of the Ark, wearing loose-fitting anoraks and faded jeans. "Noreen McConathy, the one they call Mother of God. The baby is named Esther."

Gazing straight ahead, Elmo said, "Next to her, the thin guy. The boy on his left is *handcuffed* to him."

"That must be Earl Cherry. The boy's name is Jeremiah. His son."

". . . the Day is coming, my white brothers, my white sisters, when we will finally have the chance to fight for our race against the New World Order—you've seen the backs of the road signs, you've seen the secret codes with your own eyes—you know that they've already moved the boxcars into Polk County—not very far away, my brothers and sisters, Copper Hill, Tennessee— the boxcars with the arm and leg shackles bolted to the walls, bolted to the floors—all ready and waiting for prisoners like us when the United Nations' blue helmets march in and take over! But they forgot one thing—the prisoners ain't goin' peacefully— the prisoners ain't goin' at all!"

A cry rose up from the rapturous lips, and Joshua, sweat drenching his face, spun to the altar and seized a jagged piece of orange cardboard torn from a box of detergent. "See this! See this!" His rigid finger striking like a snake at the black-and-white Universal Pricing Code. "What does it say in the Book of Revelation, what does it say will transpire when the end is near, when The Day is at hand, The Day of Armageddon, brothers and sisters of God's Country? 'No man might buy or sell save that he has the mark of the beast! No man might buy or sell save that he has the mark . . . of . . . the . . . beast!' Look here! Look here! The mark of the beast, on everything bought and sold!"

Erupting applause, as if Joshua had performed a great conjurer's trick.

"This is a religion on steroids," Elmo whispered to George.

"Jesus with an attitude. The woman in cammies, front row. She's Randall Tice's lawyer. Linda Pearson."

Elmo and George had appeared at God's Country a full hour before sunset, driving up unannounced in Louise Perry's green Lincoln Navigator. They were stopped at the phone-booth guardhouse by Hi Hitler, where they asked for permission to attend the sunset service. Heard a lot about it. Happened to be nearby. Using a walkie-talkie, Hi Hitler conferred with someone, then escorted them to the Ark, which was empty, and left them alone. With time to kill before the service, as they had planned, Elmo and George strolled out of the Ark and ambled openly about the compound, pushing the rusty swings for a few children, making friends with a few dogs. The layout was fresh in their minds from the photographs taken on Henry Wood's overflights that morning. Their seemingly aimless wandering covered a precise route—the cluster of trailers on the eastern end of the semicircular compound, the cream-colored van near the hut made of bales of hay, the gleaming silver trailer set off from the others which was the home of Joshua and Mother of God and Esther, the two polyurethane outbuildings in the trees near the generator. Before long, Hi Hitler came running up and stayed with them until Spiderman, wearing a long-sleeved brown shirt that concealed his tattoos, took over. Elmo and George were genial, talkative, knowledgeable about Randy Weaver and Ruby Ridge, about David Koresh and Waco, hostile to the FBI and the BATF. As he listened to the two strangers, Spiderman gradually relaxed, and finally couldn't resist a little boasting: God's Country wasn't some backwater Podunk, no sir, it was on the underground map. On the Internet. Militiamen always passing through. Fugitives from here and there. Spiderman drew himself up to full height, inflated his chest. A man named McVeigh. Through clenched teeth, Elmo and George struggled with their faces.

Spiderman noticed nothing amiss, even as they strolled back past Joshua's silver trailer and Elmo broke into a sudden coughing fit, bent over double, dropped the blue anorak which had been slung over his arm, and stumbled away from the other two, heaving. George explaining about the allergies that hobbled his friend every fall, George retrieving Elmo's anorak and distracting Spiderman for a moment as Elmo Finn made a furtive move at the edge of the silver trailer. Then they went on. Before the sunset service began, Elmo and George had managed to see everything they were interested in.

Joshua's face was fire-red now, his black shirt soaked through with sweat.

". . . as Jesus teaches in the gospel of Luke, 'He that hath no sword, let him sell his garment and buy one.' "

"Swords our law, swords their law," George muttered.

"A white thunder is rolling across the land!" Joshua roared, thumping back and forth along the edge of the raised platform between his stiff-legged honor guard in the brown shirts. "A white thunder is rolling across the land—and we are the lightning bolt!" Joshua froze dramatically, his icy blue eyes leering at Elmo Finn and George Graves. He held the pose and a few heads turned to look at the strangers who sat motionless, staring back.

"But! But! For the benefit of our visitors, whom we welcome, let me hasten to add that we are not an *offensive* lightning bolt, we are *defensive!*" His mouth curled into a teenager's smirk.

"We are peaceful unless attacked, peaceful unless attacked. When you think about it, God's Country is just one big happy *neighborhood watch!*" The smirk dissolved into a calculating grin and a wave of snickering rippled through the Ark.

Joshua slowly lifted his eyes to the ceiling and flung his arms wide in a crucifixion stance, frozen, until his spellbound parishioners began to applaud. Still frozen, applause swelling, still frozen, one rapturous shriek followed by another, until at last he lowered his head inch by inch to cast a beaming, toothy, self-possessed smile beneath the ice-blue glare.

"Blood, soil, and honor!" Joshua roared, snapping a Nazi salute.

"Blood, soil, and honor!" returned the others, leaping to their feet and stiff-arming back.

"Blood, soil, and honor!"

"Blood, soil, and honor!

"Eighty-eight!"

"Eighty-eight!"

Joshua leaped from the platform and embraced Noreen and the baby as the others pressed forward to touch him. Young Jeremiah, still handcuffed to his father, was skipping on one foot and pawing with his free hand at the black-clad preacher.

"George." Elmo had stood up slowly at the end, and was staring at one of the four brown-shirted altar guards. Instead of coming forward like the others to join the circle around Joshua, he had hurried out the far door. Before he got away, both Elmo and George clearly recognized the brawny, sandy-haired figure of Sgt. Clay Jennings of the Tennessee State Police.

"What brings you old boys to God's Country? Let's get down to it. Y'all been talkin' the right talk, but the question is, are you walkin' the right walk?" Joshua snatched a folding chair from the front row and swung it up onto the raised platform with a clang. He mounted the platform and plopped down, leaning the chair back on two legs, gazing down at the others. "Especially walkin' the walk all around our property, nosin' around. Like you're lookin' for somethin'." He cocked his head with a sneer.

"Heard about you," Elmo said innocently, one foot propped on a chair. "Thought we'd check it out. We got here early so we took a walk around. Your man was with us, we didn't steal nothing."

"Heard about us."

Encircling Finn and Graves were three brown-shirted altar guards, including Spiderman and Hi Hitler, and the big woman in camouflage attire. Everyone else had left the Ark.

"We ain't the only ones who've heard about you, Joshua. That's really why we came by."

Joshua raised an eyebrow. "Well now. Let's get down to it."

"Search 'em," Linda Pearson snapped. She seemed accustomed to issuing commands, but the brown shirts held back, looking to Joshua.

"Let's get down to it," Joshua repeated.

Elmo Finn said, "Fine. I'll just say that we have some contacts who also have some contacts. Friends of friends. Including people inside various so-called law enforcement agencies, like the Federal Bureau of Investigation. Like the Bureau of Alcohol, Tobacco and Firearms. I'm sure you know, Joshua, that God's Country is under surveillance by the federal government, like all patriot groups, because basically they're afraid of you, and we may be able to get our hands on certain products of that surveillance . . . if you would be interested."

Elmo spread his hands like a blackjack dealer. No tricks.

"Like what?"

"Like aerial photographs."

"Taken when?"

"Recently, I believe. Certainly not too long ago."

The side door opened and Earl Cherry came in. His long legs crossed the floor quickly and he took a position next to Hi Hitler, whose bulky frame accentuated Earl's gauntness. His sharp Adam's apple appeared and disappeared as he shot glances at Elmo and George.

"Earl, you had a chance to check your rat traps?" Joshua asked.

"Yes sir, yes sir." Earl Cherry's hand crept inside his shirt.

"Everything okay?"

Earl cleared his throat. "Yes sir."

"You sure, Earl?" Linda Pearson snapped. "Absolutely sure?"

He reached inside his shirt again, then looked at her and nodded slowly.

She said, "Earl, you were supposed to disappear. Where's Jeremiah?"

Earl Cherry made a circle with his arms and crossed his wrists.

"The usual tree?"

He nodded slowly.

"Very good, Earl," Joshua said. "Keep a close check on your traps. You're doing a good job, Earl. Now, boys, I don't believe I know your all's names."

"Well," Elmo Finn said indifferently, "we have names, Joshua, and we have identification, but they're both false. We got 'em by readin' one of the books you sell on your Web page. *Building a Legend.* Maybe some of your good citizens here at God's Country did the same thing. Get a fresh start. Maybe even you did, Harlan."

A bolt of surprise flashed across Joshua's face. The pale blue eyes glimmered and narrowed. He slowly lowered the chair to the floor and assumed a showy grin.

"What'd you boys think of our Web page? Our lawyer here runs it. Linda Pearson. God's Country On Line."

The big woman jumped onto the platform and took a wide

stance next to Joshua, her boots angled outward. Elmo and George said nothing.

"So. You boys know my former name." Joshua rubbed his hands together. "That's very interestin'. And I don't know your old names or your new names. Building a legend. Why do y'all need new names, I wonder, you legends you."

"The past was catching up on us. Gettin' a little too close."

"Gettin' real close," George said.

"Well, you legends, I can't say that I am unfamiliar with that particular problem. How'd you get the aerial photographs?"

"Some contacts who have some contacts. You know, Joshua, not everyone in law enforcement thinks you're the enemy. The Patriot Movement, Posse Comitatus, Christian Identity, God's Country—you've all got friends and sympathizers. Here and there. Inside ZOG, you might say. With access to top secret stuff. And we have access to them."

Elmo reached inside his shirt and slowly drew out a photograph. He stepped up onto the platform and went to the altar. At first, Joshua didn't move, but at length he stood up and gathered around with the others as Elmo spread out the black-and-white aerial photograph taken only that morning during a daring dead-stick pass by Henry Wood in the rented Cessna. There were smears of India ink blacking out certain sections.

"Joshua, look here in the lower left . . . there's your guard-house, right beside the road . . . here's a few of the trailers . . . cars up on blocks . . . now look down in this corner, Joshua, see those initials . . . F . . . B . . . I. These are the kind of contacts we have, Joshua. You can have this. As a sample. Might help you redesign your perimeter."

"Why's it all blacked out?"

"It's just a sample."

"And the ones that aren't blacked out will cost something."

"That's the idea. Let's just say we're a profit-making enterprise."

"What else can you get? We could take our own damn pictures."

"I don't know everything that might be available, just wanted to see if you're interested. And flush."

"How much?"

"Depends. Say a nice package of aerial photographs, top-secret memos, wiretap transcriptions, invasion plans, names of agents assigned, names of informers, et cetera, et cetera . . . we're talking mid-five figures here, Joshua."

The white-haired zealot turned away abruptly. "Earl, you better check the rat trap again. Go on outside, Earl, and check the traps."

Earl obeyed immediately. Joshua trained his pale blue eyes on Elmo Finn, whose expressionless gray eyes with the fire-flecks stared back.

Elmo Finn said, "Can you afford it, Harlan? No sense wastin' time if you can't."

"His name is Joshua," Linda Pearson said.

"This is very strange, you know, very peculiar. You boys showin' up at this particular time. At this particular time. Quite a coincidence, and we don't much believe in coincidences. You don't mind takin' your shirts off, do you, legends?"

Elmo shrugged and skimmed off his long-sleeved chambray shirt. George did the same. Neither wore an undershirt.

Joshua made a gesture, and they unhooked their belts and allowed their jeans to slide to their knees.

"Black skivvies. I wear those too, legends. Linda thinks it's kinda naughty."

Linda Pearson walked behind Elmo and George and peered at the backs of their necks.

"Just to make sure you're not Black Eagles," she said, running her stout fingers along Elmo's hairline.

"What's a Black Eagle?" Elmo asked.

"Hah! Didn't your *contacts* tell you? Black Eagles are goon squads—New World Order goons—who've been programmed with biochips implanted in their necks."

"Must hurt," Elmo said, and someone stifled a laugh.

Linda Pearson came around to face Elmo, dropped to one knee, and examined his jeans, then suddenly yanked his shorts to his knees. She did the same with George. She stood up, circled them again, reached between their legs, then abruptly pulled their shorts back up.

"Hide a wire anywhere," she growled. "In your package."

Hi Hitler's giggle prompted a guffaw from Spiderman. Then the others burst out as Elmo and George nonchalantly got back into their clothes. George picked up the anoraks and tossed one to Elmo.

"Hold on." A florid Linda Pearson grabbed Elmo's coat and probed it carefully, reaching into the pockets, running her fingers along every seam, repeating the process with George's. Finally she flung the jackets back at the two intruders and resumed her toes-out stance next to Joshua.

"How's *your* package, Linda?" Elmo Finn said. "You keep it strapped on permanent?"

Hi Hitler and Spiderman cracked up again, but Joshua's ice-blue scowl silenced them.

"We have some money coming in," Joshua said. "A lot of money."

"It'll take sixty thousand, you want to do business."

"We'll need to see an inventory of what you can get."

Elmo and George dropped down off the platform and sauntered away without looking back.

"How can we reach you?" Joshua called out.

"Too many people tryin' to figure that out, Harlan," Elmo said over his shoulder. As they left the Ark, a gust of cold mountain air buffeted them. As they reached the green Navigator, Earl Cherry darted away into the shadows. Then Spiderman jogged up.

"Check back soon," the tattooed minister of defense said. "We got some serious money on the way."

"Sure." Elmo opened the door of the Navigator.

"You want a phone number?"

"We don't talk on phones."

"We could use code."

Elmo got in behind the wheel and lowered the window. "We'll just check back, Dean. Or do you prefer Quincy?" Smiling amiably; all in good fun.

Quincy Dean Klepper, who had not heard someone utter his real name in four years, said, "You could have got that from the newspaper. We were all in the paper."

"I guess we could've." Elmo started the engine and smiled again. "But we didn't."

Elmo Finn, sensing the hard eyes of God's Country behind him, drove out of the compound and turned opposite to the way he had come in. He accelerated down the unmarked county road, high trees along both sides, pushing the Navigator to seventy on the straights. After two miles he slowed abruptly, swung off the blacktop, U-turned smoothly, then pulled off again into a clearing behind a stand of trees. He extinguished the headlights, and he and George sat in complete silence for almost a minute. Then there was a faint two-one-two tapping on George's window.

George tapped a response and three doors opened as one. Henry Wood and Roy, dressed all in black like commandos and wearing backpacks and gear-laden web belts, got in the side doors. Cecil Beech, also in black and wearing greasepaint on his face, shoved some canvas bags through the rear cargo door. Then, holding a rectangular device with luminous dials, he circled the vehicle slowly, pausing twice. Two minutes later he climbed into the second seat.

"All clear," Cecil said crisply, the first words anyone had spoken. "Didn't pick up no bugs at that bughouse."

The Navigator rolled forward around the trees and back onto the blacktop.

"No sign of Nikki," Elmo said. "They took the bait—almost too easily."

"There's no perimeter, sir," Roy half shouted from the rear.

"None," Henry echoed. "Just a cattle fence—three strands of barbwire. No guardposts."

"We could have penetrated anywhere," Cecil said. "Anywhere." He cracked a window and lit a cigarette.

"They may talk military," Roy snapped, "but they ain't."

"Guess who we saw," Elmo said. "Our old friend Sergeant Clay Jennings—he was one of Joshua's storm troopers. Dressed up in a brown-shirt Gestapo outfit. He ran out the back door to keep us from seeing him."

The others voiced their amazement.

Henry Wood said, "So the state trooper is also a storm trooper. And he's also one of the eight people who visited Randall Tice in prison. What the hell is this, Colonel?"

"I can't wait to ask that question of Clay Jennings," Elmo Finn said. "Roy, I got the bug planted under Joshua's trailer, close to the spot we wanted. Maybe we'll get somethin'."

"Roger that, sir. Like to get my ears on."

"Listen to this," George said. "We got half a hand job from Linda the lawyer. Inspectin' our privates for recording devices. Our packages, she called 'em."

"Didn't take all that long," Elmo said. "The inspection. I think mine took longer."

"Harder to find," George muttered.

"Ah, George, 'Small things make base men proud.'"

They were almost back to the God's Country entrance. Elmo Finn slowed down a little as they passed the elongated guardhouse. The compound itself was dark now, nothing visible ex-

cept the moonlit silhouette of the Ark and its rooftop cross of
steel.

"Where's the car, Roy?"

"One-point-two from that guardhouse—look out!"

A bundled figure lurched wildly in front of them. Elmo
wrenched the wheel to the left, then back, braking hard, pulling
off.

"Jesus!" Elmo Finn shouted as George and Roy jumped out.

The figure lay sprawled across the lip of the road, half on the
blacktop, half on the dirt shoulder. It was struggling to move
when George and Roy raced up.

"Did we hit you?" George yelled. "Are you okay?"

The figure rose laboriously to one knee, a gloved hand float-
ing up to throw off the hood of the heavy parka. Long hair
streamed out as Elmo Finn and the others appeared.

"No, I don't think so," the woman said. She gingerly tested
her arms and legs, finally shaking her head and standing upright. "No, I'm all right. I just stumbled when you came up—
didn't get off the road fast enough. There's usually not that
many cars . . ." She seemed disoriented, and looked at the men
in puzzlement.

"Where are you going?" Elmo Finn said.

"Up there a ways. Not far."

"Do you live at God's Country?"

"Mmmnh! God's Country!" She threw her arms frenziedly,
her breath turning to gasps. The men leaned away. "Yes, yes, I
do live at God's Country! Part of me lives there, my boy, my
boy lives at God's Country! The devil's country! In a straw
house! In handcuffs!"

They drove Helen Cherry to her car, hidden half a mile away
on an overgrown dirt road. Roy slipped out of the Navigator
and disappeared, but for twenty minutes Elmo and the others
listened to her story. Earl and Helen Cherry and their troubled

son Jeremiah had been one of the first families to relocate to God's Country, seeking refuge from the wicked maelstrom of modern life. Seeking escape from satanists and pornographers. Seeking communion with God and fellow worshippers. Seeking the peace and serenity of the Tennessee mountains. And a second chance for Jeremiah.

It had sounded perfect in Joshua's blue-eyed, soft-sell spiel. After praying on their knees for nights on end, pleading for a sign, they saw a rainbow in the western sky and interpreted it as God's command. They pulled up stakes, spent their twenty-two-hundred-dollar life's savings on a used mobile home, and migrated to the mountain Christian paradise they privately called Heaven on Earth. When they glimpsed the God's Country sign leaning against the guardhouse and pulled into the gravel drive, they jumped out and fell to their knees, weeping and kissing the ground, overcome by rapture. They had never been there, yet they were home.

But, for Helen Cherry, the rapture soon ebbed. God's Country proved not to be Heaven on Earth; it was hell. Young Jeremiah, who had enough problems, was soon learning and spouting racism, violence, suspicion, hatred—and mindlessly storming about shouting "eighty-eight" and launching absurd Sieg Heil salutes. Earl refused to look for carpentry work, his only skill, and began demanding military salutes from Helen and Jeremiah in recognition of his appointment as deputy minister of defense. He fawned after Joshua like a worshipper. *Joshua!* Helen Cherry broke down describing the afternoon he raped her, how cruel he was, how insatiable, how her husband Earl had volunteered her body to the Prophet in the first place. That same night, she met secretly with Mother of God, Joshua's wife whose real name was Noreen, and Noreen showed her how to escape. She had walked nine miles to freedom, and now she was fighting for custody of her son. Her brittle voice raged as she described her recent confrontation with Linda Pearson, the God's Country lawyer who dressed and talked like a terrorist and who was representing Earl Cherry in the custody suit.

"We'll help you, Helen," Elmo Finn said. "We'll help you get Jeremiah back. And I think you can help us too. Did you know Clay Jennings at God's Country?"

"Yes, he was nice. He's a state policeman."

"Does he live there?"

"No. He didn't then."

"Is he one of Joshua's lieutenants?"

"I don't know. I think so. They don't tell the women anything—we're just . . ." She moaned softly, sniffling for air, as the sobbing overcame her again.

It was nearly dark when Louise returned from still another unproductive canvass of her neighbors. Apparently, Rupert Henderson, the viscount, was the only person who had seen or who remembered seeing the kidnappers or the cream-colored van. Determined to stay busy to quell her rampant anxiety, Louise plunged into the domestic management of the command post. First she turned to Eli Korn, the governor's Yes Man who still hadn't figured out what the five grim strangers were doing in his old campaign headquarters. And why the governor and his mother-in-law had virtually moved in with them. And where the hell Nikki Gannon had gone on her so-called private trip. And why the governor had ordered a politically suicidal mass release of more than two hundred convicts. But the Yes Man swallowed his misgivings and delivered yet again, helping Louise convert the old Xerox room with its stainless steel sink and floor-to-ceiling shelves into a functioning galley. Eli's energetic volunteers speculated on what the governor and the tight-lipped outsiders were up to—the favorite theory was black ops, digging up dirt on Luke's potential opponents—as they hauled in a new electric stove, unpacked boxes of cookware and china and cutlery, and repositioned the refrigerator three times as Louise changed her mind. Then everyone trooped behind Louise on a supply mission to stock the pantry, in one volunteer's phrase, "like a gourmet bomb shelter." Baskerville the cat, after disappearing for a day, emerged from somewhere and systematically investigated the entire fourth floor between samples of Louise's beef stew and creamed chicken, with occasional pinches of buttered croissant.

It was 10:00 P.M. when Elmo called on the private line, which Cecil had swept for bugs and pronounced secure. Luke answered on the first ring.

"Okay."

"No sign of her, Luke," Elmo Finn said, "at least in the main compound. We got a pretty good look, but this is a big place."

"Understood—there's more ground to cover. Where are you now?"

"We're outside a bar called the Hog, a roadhouse, pay phone, about five miles west of target. Now, listen to this, Luke. Tonight we saw Jennings—your body man, Sergeant Clay Jennings—he was one of Joshua's *storm troopers*, brown shirt and everything, the honor guard around the fucking altar. No question it was him—he tried to disappear before we could recognize him. I suggest getting his commander in tonight—we'll be back in two hours."

"Clay Jennings is part of God's Country? *Clay Jennings*? Could he be in on this? Jesus Christ!"

"Let's talk to his commander first. And get somebody to find out if anyone ran a tag-number check on the Navigator tonight. Jennings could have done that easily."

"Jesus! They'll find out it's my mother-in-law's vehicle."

"No they won't—we replaced her plate with another one." He gave Luke the tag number.

"Where'd you get this plate?"

"We borrowed it."

"Jesus, Mo."

"No one will know, Luke—we'll return it late tonight. There's more. We need to find out about a child custody case in Boone County—a woman named Helen Cherry is suing her husband Earl, who lives at God's Country, for custody of the son. Jeremiah. Linda Pearson represents Earl Cherry."

"This is material?"

"Yes. I'll explain. Hang in there, Luke—we didn't strike paydirt tonight but at least we're on offense. Here's another thing—Joshua used the phrase 'White Thunder' in his sermon. Same as the kidnappers' code name. Another coincidence. And he told us they'll have a lot of money soon, to buy some of our FBI items. They were a little suspicious that we showed up, quote, 'at this particular time,' and they checked us for a wire. Speaking of which, our ears are on twenty-four-seven, under Joshua's trailer, Roy's staying overnight to monitor, we'll relieve him on Henry's first overfly tomorrow. Anything new there?"

"Not much. Sushi called from New York for Cecil but he wouldn't talk to me, the goddamned Jap."

"Why does he have to handcuff the boy? The other children see, they don't understand. Poor little Jeremiah . . ." Noreen McConathy fed her daughter Esther a tiny spoonful of applesauce.

"Discipline, Noreen. Earl can't manage that boy without handcuffs. He's wild, like an animal. It's not a permanent measure." Joshua sat on the edge of a straight-backed chair, leaning toward the computer screen on the small table.

"Wait'll the judge hears that. An emotionally disturbed ten-year-old, severely underweight, only clothes he's got are his father's hand-me-downs, forced to live in a straw house, for God's sake, and Earl keeps him handcuffed for disciplinary reasons.

Handcuffed *around . . . a . . . tree* while the other kids tease him. Case closed, custody to Helen."

"Shut up, Noreen! Shut up! What their courts say doesn't matter! God's Country is a separate nation."

"Harlan—save that crap for your misfits. You just wait, when some judge hears about the handcuffs and the straw house, Jeremiah will be out of here. And a lot of cops will be all over this place. And Earl Cherry will be in jail where he belongs."

Rising from the chair, Joshua crossed the small living room in two strides and struck her backhanded across the face. The slap seemed to resound in the cramped trailer. Noreen looked down at her baby daughter and fought back the stinging tears. He hit her again.

"Shut up, Noreen. Shut up. Shut up. Shut up. Don't think you can't lose custody, too, *Mother of God*. I can raise Esther without you, there's plenty of women to help. Plenty of women to help in every way, Noreen. Mother of the Week, I could run 'em in shifts."

She struggled to compose herself. Joshua went back to the computer. Neither spoke for a long time.

He said, "Linda hasn't updated our Web page in a month. Fuckin' bitch."

"I could learn about computers, Joshua, I could do the Web page."

He glanced at her over his shoulder. His face had softened. "You could. I believe you could."

"I could."

"For example, the Thought for Today. It's a good idea, gets people checking in every day—but this same one's been up for a month! 'BATF—Bureau of Arsonists, Traitors and Fascists!' That's good, but not for a whole month! Goddamn that Linda—if you call it Thought for Today, there ought to be a new one every day. People would log on to read it, then check out the other stuff. Maybe buy somethin'."

"Linda doesn't ever follow through, you ought to know that by now. She's all talk. What happened with the God's Country classifieds? That was a great idea—that was your idea—to patronize patriotic Christians. Support your own kind. Buy and sell from each other. She's all talk, Joshua. I could do the Thought for Today."

"You could, Mother. I know you could."

"I could get a whole list ready, a month's worth, or two months', then just change it every day. Like she's supposed to do but don't. It ain't hard, Joshua, you don't even have to get dressed. Nobody can see you on the Web. Nobody knows who you really are."

"Look here at Trochmann's page—look how easy it is to read! All the updates right up front! That's the way to do it, look at this, honey—'Welcome to the Militia of Montana Home Page.' How to subscribe, when it was updated, they've even got an index! Trochmann's got updates and a full index and all we got is a Thought for Today that's the same every damn day. No wonder nobody's buyin' nothin'!"

The baby made a sound. Noreen said, "Joshua, I don't want to drive again. Because of Esther . . . I'm too scared. I wouldn't be any good."

"Just once more, and this is different from all the rest. This ain't no bank, Noreen. Just once more. I need you, honey."

She let out a long sigh and held her baby close. After a while she took a pair of scissors and snipped off a lock of Esther's hair.

"Who were those two men tonight?" she said.

"They want to sell us somethin'."

"They're not local."

"They're sure not local, but they sure knew about God's Country."

"How'd they know?"

"We're not exactly anonymous, Noreen, we got a Web

page, we had those articles about us in the Nashville *Tennessean*, Knoxville *News-Sentinel*, we got Randall Tice in the penitentiary who had all that publicity—sometimes you act like we're just a backwoods pig-pickin' or somethin'."

Noreen tied the lock of Esther's hair in a silver ribbon. "I don't trust those men. They just breezed right in—"

"I didn't buy nothin'."

"It's awful coincidental, them comin' right at this particular time."

"I didn't buy nothin', I told you. Linda stripped 'em down. Full body search. We know what we're doin'."

"If you want me to drive, then I want you to carry this lock of Esther's hair. In your wallet. At all times."

He came over and took the tiny package and put it in his wallet.

"You believe in this?" he said.

"I want a lock of your hair for Esther."

"She ain't got a wallet."

"I'll put it around her neck on a string or something. My daddy and I always carried locks of each other's hair. For good luck. I want Esther and her daddy to do the same."

She made a motion with the scissors and he bent forward, allowing her to snip off some hair. She tied it with another silver ribbon.

The baby made another sound. "Joshua, I want to take her to the doctor. Somethin's wrong."

"Take her to that free clinic first. Before we pay money to some quack. But make sure you take good care of her, even if we do have to pay. You may be Mother of God, but baby Esther is Daughter of God. She's the future." He patted his hip pocket. "I like having this lock of hair. She'll take over for me someday."

———

"Mo, could we be on the wrong track?" Gov. Luke Gannon said, slumping into a metal chair at one of the long worktables. "Do you really think they've got her, or could it be somebody else? Are we doing the right thing? Let's talk it through."

Everyone except Cecil Beech, who was hunched into the computer, got plates of food from Louise's steaming buffet and brought them to the table. Louise refilled Baskerville's plastic bowl, mixed a stiff gin and tonic, and took a seat next to Luke. It was 1:15 A.M.

"Forty hours," Elmo mused, checking his watch. "Forty hours. Okay, let's assume for a moment that God's Country *doesn't* have her. Then whoever *does* have her must believe that we're cooperating. We're keeping it quiet, like they demanded, there's been no publicity. And tomorrow morning they'll see our first classified ad. Promising full cooperation. So there's no reason for them to panic or to do anything but stick to their original demand."

Elmo took a few bites of Louise's chicken and penne casserole, then put down his fork. "But if God's Country *doesn't* have her, we have no suspects. Maybe we should review all those anonymous threats that came in, Luke, to see if there's anything suggestive—"

"There won't be. I read them all very carefully."

"But there's a new context now—kidnapping."

Luke gestured impatiently. "Go ahead and read 'em yourself, then. There's nothing there. Nothing. I was an FBI agent, you know."

No one spoke for a while. They concentrated on finishing their meals. From the corner came the occasional sounds of Cecil's computer.

Elmo Finn pushed away from the table and took out his notebook. "Very good, Louise. Better than very good." The others voiced agreement.

"Are you writing down your calories?" Louise whispered.

Elmo Finn nodded. "And I enjoyed them all—all eight hundred."

"I couldn't enjoy them if I had to write them down," she said. "You're very disciplined."

"He's very anal," George growled. Everyone laughed, including Luke.

Elmo Finn got up and went over to the giant map of Tennessee with the counties color-coded according to Eli Korn's red, white, and blue scheme. He turned and faced the others.

"Okay. Luke's right. Let's review where we are at forty hours. Take a cold hard look. First, despite the fact that we saw no sign of Nikki at God's Country tonight, and no sign that anyone is being held hostage, except little Jeremiah, and no sign that they've taken security precautions, everything still points to God's Country, or elements of God's Country, or a tangent of God's Country, as the kidnappers. The object of the ransom demand—Randall Tice—has had only eight visitors in the three years he's been in prison. *Seven* of them are from God's Country—counting Sergeant Clay Jennings, and we have to count him after what we saw tonight. The eighth, the elusive Herman Page, *could* have a connection—Cecil, do we know anything yet about Herman Page?"

Cecil, a telephone cradled against his ear, gave a thumbs-down sign.

"Herman Page is the one who brought Tice the TV set?" Luke asked.

Elmo nodded. "And he has the same last name as the state trooper that Tice shot." He spread his hands and shrugged. "The point is, every visitor except Herman Page is part of God's Country."

"I can't believe Clay Jennings is part of that goddamn cult," Luke said, massaging the back of his neck with both hands. "I just can't believe it. No way."

Elmo shrugged again. "We have a white male and white female, thirty-something, who carried Nikki away inside the rug in the back of a cream-colored van, and we saw a cream-colored van tonight—"

"So you're sure it's them?" Luke said.

"Of course I'm not sure it's them." Elmo Finn's voice flared; the room became very still. "But right now, at forty hours, if it *isn't* God's Country, there's nothing we can do until we get Randall Tice in our hands and offer who*ever* it is a swap. Randall Tice for Nikki, no questions asked. Whoever's got her."

Luke arched his neck, then rolled his head from side to side. "I know. I know. And if it *is* God's Country, as it appears to be—are we doing everything we can do?"

"We're on offense, Luke. Henry and George are flying recon every day, taking photographs, comparing them. But we're limited from the air—the leaves haven't fallen yet and the infrared scopes would work better if it were colder. George and I invaded the sunset service tonight while these guys tested the perimeter. We let Joshua know that some strange new people are suddenly in the picture. We bugged Joshua's trailer and Roy's out there in the woods right now, close by. We're checking every pawnshop and Oriental rug dealer from Bristol to Memphis, if they're dumb enough to try to unload the rug. We're checking chloroform and atropine suppliers, see if anything unusual happened lately—although it's hard to do that without the imprimatur of the police. We're using private investigator credentials, and they only go so far. We're hacking into the Corrections Department's computer to add Randall Tice's name to the prisoner release. Henry's got a chopper on standby for a raid, if necessary, and we've got plenty of firepower to take with us. If necessary. We've found a potential ally in this Helen Cherry—we may be able to use her custody situation to our advantage."

Gazing off somewhere, Luke nodded perfunctorily.

Elmo began pacing the length of the room. "Luke, we could

shift to a lower gear. We could simply follow their orders, release Randall Tice with no strings attached, and hope that God's Country or whoever keeps the deal."

"That's too low a gear," Luke said. Louise nodded silently, then reached for his hand. She broke into sobs as he leaned over and kissed her cheek.

"I just want something to happen, Mo," Luke said. "I've got to get her back. I've got to get her back. There's no substitute for that."

"Luke, keep asking questions. Tough questions. So far, we've *seen* nothing at God's Country—nothing from the air, nothing from the ground—that looks connected to a kidnapping. But there are some hints. Joshua talked about jackboots in his Web page message to Janet Reno after Waco, and the word *jackboots* was in the kidnappers' first message. Tonight we heard him say, 'A white thunder is rolling across the land.' White Thunder—the kidnappers' code name—is that a coincidence? He told Noreen it was 'quite a coincidence' that we had shown up there tonight, and he searched us for wires. But I admit that that whole scene had no real edge to it. They let us walk around the place, with an escort, of course, but nobody steered us away from anything."

"Could they be that good?" Luke wondered.

"The point is, Tice gets out Monday, we snatch him, our classified ad Tuesday morning will say, Okay, White Thunder, let's swap. No questions asked. No publicity. Now, if White Thunder ain't God's Country—"

"The plan still works," Luke said.

"It has a good chance to," Elmo Finn said. "But it's your call, Luke."

"What a Jap!" Cecil Beech whooped, spinning away from the computer screen and brandishing a yellow pad. "Goddamnedest Jap—Colonel, I can now inform you and the governor that Sushi's pal Tojo is in the air with some very bogus material that may change our situation. Toward the positive." He scooted across the floor in his swivel chair and began to explain.

Fifteen minutes later, there was noise on the steps followed by impatient knocks on the door. Luke, suppressing a grin, hurried over. It was Col. Bump Hanner.

"Got here as quick as I could, Governor." The stocky state police commander was slightly out of breath. Looking around, nodding sourly to each face, he peeled off his suit jacket, revealing gaudy red-white-and-blue suspenders.

Luke said, "Bump, for reasons I won't go into at this time, and I direct you to keep this conversation confidential, my friends Elmo and George went to a sunset service tonight at that God's Country compound, over in Boone County."

Bump Hanner stood frozen, his eyes cutting to Elmo Finn and back.

"Guess who they saw, Bump. Guess who they saw at the sunset service at God's Country. Sergeant Clay Jennings. Sergeant Clay Jennings of the Tennessee State Police. Dressed up in a brown shirt like a neo-Nazi storm trooper and standing guard at Joshua's altar."

Bump Hanner was nodding slowly, his lips pursed, as if this revelation were completely expected. He looked at the floor for a moment while the edgy silence intensified, then curled his eyes toward Gov. Luke Gannon.

"He's undercover, sir. He's an agent."

"An agent? He's infiltrating them? Clay?"

"Yes, sir."

"Why?"

Hanner snorted. "Well, Governor, sir, because they're suspected of murder and bank robbery and extortion and sale and possession of illegal weapons and grand theft auto and kidnapping and harboring fugitives and drug trafficking—"

"Has he found anything?"

"Yes he has, sir, but he's only scratched the surface. When he gains their complete confidence, he'll produce much more."

"They know he's one of my body men?"

"Yes, sir—that makes him even more attractive to God's Country. They think he's *their* spy."

"Jesus. Why wasn't I told of this?"

"I didn't think it was necessary, sir. These operations are usually need to know. I'll certainly keep you in—"

"What kind of kidnapping? You mentioned kidnapping."

"There's a young boy named Jeremiah Cherry, who may be being held against his will. Certainly against his mother's will. She's filed a custody suit—and she's driving the Boone County sheriff crazy."

"Is the boy kept in handcuffs?"

"Yes, sir, that's correct." Hanner showed no surprise. "Clay's given us several reports on Jeremiah."

Luke and Elmo moved a few steps away and talked in hushed tones. The state police commander shifted his weight back and forth, gazing at the walls and the ceiling, a red snarl coloring his face.

Luke walked back. "Bump, get Clay in here. I want to talk with him."

"Yes, sir. First thing tomorrow."

"Right now."

"At two in the morning?"

"Right now."

"Right now. Yes, sir. Do my best."

The phone rang as the angry state police commander stormed out. Louise answered the call and motioned for Elmo, who went to the phone, listened for two minutes, and hung up. He called everyone around.

"That was Roy. The bug's working. Joshua and Noreen talked for a long time tonight—about the custody fight over

Jeremiah, they had a fistfight about that, about Noreen taking over the Web page because Linda Pearson's a slacker, about who George and I were, she was more suspicious than Joshua, Randall Tice's name was mentioned, apparently innocently—and all of this without a reference to Nikki or to any kind of a kidnapping. Noreen did say it was *coincidental* that we showed up, but didn't say what the coincidence might be. The baby girl, Esther, is sick and Noreen's taking her to a free clinic."

"Operated no doubt by the very government they hate," George Graves said. "Don't put car tags on, don't pay your taxes—but by God take your sick daughter to the free government clinic."

The others voiced general disgust with God's Country and the paranoid right wing. Elmo Finn was gazing into the middle distance, a milky glaze masking the fire-flecked gray eyes.

"What is it, Mo?" Luke Gannon said. "You're thinking about something."

"Luke, as of now, you're still signing off on the swords approach."

Luke nodded vigorously. "Hell yes. I just wanted to talk it all through. Swords our law."

"Swords our law!" Louise yelled with a contrived grin.

"Then let's sharpen our swords even more. I have another little idea."

"Sharpen away," the governor said.

"Luke, you don't have to know the details."

"You mean I can have deniability? No, I'm in all the way, all the way—money, marbles, and chalk. And I don't care what happens to my governorship, screw the governorship! Nikki comes first. Money, marbles, and chalk, Mo! And swords!"

Sgt. Clay Jennings wore a sheepish look on his square face. "Governor, I thought they should have informed you about my undercover assignment, but the powers that be . . ."

"It's all right, Sergeant," Luke Gannon said. "Bump was right. Need to know. But now, as it happens, Elmo and I have an interest in that place, and I want you to tell me everything you know. Even though it's three o'clock in the morning. Everything."

"Sure, Governor, whatever you want." The big state trooper who eight hours earlier had stood pillar-straight as one of Joshua's brown-shirted storm troopers smiled across the table at Elmo Finn. "You guys ought to try us again, Elmo. Give the body men another chance."

"We'd never get past you a second time," Elmo Finn said smoothly. "And I bet no one else will, either. The first time."

"You got that right. You got that right. But you shook us up, it served a purpose." He offered a big hand across the table. "No hard feelin's."

"None," Elmo Finn said, shaking the cop's hand.

"Have you seen anything suspicious out there, Clay?" Luke said.

Jennings leaned back, crossed his legs, and laced his hands around his knee. He seemed fresh and alert, despite the late hour. "It's *all* suspicious, Governor. These people, let me tell you, they're a few bubbles off plumb. They got a guy out there named Glenn Forbush who is certified dumber'n a stump, had his name *legally changed to Hi Hitler* because he thought the Nazis were saying Hi Hitler instead of Heil—"

"You haven't seen anything odd, people coming and going at odd times, covert, like they're hiding something . . ."

"I'm not an insider yet, Governor. They're still testin' me. And I work forty hours here so there's only ten to twenty I can work out there. Long drive. But that's what Bump wanted, low-key approach, don't make 'em suspicious. But I haven't seen nothin' *odd* except that everything out there's odd. There's this straw hut, made out of bales of hay—"

"Clay, if you see anything different from the usual routine out there, anything suspicious, like somebody's hidin' in a trailer or a hut or a cabin somewhere, off the beaten track, a fugitive or somethin,' prisoner, let me know. Personally. This order takes precedence over Colonel Hanner's. You're *my* agent now."

"Yes, sir. Yes, sir." The big trooper looked wary.

"Sergeant," said Elmo Finn, "I'm interested in Noreen and Joshua. Are they together? Are they a team?"

"They seem to be. Everybody calls her Mother of God 'cause she thinks God's a woman. Even so, she's not as crazy as the rest of 'em. She's pretty nice. They fight some."

"What about the boy—Jeremiah?"

"He lives in the straw hut with his father Earl who's a lowlife moron, and Jeremiah himself's backward or something. He has to wear Earl's old clothes, way too big for him. The other kids make fun of him, they stand outside the hut and yell 'We'll huff and puff and blow your house down.' I feel real sorry for Jeremiah. Sometimes Earl handcuffs him around a tree. I can't stand to see it."

Elmo Finn folded his hands on the table. "Sergeant, there used to be somebody at God's Country named Randall Tice. You ever hear of him?"

Jennings sat back suddenly, an angry glare darkening his face. "He's in prison—Brushy Mountain. One of my first jobs for God's Country was to go visit Randall Tice—Joshua thought it would cheer him up to know a state trooper was on board. Impress him." Clay Jennings shifted in his chair. His eyes were furious. "That was hard for me to do, very hard, because Randall Tice killed one of our troopers. But the case—actually, Governor, your father-in-law, Judge Perry, threw the case out. *Probable cause.*"

"I remember, Clay," Luke said.

Jennings folded his arms across his big chest. He was red-faced now. "Governor, can you give me a little better idea exactly what you'd like me to look for out there? What's it got to do with Randall Tice?"

"Clay, I can't explain right now. Just check out everything you can get close to, keep your eyes and ears open."

Jennings stared at the governor for a long moment. Then he said, "That's what I've been doin'." Another stare. "You know, they claim McVeigh was through there once."

"You believe it?"

"I don't think so. They're always tryin' to impress me 'cause I'm a state cop, they think I was part of the Zionist Occupation Government without knowin' it. ZOG. They're pretty flaky."

"You work for me now, Clay."

"Yes, sir."

"Take a week off from security, stay out there as much as you can get by with, sleep out there. Can you go back tonight? Right now?"

"Yes, sir. No problem. You're the boss."

Luke wrote a number on a business card and handed it to Jennings. "Call me on this number anytime day or night. Talk only to me or Elmo or George Graves."

"Yes, sir." Smiling once more across the table at Elmo Finn. "I'll never forget those old boys."

The Fourth Day

For the second straight night, Gov. Lucas Gannon collapsed into bed at four-thirty, exhausted, but slept no more than a half hour at a time, bolting fully awake from grotesque nightmares that he couldn't remember, his insides thundering. He leaned over the edge of the bed and sipped brandy from the bottle on the floor, buried himself beneath the down comforter, then kicked it to the floor until he began shivering, ground the top of his head into the ridged headboard to compress the whirlwind in his brain, switched the television on and off and on and off. At eight-fifteen he rose and flung himself into the shower, wobble-headed from the fitful sleep and the brandy and the galloping fear.

After three cups of coffee with the body men in the foyer and a fourth back in the bedroom laced with brandy, he telephoned his banker.

"Cliff, you know somethin' yet?"

"Governor, I was just going to call you. There's something very odd."

"What?"

"You wanted to know how much you could borrow on the equity in your house, and the answer as of now is zero. There's a lien."

"What? A lien? There's no lien on this house, Cliff—did you have some rookie handle this?"

"Luke, I went to the courthouse myself. I couldn't believe it. A lien against your property has been duly recorded—filed by a very kooky lawyer named Linda Pearson. She represents some real warpos, like that God's Country crowd."

"Goddamnit, Cliff, how can she—I've never even laid eyes on the bitch!"

"Apparently anyone can file a lien just by filing it, on their own motion, and it's up to you to get it removed."

"Somebody can just walk in and file a lien with no proof?"

"I'm having our lawyers follow this up, Luke. Don't worry—this is no more than a nuisance."

"Cliff. Are you saying that if I wanted my equity today, I couldn't get it?"

The banker breathed into the phone. "I'm afraid that's correct, Luke."

"Then it's more than a goddamn nuisance *right goddamn now*." The intercom buzzed. "Cliff, I've got to go. Figure this out for me—I may need some money soon. Real soon."

Luke punched the intercom button and was told that Elmo Finn had arrived. "Send him back and bring more coffee."

Elmo slouched in with the disorganized face of an all-night poker game refugee forced into emergency ablutions—whore's bath, cold-water shave with dull razor, aspirin, and black coffee in the car on the way to work. But beneath the despoiled face, he was costumed properly for the part he was to play—dark blue suit, white shirt, narrow striped tie that was years out of date, black cops' shoes. And, despite the fog, a glinty smile.

"Luke, Tojo made it to Knoxville. Plan B is active. Henry flew over before sunup to meet him."

"When do I call Clarence?"

"Soon as I leave. Will he cause any trouble?"

"I can handle Clarence. When I first told him I wanted to appoint him Commissioner of Corrections, he just looked at me in wonderment. Then he cried like a baby. It was very embarrassing. He said he'd be the most loyal appointee I ever had."

"Remind him of that. If anything ever called for loyalty, this does."

Luke nodded heavily. "I couldn't sleep, Mo. Maybe I should take something, Louise has some—Jesus! Where's the paper? I'm so groggy—"

"The ad's in there. So they know we're following orders."

"Any typos? I want to see it."

"It's perfect."

A uniformed maid brought in a large carafe of aromatic coffee and oversize mugs on a silver tray. Elmo and Luke fixed their coffees. Then Luke sat on the edge of the unmade bed, Elmo on the chaise lounge.

"Mo, the reason I can't sleep, I keep thinking—is she warm, is she cold, is she scared, is she hurt, is she drugged, is she being tortured—is she naked! Being abused! God, I'm going crazy just imagining—"

"I'll tell you what Nikki's doing, Luke. She's fighting back however she can. Listening for words, sounds, vehicles, anything. Memorizing voices, smells, noises, details. Playing for sympathy. Nikki is tough and smart. And scared, of course—everybody in captivity is scared. But I know she's doing whatever she can do. We've got to work as hard as she's working."

"She's a fighter, Mo. She's tough."

"Yes she is, and so are we. Now, before Henry gets back, I

want you to tell me the basic facts of Judge Perry's suicide. I don't know why I need to know this, but I do."

Luke expelled a long breath. "I don't know why, either, Mo. It was surreal—just like what's happening now. Completely surreal. Louise was in New York on some theater excursion. Nikki found the body—his clerk called when he didn't show up for court. First time ever."

"What were the details?"

"Well, you know the judge was soft on certain criminals— maybe all criminals. There was this stalking case—girl dumps boy, boy can't deal with it, stalks her, threatens her, roughs her up, she gets a restraining order that's supposed to keep him one hundred feet away. He ignores it, beats her up again, gets arrested again. And Judge Perry *lets—him—go*. R-O-R. The prosecutors freaked. Soon as this guy was out of the courtroom, he goes straight to where she works and strangles her. Her friends are trying to pull him off but couldn't. D.O.A. People got up petitions to impeach the judge—just like in the Randall Tice situation when the state trooper was killed and Judge Perry threw out the evidence."

Elmo got up and poured more coffee for each of them. He opened some blinds and bountiful sunshine streamed in.

Luke went on. "Not long afterwards, the judge was at his desk one night, apparently suffering deep remorse for releasing the stalker and thereby causing the girl's death, and he fashioned himself a noose and looped it over a beam and stuck his neck in it. There was a clipping about the stalker on his desk."

"Any note?"

"No. Most suicides don't leave notes."

"Any indications beforehand—remarks that no one interpreted correctly—"

Luke shook his head sadly. "You never know what's inside a person."

"Where'd he get the rope?"

"I don't know. Maybe there's something in the police file. But it was a suicide, Mo—Louise, of course, doesn't believe it. She can't bear the thought that her dear dear Nicholas would end it all and forgo the pleasures of living with her. But that's what he did. Living with *her* wasn't the problem. He couldn't live with himself."

"Did Nikki believe it was a suicide?"

"Yes."

"Did she accept it?"

"Eventually. It still gets to her."

Elmo Finn jumped to his feet. "Okay, pal, showtime for you, showtime for us. Let's do it."

The governor of Tennessee looked at his old friend and comrade in arms. "Mo, this is against the law. You're breaking the law. Are you sure?"

Elmo Finn smiled. " 'I am a kind of burr; I shall stick.' "

They shook hands, then embraced.

"Swords our law."

"Swords our law."

Outside the Ark the sun still had not crested the eastern ridges and only pale filaments of dawn flickered through the ersatz stained-glass windows into the Ark, where twenty-one men of God's Country stood in a circle on the wide-planked floor, holding hands, looking down on the infant girl lying naked on the coarse blanket.

Candles burned from the rough-hewn altar and around the walls, throwing a crazy quilt of cold shadows. Esther gazed upward, blinking at the circle of faces, and began to cry. Joshua bent to stroke her hair, and moved a candle closer so the dancing flames might seize her attention.

Straightening up, reclasping the hands of the men flanking him, he began to chant in his rich baritone.

"I swear on the sacred graves of our Aryan forefathers . . ."

Twenty voices repeated, "I swear on the sacred graves of our Aryan forefathers . . ."

"I swear as a citizen of God's Country and as a soldier of God's Swift Sword . . ."

Again the chorus of responsive voices, meshing into a rhythm.

"I swear upon the purity and innocence of our wives and daughters, symbolized by this perfect child . . ."

Several of the men were already weeping, voices breaking, heads lifting to the high broad beams of the ceiling and the thrashing shadows of candlelight.

". . . join with my blood brothers in this circle . . . no fear of any enemy . . . any obstacle . . . any death . . . sacred duty to deliver our race from the Jew and the mud people and to bring eternal victory . . ."

Little Esther was crying again as the Aryan warriors wept unashamedly, proudly, clutching the moist hands on either side. Joshua ignored his daughter and bore on.

"I swear to you, my blood brothers, that should one of you succumb in battle, I will attend to the needs of your family."

The twenty voices rose as one now, thundering the response.

". . . should one of you be taken captive, I will strive unceasingly to restore your freedom . . ."

The response echoed off the timbers.

". . . should a Jew or a ZOG agent cause you suffering, I will pursue and destroy him . . ."

The chorus shouting now.

". . . should I violate this oath, let me be cursed and shunned . . ."

"No! No!" Noreen McConathy had slipped in through the side door. She ran to her whimpering daughter and snatched her up. "No! She's sick! She needs a doctor! Harlan, I told you!" She ran out with the girl in her arms.

Joshua's powerful voice continued with the oath, his head

high, thrusts of sunlight now setting the stained glass ablaze. And the men responded.

". . . we gladly accept this covenant of blood and declare that henceforth and forever we are in a full state of war with the enemies of our race and our faith, and that we will not rest until we have driven them unto Satan and reclaimed, with our blood, the land of our Aryan forefathers and the land of our Aryan children to come."

The men embraced wordlessly, thrilling to the moment despite Noreen's intrusion. Tears flowed copiously, and Joshua shook hands solemnly around the circle.

"I promise," he said to each man, standing close, the ice-blue eyes raging.

"I promise," came the answers.

The last man was the towering Clay Jennings, who had not slept the night before. His eyes were dry. As Joshua and the others composed themselves and left the Ark, he circled the room and gently blew out the candles.

She emerged into the late-summer wind from the entryway of the squatty, cinder-block Boone County Medical Center, carrying the child wrapped in a blanket. As she braced her daughter on her hip and reached back to close the door, a nurse in a blue uniform appeared and followed her out.

"Make sure she takes all the medicine, Mrs. McConathy. Don't stop it even if she seems to be better. Until she takes it all."

Noreen and the nurse headed toward the gravel lot filled with cars and trucks parked in ragged rows. The wind whipped and swirled through the cramped mountain valley, lifting and tossing scraps of paper and a few brown leaves. The sky was pale and clear. As they approached the gray hatchback with God's Country plates, a man rose up between the car and the big green sports utility vehicle parked next to it. He unfolded a road map and buried his face in it.

The nurse helped Noreen put Esther into the car seat.

"You bring her back if her temperature isn't down within forty-eight hours, okay, Mrs. McConathy. You hear now?"

Peering at the stranger with the map, Noreen nodded absently, then got in the hatchback. The nurse turned to the man.

"May I help you, sir?"

The gray hatchback backed out quickly and shot away.

"No thank you, ma'am, I think I just figured it out. Musta missed a turn somewhere."

The nurse waited until the man got into the SUV. She went back to the clinic and watched from the entryway as the Navigator slowly worked its way out of the parking lot and turned onto the two-lane road. Then she went inside.

"She's gone," Roy said. "Goddamn Florence Nightingale."

George Graves scrambled up from the floor of the rear seat, where he had been hidden by blankets. "She get a good look at you?"

Roy shook his head.

When they were out of sight of the clinic, Roy gunned the Lincoln to sixty-five. The rural road had few straightaways, curling between stumpy hills and coarse brown fields with craggy outcroppings, on a generally upward slant. Hazy blue mountains loomed on the eastern horizon. Soon the hatchback was in view. Roy stayed at a constant distance behind.

"Good stretch comin' up," George said.

"Yep. That broken-down billboard is fail-safe."

Roy accelerated, closing the distance to the hatchback, nearing the billboard, ready to slam the Navigator into passing gear.

"Abort! Traffic ahead!"

An ancient pickup truck trundled into view on the curve ahead, lumbering toward them.

"Goddamnit!"

"We'll make it, we've got twelve miles."

"And the road's as crooked as a dog's hind leg, George."

"That's why you're drivin'."

The cab of the pickup was jammed with people craning to observe the Navigator's passengers. Roy and George stared straight ahead as the two vehicles passed. The pickup disappeared around a curve.

Roy accelerated again, topping a rise and plunging into a long curve, holding the Navigator tight into the curve, holding the downhill groove, then roaring into overdrive, slinging into the empty oncoming lane, hitting the straight stretch at eighty, swooping even with the gray hatchback, angling sharply right and braking hard, cutting the small car off, forcing it to the narrow shoulder in a cloud of dust and gravel.

George was out of the Navigator before it stopped, racing back to the dust-covered car, arriving seconds before the terrified Noreen tried to jam down the door lock. George yanked the door open as Noreen McConathy threw her fists at him wildly. George forced his way in.

"You're safe, Noreen. I'm a friend. Move over, move over. You're safe. You're safe. This is about Jeremiah. Jeremiah is in danger. Nothing will happen to you or Esther. Jeremiah is in danger and we need your help. We need your help."

George spoke calmly, authoritatively, easily blocking Noreen's frenzied haymakers with his forearms. She lunged for the car key but George caught her arm, held it firmly, then softly returned it to her side before releasing it. She was whimpering and breathing heavily. Esther was slumped in the car seat, the soft blanket covering half her face. Noreen unfastened the straps and lifted her baby in her arms.

"Why are you doing this?" she said in gasps.

"We need your help, Noreen. For Jeremiah."

"My baby's sick. I've just been to the doctor."

"We wanted to talk with you in the parking lot, but the nurse was there."

"She can identify you." Noreen's eyes narrowed. "I know you. You were at the sunset service. I knew you couldn't be trusted."

"You can trust us, Noreen." George spotted a vehicle in the rearview mirror and edged the hatchback farther off the road. The strange car went by. "We'll make sure Esther's all right, we'll get a doctor if necessary."

"I can't help you with Jeremiah! I don't even know where he is—his daddy took him away."

George pulled the hatchback back onto the road. When he passed the big Navigator, Roy swung in behind.

"I've got to get back. Joshua will be worried. He'll send out people—people with guns!"

"We need your help, Noreen."

"My help! You keep saying that! There's nothing I can do, you've got it figured all wrong!" She was rocking her child gently in her arms.

George was silent. Noreen whispered to Esther as she rocked her.

"You've got this all wrong, you don't know what you're doing. What *are* you doing, kidnapping me?"

"Temporarily. You're in no danger."

"Boy, you sure are. You don't know the danger you're in."

"So they had to send two of you, did they, just to pick up one piece of trash like Randall Tice."

The corrections officer wore a snugly fitting starched uniform and spit-shined shoes. Everything about him seemed regulation, by the book, except his playful eyes, which were open to interpretation.

"I quit tryin' to figure 'em out," the white man said in a bored voice, stifling a yawn with his fist.

"Any chance of seein' James Earl Ray's cell?" the black man said. "I'd like to see where you kept him for thirty years."

The playful eyes became curious. "Have to pull a few strings for that. Thought you were in a hurry, Marshal."

"Yeah, we are," the white man said.

"Why'd they cremate him and bury the ashes in Ireland?" the black man said.

"Shit, I don't know. I just work here." Corrections picked up the federal court order from his desk, scanned it again, frowning, then returned it to the pocket envelope marked United States District Court, Southern District of New York.

He said, "I hear the governor himself called. What's so important about Randall Tice? Lowlife cocksucker, come get him in a helicopter?" He looked at the black man. "Which was one of James Earl Ray's pals, by the way, Marshal Dobbs. Did you know that? It's Dobbs, right?"

Henry Wood nodded coldly and leaned back in his chair.

Elmo Finn yawned again. "Somethin' about a bank robbery, Officer, some unexpected witnesses turned up. They don't tell us much. We just work there."

Corrections's playful eyes brightened. "They say Randall Tice robbed more banks than Jesse James. Got money stashed in the hills."

Elmo Finn's lips curled into a smile. "Maybe we'll beat it out of him."

"Fine with me. You can beat him to death or dump him out of that chopper for all I care. Right on his pointed redneck head." Corrections leaned forward on his forearms. "Mind if I look at your badge again? Marshal . . ."

"Reardon."

"Marshal Reardon."

Elmo Finn stretched languidly. He produced the scuffed

black leather case and tossed it across the desk. "Help yourself."

"It's just I love badges," Corrections said, smiling innocently. "And I really love this one. Like the Wild West."

"The Wyatt Earp badge, I call it," Elmo Finn said. "Five-pointed star in a circle."

"It's a helluva badge! Wyatt Earp—he was a U.S. marshal too." He handed the leather case back to Elmo Finn.

"You oughtta take the exam, get yourself one."

"Me? No, I don't—"

"You're not thirty-seven yet, are you?"

"Pushin'."

"Well, you got a bachelor's, you're in, or three years' relevant experience, I *know* you got that. Workin' at Brushy Mountain State Penitentiary is damn sure relevant experience."

Corrections's eyes turned thoughtful, almost dreamlike. Elmo and Henry struck new poses of nonchalance.

The door to the inner office swung open and a tall, spare man in a pearl-gray three-piece suit came out. He took a few steps into the room and stopped. He was frowning.

"You boys don't believe in much notice, do you? This is irregular, say the least, I told the governor exactly that. I told the commissioner exactly that. First time the *governor* ever called on one of these."

Elmo Finn spread his hands, palms up.

"There's somethin' political behind this. I can smell politics a mile away, this one's got the smell to it."

Elmo and Henry gazed evenly at the warden, like stud players waiting for a card.

"I know it's not your fault, boys. I got nothin' but respect for the marshals service, but there's a procedure for everything. I don't like these hurry-up jobs."

"We don't like 'em either, Warden. Except we managed to see some pretty nice country this mornin' from the air, leaves startin' to turn," Elmo Finn said. "I do believe this is about the nicest maximum-security scenery I ever seen."

"You bet it is. You can't beat the East Tennessee mountains, nowhere on this earth. This is God's country."

"I guess if you got to be in jail—"

"You all know how old this prison is?"

Elmo Finn shook his head.

"Over one hundred years old."

"Man!" Henry said. He and Elmo exchanged glances, deeply impressed.

The phone buzzed and Corrections answered it. After a moment, he nodded to Elmo Finn. "They got him ready for you, Marshal. Change of clothes in his bag. Watch the little fucker good, strap him in, make sure those helicopter doors are shut nice and tight, now."

"Oh you bet, Warden. We wanna bring him back safe and sound."

They all shook hands before Elmo and Henry went out to take custody of Randall Tice.

"Federal fuckin' government," the warden grumbled behind them, loud enough for them to hear.

The man code-named Blue trickles three quarters and a nickel into the pay phone after wiping each coin clean.

"I don't like this," Red says as the connection comes through, speaking in a falsetto monotone to disguise her voice.

"You don't like anything. Two pay phones, nothing's safer. Listen up. There's a possible change, I want more of the juice and more syringes."

"Another change? Why? We had a plan—"

"Roll with the punches, little . . . little Red! This is perfect. Listen."

He explains it.

"You're wrong, Blue, nothing's perfect. But this is good. It's a good change."

"It's a work of art."

Red's falsetto has vanished. "You better worry about gettin' two motorcycles, Mr. Blue."

"The motorcycles, Miz Red, are already got. And standing by."

"You sure a four-wheel-drive can't get through?"

"Yes."

A Bell South recording comes on. "Please deposit forty cents for an additional minute."

They hang up.

Alone in his office, Eli Korn realized he was nodding demonstratively as he talked with the governor's receptionist over the interoffice phone. He almost laughed, wondering if such unseen gesticulations were an unconscious habit, and if anyone had ever noticed. But how could anyone notice an unseen gesture? He laughed out loud, and the receptionist laughed back as if she were in on the joke.

Eli said, "Wait till I buzz, then send him in."

He punched Jill Dennison's number. She answered immediately.

"Clarence is here. I wish you'd come over, Jill."

"You want a witness, Mr. Chief of Staff?"

"Goddamn right."

Jill opened Eli's private door without knocking and came in. Eli buzzed the reception room and soon they were joined by Clarence Monahan, the state Commissioner of Corrections and a political appointee of the governor.

"Here's the list, Eli," he said, handing over a sealed brown envelope. "Two hundred and twenty-six lucky inmates. Except it's moot now, thank God. Hi, Jill."

"Commissioner."

"Moot." Eli dropped the envelope on his desk and came around to the sofa, throwing Jill a cautionary look on the way. "Sit down, Clarence, you want some coffee or something?"

"I'm on the wagon. I'm down to twenty cups a day."

Eli manufactured a little laugh. "Ah, Clarence, what's your precise understanding, ah, at this point of the, ah, prisoner release? At this stage."

"That there ain't no prisoner release! Not yet anyway, not until we have to under the court order. The question's moot. The governor called me to his house this morning, don't you all know about that?"

"Only the general thrust, Clarence, why don't you fill in the details for us. Before we see the man."

The Corrections Commissioner looked from one to the other of the governor's top assistants and made one of the hundreds of tiny decisions that working politicians make every day.

"He said he had changed his mind, that my arguments had nagged at him, about the bad press, so forth, and for me to just cancel the midnight release, that's what I was calling it, privately, of course, which was easy since none of the orders had gone out anyway. So, done and done. It would have been awful—two hundred and twenty-six felons. Some of 'em violent."

"Well, Clarence, case closed."

"Case closed, which eases my mind considerable. But then he did something else that was odd."

"What was that, Clarence?" Jill asked.

"He had me call Brushy Mountain, right from his house. Then he got on the phone and told the warden some U.S. marshals were on their way to borrow a prisoner, that's how he said it, *borrow* a prisoner, he was cuttin' through the usual red tape for an old friend in the U.S. attorney's office in New York, to expedite the release, don't worry about the paperwork too much. Then I got back on and said the same thing, which he had ordered me to do, except I didn't know what the Sam Hill I was talking about. I tell you, the man's got friends everywhere. I believe he may run for president. You'll be famous, both of you."

"He runs for president, I run for cover," Eli said. It was Eli's stock line, and Clarence and Jill laughed dutifully.

"Who's the prisoner?" Jill asked.

"You'll probably remember him. Randall Tice, the God's Country bank robber. And cop killer, if the state police are right. Remember, the governor's father-in-law made one of his famous Fourth Amendment rulings and Tice didn't even get prosecuted for the trooper."

"New York wants Randall Tice?"

Clarence nodded. "And went straight to the governor to get it done. Makes you wonder."

"About what?"

"Well, the governor was in the FBI, they say he was in the CIA in Vietnam, all this hush-hush stuff, hurry-up stuff, special favors. And he looks goddamn awful, bags under his eyes—is he all right, Eli? I've even heard that he and Nikki are on the outs. I've even heard that she split."

"No no no, Clarence. He's just working too hard. He and Nikki need a little vacation, that's all."

"Who are all these strange dudes hangin' around? They really pissed the body men off."

"There've been some threats against the governor, Clarence. More than what the press reported. These people are security specialists."

"Well, good, then I'm glad they're here. But I can see why the body men are so pissed—somebody invadin' their turf."

The conversation shifted to other topics, and Commissioner Clarence Monahan decided to sit right where he was as long as possible. He was slightly heady after a morning so close to the throne, summoned to the governor's private residence where he was sure he had smelled liquor on the governor's breath, orders cancelled, orders given, then welcomed into Eli Korn's capitol office, where everyone knew the real decisions were made, and stunned to encounter the bright and beaming Jill Dennison whose long, long legs had so beguiled His Majesty that Nikki had ordered her fired months ago, which started all the domestic trouble in the first place. Or so the gossips told it.

But the conversation soon wilted, and Clarence was gone. Eli took a pack of cigarettes from a desk drawer and offered one to Jill. They both lit up.

"What the hell, Jill?" Eli reached across the credenza and raised the window a few inches. "First we're going to release two hundred felons, then we're not going to release two hundred felons. Clarence Monahan talked him out of it!"

"Clarence's ass. Something's going on. It's those cowboys—I don't know. That Elmo Finn."

"Is the boss getting squeezed here—CIA, FBI, old home week, Nikki's private trip, these crazy packages bein' delivered, all that secret stuff over there on the fourth floor. What the fuck's going on?"

"I don't know! Where is he, anyway, still at home?"

"What the hell does a U.S. attorney in New York want with a little hillbilly like Randall Tice? And why the hell is our governor handling prisoner traffic for the federal courts? That's a routine deal, isn't it? Doesn't take a personal phone call from the governor to the warden of Brushy Mountain State Penitentiary."

Jill stood up and went to the door, then turned back.

" 'Sunlight is the best disinfectant.' "

"You mean leak this?"

"Why not? If Luke's in a bind, nothing like publicity to get him out. Or muddy everything up."

"Luke would suspect Clarence or the warden. Not us."

"Think about it."

"He said 'Trust me.' "

Jill Dennison laughed sharply. "But you didn't."

The Mountain Empire Motel was wedged into the Boone County hills like an alpine village. The original section, a modest row of eight rooms and an office, had sprouted double-decker wings and ells like tentacles. Now the complex included two restaurants, a gas station, a video arcade and souvenir shop, and a heated swimming pool beneath a Plexiglas dome.

The green Lincoln Navigator pulled into the complex and headed for the newest section, farthest from the road, standing alone on a perch that had been carved out of a rugged slope. Only a few vehicles were parked outside. Roy drove to the end of the two-story wing, then turned and started back.

"That's the one," George Graves said, pointing to his flowered lavender necktie dangling from the doorknob of Room 525. Within seconds they had escorted Noreen McConathy and her daughter Esther up the middle stairs and inside. Elmo Finn was waiting.

Noreen went to one of the double beds and made a place for Esther, who was sleeping quietly. Noreen tucked her in, felt her forehead with the back of her hand, and kissed her gently. She went to the chair by the window.

"You are in no danger, Mrs. McConathy," Elmo Finn said. "Do you want us to get a doctor?"

"No. I want to go home."

"You'll be able to go home soon. But we need your help first."

"You're the other one. You were at the sunset service. Pretendin' to be sellin' something."

"We need your help, Noreen."

"I don't know where Jeremiah is—"

"Who else is being hidden at God's Country, Noreen?"

"Who else? I don't know. Nobody else."

"We're looking for someone—a woman—and we think she's there. Somewhere."

"Helen Cherry? Is that who you're lookin' for? Jeremiah's mother? She's always sneakin' in and out, tryin' to find Jeremiah. But I don't think she's livin' there. She couldn't be."

"It's not Helen Cherry we're looking for."

"Well, who *are* you looking for? Who are *you?*"

"We're not your enemy, Noreen. Nothing will happen to you or your daughter."

"So what's going on—are you holding me hostage until you find whoever you're lookin' for?"

The baby stirred. Noreen jumped up and went to her. Elmo went into the bathroom and returned with a damp washcloth. Noreen took the cloth and softly patted Esther's face, then laid the cloth across her forehead.

"Yes, Noreen."

"I'm a hostage."

"Yes. In no danger."

She made a guttural laugh and went back to her chair. "Are you cops? You couldn't be cops."

"We're not exactly cops."

"Not exactly cops." She sighed deeply and curled into a ball, her arms tight around her knees. In a small voice she said, "I want to make a phone call."

"No, I'm sorry."

"I want to call my Hello Number. Do you know what that means, Mr. Not Exactly a Cop?"

Elmo Finn froze, his skin prickling. "Who do you work for, Noreen?"

"I don't know why I trust you, but I do. The BATF—Bureau of Arsonists, Traitors and Fascists." She let out another guttural laugh.

Elmo Finn ran a dozen calculations through his mind, struggling for the best-guess answer to one question: Which course of action would most likely rescue Nikki Gannon unharmed? Nothing clicked except instinct.

"Okay. You can't reveal your whereabouts. Tell your Hello Number that I'll meet him at a bar called the Hog. Or her."

"Him. He knows where the Hog is. He goes there."

"Tell him to wear a tie around his neck, but untied. Loose."

"I have to tell him who you are—so he won't call in an assault by the whole U.S. Army or something."

Elmo brought out the leather case and flipped it open. "Tell him you're with some United States marshals who want everybody to cooperate."

She examined the badge carefully. "U.S. marshals. Not exactly cops—you weren't lyin'."

Cecil Beech was incredulous, the Pancho Villa mustache bristling, the Noel Coward cigarette making loop-the-loops as he paced and gestured.

"Fucking Jap wore a top hat. A black—silk—fucking—top—hat. Said he always wanted to look like Odd Job in the James Bond movies, d'you remember, Luke, the big stud Oriental, looked like a refrigerator, wore tails and a top hat? Threw the top hat like a Frisbee, sliced the heads off of statues. So Tojo goes out and rents a black—silk—fucking—top—fucking—hat! And flies off to Knoxville, Tennessee, on orders to be inconfucking-spicuous, and hands over the forged U.S. marshal credentials to Mo and Henry. Wearing a black—silk—top—fucking—hat! Goddamnit to Nippon hell!"

Luke Gannon managed a bleak grin. He and Cecil were alone in the command post. It was one o'clock.

"So," Luke said. His lips formed another word, then dissolved into a thin line. He gazed off somewhere.

"You can't get anywhere dependin' on Japs," Cecil said. "I

got to rethink my whole operation. I got Sushi who's never been south of Macy's and I got Tojo who now sports a top hat. A Jap in a top hat in Tennessee. Odd Job. This is starting to sound like Wallace Stevens. I placed a Jap in Tennessee—"

"Cecil, please. Elmo and Shakespeare are enough."

"It'd *take* Shakespeare to do justice to those two nippers. They need some more jail time. A fucking top hat."

"Cecil, I know what you're doing and I appreciate it. I just can't stay cheery too long."

"Sure, I'll cool it, Luke. Sorry."

"No, I didn't mean . . . we ought to be hearing something pretty soon."

They sat quietly for several minutes. Finally the phone rang. Luke grabbed it, barking "Yes."

"Governor, is that you?"

"Clay?"

"Just reportin' in, sir. I came right straight back out here like you said, didn't get to bed at all, and there's some odd things happenin'. There was a sunrise ceremony this morning with candles, very creepy, Aryan brothers and all that, they used Joshua's little baby girl as a . . . like an idol, but Noreen busted in and grabbed her up and I ain't seen either one of 'em since. And there's some strange cars around, some with Georgia plates which I've never seen here before, and that straw hut is empty, I sneaked in for a look, Earl Cherry and Jeremiah must have taken off, and then that lawyer Linda Pearson showed up and Joshua and some of the men took off with her, but of course they didn't ask me to go along. I'm still out in left field. So— my report is that some odd things are happenin', but I don't know what they mean."

"That's okay, Clay, keep at it. Where are you calling from?"

"A pay phone a few miles away. Outside a roadhouse called the Hog. Didn't trust my cell phone."

"Be careful. Don't let anyone see you making calls."

"Yes, sir. Anything specific I should be lookin' for?"

"Look for a place where someone might be hiding. Or being held as a prisoner."

"You mean little Jeremiah?"

"There could be others. Probably *are* others."

"Yes, sir, I'll look everywhere I can. I'll be stayin' the nights, they got some bunks in the Ark."

"Good, Sergeant. I appreciate it. Be careful."

"Yes, sir. After what I saw this mornin', I'll sure do that."

During the phone call, Louise had come in with a small brown package in her hand. She was pale and nervous.

"Eli sent this over, Luke. It was under a trash can outside the capitol. Someone called in."

Luke tore open the package. Inside was an audiocassette tape but there was no tape player in the command post. Luke, Cecil, and Louise ran outside into the corridor but the elevator was on the first floor, so they took the stairs down. Luke demanded the keys to the state car from the body man, Moody, who seemed to sulk when the governor told him to stay behind. Moody watched them from the rear entrance as they hurried to the car.

Inside the car they activated the cassette player. There was a lot of tape hiss, and Luke adjusted the volume. Then a female voice came on.

"Luke, they saw your ad in the paper this morning—"

"It's Nikki!" Louise cried. "Oh my God."

"She's all right, Mom! Listen!" He rewound the tape a little.

". . . in the paper this morning. Please do whatever they say, please, Luke. I am all right but they have made me do things, oh Lucas, I want to come back to you, I am so scared, so alone, like it's just me against the world, please do what they say so I can come home. Please don't try—"

The tape broke off in a crackle of static, then went silent. Cecil rewound it and they listened to it again.

Luke was beaming. "She's sending a message, Mom. 'Me against the world.' That's our motto. That's what we say to each other."

"I never heard her say that."

"It's just between us. It's our little slogan."

"They're abusing her, Lucas. *Making her do things.*"

"She's okay, Mom, she's hanging on. Her against the world! The message is, she's all right. Oh I love that lady! And she mentioned the newspaper ad, so this tape was made today!" He embraced Louise and held her tight. "Mom, we're going to get her back! We're going to get her back!"

"If my husband knew I was alone in a motel room with a black man . . ." Noreen McConathy's soft chuckles were full of wonder.

Henry Wood said, "If my ex-wife knew I was alone in a motel room with a white woman called Mother of God . . ."

Noreen cackled. "What would she do, Marshal?"

"Probably hire another detective."

"*Another* detective?" Noreen half rose from her chair beside the window and looked at Esther, who was sleeping soundly, a tiny figure in the double bed.

"She sleeps better here than at home. Our trailer's so drafty. I've got to wake her up soon for the medicine."

"She's a beautiful child, Noreen."

"I can't believe she's mine. She's the reason I became an informer—I can't let her grow up in all that hate. My daddy gave us that beautiful land, a thousand acres with a clear blue lake . . ." Her eyes were brimming with tears. "You know what happened to me at that lake, Marshal Dobbs? Henry. I was up there one morning all by myself, very early, and it was so perfectly still, so beautiful and peaceful, not a sound to be heard that was made by man, and then I heard a bird flyin'. A bird in flight—not beating its wings, just flyin' over the lake. Soarin'—I could hear it. It was the most perfect moment. And that's what I thought God's Country was going to be—a place of perfect moments—not this rancid, bitter, political thing, teachin' little children to hate the government and Jewish people and black people. So the BATF is puttin' my money in a special account, and one day I'm going to take my baby and just disappear. And I don't care what happens to *Joshua*. Who's just a backward redneck named Harlan McConathy."

"You're a brave lady, Noreen."

"Thank you, Henry. I haven't had anyone to talk to—" She began to weep and turned toward the window, which was masked by the heavy drapes. "I'm scared all the time."

"Do you want some more tea?" Henry asked.

"Yes, Henry, thank you. It's good—we never have tea."

"I carry this with me wherever I go. It's Chinese tea—I got used to it in Vietnam."

"You were in Vietnam?"

There were two staccato knocks on the door, then three knocks, then two more. Henry opened the door and Elmo Finn and a wide-shouldered man came in.

Elmo said, "Marshal Henry Dobbs, Agent Gene Kessler. ATF."

They shook hands briefly. Gene Kessler went over to Noreen and kissed her on the cheek.

"I was worried about you," he said. "First time you've ever called the Hello Number."

"I knew you'd come, Gene." She held both his hands tightly.

Elmo emptied some grocery bags on the vacant bed. "Diapers, lotion, talcum powder, baby food, teething rings, diet Cokes, Budweiser, Marlboro Lights. Pacifiers for young and old."

Everyone laughed. Noreen attended to the baby while the three men talked quietly. Then she opened a can of Coke, lit a cigarette, and sprawled across the window chair. After a few cries of irritation, Esther fell back to sleep.

Gene Kessler took off his coat, revealing a nine-millimeter semiautomatic in a holster on his hip. He slumped into one of the low-backed easy chairs and kicked off his dust-covered shoes. Elmo Finn and Henry Wood sat on the second bed.

"Noreen," the brawny federal agent said, pausing a long time as if reaffirming a decision in his mind, "the Bureau is going to cooperate with these marshals here. No questions asked, even though a few very good questions—*very good questions*—come to mind. And vice versa—they're going to cooperate with me." Kessler gave Elmo a mock glare that dissolved into a quick smile, producing laughter all around.

"All right, let's be sure we're on the same page," Gene Kessler said briskly. "Marshal Reardon and I worked this out at the Hog. My team—BATF—is looking for illegal weapons—especially a delivery that may be in progress—military ordnance stolen from Fort Bragg. Scary stuff. An ex-GI named Wendell Maloney, Special Forces master sergeant, a.k.a. Sarge, is the middleman. We know some of his sources but not all. The other team—the marshals here—are looking for certain kidnap victims who are probably being held somewhere on the God's Country property, including a ten-year-old boy named Jeremiah Cherry. We've got a spy—Noreen. So do the marshals—but they can't say who it is. Or won't say."

"Who?" Noreen blurted. "Who? There's another spy? Does he have tattoos?" She laughed wildly. "Kidnap victims! I thought I was a kidnap victim"—winking at Henry—"until Henry explained things."

Kessler went on. "Now, I don't understand why U.S. deputy marshals are staking out a kidnap site, infiltrating a kidnap site, it ain't their jurisdiction by a long shot, I don't understand why Marshal Reardon had Noreen here virtually kidnapped just to *talk* to her about—whatever—and I don't understand—nothin'.

And I don't care. We all have our little secrets, and God and the Central Intelligence Agency work in mysterious ways." He gave Elmo Finn a little bow. "All I care about is stopping some very ugly munitions from reaching these maniacs at God's Country. Just for the record, I've got reinforcements standing by. We're not as obvious about it since Waco."

Noreen lit a fresh cigarette off the butt of the old one. "I didn't smoke when I was pregnant—got to catch up now." The room was hazy with smoke. Henry got up and cracked the door open.

Noreen frowned. "I'm sorry—I forget that cigarettes bother people."

"Not me," Elmo Finn said. "I quit ten years ago and I've missed them every day since. Smells good."

"I think I'll be able to quit again when Esther and I are free."

Gene Kessler brought the conversation back to business. God's Country apparently was planning a big job to pay for the illegal ordnance—the "final job," if Joshua could be believed. He had told Noreen that it wasn't another bank, but Joshua often lied to his lieutenants. He had been buying used cars, just as he always did before a job. Noreen, who had driven getaway cars in the past but who wouldn't be prosecuted because of her cooperation, had been ordered to drive again. One last time.

"I don't want to—I'm scared. Because of Esther."

"If we discover the target early enough, we'll stop it," Kessler said. "We want you to wear a device, Noreen."

"A wire? No!"

"It's not a wire, it's not a recorder. Just a tiny transmitter that goes inside your bra—specially made for female agents. Just so we can follow you. It's very safe."

"Ho ho! Joshua tells me driving will be safe and you guys tell me wearing a *device* will be safe. All you men telling a new mother how safe it is to do dangerous things."

She crossed to the bed and felt Esther's face. "I don't *feel* safe. She's cooler already—what a strong baby."

She came back to her chair and lit another cigarette, exhaling a dense stream of smoke. She rummaged in her handbag and brought out some tissue paper, then peeled back the layers revealing something tied up in a silver ribbon. She passed it to Gene Kessler.

"Noreen, you're the best." He brandished the lock of Joshua's hair and looked at Elmo and Henry. "DNA."

Noreen said, "Okay, I'll wear your tiny little transmitter in my bra, but this is it, the last job. Last job for Joshua, last job for you. Esther and I got to get a life."

Six doors away, in Room 513 of the Mountain Empire Motel, three men were fighting a duel of mind and will.

The man in handcuffs, standing bare-chested, was slight of build, with limp mouse-brown hair and seventies' sideburns, and a mottled complexion that made him seem unwashed. His torso bore discolorations where tattoos had been removed.

George Graves focused the camera and snapped the shutter. "Randall." He motioned for the man to turn sideways; he complied. George took another photograph.

"That'll do it, Randall." George put the camera aside as Roy unlocked the handcuffs. Tice began to get dressed.

"Just for our protection, Randall." George stretched out on one of the beds, his hands beneath his head. "Just in case your friends don't keep their bargain, we'll need these photographs for the execution squad. Now let's start over, Randall, go over everything again. Somebody wants you out of prison bad enough to risk going to prison themselves. And, although they don't know it yet, to risk dealing with my group, which is far worse than any prison. Who are they, Randall?"

Dressed now in a blue shirt and jeans he hadn't worn for three years, Randall Tice shuddered a little but maintained his rigid stare at a spot high on the wall above George's bed. For the dozenth time he recited, "My name is Randall David Tice, rank of captain in the army of God's Swift Sword, serial number oh-oh-oh-oh-four-four. I demand proper treatment as a prisoner of war under the Geneva Convention."

"You can sit down, Randall."

The obdurate militiaman, who had been out of prison for four hours after thirty-two months of confinement, remained standing, his hands behind him, gazing at the spot on the wall.

"Randall, you are not our prisoner. We are simply escorting you to your liberators. It's a simple swap—they have our friend, we have their friend. So we trade, even up, case closed."

A contemptuous smile bloomed on Randall Tice's face. "Herman said he'd get me out."

"Your friend Herman Page, sure. Brought you the TV set. Visited you more than anyone else. Forty times, must be a real pal."

Looking uncertain now, Tice sat on the low dresser. Roy, who was lounging on the other bed, got out a long hunting knife and began honing it on a whetstone, producing grating metallic whines.

"You want a beer, Randall? Or a cigarette? Or both?"

Tice hesitated, then said, "Yes—I don't know your name."

"We don't have names, Randall. Help yourself."

Tice got a pack of cigarettes from the carton on the dresser and a beer from the ice-filled sink. He went over and sat on the arm of the easy chair in the corner. The raspy zings of Roy's whetstone droned monotonously.

George Graves said, "Where's the money, Randall? Three hundred thousand dollars from that bank robbery in Cookeville, never recovered. Where'd you hide it?"

Tice rolled his eyes. "You guys don't know so much after all.

I never had the money, I think some cop got it. They framed me—ZOG framed me."

"Does Herman know this, Randall? Does Herman know you don't have the money?"

Tice sneered and twiddled his lips with a forefinger.

George laughed. "Doesn't really matter. If you try to fuck us, we can follow you through the implant—don't you remember that prison doctor, Randall?"

"What prison doctor? I didn't see no prison doctor."

"You just don't remember, Randall. That's how they do it—alter your memory circuits. Is Herman Page the brother of Travis Page? The trooper you shot?"

Whhing . . . whhing . . . whhing rang the whetstone against Roy's long knife.

"No relation—none whatsoever! You can bet that's the first question I asked—and I didn't shoot no trooper or nobody else. They think I did."

"Randall, we don't give a good goddamn whether you shot anybody. Just don't make *us* shoot somebody. And the somebody in question is you, Randall, and if you end up stone cold fuckin' dead, Randall, we won't give a good goddamn about that either. Where's Herman hang out these days?"

A red flush spread slowly over Randall Tice's face. He wiped his brow with his hand. "You about done sharpenin' that thing?"

Roy squinted at Tice, then with a violent turn of his wrist flung the knife underhand. It whisked past Tice's head and embedded in the wall behind him.

"Jesus! Jesus!" Tice snapped around to see the knife still quivering in the wall, then spun back to Roy. "Who are you? Who the fuck are you?"

George Graves said, "Randall, you ask one more question and we'll cut your goddamn heart out. We ask the questions. You want another beer?"

Louise wedged a doorstop under the command-post door and wheeled in her lunch wagon—a long, narrow utility table laden with bowls and platters stacked high and separated by cookie sheets. Luke arrived right behind her and began to help, but Louise waved him away. "This is my job, son."

"Smells good," Cecil said, reaching for his cigarettes.

"Both of you, please eat something. You must eat; you can't keep going without food. Come here, Baskerville, set a good example."

"The ad's done, Mom. It'll be in tomorrow. I called it in myself."

"Oh! Someone might have recognized your voice."

Luke shook his head slowly.

"What was the final version?"

" 'To White Thunder. We have ice with us. Ready to trade for Hot Stuff no questions asked. Please contact soonest. Blind Man.' "

"You left out 'anytime, anywhere.' "

"I think this will do it. It's just right."

"It wouldn't have hurt to be more . . . conciliatory."

"What's this, Miz Perry?" Cecil was peering under the lid of one of the dishes.

"Steamed vegetables and pasta in marinara sauce. Pasta primavera. Very healthy, Cecil."

"I get most of my vegetables from R.J. Reynolds."

"Cecil! You're—I don't know what you are!"

"Endearing."

The phone rang and Luke lunged for it. "Yes."

"Governor, your spy calling."

"Clay, good—you have anything?"

"No, sir—that's what I can't figure out. It's like everybody's duckin' me. Those new vehicles I mentioned, they had legal plates but they've disappeared. Joshua and Spiderman and Hi

Hitler have disappeared. Most of the other men, disappeared. I saw Earl Cherry but Jeremiah wasn't with him. Earl's got a gadget he calls the Rat Trap, supposed to detect wires or bugs or transmitters on people. He was usin' it on me to see if I was really a ZOG agent. I almost clobbered him. He'd have to get smarter to make idiot."

"Stay at it, Clay. I feel a lot better knowing you're on the scene."

"I already nosed around a lot, Governor, since nobody was here, everywhere I could, all the way up to the cabins behind the lake. Nobody's hidin' anywhere or bein' held anywhere, far as I can tell. Even Mother of God was gone all morning—she just got back. Took her baby to the clinic."

"Keep your eyes and ears open, Sergeant. Cover as much of the place as you can. And call me anytime. *Anytime.*"

"Yes, sir. Copy that."

Luke hung up. "Now that we've got a spy at God's Country, everybody's disappeared."

"Did Noreen get back?" Cecil asked.

Luke nodded. "She just got back. Clay's been poking around but hasn't found anything suspicious. The Earl Cherry dude is running around with a so-called Rat Trap, sounds like a radio frequency detector. Looking for ZOG agents."

"Oh, God." Cecil's cigarette froze in midair.

"What!" Louise cried.

"This morning our troops learned that Noreen McConathy is also a spy—she's an informer for the ATF. Elmo met with their agent, we're all cooperating. They just sent Noreen back in. Wearin' a wire."

Eli Korn was pacing in the private corridor outside the governor's office, his bony arms poking like twigs from his rolled-up shirtsleeves and swinging maniacally as he paced and whirled.

Jill Dennison peeked in from a side door. "Where the hell is he?"

Eli looked at her wildly, as if she had spoken in a tongue.

"Goddamnit, Eli." She was gone.

The chief of staff was considering making another round of phone calls when the door opened and Luke Gannon came in. Trooper Dale Moody, today's body man, was right behind.

"Governor! Thank God."

The two men went into the governor's office. The body man stayed outside. Luke headed for the corner sideboard and began mixing a Scotch and water.

"Governor, the *Tennessean* is asking a lot of questions, serious questions. They're demanding an interview."

"Fuck the *Tennessean*."

"About your wife."

Luke drank some Scotch and squinted across the rim of the glass at his earnest young assistant.

"What do they want to know?"

"They've heard . . . rumors."

Luke finished the Scotch in two gulps. "Round 'em up—I'll be in the press room in fifteen minutes."

"Governor—"

"Fifteen minutes, Eli. This is an executive decision by the chief executive of the state of Tennessee."

"Yes, sir. That tie, Governor, it'll really bloom on TV." Eli scampered away, his etched-in frown giving way to something else.

In fifteen minutes the press room was overflowing. It had been chosen as the press room precisely because it always overflowed—Eli Korn wanted standing-room-only settings when his governor confronted the press. Five television cameras were wedged onto a rear platform that was meant to accommodate three. Still photographers were camped along the walls, elbows out. The secondary reporters and hangers-on filled all the chairs except the front row, leaving those seats by tradition for the on-camera reporters and the wire services. And the *Tennessean*'s man.

The narrow door swung open and Luke Gannon sailed in, followed by Eli and Jill. There was an immediate hush. He leaped onto the platform and strode to the lectern. He had changed ties. Eli and Jill stood against the side wall.

"No announcements. Go."

The hush persisted. The governor was known for bantering with the press—he called it foreplay—before getting down to business. But this was a different Luke Gannon—stern, magisterial, commanding.

The *Tennessean*'s man, whom the others (though they wouldn't have admitted it) were deferring to, slowly raised his hand. Luke half nodded, his eyes sharp and black.

"Governor, there have been some, ah, rumors going around, ah, there's no delicate way to put this, regarding whether you and your wife have, ah, separated and whether she has, ah, actually, ah, moved out. Would you care to comment?"

"You're goddamn right I would. My wife and I are just fine, just fine—better than we've ever been, in fact. She's on a little trip right now which is frankly none of your goddamn business, it's a private trip, and if all you've got to ask me about are rumors which run through this place every day, just like the sewer, then I'm going back to work and you can go back to the sewer."

His dark glare traveled along the front row, face by face. There was complete silence.

Finally, the *Tennessean* said, "Governor, let me try again. We understand how you feel about rumors, but this one is persistent, and perhaps you could give us some details—"

"Asked and answered. Is that all?"

Ostentatiously, the *Tennessean* snapped his notebook shut.

Another hand ventured up. "Governor, has Sergeant Jennings been fired?"

"Of course not. Is this another of your rumors?"

"It's not *my* rumor."

"Oh. You're just spreading it. Next."

Another ripple through the room. What had gotten into the governor?

One of the wire-service veterans stood up. "Governor, this is not a rumor. There was a prisoner release in the works, the midnight release it was being called, then it was suddenly cancelled. Can you shed any light—"

"I can but I won't. Not at this time. Ask the federal courts. Next."

The reporters were obviously stunned, hesitant, unsure how to combat the freshly combative governor.

"Is that it?" Luke barked.

"Who are the new people at your political headquarters, working on the fourth floor? This is not a rumor. I saw them."

"Friends of mine. No further comment. Next."

"Are you thinking about running for president?"

"No. Are you?"

The reporters looked at each other to confirm their own reactions. There was a commotion as the *Tennessean* climbed to his feet, a newspaper clipping in his hand.

"Governor, certain, ah, unusual classified advertisements have appeared recently in the personals section of the *Tennessean*. Apparently coded messages from someone called Blind Man to someone called White Thunder." He paused dramatically. "Can you tell us anything about, ah, these advertisements?"

How had the bastard learned of the ads, Luke wondered. No doubt some sharpeye had accidentally run across them—and they were obviously coded messages—and the cynics and rumor-spreaders in the capitol sewer . . .

176

Luke glared at the reporter. "I guess it means even a blind man can read the *Tennessean*."

Amid the rollicking reaction, Luke Gannon walked off the platform and out of the room, trailed by a scattering of applause.

"They're clapping!" Eli Korn marveled as they breezed toward the office.

The governor muttered, "Reporters should be struck regularly, like a gong."

The high spotlights threw tremulous shadows around the Ark. Every movement—the cocking of a head, the reaching of an arm—rearranged the ghostly patterns.

Joshua sat on the edge of the raised platform, his back against the huge altar. Facing him in a semicircle of folding chairs were Linda Pearson, Spiderman, Hi Hitler, and Noreen, who rocked the sleeping Esther in her arms.

"One last time. One last time. This is our view approaching ground zero," he said, displaying a Polaroid photograph. "This is the point of attack." A second photograph. "This is the zip." A third.

"The zip!" Hi Hitler giggled.

The others leaned forward, nodding understanding, making the shadows whirl. This was the fourth run-through.

"Okay," Joshua said, glancing at a yellow pad. "Trouble spots. Has Popeye figured out how to wear his glasses with the mask. Blind fucker."

"He's okay," Spiderman said. "He's been practicin' for three days."

"He can't wear them coke bottles *outside* the mask. They got to be underneath."

"He knows that—we made the mask a little looser."

"We never had to use Popeye before, Spider."

"He's okay."

Joshua consulted the yellow pad. "What about the Professor and the Uzi? And Earl with the twelve-gauge? Tell me again."

Spiderman snorted in exasperation. "I worked 'em at the range myself. Don't worry, Joshua."

"The Professor can make that Uzi talk!" Hi Hitler chortled. "But I wish I didn't have to be Fred Flintstone."

"Hi, shut up. You have to be Fred Flintstone." Joshua's flashing blue eyes swung back to Spiderman. "What about traffic control? Tell me again."

"We've practiced it, more'n we ever practiced anything before. I think we're ready. I know we are. Don't worry, Joshua."

"He has to worry," Linda Pearson snapped. "That's why things happen the right way, because the Prophet worries."

The side door opened and Earl Cherry entered. He stopped just inside the door.

"Where's Jeremiah?" Linda Pearson said.

"Outside."

"Is he handcuffed?"

"Yes. Around the tree. Your Jeep's running, Linda."

"Don't worry about it."

"Come on in, Earl," Joshua said. "We're going over some final points about tomorrow. You don't have to worry about anything, you'll be with Spiderman, under his command, as I told you before. You got the twelve-gauge."

Earl Cherry made his usual slow, ingenuous nod and sat down. His hand reached casually inside his shirt.

Joshua said, "We'll have ample time if we *take* our time. Don't hurry. Trust the plan. The only thing that I still question are the three skinheads. Can we trust—what is it, Earl—what is it—sit down, Earl, what is it?"

Earl Cherry was on his feet, jabbing his finger at the right side of his body. He yanked up his shirt, exposing the radio frequency detector, the Rat Trap. His head was nodding in jerky spasms, his face radiant with excitement.

"What is it, Earl? Is it vibrating? Is it vibrating? The Rat Trap is vibrating?" Joshua jumped to his feet. "Well! Well! It seems that the Rat Trap has finally caught a rat!"

Hi Hitler's shrill giggle burst off the walls. The shadows quivered and collided.

"Where are you going, Noreen?" Joshua said.

"Earl, are you sure? That damn thing . . ." Spiderman said.

The baby cried out sharply, then began bawling.

"Strip search!" Linda Pearson boomed. "Strip search!"

"Noreen!"

Carrying the wailing baby, Noreen was shuffling the length of the Ark, toward the farthest corner, her free hand groping at her blouse.

"Where are you going, Noreen?"

"She wants to nurse," Noreen yelled over her shoulder. "I can't nurse her in here." She angled to the far door and went out, leaving the door open behind her.

"Noreen, come back! Come back!" Joshua ran a few steps toward the door.

Noreen kept walking, her hand inside her blouse.

"Noreen!"

The child shrieked. Noreen stopped abruptly and spun around, flinging an arm in a gesture of exasperation. "She wants to nurse! She wants to nurse!"

"I know what it is!" Linda Pearson yelled. "My police scanner—I think I left it on." She rushed out through the side door.

The baby was wailing now. Noreen shifted her in her arms, rebuttoned her blouse, and returned to the Ark. She plodded across the long floor and sat down.

"She wants to nurse, Joshua. She's sick. She's just been to the doctor." Her own tears flowing now, Noreen pressed the baby close.

Linda Pearson came back in. "It's all right, it's all right. Rat's dead."

"Switch it back on, Earl."

Earl Cherry activated the detector. Everyone froze, breathless. The only sounds were the sobbing of mother and child.

"Anything, Earl?"

Earl's body was rigid, his face strained in concentration.

"Calm down, Earl. Easy does it." Joshua walked over and placed his hands against the frequency detector inside Earl's workshirt. Earl jumped backward.

"Okay, okay, easy does it."

Finally Earl fixed his cloudy eyes on Joshua. He shook his head cautiously.

Joshua slumped into one of the folding chairs. "All right. All right. Rat's dead."

"How do we know, Joshua?" Noreen wailed. "How do we know! Maybe Linda—maybe Linda ran out to her Jeep to do something else. Maybe—hide the evidence!"

The red-faced Joshua glared at her. "What are you saying, Noreen? Are you crazy? Have you gone completely crazy?"

"Strip search!" Hi Hitler screeched with a wild laugh.

"Why not, Joshua? Why not! Why not!" Noreen sobbed. "Why couldn't your precious Linda—" She howled like an animal.

Slowly, Linda Pearson stood up and began unbuttoning her shirt.

"Don't, Linda," Joshua said.

"You've seen 'em before."

Esther was bawling louder and Noreen's tears were streaming. She stood up. "Please, Joshua, I have to nurse her. She's sick."

He made a gesture and she turned and wobbled out of the Ark, still moaning. She made her way across the compound to the silver trailer. Inside, she stretched out on the loveseat and pretended to breast-feed her daughter. She closed her eyes for a while, then opened them at a noise. She looked behind her at the small curtainless window. Joshua was watching her.

"Oh! What are you doing! You scared me, Joshua."

Joshua came inside. He lifted the sleeping baby and laid her in the easy chair.

"Stand up."

"What are you doing?"

"Stand up."

Noreen got shakily to her feet. Joshua took her blouse in both hands and ripped it open, the buttons flying.

"What are you doing! What's wrong?"

"What's wrong with your bra? It's torn."

She looked down. "My breasts are so much bigger . . . the bra hurts, Joshua."

His fingers explored the brassiere, roaming everywhere, insistently, roughly.

Noreen, her arms at her side, began weeping. "That hurts, Joshua. My breasts are so sensitive. Please don't."

He snapped the bra open and pulled it off.

"Take everything off."

Meekly she removed all her clothes and stood before him, looking down. Joshua examined each item, then returned to the torn brassiere.

"Stop crying. Did you see the doctor today? Did he examine you too?"

"He wanted to make sure I hadn't caught something from Esther."

"Did you undress for him?"

"No, just for the nurse. For the X-ray."

His cold blue eyes slammed into hers. "Did he see your big sensitive tits?"

She looked down. "No, Joshua. He just listened to my chest with that thing they use. But I had a wrap on."

"A wrap."

"It's a little robe they give you."

"A little robe they give you."

She waited, expecting a blow, but none came.

He said, "Was he Jewish?"

"No."

"How do you know?"

"I *don't* know! I *don't* know! He didn't look Jewish. But that's the point, isn't it? Most of the time you can't tell! Most of the time the lost tribes and the found tribes and the whatever tribes all look pretty much alike—they all just look like people, Harlan! Just plain old simple people! *Harlan!*"

The Fifth Day

Her heart racing, White parks the car in a new place, farther away than usual, and jogs to the pay phone. She is early; waiting is torment. When another car cruises slowly past, she lifts the receiver and pretends to be talking, her thumb surreptitiously holding down the cradle. Her leg jiggles frenziedly despite the Valium she has taken; she concentrates on controlling the tremors, but fails. Every half minute she looks at her watch, fearing the worst.

The call comes six minutes late. She snatches up the receiver.

"Red, white, and blue!"

"Roses for you."

"The roses are dead."

"Blue, white, and red."

"There's a new ad this morning, Blue, they've changed the plan! Have you seen the *Tennessean?*"

"No. I didn't expect one today. Read it to me."

" 'To White Thunder. We have ice with us. Ready to trade for Hot Stuff no questions asked. Please contact soonest. Blind Man.' "

" 'We have ice with us'? What does that mean? They've already got him out of Brushy Mountain? I didn't think even a governor could—"

"I don't know what it means. This isn't good, Blue. It's that Elmo Finn—he was something big in the CIA."

He laughs sourly. "No, no, we're just dealing with a governor here, Red, and you don't get to be a governor without having balls."

"You didn't figure on this, Blue. This is unexpected. This is trouble."

Blue says nothing.

"Did you hear me?"

"I heard you. I'm thinking. This could actually be . . . this could actually be better than the plan."

"Better than the plan? How? That's crazy! Elmo Finn's taken control, Blue. *Better than the plan*."

"Bullshit. Nobody's taken control of anything. This could actually be better, this could be pretty good. I want to talk again in exactly one hour, after I think it through. They think they're pulling a fast one, do they? Red, be ready to deliver a message. Later today. Use City Delivery if you want to."

"Gannon had a press conference yesterday—big story on page one. 'Governor Gorilla.' "

Another sharp laugh. "He's got balls, I told you. Get to be governor, you got to have a pair."

"They asked him about his wife, had she left him. He said she was on a private trip and it was none of their goddamn business. He said 'goddamn' twice on television."

"He's got a pair. But don't you see—he's also telling us that the deal's on. By lying to *them*, he's giving *us* the go-ahead."

"He's taken over! I don't like this, Blue."

"So what's new? You don't like anything. Got to roll with the punches. We talk again in one hour from mark . . .*mark!*"

Eli Korn stared at the blinking light on his six-line telephone console, trying to guess the caller's purpose. He had an eighty percent average—he kept score on a ledger sheet taped inside a desk drawer—but this one was baffling: *Cliff at First Tennessee.* Luke's banker, good contributor, had never asked for a favor. Eli picked up the receiver—when in doubt he didn't use the speakerphone—and punched the blinking button.

"Cliff, how you doin'? How's my favorite banker?"

"Can't complain, Eli, I'm sorry to bother you but I can't get through to His Nibs—and I'm tryin' to report on somethin' he gave me to do. Will you just tell him I've been to the courthouse again and the situation's more complicated than it appeared. To remove a lien, you've got to—it's just complicated. But tell him I'm on the case."

"It's hard to remove a lien but you're gonna do it."

"*Try* to do it. There's more than one. You know this Linda Pearson, Eli?"

"The killer whale type, I understand."

"Eli, that's an injustice to killer whales."

The phone rang in Elmo Finn's room at the Mountain Empire Motel.

"Okay."

"Gene Kessler, Marshal. Just got your message."

"What about Noreen's transmitter, Gene?"

"What about it? It's been stationary, I figured she's just sacked out. All the strain."

"Our spy reported they've got a radio frequency detector at God's Country. They call it the Rat Trap."

"Oh Jesus."

"I should have realized it. When I was there, they were talking about rat traps but I didn't make the connection. Like a moron. And we had our own bug under Joshua's trailer, but it's stopped working."

"Oh Jesus. And we can't get a message to her. Unless your spy can."

A weed-strangled parking lot behind an abandoned cinder-block building with every window broken. Fading six-inch letters above the missing rear door: McConnell's Auto Repair. Trash and debris freshly raked into a pile. The hum of a nearby highway.

On this bright, crisp morning, nine men and two women clustered around two pickup trucks, applying Krazy Glue to their fingertips, then pulling on surgical gloves. They wore jeans, long-sleeve shirts or sweaters, baseball caps, and athletic shoes. With one exception, each had rehearsed a specific assignment until it had become second nature, and had visited the overgrown parking lot several times. With one exception, each carried a powerful firearm.

"Five minutes!" said Linda Pearson, training field glasses on the nearby highway, a four-lane section of U.S. 27.

"Mount up!" Joshua ordered.

Noreen and Spiderman got into the cab of the first pickup, Noreen behind the wheel, as Hi Hitler and the three teenage skinheads climbed into the back. Spiderman's shirtsleeves were taped around his wrists, concealing his tattoos. He carried a .308 Heckler and Koch semiautomatic rifle with an ammunition pouch on his hip. Everyone in the bed of the truck had nine-millimeter handguns.

Joshua was driving the second pickup. Mounted on a jerry-rigged console in the center of the dashboard were several police scanners. Three of the God's Country cadre rode in back—the Professor, who had three hundred college credits but no degree, gripping an Uzi submachine gun; Popeye, a stumpy ex-deputy sheriff with a .308 H&K laid across his knees; and Earl Cherry, wearing the deactivated Rat Trap under his shirt and clutching a pump-action twelve-gauge shotgun to his chest. Snug against the tailgate were two heavy boxes of roofing nails.

Everyone had a rubber mask.

Noreen and Joshua started the engines. Earl Cherry bowed his head and began reciting the Twenty-third Psalm under his breath. Popeye disobeyed Joshua and made a last-minute alteration to his disguise, fitting his thick prescription eyeglasses over the rubber mask and taping the temple pieces down. In the other truck, Hi Hitler giggled piercingly, and the skinheads gave Sieg Heils.

"Plus one minute—it's late," Linda Pearson called from her position at the edge of the building.

"No hurry, no hurry. We can wait." Joshua got out of the cab and went forward to the lead truck.

"Noreen, remember, this is the last one, like I promised. Just do what Spider says."

She nodded jerkily, her gloved hands gripping the steering wheel. "I don't know what I'm supposed to do! I should be with Esther."

"You know enough, Mother, just do what Spider says. You're the best driver I've got. You'll be with Esther soon."

"Plus five!"

"Stay mounted up, Hi!"

Another shrill giggle as Hi Hitler shivered himself back into place. Joshua returned to his truck.

"Target! Target!" Linda Pearson raced to Joshua's truck and jumped into the cab as Noreen wheeled the lead truck smoothly onto the gravel driveway and accelerated around the building and through the parking lot and onto the highway. Joshua was right behind. There was no other traffic except the big gray truck ahead, gearing down for the long, lazy S uphill curve as U.S. 27 wound toward the summit two miles away.

Noreen swung the lead pickup into the passing lane and overtook the truck on the upgrade. As she sailed by, Spiderman raised a newspaper to shield them. Then Noreen cut sharply in front of the lumbering truck and braked hard. The Wells Fargo driver jammed on his brakes as Joshua pulled alongside in the passing lane. The two pickups came to a full stop in the highway, sandwiching the armored truck against the narrow right-hand shoulder. The God's Country cadres leaped to their positions.

Wearing a Fred Flintstone mask, Hi Hitler stood in the bed of Noreen's truck and with both hands thrust a cardboard sign at the Wells Fargo cab: Dismount or Die. There was no reaction from the armored truck.

"He's got a phone!" one of the skinheads yelled. Spiderman raised the H&K .308, loaded with jacketed shells to penetrate bulletproof glass, and blasted three coin-sized holes in the upper center of the driver's windshield. Both Wells Fargo doors burst open and the two guards scrambled out with their hands up. Hi Hitler lunged for the driver's door and grabbed it before it closed, preventing the automatic locking. Obeying Spiderman's gestures, the two guards sprawled facedown along the shoulder of the highway, their arms stretched above their heads. Joshua complimented Hi Hitler with two pats on the shoulder, then climbed inside the cab to switch open the money compartment in the rear.

"There's another one! Another one!"

From the siderails of the second pickup Earl Cherry pumped and fired his shotgun over and over into the small square window high on the side of the Wells Fargo truck, scattering glass everywhere. "There's not supposed to be one in back!" he yelled, pumping and firing again. Then the side door opened slowly and the third guard, a short man bleeding from the neck, fell to the pavement and crawled off the road.

"One minute!" shouted Linda Pearson, leaning out of the second pickup and brandishing a stopwatch as she monitored the police scanners.

"Traffic control," Joshua said calmly as Hi Hitler and the three skinheads formed a bucket brigade and began passing the heavy money bags through the side door of the armored truck and around to the front pickup. Spiderman and Popeye walked behind the trucks where several other cars, coming upon the blocked roadway, had been forced to stop. Spiderman motioned the occupants to get out, then shouldered the assault rifle and fired into the center of the first windshield. People began abandoning their vehicles and dashing for the trees. The Professor crossed the median and waved on the opposing traffic, firing short bursts from the Uzi into the air.

"Four minutes!"

"How many more bags?"

"Six or seven."

"Hurry."

In another minute all the money bags had been transferred. Earl Cherry discharged shotgun blasts into all four Wells Fargo tires, then two volleys into the radio receiver in the cab. Noreen's pickup pulled away first, straining up the long slope with its heavy cargo. Joshua followed as Earl Cherry and Hi Hitler, who had switched to the second truck, dumped the roofing nails onto the roadway behind them. Linda Pearson stood in the bed, braced herself against the wheel housing, and squeezed off rifle rounds over the heads of the people behind. Across the median, there was only scattered traffic and a handful of bewildered rubberneckers, who seemed to think a movie was being filmed.

The governor of Tennessee was explaining how he could elude his own body man without being missed until the next day. He was pacing and gesturing as he laid out the plan. Elmo and Henry would occupy the attention of the body man at his first-floor station while Luke, disguised as a workman complete with leather belt and baseball cap, slipped down the back stairway and out to an escape car. Later that night, when the body man would expect Luke to go home to bed, Louise would phone down and tell him that the governor had decided to crash in the bunkroom. He'll see you tomorrow, she would say.

"It'll work," Luke said confidently, the others nodding approval. "I know it'll work."

Louise brought the coffeepot and filled everyone's cup. "They've seen the new ad by now, I know they have. Oh, maybe by tonight, son, maybe we'll have her back." She let out a sob.

Luke nodded grimly. Cecil Beech got up and went to the computer, checked something, then came back to the long worktable. Henry Wood reached for a bagel and slathered it with cream cheese. Elmo Finn finished his coffee, muttered "Seventy-two hours," then dropped to the floor and began doing situps.

"Waiting is the worst part," Louise said.

"I go a little crazier every five minutes," Luke said. "I keep thinking about Nikki. I keep thinking about Noreen, too, whether she's been discovered. What they might do to her."

"Kessler said it's not unknown for those transmitters to fail," Elmo Finn said. "Our bug under the trailer went dead. For some reason."

"But he's worried."

"He's worried."

"It was a good idea, Mo—kidnap Joshua's wife and add her to the swap. Sweeten the pot. Gain an edge. And then it turns out she's already on our side." Luke stood up and stretched.

"God, I hope she's all right." He added softly, "I hope Nikki's all right too."

They sat in silence for a while. Luke said, "Randall Tice must be talkin' to himself in that motel room, you imagine, George and Roy interrogating him like he's some Vietcong sympathizer. Roy did his knife thing—Tice turned completely white, like all his blood just dried up. He probably wishes he were back in Brushy Mountain State Penitentiary. In solitary. But he hasn't said anything."

"He may not know anything."

The phone rang and the hair-trigger Luke lunged for it, wrenching his back and swearing. It was Eli. Another mysterious padded envelope had arrived at the governor's office. Tested negative for explosives, but contained an unidentified object, partially metal. Should he send it to the state police lab? No, Luke said, just bring it over. Fast.

It took the Yes Man twelve minutes. He tried to linger in the command post, settling confidently into a chair, briskly whipping papers from his briefcase for the governor's attention. After a minute or two, Luke summarily sent him on his way.

Inside the big City Delivery envelope was a small hinged jeweler's box and the usual handprinted note on a half sheet of lined paper.

To Blind Man,
   You think you're so smart, see enclosed and think again. If you want Hot Stuff, find a bar on State Route 52 in Boone County called the Hog. There is a phone booth outside. Be there at 8:00 tonight. Bring Ice if you want the rest of Hot Stuff.
                                                                White Thunder

Luke opened the hinged box and gasped.

"Oh, God, oh no . . ." Luke shut the box quickly and doubled over in his chair.

"What is it, Luke?" Louise cried. "What is it!"

"Luke," Elmo said, jumping up and coming over.

"Those fucking monsters—"

"What?" Louise yelled.

Luke turned toward them, his face white, his hands trembling. He tried to open the box again but couldn't. Louise reached for it and he jerked it back, finally wedging the lid open with his thumbs.

She screamed and fell against Luke. Inside the box was a woman's finger bearing a wedding ring. It had been severed cleanly just below the knuckle, with no visible bloodstains.

"Goddamn them! Goddamn them!"

"They have to pay for this," Louise hissed between gasps. "They have to pay for this. Swords our law, Elmo Finn! Sharp swords!"

"Is this Nikki's ring?" Elmo Finn said.

Luke nodded vacantly. Louise lost her footing and slumped into a chair. She was breathing erratically.

Cecil got a bottle of brandy and glasses and poured drinks for everyone. The brandy went fast.

"They didn't like their plan being changed," Louise wailed. "This swap idea, taking charge, changing everything . . . so they cut her finger off!"

"They will pay, Mom." Luke's voice was steady and cold and far away. "They will pay with more than a finger."

Everyone sat and stood and paced despondently, saying little, drinking more brandy, Cecil's cigarettes fogging the room. Luke stared into a grim distance, embracing Louise with one arm. She was sobbing in muffled bursts.

At length Luke picked up the box and opened it. Louise jerked away, hiding her face. He stared at the severed finger and the wedding ring he had borrowed money to pay for more than twenty years ago.

Luke closed the box slowly. "She might be in shock for a

while after this. But Nikki's tough—everyone should remember that. *Remember that.* She put a message on that tape—*her against the world.* She'll hang on. She's tough, Louise, your horsey girl is tough."

They embraced again.

"The phone booth outside the Hog at eight o'clock," Elmo Finn said quietly. "Time to move. Luke, these people are barbaric and despicable, but we have to deal with them to get Nikki back. And when we do. . . . Henry, we'll take the chopper. Time to get in disguise, Luke."

The governor gave Louise a long hug and hurried down the hall, his face a snarled mask.

"Wish I were goin' too, Colonel," Cecil Beech said matter-of-factly. "Especially after this. Like to cut off a few things myself."

A flash of fetid memory seized Elmo Finn. A clearing in a wet, steaming jungle, the men of Phoenix squatting and smoking, a poncho spread beneath a tree like a net, a grinning ARVN commando emptying the contents of a drawstring bag onto the deep green nylon: severed ears.

"We could use you, Cecil, but we need a cold hand back here. Let's brief George and Roy."

Louise tried to say something but couldn't. Cecil tapped out a coded e-mail message and sent it through the open online connection to George's laptop at the Mountain Empire Motel. Within seconds there was an answer.

"They copy, Colonel. They send their sympathy to Luke and Louise. Roy requests the other night-vision scope and the bolo."

Elmo Finn nodded briskly and Cecil hurried to the storeroom. As he left, Luke Gannon reentered the room as a maintenance man—gray work clothes with cargo pockets, tool belt and boots, baseball cap, Walkman headphones, red bandanna around his neck.

"This ought to work for a five-second ploy."

"It's perfect, Luke," Elmo said as the private line rang. Cecil answered and passed the phone to Luke. It was Sgt. Clay Jennings. Luke activated the speakerphone and the state trooper's voice boomed out.

"Governor, this is Clay, just reportin' in, nobody's around much. Joshua and the key people are gone and I'm startin' to feel out of place. Conspicuous. Noreen's gone again too but left her baby here with one of the other women, which is very unusual, the woman says. She's never left that little Esther with anybody. I managed to take my four-wheel-drive up past the lake but there was no sign of anything. Nothin'. A few empty cabins. You still want me to hang around or sort of just go back and forth? I'm not doin' much."

"No, stay there, Clay. Listen now, this is very important—try to find Noreen and give her this message. A message from Gene. *Change your underwear.* You got it? *Message from Gene—change your underwear.*"

Jennings's laugh roared over the speakerphone. "Is this for real, Governor—"

"Clay! This is deadly serious. Find Noreen and give her that message, privately. If she asks you if you're a spy, say yes."

"Say yes? But I'll be blown."

"Think about it, Clay. She's with us too."

"Mother of God? Mother of God's on our side?" There was a pause. "Well I'll be damned. I wish I knew the whole picture, Governor, what the hell's goin' on out here, I might be of more use. But I'll try to find her."

"And keep poking around, Clay, as much as you can get by with."

"Yes, sir, roger that."

Luke clicked off the speakerphone. "Noreen left her baby behind. I don't like it."

"I don't either." Elmo Finn handed Luke the key to the rental car parked outside. "Let's do it, pal. Let's go get Nikki."

Spiderman entered the Hog warily and stood just inside the door, surveying the customers. The normal complement of nine-ball habitués. A dozen or so barstools occupied, mostly by solitary beer-nursers whose heads were cocked upward at the television set, where ESPN's twin anchors were kibitzing their way through snatches of videotape. The jukebox glowing silently against the wall. Alone in the last booth against the painted-over windows sat the heavyset, pig-eyed former master sergeant from Fort Bragg, an empty beer glass in front of him.

Spiderman went to the bar. "How's it goin', Harold? Take a coupla Bud drafts. And a dollar's worth of quarters."

Harold nodded indifferently and drew the beers. He gave Spiderman his change in quarters. "Merle Haggard's back, I see."

"Think I'll play some Merle."

Spiderman carried the steins of beer to the far booth, went to the jukebox and made several selections, then returned. He smiled and shook the beefy hand of ex–Green Beret Sgt. Wendell Maloney.

"Joshua couldn't make it, Sarge. But I'm the God's Country minister of defense, I can negotiate."

"Sure, hell yes, Spider. No problem. I'm havin' a little trouble with a few items on the list, not trouble exactly, that's the wrong word, it's just takin' a little longer than I anticipated. But I feel sure I'll be able to deliver pretty much one hundred percent."

"Which items?"

From the jukebox came the driving country beat of Merle Haggard and the Strangers, drowning out the ESPN anchors. The barstool customers continued to gaze at the TV screen.

"Merle Haggard—you remembered my favorite singer, Spiderman. 'Preciate it. No, there's just a little delay in gettin' the Claymores, I think I can get it worked out . . . matter of fact, I've got the M-60 and the rocket launcher with me now. Plus ammo. And ten pounds of C-4. I know you wanted fifty, but I'll have to go ten pounds at a time. You want to take possession right now, we can work on the installment plan—"

"How much?"

"Fifteen large."

Spiderman sipped his beer and glanced at the bar, where Harold was lazily washing and rinsing beer glasses.

Sarge said, "I know that's a lot of money—"

"We spent that much just the other day."

Sarge's square face clouded over. "You got another source you're workin' with?"

Spiderman laughed. "We bought various things, not exactly in your line. Bought some vehicles." Spiderman leaned across the table and whispered, "We bought some trucks, some cars, a few of 'em we didn't use but five minutes. Two thousand dollars for a car we didn't use but five minutes."

"Whoa! Last of the big spenders!" Sarge chuckled, but his pig eyes remained serious. "Lot of money for five minutes."

"My point is, we got the money if the price is right and the goods are right."

"Sure, I knew that, that's why—"

"We got the money, Sarge, if you got the goods."

"Hell, that's why I wanted to do business with you boys. Tell you the truth, when I heard on the radio 'bout that Wells Fargo hijack, I said to myself, 'Well, I know some old boys could pull that off, they had a mind to.'"

"I didn't hear about no Wells Fargo hijack."

"Down towards Dayton, broad daylight, right out on the highway like Jesse James. They got away with a lot of money. Killed one the guards."

Spiderman's hand froze on the handle of the beer mug, then drifted slowly under the edge of the table. "Sounds pretty ballsy, broad daylight."

"You'll hear about it, just watch the news. Armed robbery and murder, they better lie low."

"Damn straight. Lower'n low."

"Damn straight." Sarge drank some beer. "Speakin' of lyin' low, Spider, you ain't had no strangers snoopin' around God's Country, have you? Since our first get-together?"

"We had two ZOG agents."

"What!"

"They were renegades, don't worry. Mercenaries. Tryin' to sell us secret files about God's Country, lists of informers, aerial photographs. Shit like that."

"Be careful, be careful, Spider—that sounds phony to me. Did you use the Rat Trap on 'em? They mighta been wired."

"We used the Rat Trap and we strip-searched 'em, too—no wires. And we didn't buy nothin' and we didn't say nothin'."

"A wire don't have to be a real *wire*, you know. You can damn near wear one under your pecker."

"Linda searched under their peckers. She searched the back of their necks for implants."

Sarge snorted, stacking his blacksmith's forearms on the tabletop. "I'm just recommendin' you to be careful, Spider, I'm tellin' you, the ATF is some damn tricky motherfuckers."

Spiderman nodded indulgently, a thin smile on his lips. "I was hopin' we could get more than ten pounds of C-4."

"Sure. Absolutely. Ten pounds at a time, all I'm sayin'."

Another Merle Haggard tune came on, the whine of the electric guitars supplemented by a brass section. Some new customers arrived, and Spiderman surveyed them over his shoulder.

He said, "Lot of things you can do with C-4. Blow up more stuff than McVeigh ever thought about. More stuff than ZOG ever thought about."

Sarge let out a shaky laugh, his eyes meeting the intense glare of the militiaman, then looking off.

"So what'd you boys need a five-minute car for, Spider?"

The thin smile returned and broadened a little. "Damn quick trip, that's for sure."

Former Green Beret Master Sgt. Wendell Maloney cackled so loudly that a few heads looked over from the bar, including that of Harold the bartender, veteran of Vietnam, who was rummaging through the papers in his cash drawer, looking for the phone number of another Vietnam vet named Gene.

Clutching a large brown envelope fastened with a button-and-string tie, Jill Dennison slipped into Eli Korn's office and sat down in one of the plush chairs opposite his desk.

"You want a smoke?" she asked.

"Yes. Damn it." He got up and closed the door, then cracked the outside window before lighting up. Soon twin furrows of smoke curled toward the open window.

She unwound the string, took a photograph from the folder, and handed it across the desk to Eli.

"Voilà. The usual suspects," she said. "All rounded up."

"Criminy. This is every one of them."

"They were part of the Phoenix Project, Eli. Vietnam. Biggest covert operation in CIA history."

"Every one of them. Luke looks so young, they all look so young. Who was Elmo Finn—the commander? The black guy's gained some weight since this photograph. One, two, three, four, five, six, seven—who's this guy? He's the only one who didn't show up in Nashville this week. As far as we know."

"His name was Mason. He's the one who got killed." Jill crushed out her cigarette in a coffee cup. "You know, Eli, they say once a Company man, always a Company man."

"Who says?"

"I don't know who says. I just wish I knew what was going on and if our man's about to self-destruct."

"You think the *Tennessean* would like to see this photograph? Of all the strangers they were asking about, running loose in Music City? The Central Intelligence Agency on parade?"

"Live by the leak, you die by the leak."

The Yes Man smiled smugly. "Unless you're Noah. With the foresight to build an ark."

Randall Tice lay under a canvas tarpaulin in the back of the Navigator—blindfolded, gagged, handcuffed, hog-tied, his ears sealed with rubber plugs and duct tape.

It was nearly eight o'clock. The parking lot at the Hog was less than half full. The September light was dying fast.

Luke Gannon waited inside the phone booth that stood at one corner of the lot, angled oddly as if it had fallen off a flatbed in that very spot. Elmo Finn was just outside, as if he were waiting to use the phone. A few cars drove in but no one paid attention to the two men at the phone booth.

At two minutes after eight the phone rang. Luke grabbed it.

"Yes. This is Blind Man."

"Listen carefully," said a muffled male voice, speaking in a slow, robotic monotone. "Use—one—vehicle—only—go—west—on—52—for—two—point—three—miles—a—dirt—road—will—be—on—the—right—turn—in—go—to—white—tree—on—the—left—stop—cut—engine—instructions—taped—to—tree—understand?"

"Yes. West on—"

The phone went dead.

"Okay, Mo, I got it." He repeated the instructions he had written on the back of his hand. "West on 52, two-point-three miles. He said use one vehicle."

"Let's follow instructions—for now."

Luke nodded. "Right. For now."

They moved their two vehicles to the farthest corner of the

big parking lot and shifted weapons and gear from the rental sedan to the back of the Navigator. Tice's trussed-up body had to be moved to make room. A few customers came and went, glancing indifferently at the commotion in the shadows. George Graves carefully lowered the rear door so that it remained un-latched.

Elmo Finn got in behind the wheel. Luke took the other front seat, with Henry and George in the two bucket seats behind. Roy squeezed into the cargo area with Randall Tice and the gear.

"Two-point-three miles," Luke said. "Then turn right onto a dirt road."

It was dark now. Elmo Finn turned the Navigator around and headed west on State Route 52. Almost immediately, the road began rising and falling with the hills, stretching upward into the last lingering glimmer of twilight, pitching down into black-ness.

Elmo glanced over at Luke. "Recommend removing the hog-tie now."

"Sure. Yes. Let's do it, be ready."

George leaned over the rear seat and helped Roy strip off the tarp and cut the ropes from Tice's arms and legs. They left the blindfold, gag, earplugs, and handcuffs in place, and re-covered him with the tarpaulin.

The cell phone rang, giving everyone a start. Henry answered and listened for a few moments.

"It's Cecil," Henry said. "Clay Jennings just called from God's Country. He won't talk to Cecil—only Luke, Elmo, or George. Orders, he says."

"Goddamnit, I guess that's what I told him," Luke said. "Is Clay still on the line? I just talked with him two hours ago."

"No, he's calling back later."

"Tell Cecil to give him this number."

Henry relayed the message.

Luke said, "Will two-point three miles put us in God's Country?"

"Not in the compound," Henry said, reading his Corps of Engineers map with a pencil flashlight, "but fairly close to the perimeter. Damn close."

Suddenly a line of three cars came slowly toward them, the front car's high beams almost blinding Elmo Finn.

"Roy," Elmo said.

Roy raised the infrared glasses and took a long look. "Negative. Rednecks."

The cars passed and vanished into the blackness.

Elmo said, "Luke, just before we turn onto the dirt road, recommend Roy slipping out with the M-21."

"Uh, Mo, I don't want to be too aggressive just now, not till we get her back. Much as I'd like to be."

"Sure, Luke. I'm only talking recon. Recon only."

"Okay, that's good. Recon. Let's do it."

Roy climbed into the back with Randall Tice and tested the unlatched cargo door with his foot. George passed him the M-21 sniper's rifle with the night-vision scope.

"You got the bolo?" George asked.

"Affirmative," Roy said.

"Roy," Elmo said, "they'll be watching the white tree, which is supposed to be on our left side after we turn in. So the right side will probably be better for you. But use your judgment."

"Yes, sir, Colonel."

"Roy," Luke said in a hoarse whisper, "no Rambo stuff till we've got Nikki back, okay?"

"Don't worry, Governor."

Luke was leaning forward rigidly and peering straight ahead. Elmo Finn said, "Luke, recommend leaving Tice in place until we read the instructions. You can go get them, I'll stay behind the wheel with the high beams on. George and Henry, outside, in one motion with Luke, left and right rear. Doors closed but not latched. Okay?"

"Yes, sir. Good," Luke said.

"Yes, sir," came the answers from the back.

"Two miles even," Elmo Finn said impassively.

The Navigator crested a flat hill, then began dropping steeply into a valley.

"Two point one."

Halfway down the hill the road flattened a little, then began dropping again.

"Two point two."

They reached the bottom and started up the next hill. The sky was ink-black now, no stars, the trees black and heavy and close. In the long daggers of the headlights a narrow dirt road appeared on the right.

"Roy," Elmo stage-whispered, bringing the Navigator almost to a stop before turning and accelerating up the shallow incline. There was a ruffle of noise and Roy was gone.

Elmo dimmed the high beams to get his bearings, then switched them on again. The dirt road, barely wider than a trail, had no gravel. High weeds sprouted between the faint wheel tracks. Along the right side were remnants of a cattle fence, blackness beyond. Along the left were dense trees and foliage.

The Navigator inched forward, the big engine straining in low gear into the upslope. After fifteen yards, the road leveled out, and the men in the Navigator saw only a narrow overgrown tunnel that stretched like a mineshaft into blackness. Once it might have been a lovers' lane. A white tree loomed on the left.

Elmo Finn brought the vehicle to a stop, gunned the engine as three doors opened as one, then switched it off. Ambiguous night sounds filled the air: insects, creaking limbs, currents of mountain breeze, at once a whisper and a din. Then there was something else, a rumbling or rolling, something distant. A sound of man.

Luke edged behind the vehicle through high grass and weeds to the white tree that shone with the freshness of paint. He sensed movement to his left. He heard or felt a rustle in the weeds. A plastic bag containing a half sheet of paper was thumbtacked to the tree. With steady hands he took it down and went to the driver's window. Elmo Finn shined a flashlight on the lined paper.

Follow these instructions exactly or her finger will be all you get back. Flash headlights off and on three times to signal your compliance. Then send Ice straight ahead toward our lantern. We will send Hot Stuff toward you at same time. No tricks or we will shoot her in the back. Leave immediately.

Elmo Finn got out of the cab and peered down the leafy tunnel that eerily reflected the Navigator's high beams. When his eyes adjusted, he saw the lantern a hundred yards away, flickering like a tiny candle. He and Luke went to the rear door and raised it. Elmo crawled inside and removed Randall Tice's gag, blindfold, and earplugs.

"Okay, Randall, your pal Herman came through for you. It's time to go."

Tice scrambled out. Elmo Finn unlocked the handcuffs, grabbed Tice's belt, and marched him around to the front of the vehicle. Tice, runty and bandy-legged, was a head shorter than Elmo Finn, and moved limply like a marionette.

"Randall, can you see? Look down the headlights, all the way. See that lantern? The little flame? Do you see it? That's your target."

Tice rubbed his eyes, shielded them with the flat of his hands, rubbed his eyes again, squinted into the blackness.

"Okay. I see it."

"Randall, I'm going to flash my light three times. Then you start walking toward that lantern. About halfway there, you'll pass someone coming this way. Just keep going. Straight ahead. Do you remember the man who threw the knife?"

The rumbling or rolling noise, still distant, seemed louder now, or perhaps had separated itself from the ambient sounds of nature.

"Do you remember the man who threw the knife, Randall?"

Tice's head jerked down and up. "Yeah."

"That same man is watching you right now through an infrared telescopic sight mounted on a sniper's rifle. He's killed thirty men with that rifle. If you do anything different from what I just told you, *anything different*, he will shoot your heart out. Do you understand that, Randall?"

Another head jerk. "Yes," came the faint reply.

Elmo Finn looked at Luke and nodded. Luke nodded in reply. Elmo reached inside the cab and slowly flashed the headlights off and on three times.

"Okay, Randall. To the lantern. Go."

As Tice tottered forward, stumbling a couple of times before gaining his legs, Elmo and Luke raised their field glasses and scanned the ghostly tunnel ahead. George Graves, kneeling and braced against the white tree, watched Tice through his rifle sight. From the right front fender of the Navigator, Henry Wood swept his glasses around the dim periphery of the tunnel.

Luke staggered forward a few steps. "I see her—oh God—I see her, Mo. I see her. Oh Jesus."

"When they pass, Luke," Elmo said, moving up and grasping Luke's arm.

Coming toward Randall Tice, who was striding briskly now, was the slumping, stumbling figure of woman who seemed about to collapse with every step. She wore an unbuttoned trench coat that reached to her ankles. Her arms hung stiffly and did not move naturally. Her left hand was wrapped in something, her head and neck covered by an executioner's black hood, with tiny slits for eyeholes.

"Mo, there's a bandage on her hand. She's in bad shape. Oh God."

The cell phone on the seat of the Navigator began ringing. In the tense pastoral stillness the noise was ear-splitting. Henry lunged back into the vehicle and the ringing stopped.

As the two figures neared each other, Randall Tice veered wide to the right, creating a ten-yard gap between them as they passed. He eyed her warily, cocking his head, but the woman did not look at the man as she struggled forward in her agonized, shuffling gait. Tice broke into a trot, then a dead run.

Suddenly, Luke bolted toward her. The others followed, angling right and left to avoid blocking the twin beams of the headlights. The woman saw them coming and froze, then began to turn uncertainly, as if she might retrace her steps. She continued turning in a full circle, her hands groping the air, and fell awkwardly to the ground.

"Nikki! Nikki! It's all right now!" Luke Gannon strained to run faster, slipping twice in the coarse grass, flinging the field glasses aside, gasping for breath to press on. He fell a dozen yards from her and scrambled the rest of the way on his hands and knees.

"Nikki! It's all right now, you're safe!"

She had fallen facedown. Luke's quivering hands dug under her and rolled her over as Elmo and the others arrived. The rumbling noise roared louder, roared again, then fell away in a long growling whine.

Luke worked the black hood off her face and cast it away.

"Jesus," he said. "Mo—"

Elmo Finn fired his automatic twice into the air. Within seconds several rifle shots barked from the trees on the right.

"George, get the truck!" Elmo yelled.

George raced back into the white pool of light. Henry dropped to one knee and began removing the bandage from the woman's left hand. Rapid footfalls sounded from the right and Roy came running up, sweat and black greasepaint streaking his face, the sniper rifle lashed across his back. He glanced at the woman on the ground, then bent to peer at her more closely before turning to Elmo Finn.

"Two motorcycles, Colonel. They were too far away when I fired. No hit. There are trees cut down blocking the trail. No way to follow them in the SUV."

Luke Gannon, still breathing heavily, was lying face up next to the incoherent woman.

"Elmo . . ."

"Her name is Helen Cherry, Luke. Jeremiah's mother, the boy in the custody case. She's been drugged. All her fingers are intact."

Helen Cherry lay in the back of the Navigator where Randall Tice had lain. She was drifting in and out of consciousness, moaning, uttering unintelligible sounds as the powerful sedative wore off. In the front seat Luke and Elmo Finn stared at the felled trees blocking the trail, the Navigator's headlights stabbing futilely into the impenetrable tangle. Luke was still short of breath, gulping air regularly.

"Mo, why did they double-cross us? Why! Why! We were giving them everything they asked for—Randall Tice, no police, no publicity . . . now they're in trouble, don't they know that?"

Elmo Finn's knuckles were white on the steering wheel. "I don't know what they know. It was an elaborate charade—they committed a second kidnapping, they left us with a witness who's bound to be able to tell us *some*thing . . . maybe we shouldn't have turned the tables as hard as we did. Just stayed passive. That's my fault, Luke."

"No! I agreed to it, Elmo. It's nobody's fault. I just wish I could figure it out . . ."

They sat for a while without talking. From the dense over-growth came the shrill dissonant whines of crickets, displacing the sounds of man. There were faint noises from the rear of the SUV.

"We should probably get her to a doctor," Elmo Finn said.

"There's only one logical explanation, Mo." Luke was bent forward, his fingertips pressing into his temples.

Elmo Finn stared straight ahead, still gripping the wheel.

"Only one. Only one, Mo. We might as well face it."

"Luke—"

"She's dead, Mo! That's why they couldn't send her across, that's why they had to have an impostor. We forced them into a face-to-face swap, but since they had already killed her, they had to have a stand-in, they had to kidnap Helen Cherry . . ."

"That's only one possibility—"

"Mo! Don't sugarcoat it. I was in that Huey in Nam, Mo, Phoenix rising, remember? We shoot straight with each other, no matter what. She's dead, I've been feeling it, like ESP or something. I know she's dead, I *know* it. Did you look at her finger in that box? It was *dead*. Nikki's dead, Elmo. It's terrible, but it's almost a relief to say it out loud. I'll save the grieving for later. I've got a lifetime for grieving, and that's exactly how long it will take. But right now I want to go after them. I want to make them pay. God's Country! I'm going to make God's Country hell on this earth."

There were crunching footsteps outside as George, Roy, and Henry returned. They wedged into the rear bucket seats, each glancing behind at the prone figure of Helen Cherry.

"No way to track 'em without bikes and daylight," George said. "They picked a good spot."

Elmo Finn said, "Henry, who called back there, just before the swap?"

"Jennings. He was all excited—I told him he'd have to call back."

"Maybe he's finally found something," Luke said. "Our *spy*."

Elmo turned sideways in the big bucket seat. "Luke thinks Nikki's probably dead—otherwise, why would they send us a ringer? Why not send Nikki back, case closed? Any ideas?"

"Maybe she's alive but not in condition to be . . ."

"Then why not wait?" Luke said. "Why risk a second kidnapping and a witness? If Nikki's alive, none of this makes any sense. But if she's dead, everything does." Luke's voice was flat, unemotional, as if he were talking about a stranger.

Helen Cherry's head appeared eerily above the seat back. She struggled to bring her eyes into focus, gripping the seat, then falling back and climbing up again.

"Helen, we're your friends," George said. "You know us."

"You're friends . . ." she said sluggishly, her mouth working to gain control. She looked at everyone closely. "The other night, on the road . . ."

"How do you feel?" George asked.

The cell phone rang. "I'll take it, Luke," Elmo Finn said. He clicked on. "I know, Sergeant, we've been busy . . . I thought nothing was going on out there, Clay . . . calm down, Sergeant, just take it point by point, who you saw, what you saw."

For several minutes Elmo Finn listened to Sergeant Jennings on the cell phone. In the rear, Helen Cherry was sitting up, taking small sips of water from a plastic bottle. George was asking her questions but getting only hazy responses.

"What! Where!" Elmo Finn shouted. Helen Cherry screamed hoarsely.

"Are you sure, Sergeant, are you absolutely sure . . . where are you . . . have you seen any motorcycles . . . have you seen Helen Cherry . . . stay there for ten minutes." Elmo Finn clicked off the connection and turned to the others.

"Jennings is at the Hog—same pay phone we just used. He

didn't see any motorcycles today but he heard one. Wondered why I was asking. Hasn't seen Helen Cherry. Wondered about that too. Says God's Country has gone from being as quiet as a cemetery to Grand Central Station. New vehicles all over the place, and a strange guy they call Sarge driving an RV with North Carolina plates. Earl Cherry's having a nervous breakdown, weeping and wailing like the world's coming to an end." Elmo Finn glanced back at Helen and lowered his voice. "Jennings saw the boy Jeremiah handcuffed around a tree, Noreen's still gone, he hasn't been able to tell her to change her underwear, someone else is still baby-sitting her daughter, a bunch of skinheads are parading around doing Sieg Heils, Joshua's getting suspicious of Clay, asked him why he was poking around so much . . ."

Elmo Finn drew a deep breath.

"That's most of it. Now listen to this . . . Clay went way up into the backcountry above the lake and found an isolated cabin that he hadn't seen before. It looked like it might be occupied, so he sneaked up and peeked in. Didn't see anyone—but guess what was spread out on the floor. An Oriental rug. A big one. Clay said it was the oddest sight he ever saw."

Helen Cherry could tell Elmo Finn very little. Desperate to see her son Jeremiah, she had crept into God's Country again. Hid her car in the usual place, worked her way through the trees the usual way. At the very point where she could glimpse the awful straw hut, someone struck her from behind. She had no memory of anything else until a man was slapping her, lifting her up, telling her to walk down the grassy lane toward the headlights, that Jeremiah was waiting for her there.

Luke called Clay Jennings at the pay phone at the Hog and told him to return to God's Country, and to be up and alert at dawn. Then they took Helen to the Boone County Medical

Center where the all-night nurse examined her, taking her blood pressure three times. The nurse stared suspiciously at Elmo and George, asking why a heavily sedated woman was riding around in a jeepful of men, snorting huffily at Elmo's vague answer. She prescribed "rest, rest, and more rest," then demanded Elmo Finn's identification as George walked Helen out to the Navigator. Elmo snapped open his deputy U.S. marshal's ID.

"Nurse Wilhelm, we are grateful for your help, very grateful. If I tell you any more, I will have to arrest you for compromising a federal investigation." His battleship-gray eyes bored in hard. The nurse reluctantly retreated.

George booked a room for Helen at the Mountain Empire Motel and put her to bed, a gallon of orange juice and a cooler of fruit and cheese on the chair beside the bed. Henry Wood took the first guard shift. The others went to Elmo Finn's second-floor room with a case of beer and huge quantities of fried chicken, cole slaw, fruit, and Oreos.

Luke stretched out on one of the beds, pressing a cold can of beer to his forehead. His eyes were puffy and red.

"You guys . . . Jesus, you guys have been great. Beyond the call of duty. But what we're going to do tomorrow is a few steps beyond *that*. Giant steps. Perhaps of a felony nature. So it's not too late to get out. I'll understand."

Elmo Finn looked around the room. "Anybody leaving?" he asked briskly. "Good." He picked up the phone and dialed Henry in the other room. "Luke says you can bail out if you want. He'll understand." Elmo laughed and hung up. "Henry says fuck you. Nobody's leaving, Luke. Phoenix rising. I want you to deputize us as special representatives of the governor . . ."

"You guys are something," Luke said. "But I knew that. Jesus! I've got to call Louise. I don't know what to tell her."

"Tell her the truth—we don't know."

"That's right—we don't know anything for sure. Even though I know Nikki's dead." His voice was flat, unemotional.

He pushed up into a sitting position and reached for the cell phone. As he punched in the number, three heavy knocks boomed from the door. George and Roy vaulted up, guns in their hands.

"The code's two-three-two," Elmo Finn whispered as the others nodded. "It's not Henry."

Three more knocks, louder this time. Elmo Finn went to the door and peered through the eyehole, but couldn't make out who it was. Luke, who was speaking in muffled tones to Louise, turned his back to the door. Elmo made a gesture and Roy went to the corner near the window; George Graves flattened out on the floor between the beds, raising up on his elbows behind the nine-millimeter Browning.

Elmo Finn yanked open the door. There stood the wide-shouldered figure of Agent Gene Kessler of the Bureau of Alcohol, Tobacco and Firearms, whose quick hard eyes swept the room. Luke, the phone to his ear, made a hold-it-down gesture without turning around. George and Roy concealed their handguns.

Elmo Finn ambled outside to the narrow balcony, closing the door behind him. "Got a man on the phone in there. How you doin', Agent Kessler."

"Marshal Reardon, Marshal Reardon. Pretty crowded in there, Marshal Reardon."

"Just relaxin' a little. You hear anything on Noreen?"

He shook his head. "Transmitter's not working at all now. Our people say it's probably a malfunction. Did your spy deliver the message?"

"He hasn't seen her. She took off somewhere and left her baby behind."

"That's not like her."

The two men looked at each other. Then Elmo Finn said, "So the transmitter's either malfunctioning or it's been discovered, and you're not sure."

"I'm not sure. But I'm sure worried." He glanced at the adjacent rooms, all of which were dark, then turned and leaned on the railing with his forearms. Without looking at Elmo Finn he said, "I checked with the Marshals Service. Ain't no deputy marshal named Reardon."

Standing woodenly a few feet away, Elmo said nothing.

"Ain't no black deputy marshal named Dobbs either."

Gene Kessler's eyes seemed to be focused on a young couple in the parking area below, struggling to get their bags inside in one trip. Elmo came over slowly and put his hand on the railing.

"Gene, I'm going back inside for one minute. Then I'll be back."

Roy answered the two-three-two knock immediately. Elmo entered the room and spoke with Luke, who was still on the phone with Louise. Soon he was back outside. Kessler was standing with his back to the railing, his arms hanging loosely.

"Gene, did you see the man on the bed in there, talking on the phone?"

Kessler nodded.

"That's the governor of Tennessee. Lucas Gannon."

The federal agent's cold eyes betrayed nothing. Perhaps a flicker of interest: tell me more. This guy's good, Elmo Finn thought, and he knew Luke's decision was right.

"His wife was kidnapped eighty-four hours ago. We think God's Country did it and they've got her out there somewhere. That's what we're doing—trying to get her back safely without having a media circus. Without any publicity at all, because the kidnappers say they'll kill her if there's any publicity and we believe 'em. When I first told you what we were doing, I was perhaps slightly economical with the truth, but I couldn't mention the governor's involvement. I hope you can understand that. There's something else I need to tell you—less than an hour ago, our spy reported that somebody called Sarge is running around God's Country in a Winnebago with North Carolina plates. Sounds like the dude you're looking for. So, Agent Kessler, why don't we do a little deal?"

Elmo Finn went back inside and got a six-pack of beer and the two men walked downstairs and across the parking area to the picnic grounds. The clean night wind carried a hint of winter, distant but unmistakable. The leaves, some of which had turned, lifted and fell softly in the autumn breeze. They sat down in unpainted Adirondack chairs, side by side, and Elmo Finn told BATF Agt. Gene Kessler most of the story.

A half hour later, Kessler said, "So you guys ain't cops at all."

"We're special deputies of the governor."

"What the hell does that mean?"

"It's kind of a special concept. Reserved for certain situations."

Gene Kessler laughed sharply. "Oh yes, I can see how special it is. Impersonating U.S. marshals. Kidnapping an inmate of a state penitentiary and releasing him into the fucking underbrush. Kidnapping Noreen McConathy before you knew she was working for me as a federal informer. This is pretty fucking special indeed. Who's your spy?"

"State cop named Clay Jennings. God's Country thinks he's *their* spy."

They continued talking until Roy and George came out of room 523 and stood at the railing, watching the two men in the Adirondack chairs below.

"Some more special deputies of the governor, I suppose," Kessler said dryly, looking up. "Who once upon a time just happened to be agents of the Central Intelligence Agency."

Elmo Finn let out a quick laugh. "Chain of command doesn't work in these situations, Gene. By the time you go through all the channels, your stolen ordnance from Fort Bragg will be gone. And our stolen convict too. And Nikki Gannon may be dead, if she isn't already."

"Suppose your plan works, suppose everything goes right. I

get Sarge and the ordnance, you get Nikki back safe. You're still gonna have Randall Tice on your hands. What are you gonna tell the warden at Brushy Mountain when you breeze in one day to return their missing inmate?"

"It'll have to be crafty, I grant you that."

Gene Kessler stifled a laugh. "And what if I don't go along, Elmo? What if I decide not to ignore my oath and Bureau policy and everything else I've been taught? What if I go make a little phone call and have guys with badges and guns swarming all over this place and God's Country too?"

"Well, Gene, that really can't be an option now. No offense intended, but one more kidnapping wouldn't make that much difference."

The Sixth Day

It was still dark when the phone rang beside Eli Korn's king-size bed, but the Yes Man was awake. He answered before the second ring.

"Korn."

"Eli, this is Bump Hanner. You sound wide awake—I was fixin' to apologize for callin' so early."

"Colonel, I was just lyin' here hopin' you'd call. What's up?"

"I don't know, Eli. I don't know what's up. I don't even know if I'll be commander of the state police at the end of the day, or if I should be. We've lost Haystack."

"*Lost* him?"

"Actually, Eli, it looks like he lost us. Last night about midnight Miz Perry called down and told Moody, Moody was the body man, that Haystack had already gone to bed in that barracks room on the fourth floor, that he wouldn't be goin' home.

Okay. Fine. Moody went back to pickin' his navel or whatever. But when Devlin comes on at six, he goes upstairs and checks. The only person sleepin' in that barracks room was the little mustache, Cecil Whatever. Haystack was gone. He's nowhere in the buildin'. We don't know where he is."

"Jesus, Bump. You think he disappeared on purpose—and Louise was in on it?"

"Yes I do. I think it was arranged."

"Bump, go to your office—"

"I'm in my office."

"Good. Stay there. Don't tell anybody anything, even your own men. Wait till I call."

"Yes, sir. Eli, I'm sorry, I tried to resign—"

"Bump, stop talkin' about resignin'. We'll work this out. You can't protect Haystack if he won't let you protect him."

"Yes, sir. There's somethin' else, too—we've got the pickups that were used in that armored car holdup. Deputy sheriff found 'em behind a Wal-Mart in Calhoun, Georgia. Apparently they just off-loaded the money bags into some other vehicle right there in broad daylight. The trucks were purchased in Dalton, Georgia, with cash and phony IDs. By a woman, for God's sake. The description we've got ain't that good. We ain't released any of this yet."

"Just sit tight, Bump. If the press asks questions, say nothing. No comment."

"Yes, sir."

Eli hung up and rolled next to Jill Dennison, who was sitting up smoking a cigarette.

"So Haystack's flown?"

"Flown his own coop. How could we have expected this?"

"I don't know. But we better think of something."

———

Sgt. Clay Jennings rose before dawn from his hard bunk in the loft of the Ark. He shaved with his cordless electric razor, the tiny efficient hum a locomotive in his ears. He dressed in the brown shirt with the epaulets, clipped on the black necktie, bloused his black trousers neatly over his boots, tightened the Sam Browne belt. He packed all his personal items in a small duffel bag except for his service revolver. He snapped open the cylinder, checking that only the chamber beneath the hammer was empty, the way he always carried it. He fished out a bullet from the outside pocket of the duffel and loaded the sixth chamber, spun and closed the cylinder. Then, impulsively, he thrust the gun back into the duffel bag.

Through the stained-glass windows the sky was lightening. He went to the door and looked out. A blue dawn was creeping over the eastern ridges and above the trees. The vehicles had not been moved since last night. Everything else seemed the same, too—Joshua's silver trailer in the trees, the curtains taped to the narrow windows; the chimney-shaped guardhouse at the foot of the long slope, its door open, the wooden God's Country sign face-forward in the dust; the straw hut with the double stack of heavy sandbags blocking the entryway. He looked again at the straw hut. *Was* something different? A shiver ran through him. As he stepped out into the half-light to look more closely, he heard the helicopter pass overhead. Clay Jennings whirled and sprinted to his Toyota.

"It's the far cabin. Last one above the lake. Got to be." George Graves leaned out of the dark green Bell UH-1 Iroquois helicopter, a relic of Vietnam that a forgotten GI had nicknamed Huey. He trained the powerful field glasses on the remote cabin and surrounding area. "Something's different, too."

"Can you set down above it, Henry?" Elmo Finn asked.

"Were those tire tracks here before?" Gene Kessler asked.

"No," George said.

"They'll hear us," Henry said. "If anybody's there."

The chopper swung in a lazy arc around the two-story log cabin that sat on a graded shelf halfway up the long wooded slope. At the top of the slope was a small clearing in the trees. Manipulating the controls with musician's fingers, Henry Wood hovered sixty feet above the clearing, slowing the big horizontal rotor by gentle degrees, correcting the pitch, his eyes sweeping the gauges, nestling the helicopter down to the clumsy red earth below.

"Like a butterfly with sore feet," Elmo Finn said, drawing an approving chuckle from the others as they unbuckled quickly and grabbed their weapons. It was what Elmo Finn had said on every landing in Vietnam, no matter how rough or smooth. Even on that last mission, with Mason dead at their feet.

Elmo Finn and Roy went out first, then Gene Kessler and George Graves. When Luke appeared in the doorway, the first rifle volley tore into his chest. He fell back into the chopper across Henry's legs. Roy and Elmo hit the ground firing their rifles, emptying full magazines into the thick trees below, where the attack had come from. Then another burst of attacking fire exploded from a second position twenty yards from the first, slightly closer to the chopper. When it stopped, Roy signaled Elmo and barrel-rolled across the red dirt into the tree line. He rammed in a fresh magazine and crawled out of sight.

Elmo Finn waited for a third fusillade but none came. He flattened out and worked his way back to the chopper. There was no sign of George or the ATF agent. He crawled around the helicopter. He could hear urgent, shallow breathing and the steady whispering of Henry Wood.

"Henry, how is he?"

"One clean wound, upper right chest and shoulder. I got pressure packs on. She's a bleeder—but this old soldier'll be okay." Unlike his words, Henry Wood's voice was high-pitched, strained.

"Morphine?"

"Done."

"Mo." Luke Gannon's hoarse whisper thrilled Elmo Finn.

"Right here, Luke."

"Don't worry about me, I'll make it, Mo . . . promise, Mo . . . save Joshua for me."

Sgt. Clay Jennings was downshifting the Toyota when he heard the shots. Automatic weapons. He wheeled off the dirt road into the trees, scraping the pickup on both sides. He jumped out and hurried forward, staying low in the thinning trees. As he neared the top of a hill, he dropped to his knees and crawled forward, peering carefully over the crest.

Seventy-five yards ahead was the cabin, perched on the graded shelf like a clock on a mantel, and behind it the wooded slope up to the clearing. Jennings stretched out flat and cupped his hands over his eyes. What a decision, he thought, to leave his revolver behind. But a revolver against automatic weapons—he was sure he had heard automatic weapons.

Streaking back toward the cabin from the trees beyond came a thin, loose-jointed figure in camouflage dress, a rifle in his hands and a shotgun strapped to his back that seemed to bump his head with every stride. It was Earl Cherry. Jennings suddenly realized that Earl and little Jeremiah must have been camped out in the third cabin, hiding from the process servers. Earl fell twice as he plunged down the slope, and each time Jennings flinched, expecting one of the weapons to discharge. As Earl reached the cabin and headed around to the front, a man in black smoothly rolled over the arch of the roof and rappeled downward on an invisible cord and planted his feet and sprang out and down onto the scarecrow frame of Earl Cherry, who crumpled backward to the red dirt. Even from a distance, Jennings recognized the man called Roy, Elmo Finn's man, the man who had driven the Checker cab that first morning at the residence; the man he had fought with in the governor's workout room. Roy was bending over Earl Cherry, who lay motionless. Suddenly the first full glint of sun darted in over the trees, a pale white arrow, twinkling on the blade in Roy's hand.

When George Graves and BATF Agt. Gene Kessler saw Roy vault from the roof, they broke from their position fifty yards away in the trees and sprinted to the cabin. Roy straightened up as they arrived, a notched commando's knife in his fist.

Earl Cherry was mewling and writhing on the ground. "It was a accident! It was a . . . accident!"

"This is the specimen who shot the governor?" Kessler huffed incredulously, taking in air. He produced a pair of handcuffs, yanked Cherry to his feet, and shackled him. "You are under arrest. Anything you say—"

"No! No! A accident—"

Earl Cherry slumped to his knees and cringed pitifully. Kessler continued the Miranda recitation.

"Way to go, Roy," Elmo Finn said, appearing soundlessly from the other side of the cabin.

"How's Luke?"

Elmo Finn made a vague shrug. "Shoulder wound, mostly. We need a medic—but he wouldn't let Henry fly him out."

For a moment the wartime term *medic* froze the three men of Phoenix. Memories flared among them, registered plainly on their faces, unutterable and ineradicable and reassuring.

"This guy's crazy," George finally said. "Talking about an accident. Accidental ambush."

"No! No!" Earl Cherry cried. "The Wells Fargo truck, the guard—"

Everyone jumped as the Toyota pickup came tearing up the hill, slip-sliding to a stop. Clay Jennings in his brown storm trooper shirt hopped out.

"Did anyone get shot? I heard automatic fire—what's going on?"

Earl Cherry glared wildly and venomously at the brawny state policeman. Jennings charged over and faced him down, glaring menacingly.

"That's right, Earl, you goony fuckin' fuckhead! That's right! I'm Zaaaaahg, you goony asshole!"

Earl Cherry's face twisted into a hideous snarl of revulsion and fear. He writhed against the handcuffs. Clay Jennings laughed hysterically.

Elmo Finn said, "Sergeant Jennings, Haystack's with us, up there. He was shot by Cherry here. He'll make it."

Jennings spun back to Earl Cherry. "Shot! You goddamn ignorant redneck asshole!" His words ran together and he glared red-faced, breathing in gasps. Then he turned back to Elmo Finn.

"Is this why I was supposed to be up at dawn? What's happening? Why the chopper? Why is Haystack here—who are you?"

Gene Kessler produced his BATF identification.

"Oh you guys are real popular at God's Country," Jennings boomed. "So this is a joint federal-state operation! And I ain't got a gun or a badge, just a storm trooper shirt!" He grinned a tight-lipped grin, showing no teeth.

"Clear?" Elmo asked Roy, gesturing toward the cabin behind them.

"I didn't see anything. I could have missed something." Roy brought out a long strand of piano wire from a pouch on his leg, laced it through Earl Cherry's handcuffs, and lashed the prisoner to a jack pine stripling on the edge of the graded shelf.

"I'll go in the front with you and you," Kessler said, pointing to Elmo Finn and Clay Jennings. "You two . . ." He made a sweeping motion, and Roy and George began circling the cabin in alternate directions.

They went to the door. Kessler turned the knob and noiselessly pushed the door open, and the federal agent, the state policeman, and the consulting detective stepped into the mountain log cabin. There were two large rooms separated by a staircase, with a narrow open kitchen running along the back. The room on the left had a stone fireplace and was empty except for an incongruous Oriental rug covering the wide-plank floor. The room on the right was filled with olive-drab metal boxes and wooden crates, some of them already open, containing an M-60 machine gun, semiautomatic rifles, and enough complementary military ordnance to outfit a small army. Which was exactly the idea.

"I should be with the governor," Clay Jennings implored Elmo Finn, his brown storm trooper shirt blotched with sweat. "It's my *job*, Colonel Finn, I'm a body man. How bad was he hit?"

"A good man's with him, Sergeant. But you're right. Go straight up the hill to the clearing where the Huey is. But I may need you again—you're still our spy."

"I'm blown now."

"Only to Earl Cherry, and he's not going anywhere."

Jennings nodded grimly and hurried off. Elmo Finn went back upstairs to the sleeping loft where Gene Kessler was still searching.

"Three sleeping bags, Elmo," Kessler said. "One for Earl Cherry. One for the boy Jeremiah, who's apparently disappeared. One for somebody else—Randall Tice, maybe?"

A faint sound came from the low area under the steep slant of the roof, where blankets and rags were piled up. The two men continued talking as if they had heard nothing. They drew their weapons and using hand gestures took up positions.

"Probably *was* Randall Tice," Elmo said. "But he's long gone by now."

Elmo Finn reached down and yanked the top blanket away. "Come out! Now!"

There was another faint noise. Something ruffled the farthest corner of the jumbled mound.

"Go ahead, Gene," Elmo Finn said. "Just empty your gun into the goddamn thing. You can't miss."

A shallow cry sounded and Elmo swooped down, grabbed another fistful of cloth, and yanked hard. Heaving in terror, his face clotted with dry streaks, his bony wrists caked with blood, Jeremiah Cherry stared out into the guns. He was naked, one arm handcuffed to an eyehook.

"Jeremiah, Jeremiah, you're all right now," Elmo Finn said softly, dropping to one knee, holding the boy's bony shoulder. "You're all right now. We're your friends, it's all right. Does your father have the key to the handcuffs?"

The boy's head and shoulders were bobbing, thrashing, perhaps signaling yes. He jerked backward suddenly, straining against the handcuffs, and fresh blood spurted from his wrist.

"We'll get the key and a drink of water for you, Jeremiah," Elmo Finn said. "It's all right now. I saw your mother, I'll take you to see her. Everything's going to be all right, Jeremiah."

The boy's face calmed somewhat though he was still wheezing and pulling his cuffed wrist jerkily. Elmo Finn and Gene Kessler hurried downstairs. Gene Kessler went to get the handcuff key while Elmo grabbed a plastic cup and went outside to the well, where George was working the pump handle. George finished and headed up the slope with a bucket of water for Luke. Elmo filled the cup and he and Kessler climbed the stairs again.

"He's got a gun! Jesus! He's got a gun!" It was Roy's voice from outside.

Dropping to his knees, Elmo looked into Jeremiah's nook. The bloody handcuffs dangled from the eyehook. Jeremiah was gone.

The men sprang to the window. The gaunt naked boy, fragile and savage, was weaving and dancing before the stripling where his trembling father was bound. The boy uttering feral, prehistoric sounds that his spare body seemed incapable of producing. His skeletal hands, dripping red now, slicing the air with a small silver automatic. Twenty feet behind him Roy was creeping up.

"Jeremiah, Jeremiah," Earl Cherry pleaded, his slender body, progenitor of the son's, twisting and writhing against the handcuffs and the piano wire. "Oh God God God God Joshua Joshua—"

An instant before Roy dived the naked boy pulled the trigger. Roy knocked him down but his swipe for the gun missed, and Jeremiah rolled to his feet, danced away, fired again and again from a perfect flexed-knee stance. The boy's hollow eyes were cold slits, and with each recoil of the gun he took a little hop. Earl Cherry feinted and lunged and cowered before each volley, then slumped forward limply against his bonds before the last shot exploded. His shirt had vanished in a drench of bright blood. As the gun clicked empty Roy chopped it from the boy's hands.

Jill Dennison, perched on the edge of the leather chair across from Eli Korn's desk, was lighting a cigarette from the butt of another when the phone rang.

"Korn."

Eli raised his eyebrows to Jill and switched on the speaker-phone.

". . . somethin' you ought to know, Eli, it's a mystery to me . . . you put the speakerphone on?"

"Jill's the only one here, Clarence. She's reliable."

"Certainly, I wasn't suggestin' . . . well, anyway, both of you ought to know. That's why I'm callin', keep the governor's office informed."

The hollow speakerphone voice halted and there was a long silence.

"Go ahead, Clarence, we're with you." Eli fished out the pack of cigarettes he now kept hidden in his desk, shook one out, and lit up.

"Remember day before yesterday, I told you how the governor in my presence called the warden at Brushy Mountain, said he wanted to do a favor for a friend in the U.S. attorney's office in New York, they needed to borrow a prisoner name of Randall Tice. And later that very morning two U.S. marshals showed up at Brushy and took Tice away in a helicopter. With our complete cooperation."

There was another silence.

"So?" Eli asked.

"So. This is where it gets right peculiar, Eli. There ain't no U.S. marshals with the names they gave, Reardon and Dobbs, and there ain't no U.S. attorney in New York needin' no Randall Tice."

The only sound was a faint crackle from the speakerphone. Eli coughed softly.

"How do you know all this, Clarence? You been makin' some calls?"

"I wasn't snoopin', Eli. The people at Brushy Mountain had some suspicions, they asked some innocent questions. And the answers came out funny, that's all I'm sayin'."

"What the hell are you implying, Clarence? That the governor somehow sprang a maximum-security inmate with fake U.S. marshals and—"

"No, no, Eli, not at all. I'm just reportin'. I'm just afraid that the governor may have been hoodwinked or something. By his old friend in New York. Or those cowboys he's pallin' around with. Or somebody. And the press might get wind of it."

"The press better not get wind of it, Clarence. I'm holding you responsible for that. Personally. If what you say is true, it wouldn't look too good for your department to be releasing convicted felons to U.S. marshals who ain't U.S. marshals. Would it now, Clarence?"

"Eli, I'm on the team, goddamnit, that's why I'm callin'."

"I understand that, Clarence. My advice is to just sit tight. There's an explanation for everything in this devious disorderly world. Like that old Duke Ellington song, Clarence, do nothing till you hear from me."

"One marshal was white and one black."

"What does that mean?"

"It don't mean nothin'. I'm just reportin'. The black one was the pilot. Big guy, barrel-chested. Wanted to see James Earl Ray's cell." He paused. "Just givin' you some details."

"Let's just sit on this for now, Clarence."

"Where *is* the governor, by the way?"

"The governor is on the job for the people of Tennessee. As always."

"I've heard some things, Eli."

"Tell me, Clarence. Nothin' I like better than the latest god-damn rumor."

"I heard the governor had kind of disappeared. With his old gang of CIA cowboys. Includin' the barrel-chested black dude who's a helicopter pilot. The body men are in a state."

"That's a good one, Clarence. Thank God for rumors, keeps Nashville percolatin'. You won't be passin' on any rumors, will you, Clarence? While you're still workin' for us."

"I hear you, Eli. You ought to know by now that I'm on the team. And I think somebody sometime ought to see fit to tell

226

the people on the team what in the pluperfect fuckin' hell is goin' on."

"I expect you'll be among the first to know, Clarence."

When Eli switched off the phone, Jill Dennison realized she had two cigarettes going and crushed one out. "This thing's out of control, Eli. Like me."

The Yes Man exhaled a thick stream of smoke. "I'm afraid, darlin', you're assumin' that it was ever *under* control."

The man code-named White, ripping long strips of duct tape from a roll, retapes the opaque curtains tight around the windows. He whirls at a noise and exhales sharply.

"Jesus! Don't sneak up on me."

The woman called Red drops a grease-stained paper bag of hamburgers and fries on a table against the wall. "You can't hear much in here. It's like a tomb."

They look at each other and laugh raucously. They help themselves to the food and sit on the floor to eat, washing it down with bottled water.

"Like a tomb," he says. They laugh again.

From a distance comes the muted lowing of cattle.

"You can hear the cows," White says between bites.

They look at each other again, apprehension coloring their faces.

"What do you think?" Red asks. "You can sure hear the cows."

White puts down his half-finished hamburger. "Damn it. One more damn thing. Plus we don't know what that Cherry bitch might say."

"It'll be all right. Everything will be all right."

"Sure. I know." He picks up the hamburger and puts it down again. "The finger was a mistake, I said that all along. The finger was a definite mistake."

The morphine had done its job. In the shade of the helicopter Luke lay semiconscious on a mattress that had been dragged up from the cabin, his head resting on a stack of folded blankets. His shirt was stripped away around the shoulder wound, which Henry had bandaged tightly. The bleeding had stopped.

Jeremiah, dressed now in baggy jeans like clown's pants and an overlarge shirt that hung limply on his bony frame, had been sitting docilely on the red dirt of the clearing, his eyes fixed and glazed. Around him sat the other four men. Suddenly the boy jumped up and darted toward the trees. Roy was barely quick enough to snatch his trailing arm and reel him back. Jeremiah crumpled like a marionette.

"Jeremiah, we don't want to tie you up again. We are your friends. But don't run. You can't run, Jeremiah."

The boy rolled and squirmed in the red dirt. "Show you," he moaned, the first words he had spoken since emptying the automatic into his father's chest. "Show you, show you." He popped up and motioned to Roy with both arms: come with me.

"You want to show us something?" Roy asked.

"Show you." His head bobbed up and down jerkily. He made vague two-handed gestures toward the trees on the other side of the helicopter.

Roy and Elmo Finn followed him, staying close. Jeremiah led them into the dense growth, turning this way and that, working down and around the long slope and then up again, clambering over sharp rocks, slicing through heavy branches that snapped back. He led the way confidently. Once he angled sharply to the right and Roy caught his arm, but the boy was not trying to escape. After a while they came to a narrow path with parallel three-inch-deep ruts made by a heavy cart or wagon. Elmo Finn pointed to the ruts and Roy nodded. The men stopped for a few moments to catch their breath; the boy slumped against a tree, trancelike, a tiny stick figure in the loose shapeless clothes. Then they were on the move again. Jeremiah followed the path for fifty yards, then cut back into the trees. They went downhill for a while, crossing a busy stream with moss-covered banks, then upward again, almost straight up, higher and higher, the two men slashing like trailblazers at the branches to keep up with the wispy boy, who edged between everything or ducked under it. Once Elmo Finn looked back and realized he could not point in the direction of the helicopter. Soon Jeremiah stopped, indicating with both hands a thick grove of pine trees thirty yards ahead. He sprang forward again, as energetic as he had been at the beginning. "Show you," he said hoarsely.

Inside the pines it was easier going. The ground was soft and mossy, with a scattering of needles and cones. Jeremiah drew up short before a circular patch of ground surrounded by a ring of smaller trees. Over and over he chopped both arms forward in a violent pointing motion, but the two men could see nothing unusual. They walked over the ground slowly, herding the boy before them, their eyes adjusting to the dimness and the shadows, squinting, peering.

"Colonel." Roy's hand described a rectangular piece of ground that seemed to have been recently disturbed. It was camouflaged by an unnatural arrangement of pine needles and branches. Elmo scuffed away the debris with his boot.

"What is this, Jeremiah?" he asked softly.

The boy was sitting on the ground against a pine tree, his eyes out of focus again, his young-old face unreadable.

"Roy, should we tell Luke now?" Elmo Finn unsnapped the walkie-talkie case.

"I don't know, sir."

"No. No. He'd just have to agonize until we knew for sure."

"I agree, sir."

"Is it a grave, Roy?"

The veteran commando, who had seen a hundred unmarked graves and filled some, let out a pent-up sigh. "I don't know, Colonel." He sighed again. "It looks like a grave."

They glanced at the boy. He was paying no attention to them now, staring vacantly into the forest. Roy took out the piano wire and fashioned a long, slack loop connecting Jeremiah's belt to Roy's. Then he and Elmo Finn broke off some branches and tried to sharpen them into digging tools. After a few attempts, they gave up and decided to use their combat knives as trowels. They dropped to their knees and began digging.

The ground yielded more easily than they had expected. Faster and faster they forced the blades down, pried loose the soil, swept it aside with their hands. Sweat drained into their eyes, and they swiped at it with their sleeves. A few protesting birds fluttered higher into the branches. Elmo Finn switched the knife to his left hand, then switched back. Thirty inches down Elmo's blade struck something.

They looked at each other, then dug more feverishly, seizing fistfuls of dirt and flinging them away. Expecting to uncover a makeshift coffin, a corpse with a missing ring finger, a mass of human remains. Roy tossed his knife aside and finished the digging with his hands, flinging away the grains and clumps. Gasping noisily, they tore at the ground with their fingers. Suddenly the dirt fell away and two stenciled words stared up at them: *Wells Fargo.* The men collapsed onto the pine needles and closed their eyes.

Elmo held the boy's hand as they went back. It was very hot and they were sweat-soaked despite the relative coolness of the trees. When they needed Jeremiah to show the way, he gestured passively with one hand.

Luke was alert and sitting up on the mattress when they trudged back into the clearing. Elmo Finn gave him the two-sentence report he had practiced along the way.

"We found the Wells Fargo money buried. At first we thought it was a grave."

Luke stared at Elmo for a moment, then said exuberantly, "So we don't know! We don't know anything for sure. Not yet."

"That's right, Luke, that's right. So we press on. Phoenix rising."

But the burst of hope quickly faded on Luke's face. "But she's dead. I know that. I know that. And another man is dead this very morning." Pointing at Jeremiah, who had curled into a ball on the ground and shut his eyes, Luke whispered, "Did he show any remorse?" Elmo Finn shook his head.

Luke took a sip of water, grimacing as he raised and lowered the canteen. He looked at Elmo Finn. "Mo, you're right. Press on. Phoenix rising."

"Agent Kessler," Elmo Finn said in a strong voice, "we understand that you have to stay with the stolen ordnance in the cabin, guard it, that's BATF's interest in all this. We understand that. I would appreciate it, though, if you would also keep Jeremiah with you until we return."

"Return from where?"

"From Joshua's Ark—we're going to get Nikki. We think she's still alive and she's got to be there somewhere. Joshua must know about the firefight up here, and I just hope he's not crazy enough to start another one, or to harm Nikki in some way. But he may conclude that this is The Day he's been preaching about for so long—when the government finally attacks the patriots of God's Country. You preach enough apocalypse, sooner or later you get apocalypse now."

The federal agent stared at Elmo Finn. "Under whose authority . . . who has jurisdiction here?"

"My authority," Luke said. "I am claiming jurisdiction as governor of Tennessee."

Elmo Finn said, "We had a deal, Gene. Now we've found

your stolen ordnance, and by accident we've apparently found the Wells Fargo money, and we've got Jeremiah safely in our custody, and the man who tried to kill the governor of Tennessee is dead himself. But what we haven't got is what we came for—Nikki Gannon. So we're going in there to find her, and I'd appreciate it if you'd look after Jeremiah while you're guarding all that stuff in the olive drab boxes. We had a deal, Gene."

Kessler nodded brusquely. "All right, Colonel, I'll keep him. Safe and sound. But as part of our deal I would appreciate it if you would do the same with Noreen McConathy when you find her. She took serious risks for the government of the United States. She's a very brave lady. I'm worried about her."

"I am too, Gene. We'll protect her." Elmo Finn glanced at Luke, then back. "One more thing, Gene. We can rack a machine gun in the door of that Huey—the hardware's still in place, just like Nam. Only thing we're missing is the machine gun."

The federal agent scrambled to his feet and brushed the red dirt off his jeans. "Elmo, my nickname in the Bureau is *Book*—*Book* Kessler—because everybody says I go by the book. Always. I've always been a stickler for doing it right. Now you want me to throw the book out the window."

No one spoke. A puff of wind came up, stirred the red dirt, died. Elmo Finn took a deep, silent breath. Henry Wood walked over and began checking Luke's bandages, his long fingers probing gently.

"There's another way, Elmo," Gene Kessler said. "Bring in a whole bunch of my people, keep all this above board. Go by the book. There's one man dead already."

Luke Gannon shook his head impatiently. "It's my wife, Gene. Maybe there's a tiny chance she's still alive. I'm going to take that chance, and I'm going to take the responsibility for whatever happens. I'll protect you with the Bureau. I still have some connections." He rolled onto his good arm, nodded

Henry away, and pushed to his feet. "We're asking you for that M-60, Gene. We're going in."

Clay Jennings watched the helicopter rise silently above the trees behind Lake Joshua and bank through a soft circle, a black egg-beater against the blue-gray sky. He ran to the Ark and pounded on the door. After ten seconds he pounded again. Finally Joshua cracked the door a few inches and glared out, his ice-blue eyes venomous. He was wearing camouflage fatigues and greasepaint.

"Joshua! I need to get my weapon—it's upstairs—"

"Where's Earl Cherry?" Over Joshua's shoulder appeared the perspiring furious faces of Linda Pearson and Spiderman.

"I don't know, Joshua, I haven't seen Earl. I just need my gun."

The faint pulsing *thwap thwap thwap* of the helicopter reached their ears. Joshua's eyes widened madly as he stared at the sky.

"It's a helicopter!" Clay Jennings shouted. "A *black* helicopter! What's happening, Joshua, is this it? Is this *The Day?*"

"Eighty-eight! Eighty-eight!" Joshua made two stiff-arm Nazi salutes and slammed the heavy door. Jennings turned and raced to his red Toyota. The clattering was much louder now, *thwap thwap thwap thwap.* As the big Huey thundered into the heart of God's Country, Jennings darted into the clear waving both arms and chopping an arrow toward the Ark. Then he dived under the Toyota.

Henry circled the enclave and headed for the overgrown playground with its rusting swing set and sliding board. Just before the chopper touched down, Roy, George, and Elmo Finn, clutching Armalites with banana clips and laser sights and bipod mounts, leaped out and scattered. The Huey settled to earth; the big rotor slowed lazily but did not stop. Ragged rows of vehicles and trailers and a few outbuildings stood between the helicopter and the Ark three hundred yards away.

Beneath the blood-red cross of steel on the roof where a weathercock once stood, the Ark suddenly erupted . . . tinselly red and green stained-glass windows shattering outward in a candy-cane spray . . . gray-black barrels of automatic weapons thrusting out like cannon on a warship . . . a sheet of furious fire exploding toward the chopper with a thunderous crackling tattoo, thuds and plunks and chings, the wild fusillade tearing into vehicles, trailers, huts, sheds, trees, gravel, dirt. The barrage went on for minutes, a massive hail sweeping a hundred-twenty-degree field of fire. A car up on blocks in no-man's land exploded and burned, then another. A thin dog, trapped in one of the bare shallow depressions, bolted crazily toward the Ark and was cut in half. Leafy branches floated down around the chopper like sprays; heavier limbs split and fell. Then came a miraculous tiny interlude of silence, like the taking in of a breath, before the crash of return fire—from Roy on the right behind a shield of sandbags and firewood stacked alongside a domed hut, from Elmo and George in the big trees behind the picnic area, stretched out behind the bipod-mounted Armalites—a savage crossfire that blasted out the remaining jagged shards of stained glass and the big loft window and shredded chunks of old pine and new oak and flung up flagstone confetti from the walkway. A counterburst from the Ark, a brief deafening firefight, then Roy ducking behind the domed hut and opening up again from a clump of Scotch pines, Elmo and George slithering to new positions and laying down fresh volleys, suddenly a heavy throbbing *thwap thwap thwap thwap* as the chopper roared into the air, climbing and whirling and diving on the blood-red cross at a steep angle of attack, the governor of Tennessee in the doorway behind with the M-60 machine gun raking the Ark with murderous firepower at a rate of ten rounds per second. Great jagged holes erupted in the pine and oak planking.

As the chopper swung past the Ark and pulled up, Luke Gannon, blood seeping through his bandages, glimpsed the contorted bodies of several men lying in broken glass and splintered wood at the base of Joshua's rough-hewn altar; olive-drab ammunition boxes stacked and tumbled like miniature coffins; streaks and pools and rivers of red; and, in the crossbeams high above the altar, a limp figure in a black robe and hood, hanging by the neck from a noose.

Sgt. Clay Jennings watched the helicopter circle and descend to its former position on the drab playground. When the firefight exploded, he had managed to crawl from beneath his Toyota to a safer place in the trees. Now, in the tense lull after the helicopter attack, the big state trooper bolted toward the playground, his six-four frame bent low, his fists tight. He ran a serpentine route over open rolling ground, stumbling headlong into the ditches and depressions, digging hard up the opposite banks. Huffing and puffing, he made it to the helicopter without drawing fire.

"Jesus! This is a war!" He sank to the ground, drawing loud, deep breaths. At length he said, "This is what Joshua kept talking about. The Day. The fucking Day—when ZOG attacks."

George Graves and Henry Wood were attending to the governor, who lay on his back inside the chopper with his eyes closed. Elmo Finn sat against a tree, the Armalite across his lap, taking water from a canteen.

Roy appeared from the trees. "Good thing I recognized you, Sergeant Jennings. Might've shot you. You make a nice big target."

"Jesus Christ, Roy! Jesus Christ! I thought I might get shot by *them*! I've never been in a fucking war! Jesus Christ!"

Elmo Finn loaded a fresh clip in the Armalite and filled the ammunition pouches on his belt with extra clips from a metal box. "Clay, his wound's bleeding again, wrestling that M-60.

Stay close to him, keep him here. Then we'll fly him to a doctor."

"Sure, okay. That's my job, body man. You goin' back over there? Maybe you got 'em all."

"Could somebody have escaped from the Ark without us seein' 'em?"

"No. It would be hard. All the doors were covered . . . I'm not sayin' I saw everything, because—"

"Because you had your head down."

"Yes sir, yes sir, I sure fucking did, I was under my truck diggin' toward China. But I didn't see anybody run out. Hell, they were probably diggin' too, that machine gun. Jesus! I ain't ever been in a war."

The men gathered around the door of the helicopter. Luke Gannon, fresh bandages around his shoulder and his arm in a sling, raised up on his good elbow. His face was chalky, his lips dry and cracked.

"Governor," Clay Jennings said, "you sure were hell with that machine gun. Blew out the whole side of that Ark. I'll believe you from now on, you tell your war stories." Jennings's grin was wide but tight-lipped, showing no teeth.

Luke gazed sourly at the trooper for a long moment, then looked at Elmo Finn. "I know who it is, Mo. Hanging in there."

Elmo Finn arched his neck, his eyes darting to Jennings and back.

"Who?" Jennings asked. "*Hanging?* Where? In the Ark?"

"I know who it is," Luke muttered hoarsely, ignoring Jennings. "I know. I know who it is." He rose up a few inches more, leaning to Elmo Finn and whispering, "Just like her father, just like her father, Mo—" He began coughing hard, wincing and grunting with each convulsion of his body. "Mo. Mo. Save Joshua for me." He fell back on the makeshift pallet of towels and duffel bags.

Elmo Finn grasped Luke's hand for a moment, then moved

away from the Huey. The men of Phoenix and Trooper Jennings followed. For the next five minutes, Elmo issued specific instructions to each man. A few questions were asked, there was terse, professional discussion, causing Elmo to make two adjustments in the plan. Roy gave Jennings a two-minute lesson in firing an M-60 machine gun. Then all was ready.

"Mo!" Luke's strained whisper brought Elmo Finn back to the helicopter. He put his ear to Luke's mouth. "Save him for me, Colonel. Promise."

Elmo gripped Luke's hand again and turned back to the others, nearly bumping into Jennings.

"Colonel, I hope I can handle this machine gun. I hope I don't have to handle it."

"Just protect him," Elmo Finn said quietly.

The two men were as close as dancers, their faces inches apart.

"What's going on, Colonel? Who's been hanged? Everything else I've seen was self-defense, but I *am* a policeman, I can't—"

"Your commander is right behind you, Sergeant. We're all working for him. You're covered."

Jennings backed away a step, staring at Elmo Finn. "I'm not worried about—"

"Just protect your commander, Sergeant. You're the body man." Elmo Finn strode away, and the four veterans of Phoenix quickly fanned out. Soon it was eerily quiet around the helicopter. Luke Gannon's eyes were closed, his breathing shallow but regular.

"Governor . . ." Jennings whispered.

There was no answer.

After a few minutes, Jennings left the chopper and edged forward to a vantage point inside a stand of trees. With binoculars he could see everything.

Suddenly heavy fire tore into the Ark, splinters of wood flying and drifting down, pieces of dirt and flagstone exploding up. It was another crossfire—from Henry Wood, behind a God's

Country vehicle only fifty yards ahead of Jennings, and from the trees on the far right where Roy had gone.

"Clay! Goddamnit!" Luke Gannon, his voice hoarse but strong, was shuffling toward Jennings, bracing his bandaged arm with the good one. He was bent over slightly but moving steadily. A forty-five automatic stuck out of his belt. He leaned against a tree and took Clay's field glasses, manipulating them with one hand.

From the extreme left, near the phone-booth guardhouse next to the county road, Elmo Finn and George Graves streaked up the long incline. They were thirty yards apart, running low and hard, protected by the covering fire from Henry and Roy.

Elmo Finn dived to the ground at one corner of the Ark, George at the other. The fusillade abruptly halted. The two men crawled to the door beneath the one loft window that remained intact. Then the firing exploded again, heavier this time, a concentrated barrage from both Henry and Roy. After twenty seconds it stopped. Luke swung the glasses over but Elmo and George had disappeared. Fifty yards ahead, Henry Wood was up and running toward the Ark.

"Let's go!" The governor tossed Jennings the field glasses and pushed off from the tree. Jennings raised the glasses and scanned from the guardhouse on the extreme left to the straw hut on the extreme right. He focused tightly on the hut, then swung back to the Ark. Through the shattered stained-glass windows he saw two feet tied together, dangling beneath a hem of black. He felt nauseous, bile in his mouth. Then he saw Elmo Finn and George moving inside the Ark, vanishing and reappearing, working their way toward the altar and the door behind it, the door Joshua had slammed in Jennings's face. Jennings began running and caught up with the governor, who was still clutching his bad arm but driving forward with a strong step, completely in the open now.

"Governor, this is too dangerous—"

"Sergeant!" Luke kept moving, looking straight ahead. "My wife was kidnapped. She's hanging in that barn."

Jennings stopped dead. "Kidnapped? Your wife was kidnapped? Nikki? Jesus, Governor . . ." He ran to catch up. "Now I understand some . . . Governor, I'm sorry. Jesus. I didn't know. You should have told us—we're the police."

As they neared the Ark, Roy came running up, his AR-15 strapped to his back and a short-barreled combat shotgun in his hands. "Luke, maybe just stay out here, let us make sure—"

"Roy, I want to be there. I have to be there, Roy."

At the door of the Ark they were met by George, who also urged Luke not to go in. The governor brushed past him. Clay Jennings said, "George, now I understand what's been going on. He told me."

George's tiny twitch-smile appeared, then vanished as his mouth turned down. His eyes were wide.

Jennings said, "I don't want to go in there right now. I saw the body hanging . . . through the binoculars." He turned and began walking away, then stopped and looked back. "George, I'm goin' over to that straw hut, where Earl Cherry and Jeremiah live. Something's funny—this morning there were sandbags piled all around and now . . . I don't know, I'm gonna take a look." He turned and moved off.

"Be careful!" George yelled. "We don't know where everybody is. Why don't you wait!"

Jennings kept going, and George went back inside, where the bodies of three men and three boys lay around the rough-hewn altar in a litter of broken glass and chunks of wood and spent shells and pools of crimson. The boys with shaved heads and tattoos and black leather jeans. One man with blacksmith's forearms, another with shattered, thick-lensed glasses, the third wrapped in a shredded Nazi flag, half its swastika blown away. A line of AK-47 assault rifles pointing like an arrow in the direction of the helicopter assault.

Roy was climbing a pyramid of benches and chairs that were being steadied by Henry Wood and Elmo Finn. He almost fell twice, but finally made it to the top. He went into a crouch and sprang up, grasping the crossbeam with one hand. Slowly he pulled himself up until he could get a two-handed grip, then worked his way to a sitting position atop the beam. He gathered his strength, then scooted across the beam to the gallows. He began sawing at the noose, wielding the commando's knife with one hand and maintaining his balance with the other. After a few minutes, he yelled a warning and the body in the black hood and robe dropped silently into the arms of Henry Wood and Elmo Finn. Luke Gannon let out a sob and turned away.

"God, oh God."

They laid the figure gently on one of the long benches. Elmo Finn reached for the black hood.

"Governor! Governor!"

Everyone whirled. Sgt. Clay Jennings stood silhouetted in the doorway in the glare of the late-morning sun, bearing something in his arms. He stumbled forward with his burden.

"Someone who wants to see you, Governor."

Luke lunged forward with a cry. "Nikki Nikki oh God Nikki you're safe Nikki." His face pressed against her, tears choking his words, gasping, "Nikki I love you Nikki you're breathing Nikki."

Suddenly he grabbed for her left hand, pulling it away from her body. He studied it, brought it closer, kissed it. All five fingers.

He tried to lift her from Jennings's arms but stumbled and fell. The big state trooper bent down and laid Nikki on the wide-planked floor next to her husband. They rolled to each other and embraced, clutching, caressing, Luke ignoring his bad arm as they enfolded each other and wept and murmured softly but urgently. Then Nikki Gannon, wet with tears, pressed her hands to her husband's streaked face and kissed his eyes. Everyone heard her whisper, "Us against the world baby Us against the world Us against the world." Then she closed her eyes and fell silent.

"I found her in that straw hut," Clay Jennings whispered to Elmo Finn. "I knew something was different. She was lying on the dirt floor under a big picture of Adolf Hitler."

No one spoke for several minutes. Then Luke lifted Nikki's face in his hand, and her eyes opened narrowly and closed and opened and rolled unfocused toward the other faces, moist faces, and closed again.

"Cows," she said with an effort. "Cows, cows. There were always cows."

"Mrs. Perry, your son-in-law has been missing almost eighteen hours, and your son-in-law is the governor of Tennessee, and protecting the governor of Tennessee is ultimately my responsibility, and unless you tell me everything that's going on and tell me right now—"

"What, Eli? What! What are you going to do? Hold a press conference? Horsefeathers!"

"Louise, whatever it is that's going on, whatever it is—keeping it secret cannot help. You may think you know what you're doing, and that what you're doing is the best thing to do, but lying to the body men who risk their lives to protect your daughter and son-in-law is not the right thing to do. I can't help you if—"

"I didn't lie to the body men."

"Yes you did, goddamnit. And you're lying to me now. Wake up, Louise! Your daughter hasn't been seen for days, under very strange circumstances, and now the governor has disappeared, with or without his consent, as a result of a ruse you took part in—"

"It's none of your business, Eli. Not yet. You'll have to wait and trust Luke to do what's right. He told you to trust him."

Eli Korn sat motionless for several seconds. Then he popped open his cell phone and vehemently tapped out a number.

"Jill—get somebody from the *Tennessean* in my office in twenty minutes. I'm giving them some exclusive goodies. Disappearances, capitol resignations, strange packages delivered all over the place, ex-CIA agents all over the place, classified ads in the newspaper, kidnapping—tell 'em they better hold page one." He clicked off.

Louise asked tremulously, "What kidnapping?"

"You tell me."

"Who's resigning?"

"Me. Bump Hanner. Clarence Monahan. Jill Dennison. Among others."

"I don't believe you."

Eli Korn stood up, his thin face blotched and snarling, and delivered a violent kick to the folding chair he had been sitting in. It collapsed with a furious clang.

"Cecil! Eli's going to resign and tell the press everything he knows! He thinks he knows!"

The slight, mustachioed computer hacker was standing just inside the door. Eli tried to storm past him but Cecil caught his arm and spun him hard into the wall. The Yes Man sank to the floor clutching his arm and fumbling for his cell phone.

"You can't assault me—you can't—"

Cecil Beech leaned down and snatched the cell phone. Pawing the wall, Eli tried to climb up but Cecil pushed him to the floor again.

"Three words, Mr. Korn," Cecil Beech said evenly. Producing a Pall Mall, lighting it and taking a long drag, blowing out a thick stream of smoke. Holding the cigarette between thumb and middle finger, palm up.

"Yes. I. Can."

The woman code-named Red covers her ears with her hands.

"Moooooo!" She rolls next to the man called White and buries her face in his neck.

"Ouch! Damn it, how many hickeys you wanna give me?"

"They sound louder'n ever, like a horror movie or something. Moo moo moo moo!"

"Nothin' we can do now."

"Get out of here."

"Where to?"

"I don't know. Blue will know."

"*Blue*. We been listenin' to Blue way too long."

"What we been listenin' to for way too long is those goddamn cows. Moo—ooo—ooo! They're drivin' me crazy."

"It's a short trip."

"Put some music on so I can't hear 'em. And he can't hear us."

"So you want some more?"

"I always want more. He did too."

"Sure. He'd have fucked a bush, he thought it had a snake in it."

"Don't talk about your brother like that. I loved him."

"You know where the next hickey's goin', don't you? On your big cow tits." He gets up and goes to the player. "So whaddaya want to hear? 'Cattle Call?' Or 'Cow Cow Boogie?'"

Clay Jennings's red Toyota pickup had been shot to pieces in the firefight—every window blasted out, every tire flattened. When he realized what could have happened if he hadn't crawled to the safety of the trees, he gagged and threw up. While the others searched for the missing militia leaders, Henry Wood jogged the three hundred yards back to the Huey and flew it to the Ark. Luke Gannon, still giddy with joy, held Nikki's hands as Roy and George carried her on a makeshift litter to the chopper. She was still drifting in and out, straining against the powerful sedative. They laid her on a pile of blankets and Luke sat on the floor beside her, murmuring constantly. He gripped her hands tightly so she couldn't turn and look behind her, where the body of Noreen McConathy lay, the black robe and hood covering her grisly wounds and burns. After Roy had cut her down from the gallows, they had looked at her face, and put the hood back on.

Clay Jennings took the co-pilot's seat. Elmo Finn said, "Be alert, Sergeant. We still don't know where they are."

"I feel comfortable now, Colonel. Security's my job. Not war."

"You definitely saw Joshua, Spiderman, and Linda Pearson? In the Ark? Just before we flew in?"

"Yes! Yes! They wouldn't let me in. Thank God."

Henry finished running through his checklist. "Ready, Colonel."

Elmo Finn nodded. "Clay, have you heard any cows around here?"

"Cows? I've heard some cows from time to time. I didn't pay much attention. This is a farming area."

"Are there any cows on God's Country land?"

"I don't know of any, but this is a big place."

"Do you have any idea where Esther McConathy is? And who was baby-sitting her? And what happened to all the other people who lived here?"

"Esther I don't know. One of the women was lookin' after her, I don't know her name. Most of the residents took off yesterday. They knew somethin' bad was up. Joshua didn't care if they left—he knew that when The Day came, he'd only have about ten real fighters. The rest were sheep. Sheeple."

"Clay, have you seen Randall Tice?"

The big state trooper looked incredulous. "Randall Tice? That's the second time you've mentioned that son of a bitch— he's supposed to be in the Brushy Mountain State Penitentiary. He didn't escape, did he?"

Elmo Finn shook his head and moved back to the big open doorway of the Huey. Luke was cradling Nikki like a baby.

"You could just stop now, Mo," Luke said. "Let the cops finish it. We've got Nikki back."

Elmo Finn shook his head.

"Because of Noreen?"

"We sent her back in with a transmitter in her bra. And they found it and tortured her and killed her. And the baby's missing."

"Mo, all of you are deputized, full power of the governor. Be careful. Save Joshua for me if you can."

"Yes, sir. You take care of that lady." He coughed into his fist. "And take care of that shoulder. And start writing your speech. That'll be some speech." He came to attention and saluted the governor of Tennessee. "Phoenix rising."

Tears that had been brimming in their eyes leaked out. Luke shifted Nikki's weight off his arm so he could return the salute. "Phoenix rising, Colonel Finn," he said, his voice catching. "Mo . . . thank you." Elmo Finn turned away and the helicopter lifted off.

In the ruined Ark, George and Roy sat slumped against the wall. Elmo came in. "Roy, they may try to retrieve some of that military hardware or the Wells Fargo money before they escape. I want you to hustle back up to the cabin and stay with Gene. We'll look around here and wait for the chopper. Be careful, Roy, they could be anywhere. Far as we know, it's only Joshua, Spiderman, and Linda. But Randall Tice could be with them."

Roy jumped up. "Yes, sir, Colonel." He slung the combat shotgun on his back and popped a fresh banana clip in the Armalite. He took three extra clips from George and headed out.

Elmo Finn stood over the gory mound of bodies. "Who are they, George?"

"Here's what Jennings told me," George said, pointing to the first body. "That's the Professor, perpetual college student for twenty years, had hundreds of credits but never got a degree . . . that's Popeye, used to be a cop, deputy sheriff I think . . . these are just three teenage dropouts, three skinheads that followed Spiderman around like puppy dogs, apparently Spiderman was their role model . . . this poor devil is Glenn Forbush, another ignorant redneck who believed all of Joshua's hate stuff. He's the one had his name changed to Hi Hitler."

George looked up at the knotted rope still hanging from the beam. "His own wife," he said bitterly, "he tortured and killed his own wife. When Noreen first came here she heard a bird flying, the sound of a bird in flight. Up at that lake somewhere. Not beating its wings—just soaring. She'd never heard that sound before, that's when she knew this was really God's Country. Did you see those burns?"

"I helped send her back in here, George, with a goddamn transmitter in her brassiere. And I was too dumb to realize what Rat Trap meant." Elmo Finn's battleship-gray eyes were clouded over, the fiery flecks invisible. "She was a brave lady. She was saving her ATF money so she and Esther could start a new life. Find the real God's Country. Gene Kessler will feel terrible. Maybe as terrible as I do."

Elmo Finn and George Graves stood silently for a long moment, surveying the carnage around them.

"Haven't seen this since Vietnam," George said softly.

"Goddamnit!" Elmo suddenly leaped onto the raised platform and kicked violently at the rough-hewn altar. It buckled slightly.

"It's bolted to the floor! Stand back, George, goddamnit!" He drew his forty-five and fired three rounds into the base of the altar, then lowered his shoulder and slammed into it like a blocking back. The heavy front panel sprang open as the Ark tore away from its anchoring and toppled over.

"Only place it could have been," Elmo Finn said.

George Graves snapped on his flashlight. They stared down into the tunnel.

Spiderman watched the helicopter until it was out of sight. He waited another five minutes, then loped out of the thick, dark pines and up the narrow dirt road toward the cabin. He ran unguardedly, erect, a loose-limbed figure all in black except for a gray German helmet with a chin strap. He carried an Israeli-made Uzi submachine gun.

Halfway up the long slope to the red-clay shelf where the cabin stood, he suddenly stopped, inhaling sharply. He sank into a crouch and peered at the blanket-wrapped shape lying next to the jack pine stripling on the edge of the graded shelf. Slowly he surveyed all around him, the Uzi swinging with his eyes, then glanced back toward the trees where he had left Joshua and Linda. Bending lower, he inched forward, up the incline and finally onto the shelf, kneeling, drawing back the flap of the blanket from under the piano wire.

"Freeze, asshole! Drop it! Now!"

Spiderman dived for the bank and tried to roll, but the barrel of the Uzi caught in the soft dirt and stopped him short. He flailed his way up to one knee, frantically wrenching the machine gun into position. He was firing wildly into the ground when back-to-back blasts from Gene Kessler's double-barreled shotgun cut him in half. His torso lifted limply into the air and fell grotesquely along his legs, like the closing of a jackknife.

Kessler crouched behind the corner of the cabin, expecting gunfire from the dark pines. He held his breath. He did not look at the body of Spiderman lying only a few yards from the shrouded body of Earl Cherry. A vast silence descended. Like Nam, he thought; a hushed deadly jungle.

He heard the helicopter before he saw it, and shuddered violently. Jesus; exactly like Nam. There was another noise, this one much closer. He rapped on the wall of the cabin.

"Jeremiah! Jeremiah! It's okay, it's okay! I'll take you to your mother real soon. Don't pull on the handcuffs, Jeremiah, please, you'll only hurt yourself more."

The helicopter circled the cabin and the dark pines in ever-tighter orbits. Kessler could see Elmo Finn and George Graves behind the barrel of the M-60 that was sweeping the trees from the doorway. Dark objects were falling from the chopper and exploding in the pines. Concussion grenades, thought Kessler.

Now there was firing into the dark pines from the trees across the dirt road, and bursts of return fire from the pines. The crisp, snapping reports of automatic weapons. Gene Kessler shuddered again and stretched out flat alongside the cabin, gouging a hole in the red dirt with his chin, cautiously peering around the corner. The helicopter was lower now, swooping like a vulture in a death arc, the grenades falling in a tighter pattern. Kessler saw movement on his side of the road behind a line of trees as Roy flashed into the open and dived behind a low hill. Then a bulky figure with a hippy feminine shape wearing green camouflage fatigues bolted from the dark pines, throwing a weapon ahead of her onto the dirt road, frenziedly waving a white cloth above her head with both hands. She jumped and waved and craned her head to the sky. Then she suddenly went rigid, frozen like a hurdler at the apex of a jump. Her knees crumpled and she fell, clawing the air. Gene Kessler knew from the recoil of the body that she had been shot in the back.

Movement again, this time in the fringe of the pines. A figure running with an Uzi, jumping over shrubs and bushes, leaning back into the edge of the trees to shield itself from the menacing helicopter. Running parallel to the dirt road. Headed toward the cabin on the graded shelf and its arsenal in the neatly stacked crates and olive-drab boxes where Gene Kessler lay waiting. The helicopter rising now, then diving like a falcon between the stands of trees, diving toward the road, Roy on his feet and running hard up the center of the road, leaping over the dead female body in camouflage but still seventy-five yards behind Joshua. Elmo Finn braced in the door of the helicopter, leaping out into the air and rappeling down as the chopper seemed to brush the treetops, Elmo dangling and gripping the wire with both hands. Gene Kessler up on his knees now, watching Joshua coming, thinking, If he turns, he'll have a clear shot, scrambling to his feet and rushing down to meet Joshua, the double-barreled shotgun at port arms, knowing he wouldn't make it, thinking, If he turns, Joshua turning now, stumbling backward from his own momentum, the dangling Elmo Finn silhouetted like a target, the helicopter suddenly zooming upward yanking the dangling figure away as Joshua's Uzi spat fire. With the chopper suddenly out of sight, Joshua leveling at Roy but Roy had vanished. Joshua scurrying back to the fringe of the trees like an animal who knows his route, running again, leaping the bushes, never glancing ahead to see Gene Kessler coming with the shotgun, the chopper diving again, thunderous, knifing between the trees, Elmo Finn motionless at the end of the wire, Joshua angling back out into the road, stopping and turning, Elmo Finn releasing his grip as Joshua braced to fire, Finn's boots crashing into his chest as the Uzi crackled, Roy churning up the road with long strides, flinging aside his shotgun and Armalite and diving headlong into the bodies on the ground.

Gene Kessler, gasping for air, got there seconds later. Elmo Finn, a knife in his hand, had Joshua pinned. Roy was on all fours.

"That was too close sir!" Roy wheezed. "Too fucking close! Due respect, sir!"

"You're right, Roy. I'm gettin' older."

"Jesus," Kessler said, "Je-sus. I thought he had you, Elmo, goddamn I did. Diving into an Uzi." Kessler huffed in more air. "This is too much like the real thing, boys. I'm havin' flash-backs."

"Copy that, sir," Roy said.

Elmo Finn gave a signal to Henry in the chopper, and Henry flew ahead to the cabin and settled down on the red clay shelf. The others hiked over, Joshua goose-stepping in front, his wrists lashed together with piano wire but his legs flying antically. Kessler went inside the cabin to check on Jeremiah. No one paid any attention to the bodies of Earl Cherry, a frail shape beneath a blanket under the jack pine stripling, and Spiderman.

"The aerial photograph salesman!" Joshua was seated on the ground, his legs stretched in front of him, jerking and bouncing as if he were still goose-stepping. *Lists of informers, secret invasion plans! Hah! Jewnited States of America! All your lies! The spy from ZOG! Hah!*"

"Where's Esther?" Elmo Finn said.

"Hah! Esther! You'll never be able to brainwash her—eighty-eight!" He strained against the piano wire.

Elmo Finn smashed the butt of his forty-five into Joshua's mouth. Blood gushed out, carrying with it several teeth. The ice-blue eyes filled with tears.

"You—impure—I demand my rights, I have my rights!"

"You have no rights here, Harlan. This is God's Country, Harlan." Elmo Finn raised the big automatic and hit him again. Joshua screamed and toppled backward, groaning, but twisted and struggled back to a sitting position.

"I demand my . . . who are you? Who are you!"

Elmo Finn, his face clenched like a fist, dropped to one knee in front of Joshua. He leaned closer, then closer still.

"I am a Jew."

"Hah!"

"I am a nigger."

Harlan McConathy's pale blue eyes flickered.

"I am a spic and I am a gook and I am a raghead and I am a woman and I am ZOG and I am sheeple . . . think of me as the Neighborhood Watch, Harlan. The whole fucking neighborhood, Harlan. God's country."

Joshua's violent eyes darted past Elmo Finn to the set faces of George Graves, Henry Wood, Gene Kessler, and Roy. "I demand—"

Finn backhanded him across the face with the pistol. "Did you torture and hang your wife?"

"Hah! Hah! Traitors, agents of ZOG—"

"You shot Linda Pearson in the back."

Blood was streaming from Joshua's mouth. "Traitors! Traitors!"

"You robbed a Wells Fargo truck and killed a guard."

"That was Earl! That was—"

Finn lashed him across the face with the butt of the gun.

"You kidnapped and terrorized the governor's wife."

"Lies! Lies! Jew lies, ZOG lies . . ." Joshua's eyes were wild now, shooting everywhere.

"Where does the tunnel come out?"

"Eighty-eight! Eighty-eight!"

"Where is Randall Tice?"

"Eighty-eight! Randall Tice is a white warrior, Randall Tice is God's swift sword, Randall Tice is in a ZOG prison unlawfully but he will be free, he will be free, white warriors will rise up and awaken the sheeple—*today!*—this is *The Day!*—eighty-eight! Eighty-eight!"

Elmo Finn pistol-whipped him again and turned to Gene Kessler. "How much C-4 in the cabin?"

"Ten pounds."

Elmo Finn and the BATF agent went into the cabin and stayed for a long time. Then several trips were made from the cabin to the helicopter. Soon the big rotor was turning and Henry Wood was lifting off. George Graves and little Jeremiah Cherry watched from the ground.

The chopper flew to Lake Joshua, where the militiamen of God's Country had once strolled with Timothy McVeigh, where the sound of a bird in flight had once been heard. It dipped and landed at the base of the earthen dam, but soon was airborne again, climbing into the September sky, hovering above the flat blue lake. A spread-eagled form falling toward the shimmering water. Henry Wood maneuvering the helicopter to another position, carefully calculated, and hovering gently as Elmo Finn fired the rocket.

An hour later, at the Boone County Medical Center where Luke and Nikki Gannon had become Hall of Fame Patients One and One-A, reporters encircled Henry Wood, who had volunteered to be the decoy.

"We'll pay double! You name the price!"

"Triple! Just me and a camera!"

"Was it like a war? They said it sounded like a war!"

"Was Nikki raped? Or molested?"

"How many were killed? Did you see the bodies?"

A tall thin woman with hollow eyes made her way around the knot of clamoring reporters and entered the clinic. She was carrying a baby wrapped in a blue woolen blanket. She stood quietly just inside the entrance, unnoticed, until a nurse came over.

"May I help you, ma'am? We're very busy just now."

The tall woman thrust the child into the nurse's arms. "This is Noreen's baby. Esther." She turned and walked away.

"Ma'am!" yelled the startled nurse. "You can't just leave a baby . . . Noreen who?"

The tall woman looked back from the entryway. "Noreen's dead." She hurried out. As she circled unnoticed around the mob of reporters, Eli Korn and six uniformed state policemen appeared and rescued the amused Henry Wood. Then Eli climbed onto an overturned milk crate and faced down the reporters until they quieted.

"All of you will get everything, and everyone will get it at the same time."

"Who shot the governor?"

"Is he paralyzed?"

"What happened at God's Country? Why all the roadblocks?"

Eli Korn raised his thin arms above his head, eliciting silence. "You'll get everything as soon as we organize the information. I'll tell you this much about God's Country. There was an ark. There was a flood."

The Seventh Day

Nikki Gannon was curled across the California king squealing and groaning and holding her sides—from sheer hilarity. Sandra had hung the birdcage from the bottom of the chandelier, and Elmo Finn's red and green "imperial cockamamie," Falstaff, was perched on his tiny trapeze, preening and orating in his bright new surroundings. Macduff, the cross-eyed orange cat, was pacing along the foot of the gubernatorial bed.

"Out spot!" the bird screeched. "Out spot! Damn spot!"

Nikki and Sandra clapped their hands and Falstaff spread his feathers and turned in a half circle. Macduff stood on his hind legs and stretched up a forlorn paw.

"All a-world! All a-world!" Falstaff squawked. "All a-world a stage!"

They clapped and cheered again. "This is the best he's ever

done!" Sandra beamed. "He just needed a new audience. Tennessee royalty."

"Oh, my sides hurt!" Nikki said, curling into a ball. "I've never ever laughed so hard. *He's* the royalty. Did he just hate the airplane? Poor baby—a thousand miles."

"He travels well, especially on a charter. All I have to do is put a towel over his cage. Macduff's an old pro, he just curls up like a tomcat."

"And dreams about Falstaff."

"Barbecued."

Nikki cackled, then groaned, holding herself again. After a moment she glanced at Sandra. Tears flooded her eyes. "I never thought I'd be laughing again at anything. If it weren't for Elmo, Sandra . . . I wouldn't be here. Those guys are really something. Your Elmo Finn is . . . really something."

Sandra left the chaise, came over to the bed, and sat down. She took Nikki's hand. "Don't forget your husband, Nikki. He was ready to give up the governorship for you—for the woman he loves. Like Edward the Eighth or something. I get chills."

Nikki pursed her lips and turned her head away. "We'd been having some problems, but they seem so petty now. Sandra, you don't know what will happen in this life. You never know, it's so fragile. Here today, gone tomorrow . . . you better make that Elmo Finn marry you."

"Nikki, we're about as married as either one of us can stand. Mo says we fight like we're married and, you know, do the dirty deed like we're not. I think he's right."

"The dirty deed, the dirty deed." Nikki's smile was fleeting. "Did you hear how close it was at the end? I bet he didn't tell you."

"George told me. George saw everything from the helicopter. It looked like that maniac Joshua had Elmo point blank. He's had close calls before, but this one—" Sandra shivered. "But there were a lot of heroes, Nikki. Luke and Elmo and the guys.

That ATF agent, Kessler. Clay Jennings. Noreen. A lot of good people were on the case. And you're the biggest hero of all, for just hanging on. Was it terrible?"

"It was like dreaming a bad dream inside a bad dream. Sometimes I thought I was already dead. When they brought me food, I tried to get them to talk but they wouldn't. When they took my clothes to wash, I was naked for hours. Blindfolded. Strapped down. I sang to myself, childhood songs. 'Froggy Went A-Courtin'.' 'She'll Be Comin' 'Round the Mountain.' Then they'd give me something and I'd pass out again. Toward the end they kept me under most of the time." Nikki reached for some Kleenex and pressed it to her face. "Why didn't you bring Dr. Watson, Sandra, he's the friendliest bulldog."

"Dr. Watson, unfortunately for all concerned, has come down with gas. George says it's terminal. He has to take these pills, then he goes out and stands in the yard like a statue. George says he looks like Churchill and acts like Stalin. He wants to bronze him."

Nikki was cackling again, hugging her ribs. "I'm so sore . . ."

The door opened and Louise Perry peeked in. "Am I interrupting anything?"

"Mom, come in, you're missing the show. The Shakespearean parrot and the cross-eyed cat."

"Why don't I bring Baskerville over, he and Macduff could play."

"He and Macduff could make that squirrel sound at each other."

"The bird would unite them."

"The bird would in*cite* them. To riot."

Louise sat on the corner of the bed. "Elmo asked me again about those cows. He was very interested why didn't I mention it before. I said, *Cows?* You got to be kidding. But he wasn't. Sandra, you better marry that man."

"He wasn't kidding," Nikki said, "because the entire press

corps of Tennessee and America and most of the known world has us completely surrounded, waiting for the full story. Demanding the full story. Which isn't exactly known as of this point in time."

"Cows," Louise said with a little sob, "cows for my horsey girl." She took a Kleenex. "Thank God, baby Esther is all right. That poor woman's the real heroine, wrapping her up like Moses in the bulrushes till she could get her out of that awful place. She deserves a medal."

"They think Helen Cherry will get custody of Jeremiah. Instead of sending him to a foster home."

Macduff made a sudden leap toward the lazily swinging birdcage but missed by a foot and barely twisted upright before hitting the floor. Immediately he sat on his haunches and began licking his paw. The three women were giggling furiously.

After a while, Louise said, "Sandra, did you hear about the finger? The finger in the box? Oh my God, with Nikki's wedding ring on it—" She choked back a sob.

"I don't even remember them taking my ring off, Mother. I was so doped up, it was like dreaming inside a dream. I can't remember much of anything."

Louise said, "Why can't Lucas just have a press conference and say what he knows and get them off our backs? They're everywhere, camped out there, cameras all over the yard, I can't even go home to feed Baskerville. Rupert's doing it. The viscount. He might poison him."

"Because, Mother, there's one teeny tiny little piece of the puzzle that's missing. I don't mean the finger thing, as in Whose finger was it? I mean the question we've got to answer before facing the press."

"What question is that, darling?"

"Mom. Think about it. *Where the hell is Randall Tice?*"

———

Eli Korn said, "Governor, this was the kidnappingest week of all time. First, they kidnap Nikki. No—Earl Cherry kidnaps Jeremiah first. And Helen tries to counterkidnap him. Then Nikki. Then we sort of kidnap Randall Tice. Then they kidnap Helen Cherry. And Noreen, God rest her soul. Then that little mustachioed bandito with the faggy cigarette kidnaps me! Then we kidnap Joshua. How did Joshua escape, that's what I can't figure."

Luke Gannon shrugged, then winced and gently touched his shoulder. "Maniacs do maniacal things. Superhuman things. He took the woman lawyer hostage."

"Linda Pearson. I guess those liens she filed against you are moot now." The Yes Man grinned but drew no response. "But why did Joshua take *her* hostage, she was on his side."

"She was trying to surrender to the chopper. So Joshua grabbed her as a shield and Elmo had to let them go."

"And with her as a shield he was able to get to the dam and then shoot her in the back, and then when he tried to flood out God's Country he accidentally blew himself up? Is that how it all came down?"

"He kept explosives planted under that dam. In case ZOG attacked. That was what he called The Day. Armageddon. The end of the world. Poor paranoid, brain-dead lunatic."

Eli Korn folded his thin arms across his chest. "Governor, I still wish you had confided in me. From the beginning. I might have been able to help."

Lucas Gannon looked at his chief of staff. "When they get here, Eli, I'm going to meet with them alone. It's almost over, one way or the other."

"So I'm to leave again?"

Luke looked at the ceiling and sighed.

The Yes Man stood up. "Fine. Fine. What do I tell the press now?"

"Don't tell the goddamn press a goddamn thing! That crack about the flood and the ark, you saw what they did with that.

Old Testament! I don't care what their schedule is, or their agenda, or any other goddamn thing—I'm doing this by *my* schedule. And your little sensibilities aren't exactly at the top of my list either, Eli, you want to know the truth."

"Fine. I'm sure you'll let me know if I can be of service."

"We have to trust Elmo Finn right now."

"Fine. I'm glad you trust somebody."

A sharp knock sounded on the private door. As Luke got up to open it, Eli hurried out through the staff door, his white shirttail flapping behind him. Luke opened the door and Elmo Finn entered, with George Graves and Cecil Beech close behind. All three men were dressed in work clothes.

"How'd you get past the vultures?" Luke said.

"Roy drove a decoy van to the front and we came in the back—in a UPS truck with the regular driver."

"At gunpoint."

"At walletpoint."

Chuckling, they took seats across from each other on the big chocolate sofas.

"Mo, I can't hold 'em off much longer. We've got to find Randall Tice and wrap this up, one way or another . . . what?"

Elmo Finn bowed like a ringmaster toward Cecil Beech.

Cecil's eyes were bright. He toyed with an unlit Pall Mall. "Governor, you remember my boys Tojo and Sushi. Tojo's the Jap flew down to Knoxville with the marshal badges and wore a silk top hat. To be unobtrusive. And he's the well-adjusted one. Sushi's the one never been south of Macy's, he seriously thought he'd be voodooed if he came to Tennessee, so I gave him the job of finding our boy Herman Page, who was Randall Tice's most frequent visitor in prison, who might be related to *Travis* Page, the trooper that Tice supposedly shot—"

Luke held up both hands. "I know all that, Cecil. What's the bottom line?"

"Sushi found him is the bottom line. Goddamnedest Jap. He asked the one question nobody else thought of, and he got the fucking answer."

"Then who the hell is Herman Page?"

"He's an undertaker, Governor."

Luke intercommed Sgt. Clay Jennings and within seconds the big state trooper appeared.

"Clay, Elmo and the boys are still working on a few things. I want you to help them. They're from out of town, you know the territory."

"Sure. Yes, sir. Be glad to."

"Did you file your after-action report?"

"Yes, sir. Just like we discussed."

"I appreciate it, Sergeant. You know that."

"No problem."

A few minutes later, Eli Korn and Luke strode out of the governor's office and down the corridor, decoying the press long enough for the wide-eyed UPS driver to smuggle the others out of the capitol. Roy replaced Cecil, who returned to his computer, and the men piled into the forest-green Navigator and headed south out of Nashville on Interstate 24.

"Where we goin'?" Clay Jennings asked. He was in the back seat with Roy. Elmo Finn was up front with George, who was driving.

"South for a while," Elmo Finn said, turning sideways and hooking his arm over the seatback. "Sergeant, we need to compare notes with you—you had a vantage point nobody else had. You were there."

"We've already covered everything I know, Colonel. I've racked my brain. Joshua kept me pretty much out of the loop, I wasn't really in on anything. And, Jesus, there's a lot of cows in Tennessee. I'm tellin' you, I've racked my brain."

George was driving at the speed limit in the right-hand lane but everything on the road was passing him. It was late afternoon, the heart of the rush hour.

"Sergeant, there's one thing we can't figure," Elmo Finn said. "You knew Travis Page pretty well."

"He was one of my best friends. We were at the academy together. I was a pallbearer."

"Did you know his brother? Herman?"

"Herman? I think I met him, couple of times."

"Did you know that Herman Page visited Randall Tice more than anyone else?"

"At Brushy Mountain?"

"At Brushy Mountain. That's what we can't figure—why would a man keep visiting the man who killed his brother?"

"I'll be damned if I know. It's news to me. It doesn't make . . . maybe he was traumatized or whatever. Maybe he had to confront him, some psychological thing."

"Did the two brothers get along?"

"Far as I know. I never heard anything, but I probably wouldn't have. What is all this Randall Tice stuff anyway—did he escape or somethin'?"

"Herman Page told Randall Tice that he was not—*not*—Travis's brother. No relation. Said he didn't even spell the name the same way. Herman spelled it P-a-*i*-g-e. Put an *i* in."

"I don't know anything about that. I thought it was P-a-g-e. That's weird."

"So you don't have any idea why the murdered man's brother would pretend *not* to be his brother when he visited the murderer?"

"No, hell no, unless . . . I don't know. Maybe he was up to something."

Elmo Finn turned a little more in the bucket seat and leaned his head back against the tinted window. "Maybe Herman was making some kind of play for Tice's money—the three hundred thousand from the bank robbery. Nobody ever found it."

"I always figured he must've buried it somewhere at God's Country. But Joshua and Spiderman didn't think there ever *was* any money, or Tice would have turned it over. They trusted him, dumb sonsabitches. I bet it's deep under water now."

Elmo Finn shifted his weight in the big bucket seat. "You visited Randall Tice yourself, Sergeant. Once, according to the log."

Clay Jennings let out a long breath. "We talked about that, Colonel. Joshua sent me, he thought it would cheer him up to know that a state cop was part of God's Country. *Cheer him up.* But I wanted to go anyway, see him face-to-face. I wanted to look him straight in the eye and ask him if he shot Travis."

"What'd he say?"

"He said no. He looked *me* straight in the eye, never blinked. Then he said he never got the chance, somebody beat him to it. Then he said 'Eighty-eight,' 'Eighty-eight,' over and over. He was crazy, pure and simple. Speakin' of underwater, did Joshua's body show up yet?"

Elmo Finn shook his head. "It will."

"What is all this Randall Tice stuff, Colonel? Did he escape or something? I wish *his* body'd show up somewhere."

"You could arrange it, couldn't you?"

"Arrange it?"

"Come on, Clay. Or should I call you Blue?"

Clay Jennings froze for an instant, then folded his arms across his chest. "Blue? What is Blue?"

Elmo Finn exhaled irritably, sat up straight, glared across the seat. "This is no time for bullshit, Clay. We arrested your sister an hour ago, in the hospital parking lot. Very handy to have a nurse on your team—knockout drops, sedatives, syringes. Little sister Joyce, who also plays the organ at Herman Paige's funeral home."

Jennings, his mouth forming words, looked incredulously at Elmo Finn. He gaped at Roy, who was pointing a small black automatic at his chest, then turned back to Elmo Finn. "I don't know what . . . I want a lawyer. You can't arrest me."

"I'm not arresting you, Clay. I might do something else, because of what you did to Nikki Gannon."

"Nikki Gannon! Jesus, you're crazy, Finn—I'm the one who *found* her, for Christ's sake!"

"And you're the one who kidnapped her, Clay. Or, to be precise, you planned the kidnapping and Red and White pulled it off—Joyce and Herman. Joyce Jennings, your sister, who was Travis Page's girlfriend. And Herman Paige, who owns the funeral home, who was Travis Page's brother—Herman, who retained the old spelling of the family name, with an *i*. Thought it was more distinguished for an undertaker."

"I want a lawyer! I want—"

"Shut up, Clay. Shut up. You're not under arrest. It could be arranged."

Jennings said nothing, his hands on his knees, his face mottled red. He looked at Roy as if appealing for an intervention. George pulled off the interstate and turned east.

Elmo Finn said, "See where we're going, Clay? We're going to Herman's funeral home. Where they'll put you in a box in the ground or in a jar up on the mantel. Where little sister Joyce plays the organ at the services. Where you brought Louise on the very first day, so Joyce could do the drug test. Where Herman lives in that isolated apartment out back, the prison you kept Nikki in until you smuggled her into the straw hut at God's Country. Where Herman brought Randall Tice in the cream-colored van, along with the two motorcycles, after you'd planted the Oriental rug in that cabin. Where Herman borrowed a ring finger from one of the crematorium customers. Where there's a big dairy farm right next door. With all those cows."

George parked the Navigator under some trees at the deserted end of a shopping center parking lot only a mile from the funeral home. George and Roy got out and drifted away, leaving Elmo Finn in the front seat alone with Clay Jennings in the back. Elmo Finn reached over, turned the ignition switch on, and lowered all the power windows.

"Just you and me, Clay. I want the truth, and I want Randall Tice."

Jennings was glowering furiously. He threw his arm across the top of the seat, lowered it just as abruptly, locked his fingers around his knee.

"Why do you want that son of a bitch so bad? He killed a cop."

"You've got Tice at the funeral home, I know that. Herman's guarding him. What we don't know, is there a booby trap? Is there a password? Can we get in and out with nobody getting hurt?"

"Why don't you ask Joyce?"

"Clay, you better start thinking."

"I think I could take you, Finn. Your backup ain't here. Rambo Roy ain't here." He looked outside. There was no one in sight. The nearest car was a football field away.

"You just can't help being stupid, can you, Clay? I'm giving you the only chance you're going to get, and you're giving me jive."

Jennings's eyes narrowed. "You'll let me go if I give you Tice?"

"Have you tortured him?"

A grim smile settled on Jennings's face. "You may be just in time to save him, Finn. But *why*? You're a fuckin' cowboy, all you guys, you ain't sworn no oaths. Let us keep him, he don't deserve better."

"You're sure he killed Travis Page?"

"Yes! Hell yes! And got away with it! He should be on Death Row. That's where I've got him now—Death Row. That's justice. What's wrong with justice, Finn? What's wrong with justice?"

Elmo Finn was silent for a long time, looking at Jennings.

"I know what you'd do, Colonel," Jennings whispered. "Same as you did in Vietnam. Same as I'm doing now."

"When you volunteered to be the spy inside God's Country—that was part of the plan, wasn't it? The long-range plan."

"Got to think ahead." Jennings snickered.

"And I figure you're the one who mailed all those death threats to the governor. So they'd have to beef up the body man detail and you could get on it."

Jennings grinned through thin lips.

Elmo Finn laughed. "That's why we came to Tennessee in the first place. Those threats you sent. We were just checking security."

"I'd known you were comin', I might of dreamed up somethin' else."

Elmo Finn resettled himself in the bucket seat. "I got you figured for another thing, Clay. Nikki's dad—Judge Perry. I don't think he hanged himself. I think you hanged him."

"Whoa, Colonel, Jesus! You got some imagination. Hell, Judge Perry left a suicide note in his own handwriting. I saw it. But I'll tell you this, I didn't shed no tears. That pussy of a judge let Randall Tice get away with murder."

Elmo Finn stared at the big trooper.

Jennings said, "I sure didn't shed no tears. The *hanging* judge."

"I didn't know he left a note."

"I saw it. In his own handwriting."

Elmo Finn shrugged. "What was the deal with the finger? What'd you do, get one from the crematorium that would fit Nikki's ring? You just wanted Luke to squirm a little more?"

Jennings grinned his thin-lipped grin. "Keep the pressure on. Let him know we were very serious, a little crazy, unpredictable. Then when he got her back, he'd be so relieved that her finger *hadn't* been clipped, he couldn't help havin' positive thoughts about us. Herman and me thought about settin' up a black market in fingers, hands, whatever. He can snip away all he wants before he burns 'em. Hell, he could put dog's ashes in those urns, nobody'd know."

"You've studied psychology."

"Hell yes, psychology of the streets. People say I got a knack for it."

"Has Tice told you where the money is?"

Jennings shook his head. Another thin smile. "But I got some psychology I ain't tried yet."

"Let me guess. Fingernails. Cigarettes. Eardrums. Genitals."

"All of the above."

"It worked in Vietnam. He'll probably talk."

"He'll talk."

"Clay, let's work this out. Here's my problem—I've got to return Randall Tice to Brushy Mountain. We sort of borrowed him under false pretenses, and I've got to return him in good condition, not some slobbering nutcase looks like the V.C. worked him over. So that's my problem."

"What if I find him dead! At God's Country! I could do that easy, bein' a state trooper. It'll look like Joshua kidnapped Nikki, swapped her for Tice, then executed him. Joshua'll get the blame for everything—that's better justice than just putting Tice back in prison." The thin smile reappeared. "You got to admit, we took good care of Nikki, never laid a hand on her, you ask her."

Elmo Finn drew in a deep breath and let it out slowly. "Nikki says you did treat her well."

"I wouldn't have harmed a hair on her head. You'd get a share, Finn. I don't want any for myself, just Joyce. She and Travis were engaged—and that bastard Tice took Travis away from her. She deserves Tice's money. If there was any justice in the courts, she'd already have it and Tice would be six feet under."

"I'd want Helen Cherry to get something. For Jeremiah."

"Jeremiah, sure."

"Say, fifty."

"Fifty. I don't see why not, if we find the money."

"And another fifty for my boys. You caused us a lot of trouble."

"I can understand that. That's a hundred."

"And fifty for me. That'll still leave you and Joyce and Herman a hundred and fifty, maybe more. Who knows?"

Jennings seemed to ponder Elmo Finn's proposal. "Finn, you also got to consider this—if you arrest me for kidnapping, I'll turn in Luke Gannon for getting a felon released under false pretenses, and I'll turn you in for impersonating a U.S. marshal, and I'll turn in all you guys for starting the shooting at God's Country, I'll swear that you did that. And I'll swear that I didn't kidnap nobody. And so forth. So we could end up in a Mexican standoff. Your word against mine."

"Are you threatening me, Jennings?"

"No, hell no. I'm just speculatin'. I'd rather do a deal."

"You got to take care of Tice in exactly the right way, you got to dump the body at God's Country where somebody'll find it."

"No problem."

"It's got to look right."

"I know how to make it look right."

"You sure made Judge Perry look right. That was a piece of work. Don't pretend with me, Clay, we're down and dirty now. I know you did it. That's when you learned how easy it was to get inside his house. You used that knowledge to kidnap Nikki. I'm not stupid, Clay."

"Well, you sure got some imagination."

"Clay. We're doin' a deal here, we got to be straight on everything. How'm I gonna trust you, I don't know when you're bein' straight."

"I'm bein' straight. What're you talkin' about?"

"I'm talkin' about Judge Perry. The pussy judge. The hangin' judge. You oughtta be proud of it."

"I would be proud of it, I'd done it. That was no loss to society. I didn't shed no tears."

"We do a deal, Clay, you and me are partners for life. I got to be able to trust what you tell me. And I fucking *know* you did Judge Perry."

"That would be murder, Finn. I ain't done no murders."

"You seem ready to shoot Randall Tice."

"That ain't murder."

Finn reached inside his coat and brought out a folded piece of paper. He unfolded it and held it for Jennings to see.

"See this drawing on the left, Clay? That's a hangman's noose tied by a left-handed person. Like you. The other one was tied by a right-handed person. Look at the difference. The way the coils go."

Clay Jennings looked at the drawings, his face blank.

"Judge Perry was right-handed, Clay. And the noose he died in was tied by a lefty. I have the police photograph."

"That ain't evidence. Rope experts would contradict it."

Elmo Finn shook his head. "That's where you're wrong, Clay. Lefties and righties tie their neckties, shoelaces, everything, *differently*. The loops end up different. There's a thousand photographs of Judge Perry, and the blowups will prove he tied everything like a right-hander. Except that noose."

"Okay. Okay. Partner." The thin smile worked into a grin. "I tied it right in front of him. I made him watch. I made him beg. You satisfied now?"

"Sure, partner. Putting that clipping on his desk, about the stalker that he let out of jail who went and killed the girl. That was a nice touch. Made it look like he was suffering unbearable remorse and took the only way out."

Jennings said nothing. He leaned forward a little.

Elmo Finn said, "What'd you make him beg for? His life?"

"A bullet. He didn't want to hang. He didn't like the look of that rope at all. Wanted to swallow a thirty-eight."

"Where'd you learn to tie a noose?"

"I've seen it done. I know some old boys." Jennings smoothly drew the revolver from the backup holster on his ankle. He raised it within inches of Finn's head.

"Where's the wire, Finn? Don't move."

Elmo Finn slowly took a silver ballpoint pen from his breast pocket and handed it to Jennings.

"The recorder."

He pointed to the console between the bucket seats. Jennings raised the lid and looked inside.

"Open your shirt."

Elmo unbuttoned each button and peeled back the fabric.

"Whoa. Kevlar. Thought you'd have to shoot it out with Herman, did you?"

Elmo Finn nodded frozenly.

"That shit won't help you at close range. Get out, Finn. Walk into those woods."

Elmo Finn opened the door, stepped out slowly, and began to turn away from the Navigator. As Jennings raised his gun, Elmo flung himself to the ground and Roy fired twice through the right rear window into Jennings's head with a black automatic that had a six-inch suppressor to muffle the noise. George Graves, a blanket in his arms, yanked open the other door and forced his way in as the big green Huey sliced in above the treetops and began to nestle softly to earth.

Epilogue

by George Graves

I don't like long speeches and I hate political speeches, but I loved this one and it was both. That's what happens when you can hear between the lines.

Cool Hand Luke Gannon was sensational—calm, forthright, authentic—and damn sure needed to be. The Speech, as we had come to call it, was televised live by every station from Mountain City to Memphis, replayed again and again, and dissected and parsed and second-guessed until it could have meant anything anybody wanted it to mean. Which was just fine with us.

We watched from the governor's office—Elmo and the boys, Nikki and the girls, and Eli and Jill, who had worked around the clock helping to craft The Speech. I say *craft* instead of simply *write*, because every word, every line, every pause was purposeful. And The Speech was crafty as hell.

"Ten days ago, my wife Nikki was kidnapped."

With those eight words, the governor of Tennessee hooked a few million people. He was standing in the press room behind the podium bearing the Great Seal of Tennessee, the warm spotlighted blue drapes softly regal in the background, looking straight into a pool camera that was shooting on a slight up-angle, at Eli's insistence. The power angle. Dark suit, white shirt, maroon figured tie. The power ensemble.

"Ten days ago, my wife Nikki was kidnapped. Three days ago, thanks to some old friends from the Central Intelligence Agency, she was rescued. During the seven days in between, Nikki was terrorized, her mother was brutalized, another woman was kidnapped, and I was wounded by gunfire. But we made it through. Tragically, thirteen other people did not. They died. And another man, my wife's father who died five years ago, was part of those seven days as well. I want to tell you the story of those seven days."

Hooked wasn't strong enough, according to the postmortems. Phone usage dropped dramatically, toilet flushing dropped, traffic, everything. They could have looted most of the state, but I guess the looters were hooked too. The pool cameraman zoomed out to a wide shot revealing maps and blown-up photographs on Eli's neat arc of easels. The proof. We hoped.

Luke told a hell of a story. The perfectly executed daylight kidnapping and the bizarre ransom demand—to release a convicted felon. His difficult decision not to include the state police in the investigation, to set up instead his own task force with friends from CIA, BATF, U.S. marshals. Why no state police? A suspicion by his old colonel, Elmo Finn, that somehow the state police had been compromised, that at least one of the body men was a traitor. "Thank God for hunches," Luke said. (I felt a shiver. This was the first real stretcher. Clay Jennings, of course, *was* a traitor, but we didn't suspect it in the beginning; hell, we never had a clue. Louise looked over at me and winked, and I laughed out loud. History is written by the winners.)

The Speech overflowed with details—chilling, grisly, fascinating details—the stuff of a good story. Elmo had fought to include every tiny particular. "Let the story tell the story," he had insisted, and he didn't have to press very hard. Luke had made enough speeches to know that *telling* people things never worked, *showing* them things always did. And in crisp, vivid language, he showed them.

Knockout drops and syringes. The cream-colored van and the Oriental rug. Packages arriving by messenger, packages under marble benches in the capitol. Nikki's brassiere in one of the packages, Louise's trembling hands finding the label where her horsey girl invariably inked in her name. The infuriating note: *nice tits.* Her panties in another envelope; *nice ass.* The jeweler's box with her severed finger bearing the wedding ring he had borrowed money to pay for so long ago.

(Luke's voice breaking a little, his eyes swimming in the close-up.)

The prescribed code names, White Thunder and Ice, Blind Man and Hot Stuff, the classified ads in the *Tennessean.* And the story of Phoenix rising. "I want you to know who these men were, and why I brought them to Tennessee." And, for three million Tennesseans, Luke painted a picture of the Huey lifting from the bright jungle, Henry in the pilot's seat screaming "Wipe the blood from my eyes," Roy and me sweeping a killing arc with one of the M-60s, Elmo and Luke behind the other, Cecil flinging grenades. And Mason dead on the floor.

"We all thought we were going to die. When we didn't die, when we lived, we pledged ourselves to each other, for life. Does that sound impossibly corny and old-fashioned? I guess you had to be there, and I was there. Because of these men, Nikki is safe."

I tried to see the others' reaction without looking at them. Elmo stared at the screen. Cecil and Henry and Roy stared at the screen. I was staring at the screen.

"I realized during the agony of these seven days, seven days that seemed liked seven years, my heart pounding night and day, every minute, never sleeping more than an hour without bolting awake . . . I realized that in the final analysis, in the true final analysis, only my wife matters to me. Nothing else. Nobody else. Only Nikki. When you get down to it."

Nikki sobbed plaintively but joyfully on one of the chocolate sofas. Sandra hugged her and they giggled like schoolgirls, and Louise's hands fluttered like small white birds. I marveled at Luke's deft foreshadowing of the punchline of The Speech. The Blockbuster.

Luke's epiphany—that his wife Nikki was his alpha and omega—made his next steps seem eerily logical. Ordering the en masse prisoner release just to get one prisoner out, then aborting that plan when a better one emerged. Targeting God's Country as the chief suspect and discovering a multitude of other crimes, from the kidnapping of little Jeremiah to the Wells Fargo robbery-murder to the stockpiling of illegal ordnance for a war against the government when The Day came. The ad hoc alliance with Gene Kessler of the BATF. And infiltrating God's Country with Sergeant Clay Jennings, who turned out to be the double agent Elmo Finn had suspected, and who was using God's Country as his own accomplice. (Another shiver, right to my toes. Jennings *had* used God's Country as an accomplice, but an unwitting one. He had essentially framed Joshua and we had fallen for it. So The Speech wasn't totally factual; but, in another sense, perhaps it was true. In the spirit of Zen or something. The spirit of Zen could have been seriously undermined by the testimony of Herman Paige and Joyce Jennings, code-named White and Red, but they had been allowed to vanish, and were not expected back. Roy has a way of saying good-bye.)

Then Luke went over to the arc of easels. With professional composure, wielding a long pointer, he described the robotic voice whose commands he listened to on the pay phone outside the Hog . . . the exchange of prisoners in the long white tunnel of trees . . . the shock when Helen Cherry appeared instead of Nikki . . . the motorcycles escaping behind the roadblock of felled timber. Then the invasion of God's Country—the helicopter soaring over the perfect blue of Lake Joshua and landing in the remote clearing above the cabins . . . the bullet fired by Earl Cherry tearing into his shoulder and Henry Wood's strong hands stopping the bleeding . . . Roy rappeling from the rooftop with a notched knife in his teeth.

And the progression of death.

Earl Cherry, a brainwashed disciple of Joshua who had shotgunned a Wells Fargo guard to death, shot repeatedly by his troubled ten-year-old son Jeremiah, blood dripping from the boy's wrists where the handcuffs had been, the boy now, at this moment, finally getting the professional care he'd always needed.

Noreen McConathy, Mother of God, a courageous agent of the BATF who desired only peace for herself and her daughter Esther, hanged by her husband Joshua when her treachery was discovered. (No mention of the transmitter in the brassiere.)

The killings in the firefights at the Ark—Popeye, the rural lawman turned neo-Nazi; the three teenage skinheads, high school dropouts; the Professor, with three hundred college credits but no degree; and Hi Hitler, who had legally changed his name from Glenn Forbush, a fitting symbol of the vast dark malign imbecility of God's Country.

And the killings on the red dirt:

Spiderman, another high school dropout born Quincy Dean Klepper, Joshua's top lieutenant who wore white shoelaces to proclaim white supremacy, shot in self-defense by federal agent Gene Kessler.

Linda Pearson, Linda the lawyer, who had filed false liens against the governor's assets, who tried to surrender to Elmo Finn in the chopper but was seized by Joshua as a body shield for his attempted escape, before he shot her in the back. (My pulse spurted; more Zen, to the highest power.)

Joshua himself, the so-called prophet of a religion on steroids who was sure The Day had finally come, The Day of Armageddon when the white soldiers of Jesus Christ and Adolf Hitler would rally and repel the New World Order and the mud people and the Jews, drowned when something went wrong with his explosives at the base of the dam, the cold blue water sweeping him away. (A fine torrent of Zen.)

And Sergeant Clay Jennings of the Tennessee State Police, who five years before had hanged Judge Nicholas Perry and made it look like suicide, who had mailed in anonymous threats against the governor, then politicked within the state police to become a body man, who had pretended to infiltrate God's Country . . . shot dead before he could level his own pistol to shoot Elmo Finn in the back. His full confession was on tape.

"Thirteen dead," Luke concluded somberly. "Fourteen including Judge Perry. A lethal line of dominoes that began to fall when Nikki was kidnapped. Most of the deaths would probably have occurred anyway, sooner or later, as Joshua and God's Country escalated their deranged, illegal, sociopathic activities. But we cannot deal with what might have happened, only with what did happen. In the battle to rescue my wife, I may have set in motion this horrific chain of events. Or accelerated it. That is why I am resigning as your governor. Effective as soon as practicable."

I was watching Eli and Jill. They were astounded. Overwhelmed. Nonplussed. This was the part of The Speech they hadn't crafted and hadn't heard. Eli whirled toward Elmo, glaring. Elmo looked back blankly. After a few seconds, the chief of staff made a little bow and a little salute to Elmo with the back of his hand, and turned back to Jill. He put his arm around her.

". . . I learned this lesson," Luke was saying. "Don't lose sight of what matters most. It can disappear in an instant. So, my last appeal to you as governor, is . . . hold each other close, remember what life is really all about, let love grow so strong that hate will have no room. I saw little Jeremiah, twisted by hate, shoot his father dead." (Mild Zen; Luke didn't actually see it.) "So take your children in your arms tonight. Your wives, your husbands, your lovers. Nothing else matters. That's what I learned in seven days."

Eli Korn jumped up. "Listen! Can't you hear the Kleenex snapping? This is better than LBJ in sixty-eight. Now the voters can tell Luke whether they want him back." He grinned slyly, planting his bony arms akimbo.

"Did you know, darling?" Louise whispered to Nikki, who nodded and embraced her mother. "Oh it's so wonderful. No more, no more."

The door opened and Luke came in. The new body man, Devlin, was with him. Everything froze for a moment, then we swarmed forward, the women embracing him, the men pumping his hand. Devlin stepped quietly into the corridor and closed the door.

Eli was last in line. Everyone fell silent when he and Luke came face-to-face.

"Did you guess?" Luke said softly.

Eli shook his head. Jill came over beside him and they held hands.

"Governor . . . Curtis," Eli said, referring to the lieutenant governor who would step up to the governorship.

"He's been whispering those words to his mirror for years," Luke said.

"He's the *only* one. Will you run in the next election?"

"Eli, I just quit. I don't think I should run for the job I just quit."

"No, Eli, he won't run," Nikki said, appearing with a glass of dark bourbon for Luke.

"It would be perfect," the Yes Man said.

"Perfect," Jill echoed. "Let the people decide. A referendum on Luke Gannon, the governor who gave up his office for his wife."

Luke's smile bore a trace of indulgence. "It's not bad, is it? A ploy. It never occurred to me—I'm not a politician."

"You're the best politician around these parts," Eli said. "We'll talk in the morning."

"I'm going to Bermuda in the morning, Eli. With Nikki and Elmo and Sandra and these crazy guys and anybody else who wants to come. Except a body man."

Actually, it took five mornings for all of us to get to Bermuda. The next afternoon we were still in Nashville, so we held a final session in the old fourth-floor headquarters.

Luke walked to the windows, untaped the heavy curtains, and pulled them apart. Light burst into our lair for the first time.

"I wanted you to save Joshua for me," Luke said, looking at Elmo. "I'm very glad you didn't."

"We'd known you were quitting politics, we might've," Elmo said.

"He almost got you with that Uzi, Mo."

"Almost doesn't count."

"Did he almost get away when he took his own lawyer hostage? Linda Pearson."

"Almost doesn't count."

"What if he hadn't screwed up the explosives? Would he have escaped?"

"No."

"You can't be sure."

The rest of us tried to keep from smiling, with indifferent success. Luke finally smiled too. He knew he'd been told a very Zen-like version of the actual events, and that it was the only version he'd ever hear. He went back to the windows and shook the curtains.

"If Jennings hadn't made that one mistake . . . he almost pulled it off."

"Almost doesn't count," Elmo said. "He thought he was in control, he could risk calling our cell phone from his cell phone—right at the moment of exchanging Tice for Nikki who of course turned out to be Helen Cherry. He couldn't resist such a perfect touch. He was sure we'd think the call came from the Hog, like all the others he'd been making. He was sure we wouldn't check."

Luke let out a breath. "And when Cecil finally found the real Herman Paige, Paige with an *i*, which led to the funeral home . . . it adds up fast."

Cecil made his sweeping Noel Coward bow, cigarette palm up.

Luke said, "I wasn't worried about any investigations or prosecutions for the firefights, or even impersonating the marshals—though I did think we'd have a problem with Randall Tice. But they tell me he's become famous at Brushy Mountain. They call him James Bond. He claims he was part of a CIA operation, very proud of it. Hasn't made a peep. Go figure."

We were grinning like cheshires, peeking at Roy behind our smiles.

"I had a little talk with him," Roy said.

A whoop went up.

Luke shook hands with each of us, even though we were all going to Bermuda together. I think he wanted to close the adventure formally, like soldiers, in the command post. Lower the flag.

The handshakes became embraces, and six ex-commandos shed some more emotional tears. I thought we'd done enough goddamn crying for one operation, but I couldn't help adding mine to the mush. All we needed was Oprah.

Then, eye to eye, Luke said to Mo, "Almost does count sometimes, Mo. Jennings almost shot you in the back. Did you expect it to be that close?"

Elmo couldn't shrug off the question. "It came out about right."

"You knew he'd try to shoot you. You wore a vest. You wanted him to."

"I didn't want him to actually *shoot* me."

"You wanted him to try."

"Luke . . . I guess it doesn't fit the letter of the law very well. But maybe it fits the spirit of the law. Maybe it fits justice. *Strong arms be our conscience, swords our law.*"

They looked at each other.

"Phoenix rising."

"Phoenix rising."

My route to Bermuda went through Longboat Key, of course, because someone had to restore the goddamn parrot and the goddamn cat to their goddamn rightful thrones. Dr. Watson met us at the door, his sawed-off stub of a tail wagging maniacally, but when he realized that I wasn't Elmo he plopped down with a big burp like a punctured balloon dog. And put on his suicidal airs.

Before gathering up the golf clubs and heading to the airport, I tried to call Gene Kessler. I learned that he had taken early retirement from the BATF, cleaned out his desk, disappeared. The secretary said he was despondent and, she thought, seeing a shrink. Something terrible had happened in Tennessee, involving a woman named Noreen. I left all our phone numbers.

Back in his familiar cage, Falstaff roared into fits of broken Shakespeare, feathers fluffed and quivering, and Macduff cast a cold eye and sharpened up on the leg of the sofa. It was my best chance ever, all alone with the miscreants, poisons aplenty under the sink; but like Hamlet I wavered. Didn't cudgel my brains about it, though. Forsooth. Catch the roadrunner, no cartoon.

DATE DUE

NOV 3 '00			
NOV 23 '00			
DEC 26 '00			
JAN 31 '01			
FEB 17 '01			
APR 2 '01			
APR 13 '01			